Also by Milly Johnson

The Yorkshire Pudding Club
The Birds & the Bees
A Spring Affair
A Summer Fling
Here Come the Girls
An Autumn Crush
White Wedding
A Winter Flame
It's Raining Men
The Teashop on the Corner
Afternoon Tea at the Sunflower Café
Sunshine Over Wildflower Cottage
The Queen of Wishful Thinking
The Perfectly Imperfect Woman
The Mother of All Christmases
The Magnificent Mrs Mayhew
My One True North
The Woman in The Middle

Novella:
The Little Dreams of Lara Cliffe

eBook only:
The Wedding Dress
Here Come the Boys
Ladies Who Launch
The Barn on Half Moon Hill
Now available as an audio collection called *Petit Four*

Milly Johnson

I Wish It Could Be Christmas Every Day

SIMON &
SCHUSTER

London · New York · Sydney · Toronto · New Delhi

First published in Great Britain by Simon & Schuster UK Ltd, 2020
This paperback edition published by Simon & Schuster UK Ltd, 2021

1 3 5 7 9 10 8 6 4 2

Simon & Schuster UK Ltd
1st Floor
222 Gray's Inn Road
London WC1X 8HB

Simon & Schuster Australia, Sydney
Simon & Schuster India, New Delhi

www.simonandschuster.co.uk
www.simonandschuster.com.au
www.simonandschuster.co.in

A CIP catalogue record for this book
is available from the British Library

Paperback ISBN: 978-1-4711-7856-6
eBook ISBN: 978-1-4711-7855-9
Audio ISBN: 978-1-4711-7882-5

Typeset in the UK by M Rules
Printed and bound by CPI Group (UK) Ltd, Croydon, CR0 4YY

MIX
Paper from
responsible sources
FSC® C020471

For Luke, who is up there riding horses, walking dogs, driving his Mercedes, eating steak and chips, looking dapper, pulling the ladies, being a regular lad, making everyone laugh and breathing deep lungfuls of heavenly air.

23 December

He who does not have Christmas in his heart

will never find it under a tree

Chapter 1

Bridge Winterman, of course, blamed the weather on her husband. But then, they had been so used to fighting that he was in pole position to be held responsible for everything that went wrong, and she knew that he afforded her the same negative importance in his life. When she took a breath, and with it inhaled some sense, she did concede that Luke was probably less at fault than the idiot meteorologists who had failed to forecast the whole country would be plunged into a nuclear winter. How could they do that in this day and age with all the highfalutin technology at their disposal? Then again, in 1987, two years after she'd been born, one particular well-known weatherman had assured the British public that the rumour of a hurricane heading towards the UK was utter nonsense. A few hours later, the worst storm in three centuries began to batter the southern half of the country and more or less decimated it, so this wasn't exactly a one-off situation.

Bridge cut out peripheral thoughts of infamous weathermen and Luke to concentrate on driving. All she could see through the windscreen was a sheet of white and those snowflakes flying towards her were starting to have a hypnotic effect on her. But stopping wasn't an option, not when she was only five miles from her destination.

She'd suggested the meeting should take place at a country house hotel, near enough to the A1 but at the same time off the beaten track. She wasn't sure if she'd picked the venue because it was grand enough to be a suitable place to begin the end of their divorce proceedings, or because of its awkward-to-get-to location. Either way, Bridge would be coming home from the Borders after spending three days viewing derelict properties for sale, Luke was at a convention on the east coast, and the hotel would be equidistant between them on the 23rd, the planets perfectly aligned for once in their busy schedules. The meeting would be brief, five minutes tops; just enough time for them each to sign a piece of paper, then swap them over to return to their respective solicitors. Then Bridge could go back to Derby and Luke could head home over the Pennines and they could both enjoy a merry Christmas. Job done.

The 'negotiations' to end their marriage cleanly had not gone smoothly so far. For almost five years they had spat and fought with each other to exit their union, raged over the phone, pinged off both frosty and heated emails full of recriminations, demanded statements, information, accounts, reports. At least neither of them was stupid enough to have employed solicitors to do the bulk of the battling for them or they would have been bankrupt long ago. But handling it all personally had long since taken its toll and now they were burnt out with it. The letters of intent had been Luke's idea. 'Look, Bridge, you have Ben in your life now and I have Carmen so let's just end this for their sakes as well as ours and move on,' he'd said in an email. 'Get your solicitor to draft something to the effect that you agree to a no-fault divorce and then sign it. I'll get my solicitor to do the same for me and then we'll exchange them. If it makes you feel more secure, we'll do it face to face so there's no room for any more nonsense.'

She'd said yes. Even though she didn't want to see him. And also, she did.

'What the f—?' She curbed the expletive as her eye took a screen grab of the satnav, which was now saying she had sixteen miles to travel; how the hell could it have shot up from reporting five after her car had barely crawled a hundred yards? There was absolutely no way that Bridge could go another sixteen miles in this, and five wasn't looking good either. It appeared as if a god were emptying giant boxes of Persil over the earth. She was a competent driver but there was a breeze of anxiety blowing into her confidence now, making it flap as surely as the sign at the side of the road in the near distance was doing.

'Hey, Siri,' she said to her phone.

'What's up?' Siri answered.

'Where the buggery bollocks am I?'

Siri's answer, to her surprise, was not, *In the middle of nowhere, love. Two hours away from dying of hypothermia, so that'll teach you for not driving a sensible car*, but a reasoned and encouraging, 'You are on the A7501, south-west of Whitby.'

'Where's the nearest town?'

'I couldn't find any matching places.'

'Where's the nearest village?'

'I couldn't find any matching places.'

Bridge growled impatiently. 'Siri, I know you're a thing that lives in a phone but help me out here. Where's the nearest farm, stable, shelter . . .'

'The closest one I see is Figgy Hollow in two miles to your left.'

Well that's more like it, thought Bridge, drawing level with the flapping sign and making out the words 'Figgy Hollow' and a left-pointing arrow backing up what Siri said. She would be stupid if she didn't go there and stay put until this infernal snow cleared, even if Figgy Hollow was one of those places inhabited by strange country folk who bred werewolves and married close relatives. There was bound to be a church and, in the absence of a hotel or a pub or something, she'd throw herself upon its mercy like Esmeralda seeking sanctuary in *The Hunchback of Notre Dame*.

'Make a U-turn where—'

'Oh shut up, you annoying unreliable tart,' Bridge spoke over the satnav voice as she swung a left. She had lost all confidence in her after getting the mileage wrong. 'I'm ignoring you in favour of Siri so save your breath.'

The road was narrow, deserted; she kept crawling forwards until she was rewarded by the sight of buildings, which drew a weary sigh of relief from her: a small church, some cottages, the roofs thickly iced with snow and – deep joy – the Figgy Hollow Inn. She projected herself forwards in time ten minutes, sitting in front of a log fire defrosting the outside of her while a large brandy warmed up her insides.

The ignition on her Porsche cut out as soon as she braked near the 'car park' sign; it might as well have held up a limp hand and said, 'No more, I need to rest.' It was like a racehorse of the car world, lovely to look at, fine on a familiar course but throw in some hardship and it became a proper wet blanket. Bridge slipped on her suit jacket, opened the car door, trading the cosy warmth for a blast of Arctic wind and hurried across to the front door of the inn, only to find that it was locked. *Oh, bloody marvellous,* she said to herself, noticing that in the window stood a square of cardboard with the words, 'Open for pre-booked reservations only. Christmas Day fully booked' written on it. But one thing was for sure, she couldn't sit here for two days waiting for someone to open up.

She peered in the window, hoping to see a cleaner vacuuming around or a barman polishing tables, but there was no one. She rapped on the glass in a vain attempt to summon somebody who might be hidden out of view – a cellarman perhaps, having a crafty indoor cigarette. No response. She banged hard on the door with the side of her fist. Still nothing. Pulling her jacket tight around her she stepped, but mostly slid, in her snow-unfriendly Jimmy Choo boots around the side of the building, almost falling over a large iron ring attached to a cellar access door in the ground, hidden by snow. She bent and pulled it, but it was firmly secured from the inside. There was a shed full of logs opposite and at the back of the property she found another door with an iron grille over it and a long, narrow window to its right. She tapped as hard as she dared on the glass, hoping against hope that someone was lurking in the back half of the building, but really she knew she was on the road to nowhere with all her efforts; the place *felt* empty as well as looked it.

There was always the church, she supposed, making her way to it across the car park and the single-track road, traversing a short bridge that stood over a deep, thin ribbon of stream, slipping and sliding with none of the grace of Jayne Torvill. She tried the great arched door, twisting the rusted ring, then engaged in a bit more banging with various parts of her hand to absolutely no avail. So on it was, to the row of six adjacent cottages; she peered through the small window of the first of them, but it was too dark, the glass too dirty to see through. A knock on the door yielded the same result as every other knock she'd tried in the past fifteen minutes. She repeated the process with the remaining five houses – nothing; summer holiday cottages no doubt, abandoned until the start of the season. She returned to her best – well, only – option of shelter; the inn. And if she couldn't find a way into it, she'd have to make one and risk the consequences. Better to be prosecuted for breaking and entering than be found frozen to her steering wheel, she reasoned.

Thanks to a delinquent spell as a teen, Bridge was deft with a lock and a screwdriver, and she always carried a toolbox with her in the car. A dysfunctional, unorganised upbringing had led her to find solace and stability in being prepared for most eventualities, although that did not extend to her having her waterproof coat and snow-worthy wellies with her today. They were currently sitting in the back of the sturdy four-by-four she would have driven if a) she hadn't been intent on trying to show Luke Palfreyman that she was more than a match for him in the financial stakes and b) the weathermen of the UK hadn't been such inept pillocks.

She swung open the boot, hoisted out the metal box stored in the compartment under the mat and pulled out a flat-blade screwdriver, her breaking-in implement of choice. If this didn't work, she'd smash a window and gain entry that way, but she was pretty confident in her abilities, and rightly so; even after all these years, she still had the touch. A couple of artful prods and twists in the keyhole and there was a satisfying click. She gave the door a heavy push to open it and a rush of air came out at her with a sigh, as if it had been trapped and was thankful for its freedom.

She called hello, apology cued in her mouth just in case she'd been mistaken and there was someone within after all, but, not surprisingly, there was only silence and darkness to greet her.

Chapter 2

'Is that the fastest the wipers will go? I can't see the road and if I can't, you can't, which fills me full of confidence,' said Charlie, for once not the happiest of passengers.

'Yes, it is the fastest they will go, Charles,' replied Robin, a pronounced and annoyed space between each word. Plus he only ever called Charlie 'Charles' when he was in a heightened state of emotion.

'I'm only saying—'

'Do you want to drive?' Robin snapped. 'I can stop the car and we can swap places. Or rather you can drive and I'll get a taxi because your driving is bound to see at least one of us off before our time.' He took a deep breath in an effort to deflate his rising temper. 'Please sit back and let me handle the wheel and all the other instruments.' He huffed, then restarted the argument. 'The cheek of you, Charles Glaser. How long have I been your chauffeur? How many crashes have I had? Speeding tickets, parking fines? Not one. I wish this car had an ejector seat sometimes. I'd press it and gladly see you blasted into orbit.'

A charged silence hung in the air for a few seconds and

then both men burst out laughing. Life had always been too short for serious disagreements between them, but gentle squabbling was part of their relationship's DNA and had been for the last thirty-two years. *Thou shalt bicker to thy heart's content* was written into their constitutional ten commandments, along with *Thou shalt not hold grudges* and *Thou shalt compromise wherever possible.*

'I can't see a thing,' conceded Robin. 'This is total madness.'

'Who'd have known this was going to happen?' said Charlie.

'The bloody meteorologists should have,' replied Robin with more than a touch of impatience. 'It's the 1987 debacle all over again. How come they can send people to the moon but they can't predict this?' He threw one hand up, and then quickly replaced it on the wheel as the car threatened a rogue skid.

Charlie cleared his throat before speaking next. 'It's probably not the time to tell you that there's none in Scotland.'

'None of what?'

'Snow.'

Robin's grip of the steering wheel increased as if he was holding on to something that might stop him falling off the edge of the world. He really hoped he'd heard Charlie wrong.

'Please tell me you're joking.'

'I'm not.'

Robin's neck started to mottle red, Charlie noticed. This usually signified his partner was about to enter meltdown mode.

'And when were you going to let me in on this particular nugget of information, Charles? When we got up to Aviemore and noticed everyone in bikinis?'

'I don't mind about the snow, it didn't matter anyway.'

Robin knew that was a lie. 'It was the most important thing of all, Charlie.'

'It's forecasted though. For the new year apparently.'

'Yes and the whole of England was "*forecasted*" to be mild and dry for Christmas. They obviously couldn't forecast a puddle if they were stood in it. Are all the weathermen on acid trips?'

Robin growled like a frustrated bear, then his attention was snatched away by the satnav, which picked that moment to freeze. 'Oh great, that's all I need.' He stabbed at it with a demanding index finger, spoke nicely to it then swore at it but nothing would coax it to work.

'Charlie, get maps up on your phone. Look for the nearest town, pub, hotel, anything.'

Charlie tried, but maps couldn't seem to pick up where they were as a starting point. 'This is the trouble with modern technology,' he said. 'It works until it doesn't.'

'Very profound, my love and *so* helpful.'

'You can't go wrong with a paper map. I would have known where we were if you hadn't thrown the road atlas away.'

'It was years out of date, Charlie. It showed the M1 as a mud path.'

'Oh, very funny.'

Robin braked and felt the car struggle for purchase on the road. There was no way he could drive up to Aviemore in this, it wasn't safe.

'Mad fools and Englishmen,' he said, not quite under his breath.

'That's midday sun. And it's dogs.'

'What?'

'*Mad dogs and Englishmen go out in the midday sun*, and it's by Noel Coward.'

'Mad fools and bloody Englishmen go out in the bloody snow two days before bloody Christmas, heading for the bloody highlands of bloody Scotland and that's by Robin bloody Raymond.' Robin's neck was now completely red.

'Shh, having a fit won't get us anywhere sooner,' said Charlie, attempting to pour some oil on Robin's troubled waters. 'What's that over there?' He squinted at something in the distance. 'You know, I think it's a sign.'

'What? Like a burning bush?' replied Robin dryly.

'A wooden signpost I mean, as well you know. Drive on a touch.'

For a man six months short of his eightieth birthday, Charlie had eyes like a hawk.

Robin pressed down the accelerator softly, crawled forwards: 'Oh yeah, I see it now, what does it say?'

Charlie opened the window and snow flew in so he read quickly and closed it again.

'It said Figgy Hollow, half a mile and a right arrow.'

'What's that? A village?'

'I've never heard of it,' said Charlie. 'And I know these parts like the back of my hand.'

'It's a no-brainer, we'll have to go there then.' Robin just hoped the car would make it and not choke, splutter and stop as if they were in an old horror film, leaving them stranded at the mercy of some Yeti-like creature. 'Someone's bound to take pity on us and invite us in for some soup. Practise looking old and vulnerable.'

'I am old and vulnerable. Figgy Hollow here we come then,' said Charlie, annoying Robin even more by making it sound as if they were about to embark on a jolly adventure with the Famous Five and lashings of ginger beer.

*

Mary Padgett tried to concentrate on the road and not on her boss talking on the phone in that way he had when he was trying to hang on to his temper. She flashed a look at him in the rear-view mirror. Driving gave her the perfect excuse to glance at him every few seconds and she doubted she'd ever get tired of the sight. Jack Butterly was ten years her senior, just developing silvery sprinkles in his dark, cropped hair, and crinkles around his gorgeous grey eyes. He seemed to grow more handsome with each year that passed, as she seemed to grow more invisible. She loved her boss. Loved him with all her heart and not in an 'I like working for him' way, but an 'I wish he'd lock the door, shove me on his desk and have his wicked way with me' way, which is why she offered to drive him to a hotel in the north-east when Jack's chauffeur Fred went off sick with his back – again.

Jack had been trying for months to fix up a meeting with the head of the Chikafuji Bakery company in Japan and the only time in the calendar Mr Chikafuji and Jack were both free was the early morning of Christmas Eve. Despite being very keen to hook up and make beautiful bun business together, Mr Chikafuji had been more difficult than a greased eel to pin down, so Jack wasn't going to miss the opportunity to meet with him when he was over on a flying visit to the UK. Mary seized her chance to spend an evening in a gorgeous country house four-star hotel with Jack Butterly, an opportunity that looked set to crumble into dust, from what the fragments of conversation she'd overheard had intimated.

'Yes, I can come over to Japan instead, do you have some dates ... May? Is Mr Chikafuji not free before then? ... Oh I see, he's very busy is he? ...'

Jack ended the call on his mobile with as much annoyance as it was possible to execute with one finger. It was an end to a call better suited to a heavy desk phone with a receiver that could be crashed down onto its cradle.

'Would you believe it,' said Jack. 'Chikafuji's plane has been cancelled from Brussels, so he's going back to Japan instead and he hasn't got space in his diary for a head-to-head until May. We might as well turn back. Ha.' The note of laughter was anything but one of amusement.

Mary didn't suggest that they should have had a video call. She had learned over the years that Jack *needed* the whole meet and greet experience, to make that initial face to face connection with a potential client, in order to absorb their essence, especially one of Mr Chikafuji's calibre, and he was adamant that he couldn't do that via a screen. Mary thought he could have made an exception in this case, seeing as Mr Chikafuji was so hard to get hold of in person, but she kept quiet so as not to exacerbate his mood. Jack scared some people, she knew. He was physically imposing, tall, with broad shoulders, a man who looked after himself and spoke with an impeccable private-school accent that had a tendency to make those with a dent in their confidence feel inferior. He was a hard-nosed, hard-working businessman who believed in his product and gave off an air of self-assurance like expensive cologne. His face had a default serious set; Mary had heard a few people say that it would shatter like stressed glass if he smiled, but she didn't think that was true and how she wished she could be the one who made him smile. He didn't scare her in the slightest either, because she could read him like a favourite book and she knew under that stiff, polished veneer was someone lonely, vulnerable, sad, mixed up.

Mary dabbed her foot gently on the brake, felt the Maserati skid slightly as it tried to hold traction. There were no other cars in sight but she wasn't sure any more how much was road and how much was ditch. She made a measured five-point turn, set off back down the road they had just travelled, their freshly made tracks half-filled with snow already. She tried to keep her focus on driving and not on lamenting that her big chance to make Jack see her as something other than the PA who brought him coffee, fielded his calls and organised his diary and his dry-cleaning was now gone.

She'd bought a stunning red dress especially for the dinner they'd have had together in the hotel restaurant. She'd chosen it with care to make the best of her slender frame, to colour-contrast with her long, pale-blond hair and make her large, green-blue eyes pop. She'd bought red suede boots with heels that elevated her five-foot-three height without reducing her ability to walk in them. She'd blown almost the equivalent of her month's wages on clothes for this one night, a stupid gamble. Thank goodness they were still in the bags with the tags and stickers on them so she could get a refund. But she didn't want a refund, she wanted to wear them and have her night in the Tynehall Country Hotel ripping the scales from Jack's eyes.

She had known it was 'now or never', and so it seemed that it was going to be never, thanks to the double whammy of the ever-unreliable Mr Chikafuji and the damned weather. She had known it was too good to be true: an all-expenses-paid night in a swanky hotel, Jack all to herself for a full twenty-four hours. One of her dad's many sayings was that if a thing looked too good to be true, then that's because it probably was and once again he was right. Mary sighed audibly then quickly checked the mirror to see if Jack had heard her, but he was too busy hunting for something in his briefcase to have noticed.

Mary carried on down the road, steadily. Her dad had taught her and her siblings to drive when they were fifteen on a patch of nearby farmland. By the age of sixteen, she could throw cars around corners and handle any motor with the skill of a copper chasing a drug dealer up the wrong side of the motorway. She drove much better than Fred did, who tended to press down on the pedals as if he was stamping on a cockroach with a lead boot. He'd been Jack's father's chauffeur, employed more for being on the old boys' network rather than for his abilities, which was par for the course with Reg Butterly. Mary's eyes flicked towards the satnav when it gave her an instruction to leave the motorway at the next junction and follow the A379 to Exeter. On the screen was a map of the south-west. Even brand-new Maseratis had their glitches, she thought. Luckily she knew she was heading in roughly the right direction, back to South Yorkshire, not Devon. Sadly.

Less than a mile along the way, Mary could see there was a problem in the shape of a rockfall ahead. The weight of snow on the hillside must have dislodged stones and boulders at the inconvenient point where the road narrowed to a single track. There was no way around the obstruction, she could tell that even from a long distance away. Jack's attention was dragged to the scene framed by the windscreen when he felt the car slowing.

'Oh, please tell me this isn't happening,' he said.

'I'll have to turn back,' said Mary, stating the obvious. What else could they do? The road was completely blocked.

'Goodness, the snow really is bad isn't it,' said Jack. He'd raised his head at various points and glanced at the weather but his mind was more on the presentation to Chikafuji; now he was *seeing* the white-out. 'I think it would be sensible to pull in at the first place we can, Mary.'

Mary did another about-turn and headed for Tynehall yet again, even though they had no chance of making it that far. There had to be somewhere nearby. They were in Yorkshire, not an Arctic tundra, even if it did look like it. Then, in the midst of all the white in front of her, she spotted a wooden arrow-shaped sign coming up on the left, pointing across to a turning that wasn't showing up on the satnav, with crude black lettering: *Figgy Hollow 3/4 mile*. She couldn't remember seeing it on either of the two times she'd passed this spot before, but she hadn't been looking for shelter then.

She hadn't a clue what Figgy Hollow was: a local beauty spot, a farm; a hamlet with a welcoming hotel and a cosy log fire, she hoped, but in case there was nothing else around for miles, she took the risk and swung a right. *Nothing ventured, nothing gained.* Another gem from her father's book of sayings.

Chapter 3

Luke Palfreyman wished he was travelling in his trusty four-by-four instead of his boy-toy vintage DB5 Aston Martin, which didn't perform at its best in snow, especially super-freak snow like this, which seemed to be heralding the birth of a new Ice Age. He, alas, was no James Bond, so the car didn't suddenly project wings – or better still skis – to get him smoothly to his destination; instead he was stuck with driving it manually and praying it got him safely to where he needed to be. He'd spent the last couple of years trying to acquire the art of being reasonable and sensible – give or take buying a 1960s dream car – only to agree to head for a place in the arse end of nowhere just because his wife clicked her fingers. Or soon to be ex-wife, to give her the proper title. It wouldn't be beyond credibility that Bridge had engineered this weather to inconvenience him further. Few things had ever run well for him where she was concerned; she was a walking jinx, quite the opposite to his present fiancée. Everything was so easy with Carmen, everything *flowed*, like a peaceful river, whereas Bridge was a whirlpool full of piranhas.

He could have replied to Bridge's shouty text (STOP PRESS, DIVERT TO FIGGY HOLLOW INN. OFF THE A7501, SW OF WHITBY. ASK SIRI IF SATNAV CAN'T FIND IT) that they do this at another time, i.e. one less treacherous and more sensible, but he knew it meant a lot to Carmen to start off the new year with things moving forwards out of what had felt like an eternal impasse. As Bridge had foreseen, his TomTom hadn't recognised the name Figgy Hollow, which was just plain weird and if Siri hadn't helped him out, he would have put his substantial personal fortune on all this being Bridge playing more stupid games. She always could get under his skin more than anyone else ever could; like a sharp, thin splinter that managed to wiggle far enough in so that using tweezers to hoick it out was ineffectual and a serious incision was needed. He could feel his default setting these days of cool slipping by the second and, despite himself, he laughed aloud. There really was no one like Bridge on the planet. He looked up at the thick grey clouds through the windscreen, expecting to find her on a broomstick circling above like a malicious crow.

The snow had come from nowhere, impossible as that might have seemed in this day and age; yet it had happened. Luke had been half an hour into his journey when it started, drops of sleet falling onto his windscreen, smudging his vision. Within five minutes they'd turned to snow, within ten that snow was settling on the country's grid of ungritted roads. He'd presumed, like everyone else had, it was only a few flurries that would quickly melt away, but those flakes kept on dropping, thicker and heavier and the traffic got slower and slower. It would have been the only sensible thing to do to rearrange the meeting, but he *had* to get this divorce properly underway. He didn't want to go into a new year with this hanging over his head like the sword of Damocles, not when he planned to be remarried by late summer. He needed to pack up his old life with the old year and he had to see Bridge in person in order to do that and on both counts he was determined that nothing would stop him. Nothing.

*

Bridge lifted her glass to the optic, pressed upwards and stood until a double brandy had been delivered. There was definitely no one in the inn, she'd shouted loud 'hello hello's up the stairs and into the area behind the bar. She'd even stood at the top of the cellar steps and shouted down into the black silence and not even an echo of her voice had come back at her.

Someone must have been there recently though because the bar area was spick and span, the tabletops were gleaming and a faint smell of polish still hung in the air. There was an enormous fireplace, logs banked up on it ready to light, for the Christmas Day diners, no doubt. A large Christmas tree occupied one far corner of the room, thick green branches ready for their drape of tinsel; baubles and lights sat patiently in a cardboard box tucked underneath it, with packets of paper-chain strips, waiting to be constructed and tacked with drawing pins onto the picture rail. They were the sort Bridge remembered making at school, with a gum line at one end that tasted awful. Another memory flashed in her head: sitting on the floor putting such a chain together, in front of a fire fuelled with wood that they'd gathered illegally from the nearby park because they were too skint to buy it. She and Luke. He leaning over towards her, crushing the chain as they started kissing, tearing off each other's clothes, then making love, which had given her bum major carpet burns. She shook her head to disengage those images, stamped the mini-film of chain-making in Joseph Street junior school back over them, sitting next to Michael Butler who used to pick his nose and wipe it on any available surface other than a handkerchief.

She sat down at a bar table next to the middle of three windows and took a swig of brandy before picking her phone out of her handbag to find she'd had two missed calls from Ben. She rang him, it didn't connect the first time. She tried again.

'Are you okay? Thank goodness,' he said. 'Where are you?'

'I couldn't get to where I was heading, so I've had to make a diversion. I'm in a pub, I'm safe, no need to worry.'

'Is Luke there with you?'

'Not yet. He's on his way—'

'What did you say? You cut out.'

'HE'S ON HIS WAY I SHOULD IMAGINE.'

Luke would be here, she had absolutely no doubt about that. He was nothing if not reliable. Well, at least he was these days, by all accounts. Plus, she knew how much he wanted this divorce to go ahead. He'd drive through fire for it, never mind the new Siberia.

'I wish you'd just come straight home.' The weight of concern in Ben's voice brought a smile to Bridge's lips.

'I might have done if I'd known this was going to happen.' She said it but she wasn't sure if it was strictly true.

'You must not even think about trying to drive back in this tonight,' Ben warned her, having to repeat it twice because his voice kept dissolving into crackles and silence.

'I promise you, I won't,' Bridge replied. 'I'm on the sensible side of mad.'

'What?'

'I said I won't. Line's awful.'

'But you're all right?'

'Yes, I'm dry and safe.'

'Good.' She could feel his sigh of relief whisper into her ear.

'I'll ring you later to let you know how our meeting goes.'

'Can't hear you, Bridge. Hello? Hel—'

The line died. Modern technology was great until it wasn't. She tried to reconnect the call, but no luck. She sent a text but the message wouldn't deliver. She noticed an old-fashioned rotary dial phone on the bar in a stunning shade of mustard. She lifted the receiver to hear absolutely nothing; the landline was also deceased, it seemed.

No, she would definitely not be driving back tonight if the snow carried on falling, but at least she had been able to tell Ben that and stop him fretting, because he would worry, bless him. He was a sweet, caring person and she was lucky to have him in her life. Luckier than he was, because she was all too aware that she'd taken her phone out of her bag primarily to check if Luke had been in contact and not to tell Ben she was okay. Once again he was at the top of the *important!* list in her head and she hated that he was. The sooner they did what they had to do and could conclude their business, the better.

If she had to stay here tonight, then so be it. With any luck there would be an overnight thaw and she'd excuse the mild inconvenience and look forward to being in her own bed before midnight tomorrow so that Santa wouldn't pass by her house. She laughed to herself at that thought. She'd always been in bed before midnight on Christmas Eve as a child but it seemed Santa's sack was empty by the time he got to her chimney. Year after year her hope in his existence dwindled a little more until she lost it altogether at nine. And one day she met Luke Palfreyman and then all her lost Christmases landed in her lap in one sparkly, candy-cane-flavoured, tinsel-wrapped lump.

She took another sip of brandy, listening for the slightest sound in the muted silence. There had to be someone around in this godforsaken hole. She put down her glass, deciding to undertake a more detailed search of the premises, starting with the area behind the bar where she found a small galley kitchen and what was probably a pantry off it. No human in there, though. The ladies' and gents' toilets were identical, apart from their walls, which were pink in one case, blue in the other. They each contained a single cubicle, one sink, a bowl of spicy potpourri gently scenting the area. Bridge caught sight of herself in the mirror to find her straightened hairstyle hadn't held firm after her outdoor exploration and had reverted to its natural kinks, making her appear less serious, more casual, a look she didn't want today. She left the cloakroom and went up the narrow, steep staircase, which creaked and groaned as if protesting at the weight of her, all eight and a half stone of it.

Still calling 'hello', she pushed open the doors and checked each of the three bedrooms up there: two with twin beds, the other a double, all unmade; each room had an en-suite with shower. The décor was chintz city: dusky pink carpets, flowery walls and curtains; crocheted dolls in crinolines sat on top of each loo hiding a toilet roll, with more of that Christmas-spicy potpourri in bowls dotted around, but the effect was charming rather than vomit-inducing. The owner had taken care to provide his guests with comfort, as each room had a velvet-upholstered chair next to a table with a fan of well-read books on it, a box of pastel-coloured tissues on the dressing table with a tray of complimentary single-use toiletries, a thin notepad and pen on every bed-side cabinet all bearing a line drawing of the Figgy Hollow Inn. A fourth smaller room opposite the end bedroom was filled with stocks of duvets, pillows, sheets, towels, more of those tiny soaps and bottles of shower gel and shampoo, individually-wrapped toothbrushes with a minuscule tube of toothpaste, pads, pens, notepaper, envelopes, boxes of those coloured tissues and a motherlode of toilet rolls. There might not have been anyone around, but, on the positive side, there were enough toiletries to see her through until May if things got really bad.

Bridge went back downstairs, noticing things she hadn't seen now her brain had started to switch to full-on obser-vant survival mode: the lights on the wall, fashioned to resemble old oil lamps, the seasoned timber beams, which were probably original, given that the ceiling was bowed in places and the walls hadn't been built by anyone with a plumb bob. She hated that Victorian colour palette usually, of chestnuts, maroons, heavy oppressive shades, but the deep red paint on the walls worked well here with the bright white-glossed picture rails and skirting boards, maybe because it had been expertly applied and not just slapped on by an old bloke down the road who got paid in pints. The bar area wasn't that large: twelve dark wooden square tables to serve customers seated on the motley selection of wooden chairs, upholstered benches or leather-studded wing-back armchairs. The dark brown and red carpet had seen better days but it sat quietly underfoot without drawing attention to itself, letting other features take the glory, none more so than the massive inglenook fireplace. If ever there was a fireplace suited to a visit from Santa Claus, it was this one.

There was an old stack system stereo near the Christmas tree with a cassette tape deck and a radio. She plugged it in, switched it on, twiddled a knob trying to tune it to a station that would give her some news.

'... Met office has offered no explanation for failing to forecast the Arctic weather conditions but has issued a warning not to go outside, but to stay indoors ...'

No shit, Sherlock, said Bridge to herself. She turned the radio off, thought of Luke arriving at the inn door any moment now. Just the two of them snowed in, alone together. It wouldn't do. It really wouldn't do at all.

Chapter 4

Bridge had been there for over an hour trying to read a dated, yellowing periodical taken from a stack of vintage magazines by the fire, when the noise of a car engine pulled her thoughts away from the running sore that was Luke Palfreyman. Outside, she could see that an impressive peacock-blue Range Rover was nosing slowly into the car park. *Nice.* Surprising, though. She'd imagined Luke rolling up in the vintage Aston Martin he'd always said he'd buy if he won the lottery. He might not have won millions, but he'd certainly earned them these past five years, selling his veggie burgers. She quickly reached for her bag, pulled out her mirror and refreshed her red lipstick. She'd hidden behind this same shade (*Rich Bitch*) for years. It didn't go with her flame-bright hair, she knew that, but it made her look potent, in control, even if she didn't feel it. Like now.

She gave her hair a quick brush hoping to restore it to its artificially straightened glory, but that was a hope too far. She returned her attention to the Range Rover outside and saw that there was someone sitting in the passenger seat. *Surely he hadn't brought Spanish Carmen with him. Not to discuss his divorce.* That was the sort of shitty trick he would play, two against one. She felt her ire rising and prepared to do battle by summoning up her inner Boudicca.

The car drew up next to her Porsche, and the driver got out: a tall, solidly built man in his fifties, was Bridge's rough guess, wearing a bright orange jacket with the hood up. He tripped and slipped around to the boot to retrieve a large bag, then went round to the passenger side to open the door for an older, thinner gentleman wearing the same style ski jacket but white with colour splashes on it. They clung to each other as they battled their way through the snowflakes towards the inn door, blasting in gratefully, bringing the weather with them.

'Thank God,' exclaimed orange jacket, putting the bag down before shaking off the snow that had settled on him. He noticed Bridge then. 'Hello,' he said, politely, his eyes honing in on the brandy on the table in front of her. 'Isn't this weather awful. I bet that tastes extra nice sitting in here, looking out there.'

'Are you the landlord?' asked Bridge, ready to apologise for breaking in.

'No, just weary stragglers,' said the older man, dropping heavily onto a cushioned bench.

'So you don't work here then?' asked orange jacket, flipping back his hood, unzipping his coat.

'Nope. I'm a weary straggler too.'

'Lucky you found it like we did, then. I dread to think what would have happened if we hadn't.'

He approached the bar.

'There's no one around,' said Bridge. 'Seems the place is only open for pre-booked dinners. I helped myself to this, in case you're wondering. I've started my own tab under the circumstances.'

'What, the door was left open?' asked orange jacket. His accent was unmistakably East London, his voice gentle and at odds with his big build and shaved head. Bridge had always been good at picking out where people hailed from.

'I broke in,' said Bridge. 'It was either that or freeze to death in the car.'

'Good grief,' said the older man; by contrast his voice was refined and rich as a rum-soaked fruit cake. 'You could have died if you hadn't engaged in criminal activities. And so could we, no doubt. Dear lady, we are indebted to you.'

His response coaxed a smile from Bridge.

He unzipped his coat, then freed his arms from the sleeves. He had a lot of hair for an elderly gent, was Bridge's initial thought: salt-and-pepper curls that fell softly past his shoulders, and his thin face suited the beard and moustache combo. He was wearing a dapper waistcoat and a Chanel scarf tied at his neck as a cravat. He looked not unlike the illegitimate child of Charles I and an aged Laurence Llewelyn-Bowen.

'Looks like we will be here for quite a while, surviving on those packets of crisps until we are discovered at Easter, draped over the bar,' said the younger of the two men, taking both jackets and hanging them up on the hooks at the side of the door.

'Well, seeing as it appears we will be spending some hours in each other's company, I shall make introductions; my name is Charlie,' said the elder of the new arrivals. He made an extravagant hand gesture towards his companion. 'And this is my husband, Robin.'

Husband, thought Bridge, glad she hadn't had the chance to put her foot in it, because she'd presumed they were father and son.

'I'm Bridge. Short for Bridget, but no one has ever called me that.' *No one she wanted to remember,* amended an inner voice.

'I'll find a kettle and we'll have a nice cup of tea, shall we?' said Robin.

'No, I want what she's having,' Charlie replied with definite protest.

'Not a chance,' Robin came back at him.

'Purely for medicinal purposes,' said Charlie, in a wheedling tone. 'Oh go on, you miserable fart.'

'A very very small one then,' Robin relented with a tut.

'I presume that's your Porsche next to our car,' said Charlie as Robin called out a few cautious hellos at the bar in case what Bridge was telling him wasn't true.

'Yes, it is.'

'Very nice, love the red colour. But I imagine it wasn't great in the snow.'

'Crap,' replied Bridge, moving to sit across the table from Charlie, hoping it would be warmer away from the window. 'I consider myself lucky that I made it this far before either crashing into a tree or being buried under a drift.'

'So what are you doing up here then?'

'I was meeting someone,' said Bridge without giving details, before taking a large gulp of brandy. The mere thought of what she was here for had the tendency to drive her to drink.

'Oh dear, I hope they found somewhere to take shelter,' said Charlie.

'I hope so too,' said Bridge, but she wasn't convinced that Luke would have. This was too important to him. Winkling her out of his life was too important to him.

Robin went behind the bar. He took two glasses, held

one up to the brandy optic and one up to the malt whisky, then he delivered the glass containing the brandy into the eager hands of his partner. Charlie lifted the glass, savoured the fumes and sighed.

'Oh, darling, it's been too long,' he said, addressing the contents before sipping.

Robin crossed to the window, gazing out onto a landscape of dark skies and snow. The flakes were falling large as pennies. 'Looks like we're here for the night,' he said.

'They have three bedrooms upstairs,' said Bridge. 'The beds aren't made up, but there's plenty of duvets and sheets. I went for a snoop.'

'I can see headlights in the distance,' said Robin, squinting.

Bridge's heart made a treacherous bounce in her chest as if preparing to break out and lay down a red carpet. Hearts could be terribly immature at times.

'It's a *voiture splendide*,' Robin said. 'Maserati I think. Emerald green, beautiful.'

It had to be Luke, thought Bridge. He was not only a Maserati sort of guy these days but he'd always had a thing about green cars.

Robin's running commentary continued. 'Yes, it's pulling in. Man and a woman from what I can see, unless my eyes deceive me.'

Luke and Carmen, thought Bridge. *Great.*

Charlie was fiddling with his phone. 'I can't get a signal.'

'No signal, no internet. I just managed to get through to someone to let them know I was safe but then the line dropped and I haven't been able to get it back,' said Bridge. 'There's a phone on the bar, but the landline's dead too.'

Robin left his space by the window to open the door for

the newcomers. In rushed a young blonde-haired woman followed by a man and half a ton of snow, as if the weather sought to take refuge with them. The wind whistled a howling protest as Robin shut it out. The male newcomer had very dark hair. Definitely not Luke.

'Thank goodness this place is open,' said not-Luke.

'It wasn't, this young lady had to break in,' said Robin, bobbing his head towards Bridge.

'An obvious emergency,' said Bridge quickly in her defence. 'It doesn't look as if it's open again for another two days, at least that's what I gathered from the note stuck in the window.'

'It's mad out there,' said the blonde, putting down her handbag and a red suitcase to peel at strands of her long hair that had glued themselves across her pale-skinned, pretty face. Bridge's brain was quick to sum people up, always had been: the blonde was reed-slender, young, not one who had embraced the present trend for slug-eyebrows, spider-leg eyelashes and inflated lips, which was refreshing to see. The man, tall with the sort of build that suggested he worked out in a gym, but not obsessively. Dark hair cropped just at the point where it had begun to curl, light grey eyes, an attractive rather than handsome face with his nose a little crooked, maybe from an old rugby injury. Bridge wondered what their relationship was: brother and sister, friends? She didn't get the couple vibe from them, but they looked good together.

'We should hole up for an hour or two until this subsides and then try and get back home,' said the man, his accent polished private school, confident and deep in tone. His overnight bag, Bridge noted, was black leather, stylish, understated.

'Unless home is within skiing distance, I wouldn't bet on it,' said Charlie. 'I think it's wise to presume you're here for the night with me – I'm Charlie – my husband Robin over there and our new friend Bridge.'

'Jack and Mary,' said Mary, liking how their two names sat together in a bracket.

'Hello,' said Jack, in the manner of someone who thought introductions were unnecessary because he wouldn't be there long enough for them to mean anything.

'You certainly won't be going anywhere for a while, so I'd take your coat off if I were you and relax with us,' Charlie continued.

Mary took off her pink mac, a fashion rather than a practical piece, Bridge surmised. Jack, realising that what Charlie said was probably true, removed his coat, shook the wetness from it. A vintage Crombie; Charlie recognised it because he knew class when he saw it.

'Where's home for you two then?' asked Charlie.

'Place called Oxworth, you won't have heard of it,' said Jack.

'Oxworth in South Yorkshire? I know it well. In fact, I know every bit of Yorkshire. I was born in Whitby. I had an aunt whom we used to visit, she lived in Penistone, which isn't far from Oxworth, is it?' replied Charlie, before taking another sip of brandy and giving a shimmy of delight.

'That's right,' said Mary, hanging up both her coat and Jack's. 'It's very close to Penistone. What a small world.'

'What about you, dear?' Charlie asked Bridge. 'I can't place your accent.'

'I'm originally from just outside Derby,' said Bridge, although over the past years her accent had been ironed to neutral. She'd forced herself to talk like that at first; now she spoke that way naturally. The name Bridget and the accent that went with it belonged to a past that she had little fondness for.

'This snow is here to stay, and I imagine a road like this would be way down on the pecking order for gritting,' said Robin, from his place by the first window, his legs drawing a modicum of warmth from the old-style radiator fastened to the wall underneath it. 'There's no light coming from those cottages across the way, is there?'

'They're all empty,' said Bridge. 'I walked across before I took a screwdriver to the door lock. No one in at the church, either.'

'Then there's no chance of them clearing round here, is there?' Robin surmised. 'Any snow ploughs will be concentrating on the major roads, not single-track country lanes.'

'I have a meeting I can't miss tomorrow lunchtime,' insisted Jack.

'Well you'd better pray for a quick thaw, mate, or an AA man driving Chitty Chitty Bang Bang.' At the rate the snow was falling, Robin thought that the second option seemed the more probable.

'We're supposed to be halfway to the Cairngorms for Christmas by now,' said Charlie. 'Five-star hotel and all the snow you can shake a stick at, except there isn't any up there, it's all down here. The world's gone insane.'

'I thought everyone was more worried about global warming than this sort of thing,' said Mary.

'I could do with a bit of global warming now. It's not very warm in here, is it?' said Charlie, with a shudder.

Robin was instantly alerted to the comfort of his husband. 'Anyone mind if I light that fire?' he asked.

A general rumble of 'No' and 'Go ahead'.

'There's a box of matches on the mantelpiece,' Bridge pointed out.

'Thank you,' said Robin. He took one out of the box, struck it then poked it at the twists of newspaper under the front logs until the flame transferred.

'So, there's no landlord here then?' asked Jack.

'Not unless he's hiding,' replied Bridge. 'I gave the place a once-over when I arrived, apart from the cellar, but I did shout down and there was no answer. In short, there's no one here but "us chickens".'

'Which way to the ladies' loos?' Mary asked Bridge.

'I'll show you,' said Bridge, 'I need to go myself.'

'Mind if I go first?' asked Mary, when they got inside. 'I'm absolutely bursting.'

'Be my guest,' said Bridge.

'Thanks.' Mary rushed in, locked the door, made an eventual 'ahhh' of relief sound.

'I've been holding on to this for miles,' she said through the door. 'I was on the brink of having to stop the car at the next available set of trees. I'd have been mortified to have had to pull up for that reason.'

'You were driving?' asked Bridge.

'Yeah. I like driving. Especially that car.'

'So much easier for men, isn't it?' said Bridge. 'I do envy them the ability to just whip it out and syphon off. Where were you going?'

'Jack had a breakfast meeting in Tynehall first thing tomorrow morning. The plan was to get there today, rest up, have the meeting and then drive home straight after.'

'Tynehall? You're way off course. Were you travelling on the A1?'

'We were until a lorry blocked it. There was a diversion, then that diversion got diverted ...'

'Similar thing happened to me,' said Bridge. 'Got totally lost. Me and the satnav.'

Mary flushed the loo, opened the door.

'Is that your partner you're with?' Bridge asked.

'Jack? I wish. Oops.' Mary slapped both hands over her mouth. 'Sorry, I shouldn't have said that.'

Bridge chuckled as she went into the cubicle. 'I won't say a word. Promise.'

'Jack's the boss, I'm the lowly PA.'

'Nothing lowly about being a PA,' Bridge corrected her. 'The oil in the machine. Some of these execs don't know how much their "lowly PAs" actually do for them behind the scenes.'

'You sound as if you've been one yourself,' said Mary, turning on the tap to wash her hands.

'I was. Once upon a time. Among other things,' Bridge replied. The list of 'other things' was long: factory worker, cleaner, dish-washer, barmaid, telesales operator, till operator, auction house administrator, PA to the owner of that company ... MD of her own property company.

'I've only ever had one job, apart from a Saturday job in Tesco,' said Mary. 'I love it though. I wouldn't want to change. I think I found my perfect niche early. I've worked for Jack for six and a half years since I left college. Well,' she began to correct herself, 'I worked for Jack's dad Reg for two and a half years at first and then when he retired and Jack took over, I became his PA.'

'So that would make you about twenty-five?' asked Bridge, waiting for the answer before flushing.

'Yep. At least, I will be on Christmas Day.'

Bridge thought back: she'd been selling advertising space at that age. Working long hours selling a sub-standard product for a sub-standard rate of commission, then she'd stay behind when the others had gone to clean the building so she could at least take a semblance of a wage home. She emerged from the cubicle, went over to the sink, pushed some soap onto her hand from the dispenser before turning on the tap.

'What line of work is Jack in that you needed to travel so far for a meeting on Christmas Eve morning?'

'Scones,' replied Mary.

'Scones?' Bridge couldn't help the hoot of laughter that escaped from her. She'd been expecting the answer to be on the lines of national security.

'Yep, scones. Just scones, nothing else. Butterly's Scones. Jack's grandad Bill set it up. Jack's the third generation to run the company. Since he's been top dog, he's taken it to heights his dad and grandfather wouldn't have even dreamed of. Anyway, a bakery owner in Japan contacted us to do business with him and I can't count the number of times I've fixed up meetings only for him to drop out at the last minute. But he was bobbing over from Brussels on business today and I managed to persuade him to squeeze in seeing Jack in the morning before his plane left Newcastle, but he backed out yet again – just before we found this place. Jack's furious and I can't say I blame him.'

Bridge made a whistle. It all sounded very big business. 'I didn't realise there was such a demand for scones that you needed a whole factory to produce them and nothing else.'

'Oh goodness me yes,' said Mary with emphasis. 'At capacity we can produce two million scones per day. We do every sort too, raisin, cheese, cherry, treacle, gluten-free, vegan, different grades and prices and more long-lasting ones, which we export. We run machines twenty-four-seven. There's the demand all right, and it's growing.'

It was on the tip of Bridge's tongue to say 'You must have a word with my ex about the vegan scones,' but she stopped herself. Why should she give Luke Palfreyman any mention where a possible business venture was concerned?

'Why are you here then?' said Mary, trying not to stare too much at Bridge's face. She thought she was beautiful, with her large hazel eyes and her brave red lipstick. It should have clashed with her fire-flame hair, but quite the opposite. It was amazing what a bit of chutzpah did for you. Her dad had taught her that word. Maybe one day she'd have some too.

'I'm meeting my husband,' Bridge said, still washing her hands with the thoroughness of Lady Macbeth. 'Soon to be ex-husband.'

'Oh, I see,' said Mary, though she didn't really.

'Our marriage took a lot of . . . deconstructing.' Bridge chose the word carefully. It was a tame one to use to describe a war. 'But we got there.'

'Good that you were able to sort everything out in the end though,' said Mary with a little smile.

'We both figured we didn't want the solicitors creaming off all our hard-earned cash, so we did most of our fighting without involving them, which was hard and probably stupid, but we managed eventually to come to an agreement that works for both. Neither of us wanted to step into another new year without resolving everything, as we both intend to be married to our new partners sooner rather than later.'

'It's a bit easier when you've both got someone else,' said

Mary. 'When my aunt and uncle split up, he got himself a young, glamorous girlfriend and my auntie was so bitter and jealous about it. She still is and it's been ten years since they got divorced. In fact she's worse now than she was then. She can't let it go.'

'Yes, well, neither of us wants to be like that.'

'Much better to be sensible and cut finally and cleanly,' said Mary, nodding with a sagacity that belied her age.

Bridge snapped out a paper towel to dry her hands. 'Do yourself a favour, love, and stay single. The St Georges of today are the dragons of tomorrow.'

Which was an odd thing to say for someone about to get married to a new partner, thought Mary as she followed Bridge out.

Chapter 5

'Anyone fancy a coffee?' asked Mary, when they rejoined the others. The fire had taken hold of the logs now, flames licking upwards with golden eagerness. Outside, the snow was falling relentlessly and it all looked very festive on both sides of the bar lounge windows. The whole indoor scene could quite happily have sat on a Christmas card if it wasn't for the five disgruntled, inconvenienced faces; Jack's claiming first prize.

'Yes, I'll have one, love. Shall I come and help you?' said Robin.

'No, it's fine,' said Mary. 'I think I can manage a few coffees.' It was what she did, after all. She made a lot of coffees in her job, arranged a lot of biscuits on plates. At least Jack always said thank you, however distracted he was, unlike his father Reg.

'If you can find any biscuits backstage, I'd be awfully grateful,' said Charlie with a cheeky, hopeful grin.

'Cholesterol!' barked Robin.

'Oh shut up, you miserable queen,' replied Charlie and flapped his hand at his much younger husband.

'You can have *one*, if Mary finds some,' Robin relented.

'I'm starving. I saved up my calories for the lovely meal we were going to have in Aviemore tonight. I've only had a porridge in the service station. It was supposed to be maple syrup flavoured,' Charlie explained to Bridge. 'Tasted of fish to me.' He pulled a face and she laughed. As people to be trapped in a deserted inn with went, Charlie would have been a good choice, she thought. He had a benign air and twinkly, mischievous bright blue-grey eyes.

Bridge was peckish too. She hadn't eaten all day because the thought of meeting Luke had wiped away any appetite she might have otherwise had. She regretted not stoking up on breakfast at the Hilton where she was staying. She wondered where he was now. Maybe he was holed up in some service station. Maybe he'd broken down and was currently freezing his nuts off in the driver's seat of his no doubt very posh and totally impractical car. It would serve him right, just for being Luke Palfreyman. She also hoped he was safe.

'Well this is very Agatha Christie,' said Charlie, after a few minutes of them staring silently into the mesmerising, dancing flames. 'And then there were five. One by one, we'll be getting picked off by a murderer who sits among us. Or perhaps is presently hiding in the cellar.'

'You'll be the first victim, I bet,' said Robin. 'We'll all be queueing to shut you up before too long.'

Charlie chuckled.

'So what line of business are you in then, Jack?' asked Robin.

'Scones,' came the reply.

'Ooh, I would kill for a buttered scone right now,' said Charlie with relish.

'You're getting a biscuit with any luck, be grateful for

that,' Robin said in reply, before turning back to Jack. 'Just scones? Nothing else?'

'Just scones. Different recipes for home and export and different flavours but all just scones,' Jack answered him. 'What about you two?'

'I was a jeweller before I retired,' said Charlie. 'Mainly I dealt in diamonds. I always had an instinctive eye for quality.' He turned his eyes towards Robin.

'I was his chauffeur,' said Robin with a sniff. 'I'll tell you before he does, because he will try and insinuate that I married him for his money.'

Charlie hooted with laughter. 'Anyone who has been in my company for more than five minutes, though, will realise that it must have been my sparkling personality that drew you in first and foremost, before my sparkling diamonds.'

'Yes, and I've been promoted via marriage to general dogsbody,' said Robin, dryly. 'Charlie is twenty-four years my senior and we've been together for thirty-two years. We've had a lot of pleasure out of proving all the cynics who said it would never last completely wrong, haven't we, Charlie?'

'Oh, we have indeed,' Charlie confirmed.

Bridge found herself smiling. They were an odd couple, Charlie so much more refined than Robin, Robin so much younger and yet, from early deductions, it seemed as if they fitted together like a dovetail joint; banter passing between them as if whacked over a net by a tennis racket, back and forth in an endless joyful rally.

Mary emerged from the kitchen behind the bar with a large silver tray set with refreshments.

'I couldn't find biscuits so I hope mince pies will do,' she called out ahead of her arrival.

'Ooh, mince pies,' said Charlie.

'The good news is that we aren't going to starve, I can assure you of that,' said Mary. 'The larder and cupboards are absolutely crammed full back there. And I've got the coffee machine up and running, so this is fresh from the bean.'

Jack walked to her to take the weight of the tray and set it down on a table. Charlie immediately reached for a mince pie and Robin slapped his hand.

'If I weren't here to steer you, you'd end up crashed on the shore,' he said to his husband.

'Robin. It's medicinal. I need calories,' came the response.

'Medicinal my arse,' said Robin with a humph, but he didn't stop Charlie's hand when it reached out the second time.

They all sat quietly, sipping the coffee, biting into the buttery pastry of the mince pies. None of them realised they were as hungry as they were until they started munching.

'I don't know if it's because I was desperate for a coffee and a bite to eat or you're an angel in disguise, but this tastes divine,' said Charlie. 'Thank you, Mary. And what a very Christmassy name you have, may I say. Like my Robin.'

'That's because I was born on Christmas Day,' replied Mary. 'Mary Holly Clementine Padgett. I'm just glad my parents stopped there. Mum said that Dad wanted to squeeze in a poinsettia as well.'

'Oh you are funny, Mary,' said Charlie, having a chortle at that.

'Is it really your birthday on Christmas Day?' asked Jack.

'Yep,' said Mary, trying not to let her nip of hurt show, that he didn't even know that fact after she'd been working for him for four full years. She knew his birthday was on the twelfth of February, she always sent him a card that she'd spent time choosing.

'Well, if we're still here, we'll have a party for you,' said Charlie. It was a joke of course. It was unthinkable that they would all still be there on Christmas Day.

'What line of work are you in, Bridge?' asked Robin.

'Land and property,' she answered him. 'I buy derelict houses to renovate, but mostly I buy cheap auction lots of land that no one wants and try to sell them on.'

'That sounds like a lot of gambling,' said Jack.

'It is, but I'm prepared to play a long game for a good profit.'

'Are you very successful?' asked Jack in a way that implied he doubted it.

'Very,' she replied.

She'd been badly advised in the beginning, at a time when she wanted to prove to the world that she was in control of things, knew what she was doing when she didn't at all. *Buy that plot of land and you* will *get planning permission on it, trust me*, said someone whose word she did trust at the time, until she realised he was a friend of the person who owned the land and the pair of them were laughing up their sleeves when her bid was successful. She'd sunk everything she had into that land. All because she wanted to be the big 'I am', and show Luke Palfreyman that she was doing fine without him, had a life plan, was as good at big business as he was proving to be.

Then Derbyshire county council approached her because they wanted to open up the adjacent plot of green-belt land for building, but they'd need her plot to use for access. It had to be a miracle that suddenly she was the one laughing, signing on the dotted line, banking the big cheque. That experience made her a little more savvy as well as rich. From then on, she did her homework properly, trusted no one blindly. Some plots of land were still in her portfolio, useless fields that she rented out for peanuts to people with cows or horses, but she could afford to wait for tides to turn. She had an inbuilt radar for a good investment and she had no idea where it had come from, but she was glad it had been gifted to her.

'Wonder who owns this place?' said Charlie. 'I mean Figgy Hollow. I thought I knew this area, but I've never heard of it. It's most odd.'

'I hope it isn't haunted,' said Robin, throwing another log on the fire. 'It looks like one of those places that could be.' He shuddered involuntarily.

Jack went over to the window, clearly frustrated, saw the snow falling. Their three cars were completely covered now, looking like bumps underneath fondant icing.

'This is ridiculous. The whole bloody country goes to pot when there's a bit of snow. We export to Finland and they live with snow day in, day out. Doesn't affect their lives one bit.'

'In Tromsø in Norway, between November and January, the sun doesn't even peep over the horizon,' put in Mary. 'You have to change your mindset when you live with months of dark and snow. That's why they don't get a seasonal depression.'

All eyes turned to her and she felt her cheeks heating up.

'That would make perfect sense,' said Bridge, feeling the need to rescue the younger woman, who she suspected wasn't in the spotlight much. 'Have you been there?'

'My mother's Norwegian,' said Mary. 'I've spent a lot of time there.'

'Really, Mary?' asked Jack, raising a brace of surprised eyebrows.

Something else he doesn't know about me, thought Mary. But then, why should she be of any interest to him?

'That explains your colouring then,' said Charlie. 'Those lovely light eyes and pale golden hair.'

Mary's blush deepened, but she carried on speaking. 'The Norwegians don't stay in and mope, they go out. One of their sayings is that "there is no such thing as bad weather, only bad clothing".'

'They're right of course, but I'm staying put in front of the fire,' said Bridge.

Charlie laughed. 'At least Robin and I have brought plenty of good snow clothing with us. One of our suitcases contains only boots.'

'They don't moan about the weather and bring down their mood,' Mary went on. 'They go for a walk, breathe in the lovely fresh air, build snowmen, go skating and skiing. Then they come home, kick off their boots, drink hot chocolate and eat cake.'

'That sounds fun,' said Charlie. 'I want to go to Norway now, not Scotland. Have we time to change the booking, Robin?'

'Don't be silly, Charlie,' Robin answered somewhat gruffly, before standing and announcing that he was going to the loo.

'Poor Robin,' said Charlie with a sigh, when poor Robin was out of earshot. 'I drive him mad. He booked the Scotland trip especially for me and I know he's worried we won't get there.'

'Well, we're going to have to acquire some of that winter Norwegian mindset, certainly until tomorrow,' said Bridge, her turn to get up and look out of the window now, to try and peer through the falling snow in the hope of seeing a pair of headlights. It was half-past eight but felt like the middle of the night. It was brutal out there now, the road impassable. So why couldn't she shake the feeling that Luke wasn't holed up in safe shelter and he was still doggedly on his way?

Chapter 6

Half an hour later, Robin's phone began to beep-beep loudly in his pocket. He took it out to cancel the alarm then went over to his bag, unzipped it and rifled through it. When he came back to the fire, he had two tablets in his hand that he gave to Charlie, who grimaced.

'I hate these chewy ones,' he said.

'You don't chew those, you swallow them whole. I'll go and get you something to eat because you're supposed to take them with food. Proper food, not mince pies.'

'The mince pies were lovely and tasted like proper food to me.'

'You know what I mean, Charlie. I'll see if there's anything I can make a sandwich with. Anyone else want one?'

'I'll come with you and make some for us all,' said Mary. 'The mince pie was very nice but it didn't fill me up.'

Bridge stood, held her palm flat out towards Mary to stay put. 'You did it last time so I reckon it's my turn now.'

Jack stood also, put his phone in his pocket after checking it yet again for activity. 'I'll help. I need to do something else rather than just look at a fire. I'm going stir-crazy already. So who's for coffee and who's for tea?'

Bridge led the way to the kitchen, sneaking another peek out of the window as she passed it. She wished she knew for certain that Luke was all right, hoped her instinct was wrong and that he was sitting in a service station with a hot meal and the prospect of a bed for the night, but there were no car lights out there, no hint of Luke, nothing but snow.

'Blimey,' Bridge said, pushing open the door to the pantry, switching on the light and having a proper look inside. It was like a walk-in festive hamper. There was everything anyone could want for Christmas dinner on the shelves and in the fridges: an alp of sprouts, chestnuts, turkeys, Christmas puddings, brandy butter, rum cream, Christmas cake and a lot of mince pies.

'I'll butter some breadcakes, shall I?' said Jack, lifting up a bulk bag of them.

'I'll be on filling duty,' said Bridge. She peeled the wax off a truckle of Wensleydale cheese and cut it into chunky slices, then she carved some ham, spooned some pickled red cabbage, onions and piccalilli into dishes and set it all on a tray. She thought an accompanying mug of soup might be a welcome addition, and tipped some tins of cream of tomato into a pan. It was cosy fare, the stuff to warm spirits as well as feed stomachs.

'Am I in a dream or is all this really happening?' asked Jack, searching around for a jar of coffee. He had taken one look at the large complicated coffee machine and decided that the ones who hadn't plumped for tea would have to be grateful for instant on this occasion.

'No you aren't dreaming, yes this is really happening,'

returned Bridge. 'We are cut off from the known universe, about to spend the night with a bunch of strangers.'

Jack gave a long outward breath. He'd had to accept that he was indeed here for the night and frustration was coming off him in waves as a result. He hoped Chikafuji was similarly inconvenienced. Then he thought of poor Mary who had volunteered to drive him to the meeting, and it shamed him a little that he was more annoyed at Chikafuji than he was concerned for her being stranded with all these people.

'Can't see any scones in the larder, but I suppose you'll be sick of the sight of them,' said Bridge.

'I never get sick of them,' said Jack. 'I can't say I eat masses of them myself, but they've given me a very good lifestyle.'

'That a private school accent?'

'Afraid so. St Christopher's in Cumbria.'

A very good lifestyle indeed, thought Bridge. She knew the area. She'd bought a dilapidated church up there the year before last. St Christopher's was a boys-only boarding school set in acres of prime ground, exceedingly high fees. There was obviously a lot of cream in scones. She imagined his factory to be one that hadn't moved on since the 1940s though. There would be a typing pool full of young girls not allowed to wear trousers and fat old leery men who smoked at their desks.

As Jack swooshed the large teapot around to assist the brewing process, a thought came to him, landing in his brain like a bee bumping down onto a flower.

'Do you know, this will be the first time I've made Mary a drink in all the years she's worked for me,' he said.

Bridge wasn't in the least surprised by that. 'You should be ashamed of yourself then,' she said, thinking, *posh twit*. 'In my office, we have a tea rota and I'm on it along with everyone else. I've worked in too many "them and us" places in my life and I vowed I'd never be the sort of boss who didn't say hello to cleaners or put the kettle on occasionally for my workers.'

Them and us. That's exactly what Butterly's was like, thought Jack. The white collars were separated from the blue collars by a virtual barbed-wire fence. And only one side of it made the tea.

Cowed by Bridge's verbal slap-down, Jack took a tray of drinks through to the bar lounge without saying anything else, but he was wondering when he'd ever said hello to one of the cleaners. His mind was always so full of work, he couldn't even remember lifting his head up and registering them. Why had that never struck him before?

Robin watched Charlie pick up a cheese sandwich, part the slices and add a large spoonful of pickled red cabbage to it before squashing it shut again. He opened his mouth to warn him about heartburn but stopped himself before the words came out. Sometimes he realised how much of a nag he was; and though Charlie understood he was merely caring for his welfare, he even bored himself sometimes being Mr Goody Two-Shoes.

'My, this is a feast,' announced Charlie, patting crumbs away from his mouth. 'I can't remember the last time I had sandwiches and soup sitting by a fireside being snowed in. I think I was a small boy in my grandmother's house. That must be nearly seventy years ago.'

It certainly was a feast. Washed down with many coffees and teas, huddled around the great fire, the food acquired a deliciousness equal to far more than its components.

'Wonder what's happening out there in the rest of the country,' said Robin, nodding towards the window.

'The radio works, I tried it earlier. Shall I see if I can bring up the news?' suggested Bridge. She didn't wait for an answer but went over to switch it back on. There was only static when she turned up the volume; the station she had left it tuned to had dissolved into the ether. She twiddled the knob round and round to not much avail, heard the traces of a few distant foreign stations, then – at last – the crystal-clear strains of a tune with bells at the end, followed by the northern tones of a man who seemed to be devoid of his top or bottom set of teeth, possibly both.

'You're listening to BBC Radio Brian. That's Brian Bernard Cosgrove, not the British Broadcasting Corporation. Coming to you from the snowy Yorkshire moors. I hope you're all safe and sound in your houses with the fire on. Like being in the war, isn't it?'

'I'm sure in the war the BBC announcers had their teeth in,' said Charlie before Robin shushed him.

'Welcome to my gentle world of yesteryear with me, chit-chat and good music,' Radio Brian continued. 'In a moment, we're going to have the festive voices of the King's Singers and "O Holy Night", but first a weather update for this region, which stretches, I do believe, as far south as Bridlington, and we have had reports of a listener in Newcastle. "Stay where you are" is what the other BBC is saying. A snow plough in Whitby has got stuck and is blocking the road, which more than adequately sums up the hopeless situation we're in. There will be no let-up tonight. So without further ado . . .'

'Does that include where we are?' asked Jack, talking over toothless Brian.

'Yes, we're most definitely in the middle of that area,' replied Charlie. 'I spent a lot of my childhood years in

Whitby, before we moved down to London when my father died. That's why it's so odd that I've never heard of Figgy Hollow.' His brow creased as the brain behind them sifted through years-worth of information in a bid to find a mention of it.

'The King's Singers?' said Jack as the music drifted out of the radio speakers. 'My dad used to have their records.'

'I think they've been together about twenty-five years,' said Radio Brian.

'Wrong,' Charlie countered. 'They've passed their fiftieth anniversary. We know because we went to see them in Carnegie Hall. Superb venue, perfect acoustics.'

He stopped talking then and they all listened to the hymn, the music sinking into them along with the heat from the fire. Bridge tried not to think that 'O Holy Night' was the song carol singers were performing outside the town hall when she walked out of it as a married woman on her wedding day. She hadn't been able to bear listening to it for the past few years. It was so beautiful that it felt like a sharp pin in her breast, memories hung from the notes like decorations from Christmas-tree branches.

As it drew to a close, Mary sighed. 'How lovely was that?'

'Yes it was, but I'm not sure I can listen to any more of Radio Brian babbling on. Okay to turn him off for now?' asked Bridge, who sounded as piqued at Brian as if he had deliberately picked that hymn to annoy her. She hit the off switch with a 'Thank you for the info, other BBC. We know where you are if we want a weather update.'

Charlie yawned and set off a chain reaction. 'I think I might have to go to bed soon,' he said. 'I'm absolutely—'

'Shh,' said Mary, suddenly. 'What's that?'

Everyone fell silent. There was nothing to hear. Jack was

about to say as much when he heard something too. A noise outside, faint; it sounded like someone singing 'Jingle Bells'. He walked over to the window and peered out, then he leapt to open the door.

'There's someone there,' he said. In the distance, he could make out a lumbering shape covered in snow. He ran out towards what looked like a snowman carrying an overnight bag and Robin followed to help. The pair of them took the weight of the exhausted figure and half-carried him to the inn.

'Quick, let's get him to the fire,' said Jack, his words blowing back at him in the wind.

They bundled the shuddering man inside, pushed him into the chair nearest the fire. Jack stripped off his sodden suit jacket and pair of sheepskin mittens, Robin then draped one of the throws from over the armchairs around his shoulders. Bridge saw the shock of white-blond hair as Jack pulled off the man's wet, white, furry hat, which had a cat's face stitched on the front and wiry whiskers.

'Hello, Bridge,' said her husband, shivering out a smile. 'Have I d-d-died and landed in hell?'

Chapter 7

'This is Luke,' said Bridge, as Mary pushed a mug of hot reviving coffee into the new arrival's hand. As he sipped at the liquid, he could feel the warmth spread to his grateful insides.

'You know each other?' said Charlie. 'What a strange coincidence.'

'We should do, we've been married for fourteen years,' said Luke.

Did he wink at Bridge or was she seeing things?

'Fourteen very, very long years,' she added to that.

'I never thought I'd be so glad to see you, Bridge.'

The 'likewise' came to her lips too readily; she stopped herself just in time from saying it.

'Car couldn't go any further, there was a landslide of snow so I p-p-parked up,' stuttered Luke, trying unsuccessfully to stop his teeth from chattering. 'I waited, hoping for someone to pass, then, when no one did and the car was getting buried, I decided I should try to walk the rest of the way. Thank g-goodness I saw the sign for this place on the main road or I might have given up and become an ice mummy.'

'You could have died, you idiot,' said Bridge.

'You know me, Bridge, l–luck of the devil,' Luke said and grinned at her. 'My trusty Timberlands, and the hat and mittens I found in the glove box, excuse the pun, all saved me from the jaws of frostbite. Well, my extremities, anyway.'

That stupid grin, thought Bridge. He'd be grinning if a Yeti had appeared and started ripping him limb from limb. All that would be left of him was a pile of bloody body parts and his lips curved into that perma–grin like a really annoying Cheshire Cat. *The lips you once believed you would never tire of kissing*, came a rogue thought that she batted away.

'Thank goodness I found you,' said Luke, settling into the delightful process of defrosting. 'I was giving up the ghost when I saw the lights from a distance, but they didn't seem to be getting any closer and I wondered if it was a mirage.'

'I thought it was the abominable snowman out there for a minute,' said Robin.

'Definitely abominable,' said Bridge, deliberately not under her breath.

'Get the man a scotch,' said Charlie.

'I wouldn't say no to that,' Luke answered.

Mary bobbed behind the bar, returned with a large whisky in a glass. 'I shan't ask you if you want ice,' she said with a little chuckle.

'Alcohol has no restorative powers whatsoever, you know,' said Bridge as Luke took a gulp, felt the fire trail down his throat.

'My internal organs would be inclined to disagree with that,' said Luke.

'The place wasn't open; we were very lucky that your wife broke in, otherwise goodness knows where we would all have ended up,' said Charlie.

'Did she now?' said Luke with relish. 'Why doesn't that surprise me?'

Bridge's hand twitched. She would love to wipe that smile off his face.

'Are you hungry?' asked Mary.

'Absolutely ravenous,' said Luke. 'I was hoping to have a lovely romantic dinner for two tonight.'

He was being inflammatory by design, thought Bridge, who was determined not to let him show that he was needling her. He had always been able to get under her skin, he was an expert at it.

'That's a shame,' said Robin. 'But at least you're together now.'

'Together again,' Luke tilted his head and sighed as if he'd just watched the ending of *Bambi*.

'He's jesting, of course,' said Bridge, deciding that enough was enough. 'We were meeting up to sign our divorce papers.'

'Oh, I'm so sorry,' said Robin, hoping he hadn't said anything to put his foot in it.

'I'm not,' answered both Bridge and Luke together.

'It's very . . . mature that you can go your separate ways amicably,' said Robin, trusting he was saying the right thing now.

'Mature, ha,' Bridge said with an added tut of sarcasm.

'Amicably.' Luke echoed the word as he squeezed the top of his nose, a small laugh escaping from between his lips.

'It's fine,' Bridge added breezily, not wanting any of the others to feel discomfited. 'Just dotting the "i"s and crossing the "t"s. It's all very dignified.'

'So dignified that we're both up for a Nobel peace prize,' said Luke with the sort of smile that Rock Hudson used to give Doris Day when he was being playful.

Bridge knew that he knew she had a short fuse so she would not give him the satisfaction of his match reaching the full pack of her dynamite.

'Here you go,' said Mary, passing Luke a plate of some of the remaining sandwiches and a mug of soup. The look on his face as he tucked into the first was that of Henry VIII tucking into a roasted stag's leg.

'Oh my, that cheese is good. It's very good in fact,' he said, through a full mouth of food. 'I haven't eaten since last night.'

'How stupid,' said Bridge, who wouldn't have missed the opportunity to say so.

'Did you see any more cars on the road?' asked Jack.

'None. Apart from one – abandoned. It was mad out there. The satnav was no help, leading me one way and then changing its mind.'

'Same happened to me,' said Bridge.

'And us,' said Mary.

Did it? thought Jack. He'd been oblivious to that, trusted implicitly in Mary to get them where they should be and never thought she'd encountered any difficulty. Fred, his usual chauffeur, would flap at the merest hint of a problem of course.

Jack held out his hand to introduce himself to Luke. 'Jack Butterly. And this is Mary, my PA.'

Why not just Mary? thought Bridge. *Why do you have to introduce her as the hired hand? Posh twat.* She elevated him from twit.

'Hello, Jack. And Mary,' said Luke, with a wave at her.

'I'm Charlie and this delightful young gentleman is Robin.' Charlie inclined his head by way of greeting while Robin gave Luke his best jazz hands. 'We were en route to Scotland for a snowy mountain Christmas.'

'I heard on the news before it cut out that Scotland was strangely devoid of snow,' said Luke.

'Yes, just our luck,' said Charlie. 'Good job we found this place. I'll have nightmares thinking about what would have happened if we hadn't.'

'What are we doing about paying for everything then?' asked Mary. 'I have a notepad and a pen in my bag . . . should we write down what we've eaten and drunk and then settle up with the landlord when we can get hold of him?'

'That seems the best solution,' said Bridge. 'I don't think he'll blame us for making a small dent in his supplies. And if he does, tough. He's not getting them back.'

Robin stoked up the fire for Luke. The newcomer was very pale and Robin wasn't sure if that was his natural skin colour or all the blood had rushed away from the surface to keep snug and warm in his nucleus.

'This is bliss,' said Luke, through another mouthful of sandwich. He didn't add that it would have been even better were his fiancée there and not his wife. So far this was the longest time in the past five years that he and Bridge had been in the same room together without trying to kill each other.

'Happy to help,' said Robin. 'I hope you remember where you left your car for the morning.'

'Don't think this weather will have gone by then,' replied Luke. 'And yes, it's safe enough, I'm sure. I hope.'

'What are you driving these days?' asked Bridge.

'A boy toy,' said Luke with another grin.

Bridge tutted. 'Don't tell me . . .' she started to *da da-da-daaa* the James Bond music and when Luke clicked his tongue and stuck up his thumb, Bridge shook her head resignedly. '*Quelle surprise.*'

He wouldn't have bought any old Aston Martin, she thought, he'd have picked the one he used to dream of owning, the vintage one. In which case, he was doing *really* well. Maybe she should have carried on fighting for a chunk of his fortune.

'So . . . sleeping arrangements?' enquired Robin, noticing that Charlie looked tired. 'I think we'll have an early night, we were up at the crack of dawn this morning. My, that seems like another lifetime ago.'

'There are three bedrooms, two twins and a double. There are plenty of sheets and duvets and towels et cetera in the room opposite the last bedroom,' said Bridge. 'It would make sense if you two had the double, Mary and I shared and Jack shared the other twin with . . . Luke.' A pause before his name, as if her mouth didn't want to say it.

'That does seem the only option,' said Jack.

Inside Mary a little sigh rose and sank.

'I think we will say our goodnights now,' said Robin, hovering over Charlie to help, as he levered himself to his feet. 'Sleep well, everyone.'

Their words were reciprocated.'Yes, sleep well.'

'I'll come up with you and show you where the bedding is,' said Bridge. 'There's an ensuite in each room, so fingers crossed there's some hot water.'

The double room was the largest of them, snug and quaint with fussy, floral curtains hanging at two picture windows, which afforded views of snow as far as the eye could see. And it was still falling hard.

'Deep joy, my lovelies, we have hot water,' proclaimed Charlie from the bathroom as Bridge helped Robin fit a bottom sheet and pillowcases, dress a duvet with a starched white cover. There were plenty of towels; the fluff factor was lacking but they were soft enough, and smelled newly washed. Bridge also found a quantity of folded white towelling robes, all in monster-large size.

'I shall look like the bastard child of a snowman and Noel Coward in this,' chuckled Charlie. 'Thank you for all your help, dear girl.'

'Let's think positive: we'll wake up tomorrow to green fields and clear roads and then we'll be happily on our way,' said Robin to Bridge at the door, both hands raised with crossed fingers.

'Of course we will,' she agreed.

Downstairs in the bar, Mary was collecting the plates and glasses to take through to Jack who had volunteered to wash up. Luke was sitting by the fire, thinking that it would be so easy to nod off in this large wing armchair. At one point, when he had face-planted into some snow outside, he really had wondered if he would ever make it to the inn; it was no exaggeration. But the thought of obtaining Bridge's signature on the divorce agreement spurred him on so much, he could probably have reached the Arctic Circle if necessary. The prospect of seeing Bridge in person again drove him on too, because he was intrigued by what he'd find. She looked thinner than he remembered; her cheekbones were more pronounced because of it and she'd had her inferno of wild hair cut to just below her shoulders. It suited her, made her appear older and more sensible. She looked like an adult, in other words, less like the girl he'd known. He wasn't prepared for the sensation in his chest that his heart was smiling to find her safe and sound.

'So, were you worried about me, Bridge?' he asked her,

as she came down the stairs and over to sit with him, but not too near.

'I did hope you were alive, I'm not a monster,' she said, waiting for him to roar with laughter. Sarcasm had long since been a fuel that kept their relationship burning. But he surprised her.

'I'm glad you found this bolthole, Bridge. I did try to reply to your text but it kept saying the message couldn't be delivered.'

'I didn't expect a reply anyway, I was just letting you know the change of plan. I did wonder if you'd got it, but there was no way I could find out, because I couldn't get through to you to check. I have no idea what's going on with all the technology. You'd think it would be weather-proof nowadays.'

'This is madness, isn't it? It would have been far more sensible for us to do this another time.'

'It would. But I'm sure you agree, we both want this over and done with. It's dragged on for far too long.'

'Years too long.'

'Stupid.'

'Crazy.'

A beat.

'So, here we are, Bridge. Ending our relationship as we started it, with snow all around us ...'

Her heart kicked. Mary and Jack picked the perfect moment to return.

'I've turned the lights off in the back,' said Mary. 'The switch is on the left wall by the door if you need it. I'm going to head upstairs.'

'I'll come with you,' said Bridge quickly. Left alone with Luke Palfreyman was not where she needed to be.

'I'll stay for a nightcap I think,' said Jack. 'Care to join me, Luke?'

'Do bears ablute in the woods?' came the reply.

'I've left you some sheets and towels and things on your beds,' said Bridge. 'If you need anything else, check the door opposite your room, you're in the last one on the right.'

Luke saluted her.

'Thank you, ladies. Sleep well,' said Jack, going behind the bar to get the drinks. He'd always wanted a bar in his house. The trouble was he worked so hard these days that all his old friends were in danger of falling by the wayside and he'd have no one to invite to it.

'What can I get you?'

'A double neat Glenfiddich if they have it, squire,' said Luke.

'Sounds good, I'll join you,' said Jack, lifting two glasses in turn to the appropriate optic. He settled in the next arm- chair to Luke, which received him like an old friend. He sighed then, a sound of annoyance. 'I tell you, what a bloody wasted day. Plans all gone to the wall.'

'What plans were thwarted for you?' asked Luke.

'Had a meeting with a Japanese chap whom I've been trying to pin down for months and now it'll be May before I can either visit him or be visited by him. At the earliest.'

'Video call him then,' replied Luke.

'Not how I like to do business.'

'Sometimes you have to compromise. Takes the stress out of things. Why blow all that expense and time when you don't have to? Have you never heard of Zoom?' said Luke, sounding infuriatingly laid-back. He obviously wasn't au fait with the matter of multi-million-pound business modules, thought Jack.

'What line of work are you in?' Jack asked him. He guessed a teacher, one of those ultra-cool ones that teenagers idolised.

'Have you heard of Plant Boy?' said Luke, savouring the warmth of the fire on his skin and the whisky lightly fuzzing his brain, repairing his frazzled nerves. That nightmare walk to this safe haven was still too fresh in his mind.

'The vegetarian food firm? Of course,' said Jack. Plant Boy was a company growing at the rate of developing cells. Who in the industry hadn't heard of them? 'Why, do you work for them?'

'I'm Plant Boy,' said Luke, as if he was announcing he was Spartacus. 'Started the company five years ago. It's done rather well if I say so myself.'

Which was an understatement, thought Jack as he let out an impressed breath along with the single word, 'Wow.'

'I do video calls all the time, it's a perfectly acceptable way to have meetings these days, however important they are. I like being at home with my partner too much to be flying around the world when I don't have to. Why have the technology if you don't use it?'

Jack opened his mouth to speak, then realised he didn't have a viable enough answer other than to say that it was the way his father had always advocated doing business, and so he had too.

'When I do go, my fiancée Carmen usually comes with me and we make a mini break of it. I enjoy my new-found wealth, Jack. I'm master of it, not slave to it. What line of work are you in then?'

'Scones,' replied Jack. 'We produce nearly two million of them every day.'

'Impressive. Do any vegan ones?'

'Yes, and very successful they are too.'

'Interesting. We're always looking to extend our vegan range. We should exchange numbers.'

Jack nodded in agreement. 'My dad used to say there was an opportunity to do business wherever you were. And here we are, doing business.'

'Planning to do business,' Luke corrected him. 'Enjoy the enforced downtime.' He took a mouthful of scotch, let it sit on his tongue before swallowing. 'I think I'll sleep well tonight.'

'This wave of vegetarianism must be like a tail wind to you,' said Jack, intrigued by this man in the next chair. Plant Boy was *massive* and yet Luke didn't have the air of someone that successful. He was far too carefree, not arrogant enough by half.

'It is, and I have every intention of letting it propel us as far as it can. We could save the planet and it's all good stuff *and* I'm biting into the profits to keep the costs down so it's affordable to more people. Then, before I'm too old, I intend to sell up, take a stupidly early retirement and hopefully spend my time with my new wife, children and a set of golf clubs.'

'How many children do you have?' asked Jack.

Luke paused before answering. 'None,' he said eventually. He wetted his lips with his tongue. 'None yet. Tell me about the two older guys? Father and son?'

'A married couple,' said Jack. 'I think Charlie said he was a jeweller or a diamond merchant and Robin was, before they got together, his chauffeur.'

Luke didn't bat an eyelid at that disclosure. 'Hmm. Carmen worked for me in our accounts department before we became romantically involved,' he said. 'I truly never noticed how stunning she was, even though I used to see her all the time around the building. Then she said hello to me in the supermarket one day after work and I didn't recognise her with jeans and a big woolly jumper on. I thought, *Who is this gorgeous woman saying "Hello, Mr Palfreyman"?* You hear the expression "having the scales ripped from your eyes" but you don't ever think you can be that blind yourself.' He took another drink. 'What's the story with you and Mary then? Just business or . . .' He didn't finish the sentence but the inference was clear.

'Absolutely just business,' said Jack, adamantly. 'She's about ten years my junior for a start.'

'Carmen's eight years my senior. Age is but a number, my friend.'

'Yes, I suppose . . . though Mary's not . . .' *My type*, he was going to say. '. . . I wouldn't take advantage.'

'I wasn't suggesting as much, I was merely wondering if there were any romantic feelings pinging between you.'

'Not at all.'

A conversation to be continued in the morning perhaps, or maybe never if the weather miraculously improved, thought Luke. He was suddenly consumed with a wave of weariness, thanks to relief at having eventually found shelter, a soup-and-sandwich-filled belly and the generous slugs of Scottish malt. He tossed the remaining contents of his glass into his mouth.

'Time for me to hit the horizontal slab,' he said.

'Me too,' said Jack. 'It's been a long day.'

Luke switched off the main bar lights by the door. The embers of the large fire glowed gently, their orange light reaching into the dark. It was safe enough to leave, he decided. It looked as sleepy as he now felt.

Jack followed Luke up the stairs, the thought buzzing in his head that in all the years he'd known Mary, it had never crossed his mind to think of her with any *feeling*. And *of course* she didn't think of him in that way either. She worked for him, he paid her salary, that's as far as it went. Mary was as much part of the office furniture as his desk and his stapler were. How could there be anything more to it than that?

Chapter 8

Bridge and Mary had snuggled down into their twin beds, warm as toast. The central heating was underpowered, which made the beds extra cosy. The mattresses were soft, probably terrible for the back, but bouncy-comfy. It felt not unlike a teenage sleepover, as they started to talk in the dark.

'He's very good-looking, your boss,' said Bridge. 'Not quite modern man enough for me, plus he's too tall. I like someone I don't have to climb in order to stare into their eyes.'

Mary chuckled inwardly at the image of Bridge scaling the north face of Jack. 'Yes, he is tall. Funny that, because his dad wasn't much taller than me and I think his mum was pretty short from what I hear.' Jack was nothing like Reg Butterly to look at, who was stubby and thickset with a permanent scowl on his face, unless he was talking about his son.

'Jack said in the kitchen that he realised he'd never made you a drink before, that true?'

The thought of Jack making drinks in the office tickled Mary.

'Butterly's isn't the most progressive place on earth, I'll give you that but it's gradually coming out of the dark ages. I wonder sometimes if Jack is afraid to change things in case he thinks he's betraying his dad by doing so. Reg Butterly wasn't one for change. He was very much an "if it isn't broke don't mend it" kind of bloke.'

'He sounds an amazing businessman,' said Bridge with a sarcastic humph.

'The scones sold themselves for him, he was lucky, but it was only when Jack took over that it went massive, because he's not the type to sit on any laurels. Slowly but surely he's changing things. At least he always says thank you, which is more than Reg used to. I don't think he said it once to me in all the time I was working for him.'

'Rude pig,' said Bridge. 'I hate that sort of entitlement. I worked in a factory where the quality-control boss used to slap your bum when you took his morning coffee in.'

'No way.' Mary gasped.

'Notorious for it. He only did it once with me, mind.' She could still see a slo-mo mini video of his blubbery cheeks wobbling when her nineteen-year-old self twirled around at speed and slapped his face. She was never sure who was more shocked – him or her. He was extremely frosty to her after that, but he never put a hand on her again.

'Reg wouldn't have done that,' said Mary, with certainty. He gave off a vibe that he didn't like women. Especially brunettes. She was told by someone when she first joined that if she'd had dark hair, she would never have got the job.

'I was working at that factory in the early noughties and you would have thought it was the 1970s the way some of the bosses carried on,' said Bridge.

'Where was it?' asked Mary.

'In Derby. A massive place that manufactured plumbing parts.'

'That where you live now?'

'Yes, but at the other side of the county. I live in the countryside, it's lovely.'

'Is ... your husband there too?' His name temporarily escaped Mary.

Husband? It was funny to think she was still married to Luke. Bridge had shifted him into the 'ex' box in her head long ago, but legally they were still very much husband and wife.

'No, he moved to Manchester. Have you heard of Plant Boy?'

'Oh yeah. I'm vegetarian, well, pescatarian if you're going to be pedantic. Does Luke work for Plant Boy then?'

'Luke *is* Plant Boy.'

'No way.' Mary sounded well impressed. 'I buy loads of their stuff.'

'You've helped to finance his Aston Martin in that case,' said Bridge. She remembered their first car – a red fifth-hand Ford Fiesta with a replacement blue passenger door, more rust than paint. It never let them down though, not once.

'Jack's got a magnificent Maserati.'

'I bet he has,' Bridge said. 'How come he's single, presuming he is?' She had known Mary only a couple of hours, yet she didn't seem like the sort of girl who'd be lovestruck over a taken man.

'Oh, Jack's married to the job,' replied Mary. 'He's had plenty of girlfriends over the years but they haven't lasted very long. I think ...' She paused, was about to say something that was bordering on the indiscreet.

'What?'

'Nothing . . . only that he hasn't found the right woman yet,' Mary said.

'Oh come on, you were going to say something else. What's his usual type? No – let me guess. Glamorous, great figure, big lips and tarantula-leg eyelashes,' said Bridge.

Which was pretty much spot on. Leggy, pretty women with a ton of make-up and flicky hair extensions, heels that hurt Mary's feet just to look at. Trophies, all in the same mould. They occasionally called in to the office, some friendlier than others, and every one stabbed her a little in the heart in case *this* would be the one who hung around longer than a month. They never did though, because they were more attracted to Jack Butterly's cash, house and car than they were to Jack Butterly. He was a castle full of goodies with the portcullis firmly down and she'd been at Butterly's long enough to have heard via the gossip machine why that was.

Mary knew that he needed someone who saw past the Hugo Boss suits and the successful businessman image because at his core there was still a lonely boy frightened of having his heart mashed. It was clear to her young, but incisive mind that Jack Butterly put all his emotion and effort into the business when really he wished he could find a person to put it into.

Mary didn't want to talk about him any more. This road trip had so far told her everything she needed to know in order to do what she had to, and that would make her crumple if she thought about it too much.

'That's his type in a nutshell,' she said and shifted the spotlight away from him. 'So, are you and Luke managing to keep things civil, then?'

Bridge laughed, a hard, brittle sound, before she spoke.

'This is the most civil we've been in the five years since we split,' she said, as a vision visited her of throwing an A4 file at him four years ago, a point in her life when she had considered getting up an hour earlier in the mornings just to hate him a bit more each day.

'You've been trying to divorce for five years?'

'It feels much longer, let me tell you.'

'How long were you together before you broke up?'

'Ten crazy, mixed-up years.' A decade-long breathless fairground ride. No wonder she felt sick when she got off it.

'What made you split?' asked Mary.

There was a question. Small niggles that grew into big arguments, all the opposites that initially drew them together finally driving them apart. Her past indelibly staining their future. Plus that one big hurdle that neither of them could clear.

'Oh, too much to talk about now, it would take all night. Sleep well, Mary,' said Bridge, shutting the conversation down, politely but firmly. She didn't want to think about where it had started to go wrong. Because it hurt too much.

*

'Are you warm enough, Charlie?' asked Robin, tucking the quilt around him.

'Snug as a bug,' said Charlie. 'What a lovely comfortable bed.'

'I'd booked a waterbed for us in Aviemore.'

'Ugh no, I'd have been seasick,' said Charlie with a schoolboy chortle.

'Silly old fool. Goodnight. Sweet dreams.'

They settled into sleep mode then Charlie piped up.

'Robin, before you nod off, please talk to me.'

'What about?'

'You know what.'

Robin turned over. 'No, Charlie. Not tonight. Go to sleep, it's been a hard day, I'm done in.'

'Five minutes, that's all I'm ask—'

'I'm already asleep,' said Robin.

Christmas Eve

It's Beginning to Look a Lot Like Christmas

Chapter 9

'Dear God in heaven,' were the words that woke Charlie up. Robin was standing by the window, in his complimentary robe. He stood by windows a lot. Even when they were at home, he stood by the French windows and watched the magpies and sparrows, the chaffinches and collared doves, took joy in them skipping onto the bird table, bathing in the large stone fountain they had in their garden. Charlie had a photo framed and hanging in his office that he'd taken of Robin years ago in that position, when he didn't have so many lines weighing down his brow, when he smiled more, when he didn't have worries that weren't going to go away.

'What's the matter?'

'Remember last night when we said we'd wake up to green fields and clear roads?'

'Yes.'

'Well, we haven't. We've woken up in bloody Narnia.'

Charlie heaved himself out of bed and over to the window. Robin wasn't joking. And it was still falling in soft flakes. A bleak midwinter, snow on snow, snow on snow.

'What are we going to do?' asked Charlie.

'Do you think we have a choice, Charles? We'll have to stay put. Maybe – hopefully – drive up to Scotland tonight or even first thing in the morning if the roads clear.' It was a very big 'if' if this scene was anything to go by.

'I'm ready for some breakfast, are you?' said Charlie. 'I'm ravenous.'

'You eat more than a starving horse.'

'I could murder one of those mince pies.'

'Cholesterol, Charlie!'

'I hope there isn't a box of All Bran in any of the cupboards. I'm sick of the sight of it. I've eaten so much of it, I'm starting to crunch when I move.'

Robin opened up his mouth to extol the values of bran then surrendered at the sight of Charlie's petulantly curled lip. 'Let's go and find something else to satisfy your appetite then. Chop-chop, Captain,' he said.

Jack was already downstairs, building up a fire. The lounge was chilly because the huge iron radiators weren't kicking out much heat. They needed either bleeding or bashing with a mallet, that was evident.

'Morning,' Charlie greeted him cheerfully. 'Sleep well, did you, Jack?'

'Yes, I did actually. Like the proverbial log,' came the reply.

'You sound surprised by that,' Charlie said, with a little laugh.

'I don't normally sleep well in strange beds,' explained Jack. Usually because he was in a hotel either the night before or after a meeting and his mind was spinning. Here, he had no access to a phone line or emails; cut off from the world of business, cut off from the world of everything, his brain had taken the rare opportunity to power down properly and it had rested.

'Did you two?' Jack bounced the question back to Charlie and Robin.

'We did.' Charlie answered for both of them. 'Out like a light.'

'And the shower's good as well,' Robin added to that. 'Who would have thought such a little head could power out water like that? I feel positively pummelled.'

'Yes, it was better than I expected,' said Jack, who'd had much the same thought.

'Thank goodness you're making a fire,' said Charlie. 'It's not very warm in here, is it?'

Robin swept a throw up from one of the chair backs and deposited it on Charlie's shoulders. 'Here, this will do until the flames take hold.'

'Oh, Robin, you do fuss,' said Charlie, mock-annoyed.

'It's a good job I do, isn't it? I would prefer people thought I cared about you more than your money,' Robin threw back at him.

'So you say.'

'How dare you, Charles Glaser.'

'Ha. Sorry about us having a spat in front of you, Jack.'

It wasn't a fight, thought Jack. He'd seen fights between people who were supposed to love each other and this was at the other end of the scale. The shouting, the accusations, the violence . . . No, this wasn't fighting here today.

'Luke up yet?' asked Robin.

'He was in the shower when I came down.'

'Ah, good morning, girls.' Charlie beamed at Bridge and Mary as they appeared at the bottom of the stairs. 'Sleep well?'

'I did,' replied Mary.

'Yes, not too bad,' Bridge answered at the same time.

Mary didn't like to say that Bridge must have slept *very* well because she'd been snoring. Not too loudly, but the sort of snore a contented sleeper made.

'I'm going to make breakfast for everyone,' said Robin, clapping his hands along with the announcement. 'Bacon, eggs, sausage, beans, lashings of coffee if I can find it all.'

'Full English,' said Charlie. 'Drenched in tomato sauce, thick white toast slathered in butter.'

'You'll get what you're given,' said Robin. 'Porridge if I can find some. Or a nice yogurt.'

'You care too much. Pretend you hate me and give me something fried,' returned Charlie with his best disarming eyelash-flutter, which Robin duly ignored.

'Where's Luke?' asked Bridge.

'I'm here,' said a voice from up the staircase. The sound of footsteps, followed by the man himself. Wearing his trademark grin, as per usual.

Bridge swallowed. She hadn't had much of a chance to look, really look, at Luke yesterday other than to see someone bedraggled, damp and grateful to be alive, but here he was, showered and fresh, lean, healthy and fit as a Wimbledon men's singles finalist, albeit one with sticky-out mad scientist hair. He looked taller than his actual five foot ten, his shoulders wider than she remembered and as if he had aged in the best sort of way, like a lanky teenage boy grown into his limbs. Her brain wasn't making sense with how it was thinking but something inside her was admiring him too much, feeling too much.

'I'm going to cook breakfast,' said Robin, after wishing Luke a good morning. 'Bacon, eggs, you know the sort of thing. That suit?'

'I'm vegetarian,' replied Luke. 'So if you can work with that?'

'I'll come and help you, Robin, I'm a veggie too,' said Mary.

'Are you?' asked Jack.

There was no reason for him to know, of course, but still his question felt like a painful flick against a sensitive part of Mary's skin. *Does he know anything about me apart from my name?* she thought suddenly.

'So, here we all are,' said Luke. 'Doesn't look as if any of us are going to be driving anywhere soon, does it?'

Jack lit a match, placed it against the newspapers he had ripped apart and scrunched up. A stack of twenty-five-year-old *News of the World*s among them; the salacious headlines made for interesting reading.

'Anyone tested their phones?' asked Luke.

'Yes, and zilch,' said Bridge.

Jack nodded to affirm. 'Landline is still dead too. I checked when I got down here.'

'Looks like we need Radio Brian then,' said Charlie and crossed the room to switch him on. 'It's Beginning to Look a Lot Like Christmas' rang out from the speakers.

'That's the only thing with radio, there's no fast-forward button,' said Jack, standing up now and proudly viewing his fire tasting the logs.

'The trouble with anyone born after 1980 is that they have forgotten how to wait for things,' said Charlie, gently admonishing him. 'Let Brian play his song; you can't go anywhere, so enjoy the delightful voice of Perry Como in the meantime.'

Perry Como. Jack remembered his dad playing Perry Como vinyls on his record player, always skipping over the track 'How Insensitive' because the words were too hard to listen to, someone with ice for a heart finishing a relationship with a partner. It was as if his mother was singing it about his father via Perry Como's vocal cords.

'And you're listening to BBC Radio Brian. That's Brian Bernard Cosgrove, not the British Broadcasting Corporation. Coming to you from the cold and frosty Yorkshire moors. And that was Perry Como with "It's Beginning to Look a Lot Like Christmas", because it is, isn't it?'

'I see he hasn't found his teeth yet,' said Bridge.

'Shh,' said Luke, holding a shushing finger up against his mouth.

'The news on the street is that severe weather warnings have been issued. More snow on the way. Stay indoors and I hope you've got enough milk and bread because the temperatures are recorded in this area as minus ten, so that would indicate the snow is going nowhere fast. And here's Dean "little ole wine drinker" Martin with "Let It Snow".'

'The weather outside is indeed incredibly frightful,' said Jack with a growl, checking his watch. He should have been in Tynehall now, presenting his case on why Chikafuji Incorporated and Butterly's scones should be married in fruitful union before a speedy drive back to the office for a debrief working lunch with the heads of finance and marketing. The office would be closing early, but he'd stay on for longer. There was nothing to rush home for. No one to rush home for.

'Beautiful though, isn't it?' said Luke, taking up Robin's default position by the window. 'Spectacular, even. Like a postcard. So long as our loved ones know we're safe and there's nothing we can do about the situation . . . we might as well just relax into it.'

He felt able to do that because he'd managed to get in touch with Carmen before all the mobile networks crashed and burned yesterday, though he'd lied slightly to save her worrying about him and told her that he was 'only around the corner' from the meeting place. The relief in her voice was palpable and warmed him right through. Her sister and parents had come over for Christmas, so she wasn't rattling around in their large house alone. She was safe, protected by them but he wished it was him who was protecting her instead.

Bridge went over to him at the window as behind her Charlie and Jack started up their own conversation about scones.

'Does Carmen know you're okay?'

'I hope so. I told her I was almost here and I promised I'd stay put until it cleared if the weather got worse. She wouldn't want me to take chances.'

'And where does she think you were driving to?' asked Bridge, her interest piqued.

'If you're asking did I tell her I was coming to meet my wife then yes, she knows where I was driving to.' A smile.

'Really?' Bridge seemed surprised by that.

'Yes, really. We have no trust issues.' As soon as he said it, he realised he might as well have given Bridge a sucker punch to her kidney. 'Did you tell your fiancé you were meeting your husband?'

'Of course I did. Ben doesn't see you as a threat.'

'Touché.'

'It's not as if anything's going to happen between us because we'll be in each other's company longer than planned. We're history. Ancient history,' said Bridge, sounding more sure than she felt.

'Totally in the past. Dead in the water,' Luke appended, feeling that somehow he had slid back years, was returning to getting-the-last-word-in territory. A treacherous landscape he never wanted to venture near again. '. . . Hence why I'm glad we managed, against the odds, to meet up. I thought it was best we finalise things between us before the year ends, leave no threads hanging . . .'

'. . . *to be retied*.' Bridge's brain ended his sentence for him. A ridiculous thing for it to think.

'Well, I thought exactly the same. Which is why I suggested it and—'

Luke interrupted her. 'I asked for the meet, Bridge. Before you.'

'I don't think you did. If I check my diary I—'

'Look . . .' Luke held his hands out, palms flat as if pushing a fast-sprouting argument away. 'Let's not bicker and fall into our tried and tested bad habits. Whatever the truth, we both want the same. I don't want anything from you, you don't want anything from me and now that . . . Sabrina's . . . gone, there's nothing that we need to argue about any more, is there?'

His voice faltered on the name; it was still wrapped up in raw grief for him.

'Yes,' the word softly spoken by Bridge. Sabrina, their beautiful Belgian Malinois dog, who loved them equally. They'd shared custody of her, a month at each house. She'd been at Bridge's when she died, in her sleep. A massive heart attack, the vet diagnosed. That it would have been quick was of no comfort, neither was her 'good innings' age of fifteen. They'd adopted her from a rescue centre when they were newly married. She'd been achingly thin and distrustful then, aggressive, frightened, vulnerable. She'd reminded Luke of Bridge, which is why he was drawn to her, a cause to rescue. She'd been with them through it all, the highs, the lows, the even lowers. When Bridge found her dead in her bed, she'd howled like a wolf, wished Luke had been there to hold her because however much she hated him, she knew his heart would have broken like hers had and Sabrina was *theirs*; the last link holding them together, gone. It hurt still, months later. Hurt like hell.

'So, what's he like?' asked Luke, butting into her brief reverie.

'Who?'

'Your fiancé, durrr?' He nodded towards the ring on her finger. A stunning, sparkly solitaire square diamond. Ben wasn't without a few bob himself, Luke figured.

'The best way to describe him is . . .' Bridge mused, rummaging around in her head until she found the words that fitted. 'He's . . . the exact opposite to you, Luke.' Then she turned her back on him and went to join Charlie and Jack by the fire.

'All I can find are these in the sausage and bacon department,' announced Robin after a thorough search in the fridge, holding up a monster-sized polystyrene-wrapped tray of pigs in blankets and a packet of 'Hollybury Farm' plump vegetarian sausages.

'I'm sure they'll both go down a treat,' said Mary, who was whisking eggs.

'I wonder if we'll still be here tomorrow,' said Robin, reaching for two frying pans. 'What were your plans for Christmas Day, love?'

'Bit of a funny one this year, actually,' Mary answered him. 'We usually all spend it together at Mum's but her friend has taken her away to the Canaries this year. One of my brothers is on holiday in Australia with his pals, the other one's spending Christmas Day with his girlfriend and her parents and my sister's got a full house as her husband's family are over from Ireland. They're a lovely lot but I didn't want a big, loud Christmas, so I was just going to have a quiet one by myself.' She answered Robin's look of sympathy. 'No really, it would have been nice, that's what I wanted. I'd bought lots of lovely things to eat and was going to hole up with Christmas films and have a proper rest. I'm kind of okay with my own company. My brothers and sister were all grown up by the time I was born, so I'm sort of an only child ... but with siblings. Mum and Dad had me late, you see. I was a menopausal surprise. Mum said her ovaries had one last-ditch attempt to appear useful and I'm the result. My brother Sean calls me "the mistake".'

'How very cruel of him,' tutted Robin.

Mary chuckled. 'He's joking. There are four of us and we're super close. We take the mick out of each other a lot, but it's all good-humoured and great fun. They're a bunch of comics, my lot.'

'No sweetheart for you?' Robin cocked his head at her. She truly was a beautiful girl; pretty heart-shaped face, a flawless cream complexion with a mere hint of pink on her cheekbones, and beautiful sea-greeny-blue eyes. And the most alluring thing about her was that she obviously didn't realise how attractive she was.

'No,' said Mary, with an unconscious sigh.

'Men must be blind,' said Robin.

Mary shrugged that conclusion off. It wasn't as if she hadn't had her chances. Someone in marketing had made it abundantly clear that he would be in like Flynn if given the opening and another in finance was very flirty, but neither of them nudged her heart rate up one single notch and she had a whole family who would have been furious had she settled for anything less than she was worth. Sean was always giving her lectures about her potential love life; he'd taken over paternal duties from their father. He even looked like him, with his bright blue eyes and 'the Padgett nose', which Mary had managed to avoid inheriting. Plus her heart was already engaged because she had been stuck on Jack Butterly since she came to work for him. Sean called him 'the Boy from Ipanema' because he was tall and tanned (well, olive-skinned) and long and lovely, and he was totally oblivious to the fact that Mary was sitting on her beach towel and sighing over him walking past her. She deserved a real man who sighed over *her*, Sean told her. Mary knew this. At least Mary's head did, but her heart continued to hold out for a change in the status quo, quickening in beat every time it felt Jack's presence nearby.

'That's a pretty bracelet,' said Robin, flicking his finger towards Mary's left wrist. 'Very artisan.'

'Oh, this?' said Mary with a modest shrug. He and Charlie dealt in diamonds and he thought her daft little handmade bracelet was worthy of comment? 'It's just something a friend gave me once.'

'It suits you. It's delicate,' said Robin, 'Let me see.'

Mary lifted her arm nearer to his eyes so he could take a better look. The bracelet was made up of blue cord, silver beads and seven tiny wooden blocks each bearing a letter: C.M.W.Y.N.A F.

'Is that Welsh for Mary?' joked Robin.

Mary smiled. 'It stands for *Call Me When You Need A Friend*. A pal of mine sent it to me when my dad died. She said it was a licence to ring her whenever I needed to chat and if I wore it, it would be a reminder that she was there for me at any time of the day or night.'

'How very sweet and thoughtful of her. When did you lose him, love?'

'Two years ago,' replied Mary. 'I ended up ringing her quite a lot as it happens. I had my family to talk to but sometimes it helped just offloading onto someone else who had been through it and come out of the other side. You know, losing someone really close.'

'Yes, that's exactly what you need,' said Robin and smiled back at her.

'I'm surprised it hasn't dropped off my wrist by now.'

'Delicate but strong then.' Robin suspected Mary was very much like her bracelet. 'It's amazing the staying power of some things that others presume will snap at the slightest pressure. Like Charlie and me. The amount of "it won't last" gossip we had when we became a couple. All the bitches came to the surface like scum, let me tell you.'

'How long have you and Charlie been together?' she asked.

'Too bloody long,' he said, causing her to laugh because it was obvious he didn't mean it.

'Thirty-two years and counting. Married three years ago. We were the first homosexuals to be married in our village church. Caused quite a stir. It's very old England where we live. They were still burning witches up until last year.'

Mary chuckled at that.

'Yes, a lot of people presumed I was after Charlie's money. A gigolo with no heart, a lowly chauffeur with his eye on the golden goose.' Robin shook his head, in marked disgust. 'It has been our pleasure to prove them wrong.'

'Thirty-two years is a long time to stay with someone if you don't love them,' agreed Mary.

'Precisely. But I was still quite apprehensive to accept his marriage proposal even after all those years.'

'What made you change your mind then?'

'Charlie is a very lovable man,' said Robin, aware that he hadn't directly answered the question. 'Always kind, generous with his feelings, his time, his wisdom. Your family sound lovely and you've only told me a couple of sentences about them.'

'My mum and dad were both good people with strong values. They worked hard and tried to bring us up the right way. And Dad always had a lot of sayings. He used to call them "*the Roy Padgett book of wisdom*", and then he'd tell me a pearl to get me through whatever it was that was bothering me.'

'Oh God, he sounds like Charlie.' Robin laughed. 'He's like the bloody Dalai Lama sometimes with his sayings.'

'There's a lot of love in our family, I'm lucky.'

'That's nice.'

'And we've never been afraid of telling each other, either. Some families don't, do they? Mum and Dad didn't come from very loving homes, and so they knew how important it is to say the words and always said them to us.'

Robin gave a little shrug. 'Harder than it should be sometimes though, isn't it? Saying the words.'

'Jack . . .' Mary began, before pulling herself up short. She had no right gossiping about him. Even to someone who would probably never even think of him again when the snow had cleared and they were all on their way.

'Go on, you were saying,' Robin prompted, nudging her then whispering, 'I promise, what happens in the kitchen, stays in the kitchen.'

Mary smiled. 'Jack's dad Reg really loved him and it was obvious how proud of him he was, but I don't think he ever actually told him to his face.'

'Oh, what makes you think that?'

'Jack's always been so driven and I'm sure it's because he wanted his dad to notice him. Even now, when Reg isn't alive any more, it's as if he's still trying to make his dad acknowledge his efforts, the pressure he puts himself under . . .' An alert went off in her brain to shut up, that she was talking too much and that Robin might think she was a know-it-all. 'I may be wrong of course,' she said to end it.

Office gossip said that when Reg's wife left him, he pulled up his drawbridge and wouldn't let feelings in or out, or at least any display of them, as if showing them was akin to showing a soft, vulnerable underbelly and inviting damage.

'But you know you're not wrong, don't you?' said Robin. Mary was astute beyond her young age, that he could easily tell.

Mary sighed and poured her whisked eggs into a pan with some butter.

'I just think it's important to say the words as well, specially to the people who need to hear them most.'

'Do you really think they matter that much?' asked Robin, taking interest. 'Isn't it enough to show rather than tell?'

'Yes I do. My dad wasn't one for slush but it meant a lot that he could say he loved me as well as showing me. I think Jack might have been a bit easier on himself if he'd heard them from Reg. He won't stop until he conquers the world and yet he'll never catch the words he's chasing.' Another inner warning sounded. She'd talked enough about Jack's personal business. 'Shall I open up a couple of cans of those plum tomatoes?'

'Oh yes, why not.'

Mary's words turned over in Robin's mind as surely as he turned over the sausages in the pans.

Robin and Mary's Christmas Eve breakfast feast, as Charlie named it, went down a storm. Jack and Luke pushed tables together to make one big one and put six chairs around it for them all to sit at. In the background Radio Brian played, in between his inane ramblings, a series of songs from a bygone age that existed long before the millennium.

'I can't remember the last time I had butter that I could actually taste, and on lovely thick white toast,' declared Charlie, gleefully wiping warm dribbles from his chin. 'When Robin makes toast – always brown – he scrapes off the excess. And he buys that margarine stuff that is supposed to lower your cholesterol.'

'It's been proven to lengthen your life,' admonished Robin.

'It's been proven to make your life *feel* longer,' said Charlie.

'Every little helps.' Robin bit down on his toast as if taking out his annoyance on it.

'My grandfather lived all his life eating red meat, cooking with lard, drinking to excess and smoking like a chimney,' said Luke.

'There you go, Robin,' said Charlie. 'Proof that life is a lottery.'

'And exactly how old was he when he died?' asked Robin.

'Twenty-two,' said Luke, dissolving into a guffaw. 'Sorry, it was a joke. He didn't really, total lie.'

'How hilarious,' said Bridge, casting him a look of disdain.

'I'm just trying to keep things light,' said Luke, his tone playful. 'We're stuck here together, possibly for some considerable time, so we might as well ... chill, if you'll excuse the pun.'

From one side of the room, Radio Brian gave an updated weather report.

'Don't be fooled by the fine flurries, heavier snow is forecast after lunch. Looks like we are all going to have a white Christmas this year.'

Chapter 10

After the breakfast plates had been cleared away, they gravitated to the fire, sat around watching the flames, all except Jack who was fiddling with his phone. Luke watched him pressing and swiping at the screen.

'You can't leave it alone, can you?' he remarked.

'What?' asked Jack.

'Your phone. Picking it up and scrolling through pages is not going to miraculously produce a signal.'

'I just thought I'd check.'

'We should take this time as a gift,' Luke went on. 'What fruits will we all yield from it, I wonder? Maybe it will bring balance to those in whom it is sadly lacking.'

'How very zen,' said Bridge with a sniff. 'But I want to get back to my other half, even if you aren't in as much of a hurry to get back to yours.' *One-nil to me,* she thought.

'Ouch. Worrying isn't going to solve this problem, so there's no point in doing it,' Luke batted back, as calmly as his voice could manage because he realised this would piss Bridge off more than picking up any weapon.

'You have a Norwegian state of mind,' said Mary.

'That'll be my Viking blood,' said Luke. 'You don't get this colouring from Anglo-Saxons.' He pointed to his pale-blond unruly mop. 'Or mad red-headed Celts.' *One-all*, he thought; that levelled up the score in his eyes.

'Mary is half-Norwegian. She *really* knows what she's talking about,' said Bridge, the inference that Luke didn't clearly implied.

Luke didn't rise to the bait this time either but sent an air fist-bump across the table to Mary. 'Go us Scandinavian pale and interesting types.'

'Pale and uninteresting in my case,' said Mary with a little laugh.

'I totally refute that,' said Robin. 'We had a lovely chat in the kitchen. I found you very interesting.'

'What do you suggest we do then to pass the time best, our dear half-Norwegian Mary?' asked Charlie. 'Although to be fair, I'm quite happy sitting in this armchair, staring into the flames and listening to Radio Brian. What a wonderful picker of music he is. I feel the most Christmassy I've felt in years.' He sighed contentedly.

'I don't know really,' said Mary. 'But Luke is right, worrying won't help. We need to work with our present situation.'

'I think I'd like to take a look across there,' said Luke, pointing to the church and the cottages positioned around what, in normal weather, was probably a village green.

'I already did and there's nothing to see,' returned Bridge.

'A fresh pair of eyes might unearth something you missed,' Luke grinned benignly at her.

'Like what? A bloke with a fully fuelled light aircraft in his front room who'll promise to fly you back to Manchester?'

'Maybe.'

Bridge shrugged. 'Suit yourself, but you're going to get cold and wet for nothing.'

'I'll come with you,' said Jack. 'Let me just get my coat from upstairs.'

'Use ours,' insisted Charlie, pointing to the two brightly coloured snow jackets still hanging by the door. 'They're Arctic-friendly. They'll keep you warm as toast. Jack, you're bigger so you take Robin's orange one.'

Luke and Jack put on the two coats. Luke laced up his boots, Jack only had the one pair of shoes with him, which were very Arctic-unfriendly, but he needed to break up the boredom. He opened the door and all the snow that had drifted against it fell in and onto the bottom half of his legs.

'Fool's errand,' said Bridge with a heavy sigh. 'Don't say I didn't warn you.'

Luke didn't answer her but Bridge knew he would be determined to find something to prove her wrong. She also knew he'd be unsuccessful. She wasn't stupid; had there been life out there in any shape or form, she would have discovered it yesterday.

'Anyone for a fresh coffee while we await the wanderers' return?' she asked as the door closed behind them, a gleeful trill in her tone.

With every step they took, Luke and Jack got wetter and colder. Jack's socks were saturated before they'd even reached the edge of where he thought the car park ended. By the time they'd crunched their way over the small bridge and arrived at the buildings, Luke had to check to make sure his nose hadn't dropped off because he could no longer feel its existence. He should have worn Carmen's mittens, which were presently sitting on the bedroom radiator, and her furry cat hat. He stuffed his hands back into the deep warm pockets of Charlie's brightly coloured Alpine jacket.

'Let's try the church first,' suggested Jack, his words leaving his mouth on a visible plume of breath. Luke stuck up his thumb. It was too cold to talk when he didn't need to.

The short squat body of the church was out of proportion to the enormous square tower and the snow sat on top of the roof like Carmen's hat, thought Luke. The large wooden double doors were locked, of course, and when Luke knocked on the left one with the flat of his hand, it didn't move at all, as if it had swollen into the frame and become one with the stonework.

Jack, at six foot three, was better equipped to look through the high-placed lancet windows but they were too narrow to allow much view.

'See anything interesting?' asked Luke.

'Nope.' Jack attempted to scale up a few notches, using the relief on the stone as purchase. It didn't work well as he lost his footing and fell backwards into the snow. It was two foot deep at least but not as soft as it appeared.

'Let's try round the other side,' said Luke, holding out his hand to pull Jack up. An unbidden picture flashed in his mind of holding his hand out to the woman sprawled in the snow, a woman with red Rapunzel hair and a green coat, her hand small and cold. What if he'd been steps in front of her instead of behind and never saw her fall, never stopped to help? He'd wondered that so many times over the years, how his destiny had been altered by a mere few yards, a few seconds.

They both strode around to the back where the silence seemed more pronounced and reverent in a graveyard that stretched as far as their eyes could see, looking eerily beautiful with all the snow-dusted crosses and stones. There was a smaller door at the bottom of the tower, the wood peeling and long stripped of its varnish, and banging on that yielded no response either. There remained only the row of cottages to try.

'Can I ask what we're actually going to do if we do find someone in?' said Jack. 'Apart from enquiring if their phone is working?'

Luke's pace slowed as he pondered an answer. It was a fair question. They had food, warmth and shelter over at the inn. They were in more of a position to give than to receive.

'I have no idea,' he said eventually. 'Let's just see if there's anyone around first and then when someone throws open their door and invites us inside, I'm sure we'll think of something to ask them. Like, do you happen to have a spare snow plough or are you okay for mince pies because we happen to have plenty?'

There wasn't a single occupant in the cottages though, just as Bridge said. Peering into windows revealed either empty or sparingly furnished rooms. The cottages, it seemed, were abandoned for the winter, awaiting the summer season. There was no one in Figgy Hollow but them. Luke drew in a deep breath before he took his first step back in the direction of the inn, as he imagined the smug, told-you-so look on Bridge's face.

'Well, Bridge was right,' said Jack, which did nothing to help.

'For once,' said Luke with a humph. 'She does love a gloat.'

'Can I take it that you aren't divorcing on the best of terms?' Jack dared to ask. 'Just a vibe I picked up, despite the banter between you.'

'That's an understatement and a half. It's been an uphill slog to get where we are and I'm still not convinced that she won't refuse at the last fence. Oh bollocks.' Luke stood on a patch of ice that gave way and freezing water gushed over the top of his Timberland boot. Every mention of Bridge brought a small curse with it, like a free gift. 'You ever been married, Jack?'

'God no,' said Jack, toppling against Luke as a gust of wind surprised him from the side. 'I don't seem to be able to find anyone who's my type.'

'Ah, beware of holding out for "the type",' said Luke. 'If I'd have held out for Heidi Klum I'd have missed all the happiness that I've found with Carmen and yes, I'll admit it, the wild and wonderful years I had with Bridge. Two very different women, neither of them "ideal-type-Heidi". There are plenty of soulmates out there waiting for you, Jack. Don't paint yourself into a corner waiting for "the type".'

Jack had no idea what Carmen was like, but Bridge was tiny with hair that could probably be seen from Mars and, give or take the common numbers of head, arms and legs, about as far away physically from Heidi Klum as it was possible to get. She was also, he suspected, quite terrifying if provoked, not the sort of woman he would match with the laid-back Luke. Or himself, for that matter. Small, dark-haired and scary was how he remembered his mother being, although the image he had of her was probably coloured by the portrait his father had painted of her over many years.

Sometimes Jack wondered if he'd ever find this mysterious creature: the soulmate. Looking at the weather, worsening by the second again, he had more chance of finding Bigfoot.

Chapter 11

Bridge stood at the window watching Luke and Jack heading back. She decided she would try her very best not to gloat, mainly because Luke would expect her to. The snow had definitely increased in droppage from when they set off across the way and judging from the amount of times they were replacing their hoods as they walked, the wind was building too. The skies were a mass of ominous dark-grey cloud that no sun in its right mind would even try and penetrate.

Robin heaped logs on the fire in readiness for the wanderers' return, as Bridge had phrased it.

'Oh that's blissful,' said Charlie with delight as the flames blazed and quivered.

He felt the cold so much more these days, thought Robin. The central heating was always on full blast at home, it was hot enough to grow bananas in their parlour, wilting everything but Charlie. But he never mentioned it, just went along with agreeing that there was a need to turn up the thermostat, blaming their large old house for its draughts.

Mary opened the door for Jack and Luke who rushed in gratefully.

'Here, let me help you,' she said as Jack's fingers were too frozen to grasp the tab of the zip. She had a sudden picture of herself reaching up to straighten his tie before they went out to some posh function as a couple. It was never going to happen. Not after all these years. The sand in her egg-timer was almost entirely at the bottom now.

Luke kicked off his boots then peeled his saturated socks away from his feet, surprised that his toes hadn't come with them. His soaking wet trousers plastered themselves to his bare legs and he shuddered at the sensation.

'I need to go upstairs and change,' he said.

'You'll dry out in no time if you sit here,' said Charlie, patting the armchair next to him. 'Bring your boots over and set them down in front of the fire.'

'Thank you, Charlie, but I really do need to change my trousers. Had there not been ladies present, I'd have gladly sat beside you, stripped to my pants to thaw out my legs,' answered Luke.

'Thank goodness we're here then,' said Bridge.

'I wouldn't want to excite you too much,' Luke came back at her.

'Be still my beating heart,' Bridge replied to that in a monotone, tapping her chest with a very steady tattoo, the equivalent of a slow hand clap.

Jack was experiencing the same feeling of relief from taking off cold, soggy socks. He followed Luke upstairs to change too.

'So there *was* no one over there after all?' Bridge called after Luke, unable to resist.

'Yes, but they were all asleep. I'll go back later when they've stirred,' he threw over his shoulder to her.

*

Ten minutes later, they were all sitting around the fire, nursing cups of coffee. Luke's and Jack's feet were encased in clean socks and their shoes were drying out by the fire.

'I don't think we are going to be anywhere other than here for Christmas Day,' Bridge said, turning her head towards the window and seeing the snowflakes blowing so wildly outside it was as if the inn was sitting in a giant snowglobe.

'That would be a total disaster,' said Jack, lips contracted, clearly stressed at the thought.

'Would it?' asked Luke. 'As disasters go is this really the worst? We're warm, we've got food, shelter—'

'Brandy,' Charlie interrupted him with his own addition and laughed.

'Yep, we have enough brandy to pickle ourselves in,' carried on Luke. And his beautiful Carmen was at least with her family. They'd have a second Christmas when he got back. He had loads of presents hidden in his wardrobe to give to her. 'And we have good company of course.' He smiled, taking them all in with a slow sweep of his eyes.

'And Radio Brian as well,' said Mary. She liked Radio Brian. His lack of teeth gave his voice a soft and gentle quality that sat nicely with his pick of old records, the sort her dad always played on his old vinyl player.

'It's a bit of an inconvenience, but we are here and safe and there is nothing we can do about it,' said Charlie. 'Do you have children, Jack?'

'No.'

'Well, that's one crisis averted at least. You and your partner can have your turkey another—'

'I don't have a partner either.'

'Any dependants at all?' asked Robin.

'Not even a goldfish,' said Jack.

'So send your nerves and tensions away on holiday. Do as this very clued-up young lady says and embrace the snow,' said Luke, rolling his hand towards Mary.

Bridge looked at him incredulously.

'Are you on drugs?' she asked. This was not the Luke she knew. Someone had stolen him, put a new soul in his body and pushed him back out into the world as 'reconditioned'. This Luke should have been smelling of patchouli oil and wearing a kaftan, with his fingers permanently fixed into outwardly turned Vs of peace.

'No, Bridge, but I changed my diet, hit the gym, channelled my energies into something positive rather than negative, found—' He stopped short. It would have been crass to continue and say, 'found the right woman', but it was true. Carmen acted like a balm on his soul. She was the calmest, most kindhearted woman he had ever met. They had differences of opinion but they could dispute without throwing things at each other, name-calling, hurting, blaming, fighting. The make-up sex with Bridge had been pretty spectacular – and they'd had a lot of that – but with hindsight it wasn't worth the fall-outs they'd had to merit it. He had happily forgone urgent, fervid make-up sex in exchange for never going to bed on an argument and never having to play silent-treatment, sulking, one-upmanship, point-scoring games.

'What about your family, Mary? Will they be worried about you?' asked Robin, expecting the answer to be yes after their discussion while they were making breakfast.

'I expect they will be. I told my brother I was driving Jack yesterday but I didn't get the chance to tell him that I was okay. But they know me, they know I'm not the damsel-in-distress type.'

Jack felt a pang of guilt. What would Mary's family think about her driving him up to the north-east when he should have driven himself if Fred couldn't do it? They must have watched the snow start and panicked for her. He hoped that she'd told her family enough about him for them to be assured that she was safe with him, that he'd treat her with respect if they'd had to spend a night – or two – taking cover together. It didn't make up for the fact that she'd miss Christmas with them because of him, because he had to meet Chikafuji to talk about scones on the morning of Christmas Eve instead of arranging to communicate with him via a screen. Because of her selflessness, she was in a proper pickle now.

Mary drained her cup and said, 'I think I'll look around and see if there are some games or anything like that in a bit. They'll help to pass the time. There must be a pack of cards at least somewhere in the place.'

Charlie leaned over, picked up a log and tossed it on the fire. 'We're running low on these. Maybe we should ration them and just keep the fire ticking over rather than blazing.'

'There's a log store outside,' said Bridge. 'I saw it when I was trying to find a way into the place yesterday. There's plenty of logs in it.'

'We should get our luggage from the car, Robin,' said Charlie. 'We have a case full of boots and jumpers that we can share around if anyone needs to venture out.' He began to rise from his seat. 'I'll go and get—'

'You'll do no such thing,' said Robin, pushing him back down into the chair by his shoulder. 'You're in no fit state to do anything that will exert you, you old fart. *I'll* go and get the cases.'

'I have plenty of pairs of socks, and packs of pants, all

brand new, which you boys could have if you needed them. I do like fresh underwear for a holiday,' Charlie went on. 'I always over-pack.'

'We may have to take you up on that if we're here for the duration,' said Luke.

From behind him Radio Brian's voice drifted out of the speaker.

'Do not go out even if it's necessary, that's the advice the other BBC is giving, fully endorsed by Brian Bernard Cosgrove – the real BBC.'

Robin insisted on going out to the car to fetch their suitcases alone, but Luke equally insisted on accompanying him. He begrudgingly removed his dry socks and slid his bare feet back into his still wet boots, already counting down the minutes until he could pull them off again. When Robin opened the door, the snow swirled in along with wind noise that belonged on a 'serious winter sound effects' album. Another inch at least had fallen since Jack and Luke had been out earlier.

'Stubborn fool,' said Charlie, standing with the others and watching Robin wobbling and sliding even on the relatively short trip to the car. 'He's got a dodgy knee, a creaking hip and an arthritic shoulder and yet he still thinks he's the young ox he was thirty years ago.'

'Let me go and help them,' said Jack, feeling guilty at being a mere spectator.

'No, don't,' said Charlie, clamping his hand onto Jack's arm to stop him. 'There's nothing worse than stripping a man of self-belief in his abilities. Trust me, I know this. He'll struggle, but he's always been so very capable.' Then he added on a sighing breath: '*No one so proper, so capable as Anne.*'

'Who's Anne?' asked Bridge, brows dipping in confusion.

'That's a line from *Persuasion*, isn't it?' said Mary.

Charlie was impressed. 'How clever of you to recognise it.'

'Anne Elliot,' said Mary, explaining for the benefit of
the others. 'She's a character completely in the background,
forgotten, overlooked, who gets her second chance with
the man she loves, the dashing Captain Wentworth. It's he
who says the line because he knows she's someone to be
totally relied on. It's my favourite book of Jane Austen's.
Everyone always goes on about how fabulous Mr Darcy is
but compared to Captain Wentworth . . . *whoof.*' The sound
was heavily loaded.

'It's my favourite of hers too. Isn't it marvellous?' gushed
Charlie, delighted to have found a fellow Austen fan. 'Can
you remember the part of the story when Wentworth says
the line about Anne being capable, Mary?'

'Of course I do.' Mary's eyes glittered.

'It's when we readers find out he still has feelings for her.'
Charlie smiled a smile of literary joy.

'No, that's when he puts her in the carriage with his sister
because she's tired. *His will and his hands put her there.* Oh my,
you can just imagine him helping her in, can't you, Charlie?
His hands on her waist as he lifts her.'

Mary's smile was as broad and reached all the way up to
her eyes. Jack couldn't ever remember seeing his meek PA
so animated before. Then again, he couldn't imagine she
had cause in the office.

Charlie clasped his hands. 'Yes, of course you're right.
And when his declaration of love is made in that letter . . .
oh my!' He began to quote as if he were Laurence Olivier
at the Old Vic.

'You pierce my soul, I am half-agony, half-hope—'

Mary took over: 'Tell me not that I am too late, that such precious feelings are gone forever.'

'You see, Wentworth feared that Anne's feelings for him were dead, at the point when his for her are too big to contain,' Charlie enlightened a bemused Jack and Bridge.

'There is no more romantic book ever, anywhere,' said Mary. 'Anne is such a lovely girl, sitting on that spinster shelf, invisible, unable to truly move on from her one and only love who flirts in front of her and she's only in her mid-twent—' Mary stopped abruptly, realising she might as well have been talking about herself and Jack. Then she scrambled to find something else to say because her sudden halt made that conclusion even easier to jump to. '. . . twenties, which is absolutely no age. But back then it was . . . a very different ballgame to be single like Anne.'

'That was always my nickname for Robin: Annie, after her,' said Charlie with a fond expression. 'Because there is no one more capable than him. No one.'

'I was a Heathcliff girl myself,' said Bridge with a sniff. 'But then, I've always been attracted to twats.'

'I'm sure we have a copy of that book upstairs in the room,' said Jack. 'There's a sort of reading corner with a chair and—'

Charlie interrupted him. 'Oh, Jack, would you go and get it, please? I'd love to read it while I'm here.'

'Okay,' said Jack and promptly headed upstairs.

'You have to read *Persuasion*, Bridge,' urged Mary.

'And I will now, I promise. You've sold it to me.' Bridge had really taken to this young woman and felt as if she'd known her so much longer than she had. She turned her attention back to the window. 'Well, they've made it to the car. They're having to clear the snow so they can get in the door. I can't tell where it starts and they end, they're all white blobs.'

Jack came back downstairs, handed the book to Charlie. It had seen better days and the corners of the spine were frayed but at least the pages seemed to be all there.

'Thank you, Jack,' he said, clutching it to his chest. 'I feel as if you've just given me an early Christmas present.'

An alarm rumbled from Robin's phone on the table at that moment.

'Oh, that'll be for my tablets,' said Charlie. 'I'd better go up and get them. Robin's a stickler for regimentation. He says it throws the timings out if I don't take them on the dot.'

'Can I get them for you and save your legs?' Mary offered.

'Oh, would you, my dear, thank you, that's kind. There's a leather bag on our bed full of medication. He's colour-coded them, so it'll be the green bottle. I need two. Do you mind awfully?'

'Not at all,' said Mary.

'What a delightful girl. I bet you're glad you have her,' Charlie said to Jack when Mary was out of earshot.

'Yes, she's very efficient.'

'How long has she worked for you?'

Jack tried to work it out. 'Two ... three, yes three years ... I think.'

'Six and a half,' corrected Bridge. 'She told me yesterday.'

'Is it?' Jack pondered on it. 'Yes, I suppose it must be. She worked for my father when she first arrived. And then he retired four years ago and that's when I took over the full running of things and inherited her from him.'

'You make her sound like a chattel,' said Charlie, but not unkindly. 'I bequeath you all my worldly goods – and Mary.'

'Good PAs, and I mean *really* good PAs are hard to find,' said Bridge, a little annoyed by Jack's not knowing. 'I might be poaching her if you aren't careful, Jack.' It was only half a joke.

Mary walked into Robin and Charlie's room and was immediately greeted by a mixture of their colognes, still present in the air. It made her senses happy, made her think of her father who always smelt lovely. As a family they weren't rich by any means, but his one indulgence was a stupidly expensive aftershave, 'Pluie d'Automne'. *Autumn Rain.* She had bought him a bottle of it with her first monthly wage packet and she could see his face now, his kind, blue eyes. *'Oh, love, what have you gone and done this for?' 'Because you didn't have any left and it's too far long to wait until Christmas or your birthday,'* she'd answered him. It had brought her so much joy to buy it, there was nothing she would rather have spent her first proper earnings on. It was only in the last year that she'd been able to bear the smell of it because it did odd and upsetting things to her brain.

Robin and Charlie's scents were nothing like her dad's though, they were lighter, lavender and citrus lingering on the air. They'd made the bedroom their own, placing a hairbrush, glasses and toiletries, a book, a notepad on the dressing table and bedside cabinets. The bed was perfectly made, the white duvet cover smoothed like icing with a warm knife. There was a black Montblanc toilet bag sitting on it, just as Charlie said. Six bottles of pills inside, all with different coloured labels. She pulled out the green one, as instructed, took out two tablets, read the label before she put the bottle back into the bag.

*

'I had quite a few secretaries, as we used to call them back in the dark ages,' said Charlie. 'One had light fingers and had to go. One decided to try and befuddle me, blaming her many days off on "women's complaints" but I came from a family of ladies and I know more about gynaecology than a consultant obstetrician, so there was no wool pulled over my eyes. She certainly wasn't going to embarrass me talking about menstrual cycles and sanitary towels. Then I decided to take a chance on a young man who walked into my office with a big chip on his shoulder because he'd been hounded out of his last job by homophobes.' His voice softened. 'It was the best move I ever made.'

'Robin was good at his job, I take it?' asked Jack.

'Exceptional. Faultless. Meticulous. He started out being my chauffeur, but he quickly became more of a personal assistant. It was strictly work only for a few years, but I fell fast and hard for him. I kept it to myself, because there was a twenty-four-year age gap between us so I never thought he'd be interested in an old wreck like me. Why would I? Then I fell down the bloody stairs and he came over to the house to help me. Moved in for a week and never moved out again. People warned me he was just with me for my money, but I've always been so very good at spotting fakes.' He smiled, his eyes hopping from one to the other of them, eventually coming to a stop at Bridge.

'I was a PA once myself,' she said. 'I realise that in the cases of the best ones, you don't always know what they do until they stop doing it. If everything is in place: your diary, your train tickets – if everything is as it should be, then it's because you have a master "sweeper" on the ice, making sure that your stone runs smoothly on the curling track. Is that what Mary's like for you, Jack? Do you notice her more when she isn't there or when she is?'

'Mary is very efficient,' said Jack.

'Efficient,' Bridge repeated, her tone neutral.

'Yes, totally.'

That word again, noted Bridge. Like a rote. Cold and businesslike. Mary might as well have been a printer or an iMac.

Jack, hearing the word reflected back at him, became aware it wasn't big enough by half to describe Mary. *Do you notice her more when she isn't there or when she is?* There was a telling question. His brain pulled him down a lane in his memory to what office life was like before her, when he was his father's deputy. Carol had been his first PA, a middle-aged woman who made Glenn Close in *Fatal Attraction* look like Anne of Green Gables by comparison. Then there was Jasmina, who had a terribly aggressive telephone manner, and another whose name he couldn't recall who took slack to a whole new level. On the few and far-between occasions when Mary was absent, her replacement Kimberley never delivered that same standard of service; Jack even thought she made mistakes deliberately so that he would give her the oxygen of his attention.

With Mary as his PA he never had to worry about the minutiae. She reminded him of meetings, edited his diary, even sorted out petty factory squabbling when it occurred so he wouldn't have to deal with it himself. Coffees appeared on his desk just as an alert of dryness went off in his throat; he never had to check letters she put in front of him for signing. She was like a good fairy working magic in the background, invisible as air and ironically the least memorable of all his PAs because of her *efficiency*.

'A lovely girl, too,' said Charlie, heading for an armchair. 'Another Anne Elliot, like my Robin.' He sighed. 'If only there were more people like them in the world.'

Footsteps on the creaky staircase. Conversation about Mary immediately closed down.

'What progress, Bridge?' Charlie asked instead.

'They're on their way back,' reported Bridge.

'Here you go, Charlie,' said Mary, with a bright smile, handing over the tablets, which she had wrapped in a pastel-coloured tissue, pulled from a box of them in his room. She hadn't seen those in the shops before and wondered if they were new.

'They're the ones. Like horse tablets,' said Charlie, taking the two bulky bullet-shaped pills and popping them into his mouth.

'I'll go and get you a glass of water,' said Mary. 'You need to take them with a third of a pint at least or they won't work properly.'

'Going back to 1934 now,' said Brian from the radio. 'Can you believe that's when this song was written? "Walking in a Winter Wonderland".'

'Yes I can actually, Brian,' replied Bridge. 'Any chance of something by an artist who's still frigging alive?'

Mary returned from the kitchen just as Robin and Luke walked in, leaving the winter wonderland behind them.

'Ah, Captain Oates, you're back,' remarked Charlie.

'Oh very funny,' said Robin, depositing suitcases and bags on the floor before blowing on his hands. 'Especially after I have risked life and limb to fetch you clean underpants.'

'I appreciate it muchly, my darling,' said Charlie with a beatific smile.

'How long did you say you were going away for?' asked

Luke, also putting down two trolley cases, all matching oxblood and black. Mary saw some smart and fitting vintage-style luggage; Jack and Bridge saw at least two thousand pounds per piece.

'So we now have at our disposal: gloves, scarves, a selection of jumpers, many underpants and socks, two pairs of wellington boots, more insulated anoraks and two pairs of snow shoes,' said Robin.

'Skis would have been useful,' said Luke. 'And a Saint Bernard.' He expected a look of disdain from Bridge and was rewarded with exactly that.

'Robin, your alarm went off. Mary kindly fetched the tablets from upstairs,' said Charlie.

'Two from the green—'

'I know, Robin. Two from the green bottle. Now go and dry your very brave self out by the fire.'

Luke had removed his boots and was already plonked in an armchair, holding his feet up to the flames. 'You can't buy this feeling,' he said. 'If I could, I would at any price.'

'I'm going to have a root around now and see what I can find to entertain us,' said Mary, trying not to look gobsmacked when Jack said he'd help her.

Chapter 12

They started in the cellar. The stairs down to it were steep and Jack went first so Mary would have had a soft landing if she fell, so he said. A rare joke. She had the feeling there would be more jokes and lightness inside him if only he would release the catch and let himself go.

The lighting was excellent in the cool cavernous cellar where there were barrels of beer, stocks of wine and spirits, mixers, boxes of crisps. They could hear the others conversing above them in muted tones, Robin and Charlie having another of their pretend spats, ensuing laughter.

'I'll go left and you go right,' directed Mary.

'Righty-ho.'

Jack hunted behind the barrels, pulled out a box, but it only had rusted metal connectors and beer taps in it. He straightened up, said something that was in his mind and growing too big to keep in any longer.

'I'm so sorry about all this, Mary. Especially as you may not get home to your family for Christmas Day.'

Mary loved his voice and here, with the acoustics of the cellar, it sounded extra rich and deep. Private-school posh and cultured. She imagined that if he sang in a choir, they wouldn't know whether to put him in the bass or the baritone section.

'Oh, it's fine,' she replied. 'I wasn't doing much anyway this year.'

'I know family is important to you.'

'Yes, it is,' she agreed, 'but us lot don't need the excuse of Christmas to get together.'

'Very true,' said Jack. 'But they will be worrying about you.'

They would, and she wished she could let them know she was all right. She didn't want her mum nattering about her and spoiling her holiday in the Canaries with her 'friend'. She said she and David were simply pals who had adjoining allotments but they were both widowed and missed doing things with someone else and David was gentlemanly and good-natured so Mary hoped love would blossom between them. Her dad wouldn't have wanted her lovely mum to wear widow's weeds for the rest of her life.

'What were your plans, incidentally?' asked Jack then.

'I was going to spend Christmas by myself this year.'

'Honestly?'

'You sound shocked.'

'I hadn't got you down as a "by yourself" sort of person,' said Jack.

'I like my own company sometimes.' Mary didn't say that this Christmas she'd planned to be alone for a reason. It wasn't only Bridge and Luke who wanted to treat the new year as a fresh start.

'What about you, Jack? What events, parties will you end up missing?'

'Just some drinks with friends,' he said. Married friends,

some with babies. Die-hard bachelors who had embraced their new roles as husbands and fathers because they'd met 'their type'. Although thinking about it now, they hadn't really. Fran was far away from Zak's Jennifer Lopez ideal and Roman, who always had a penchant for ice queens, was expecting child number three with a chatty raven-haired Irish girl carving out a career as a stand-up comedian. Roman and Georgie had invited him for Christmas dinner and he'd politely declined. He wanted what they had too much to enjoy it in a spectator capacity.

'Ah, that's a shame.'

'I'll live,' said Jack. The gap between his world and that of his friends was widening with every baby that came along, he knew this. The common ground dissipating, conversation drying up.

'Well, there's no point in worrying about something we can't control,' said Mary, pulling the legs of a step ladder apart so she could stand on it to reach some high shelving.

Jack opened the double doors of a cupboard. *Result.* 'How's this?' He held up a box, the picture on the lid foxed and faded.

'Buckaroo,' said Mary with delight. 'I haven't played that for years. Yes, definitely take that upstairs.'

'It's ancient. May not work.'

'Or it might,' Mary contested.

'You're so much more optimistic than I am,' said Jack, with a small strained smile.

'"Optimism is a muscle that gets stronger with use," that's what my dad used to say,' said Mary. *Here's another gem from the Roy Padgett book of wisdom that you need to know, Mary* and she'd roll her eyes or groan. How many times had she heard him say that and what she wouldn't give to hear him say it again.

'He sounds a very wise man,' said Jack.

'He was,' said Mary. *Was*. Such a little word to have the power it did. At first, when her dad had died, thinking of him as 'was' rather than 'is' broke her. She hadn't been able to process that he was no longer around, that she couldn't ring him to tell him this or that as she always had. She loved her mum dearly, but she had always been a daddy's girl. He was the first port of call to tell when she got her A-level results, passed her driving test, got the job working for Butterly's. Still now, two years later, sometimes she thought 'I must tell my dad . . .' On those times, optimism didn't work so well.

'My dad used to say that optimism had a magic. Take that Buckaroo for instance. Neither of us knows if it'll work or not, so maybe if we presume it will, it will. And if we presume it won't, it won't,' said Mary, shifting some cobwebby demijohns to poke behind them.

'Okay, then I'll revise what I said and say . . . I can't wait to see us all playing Buckaroo.' Jack smiled again, properly this time, a smile that stretched his lips to their full extent and Mary thought how altered he looked when he did that, like a totally different person. She couldn't recall the last time she'd seen him smile in the office, his expression was usually one that implied there was a lot going on in the brain behind it and it was all serious scone business.

'That's better.' Mary smiled back at him and once again he thought how her eyes seemed to brighten when she did so, as if a light had been switched on inside her. He also thought that Mary's dad might have not been best pleased about the way she was treated by Butterly's when he died. Something that he should have been aware of and broached with her long before this.

'Ah, bingo. Literally,' said Mary, reaching up to drag over a box with a bingo set in it. There was also a cheap-looking chess and draughts set and a pack of Donkey cards, as well as some monster dead spiders, their skeletal bodies looking like the spikes of miniature broken umbrellas. She'd never been one to be scared of creepy crawlies though. She'd been brought up in the countryside where big spiders weren't uncommon. Plus, one of her favourite childhood books was *Charlotte's Web* and that had coloured her young view of spiders somewhat.

'I think this lot might suffice,' said Mary, brushing some dirt from her pale blue shirt. 'They—'

'Mary,' said Jack, interrupting her flow. 'I have an apology to make to you.'

'Honestly, it's fine,' said Mary. 'No one knew this weather was going to—'

Jack stopped her again; she'd got the wrong end of the stick. 'No, I don't mean about that.' He paused, shamed by what he was about to say. 'When your father died, we sent you some flowers, didn't we? From the company, as we always do in such circumstances.'

'Yes.' Mary nodded, slightly befuddled.

'It wasn't enough,' said Jack. 'They were just flowers. A standard company token. I never realised what you must have been feeling, not until . . . last year, when it happened to me . . . my father passed . . .'

'It's fine,' said Mary, rescuing him.

'No, it isn't fine one bit. I had no idea what it would be like. I wasn't prepared for how low I'd get.'

'Ah.' Mary understood him now. 'It's a club no one wants to join, Jack. I don't think anyone can know until they walk through its doors.'

He remembered asking Kimberley, Mary's temporary replacement, to email and enquire how she was doing and if she had an idea when she'd be coming back to work, even though there was no rush. He shouldn't have asked at all. Or at the very least he should have sent the email himself.

Mary remembered how hurt she'd been to get the curt email from Kimberley. *Jack wants to know when you'll be back.* No enquiry as to how she was. Not a word of concern. That hurt had segued into anger enough for her to reply: *I'll be off as long as I have to be.* She went back three weeks after the funeral and Kimberley was shunted off to finance again, despite hoping she'd made a big enough impression to stay in the position.

'I wondered if we'd pressured you to return to work too soon,' said Jack.

'You didn't,' said Mary. 'I came back when I felt ready. I wasn't going to rush my grief for anyone.' *Not even you.*

'Quite right too.'

Jack held out his hands to take the games from Mary. His gallantry jarred with the memory of that email now refreshed in her mind and words bubbled out of her mouth before she had time to slam on the brake.

'Actually, I was proper annoyed to tell you the truth, Jack,' she said.

'I absolutely—'

'If you'd told me my job was on the line because I was taking too long to grieve, I'd have told you to stuff it … where … the sun doesn't shine.'

Jack's mouth opened to reply, but she didn't leave a breathing space for him to butt in.

'Not even asking how I was, just *Jack wants to know when you'll be back* … yes, if I'm honest … it flipping stung.'

So Kimberley hadn't done as he'd asked. Not that it mattered, because he shouldn't have delegated the task to a PA who wasn't a patch on Mary.

'Mary, I'm so dreadfully sorry. I asked Kimberley to stress there was no rush at all, but it was insensitive of me to even ask the question in the circum—'

'Did you?'

'Of course.'

Mary's top lip curled in anger. That Kimberley really was a sort.

'I see,' said Mary. It made things slightly better, but yes, Jack should have sent the email himself. She would have done it, had the situation been reversed, and not relied on a snake in lipstick who had her own agenda.

'You should have told me to stick my job. I would have deserved it,' said Jack, contritely. Another small embarrassed smile. 'It's long overdue, but I'm sorry if that's how Kimberley's email came across, I really am. I have obviously no idea of how much you do for me in the office, but I know it's a lot, because I notice you when you're not there.' As soon as the words were out, Jack wished he could have pulled them back into his mouth, rearranged them better. 'I mean I—'

'I know what you mean,' said Mary, rescuing him once again because smoothing over stuff was instinctive, her forte, but his words rang like bells in the campanile of her skull. *Notice you when you're not there.* That said it all, didn't it.

Chapter 13

'Ah, the big game hunters have returned to the fold,' said Luke, who laughed at his own wordplay as Jack and Mary walked back into the lounge.

'We have bingo, Buckaroo, cards, chess and draughts,' said Mary, forcing out cheer when she felt like crumbling.

'Wonderful,' said Robin, whose stomach then grumbled loud enough for them all to hear.

'I think that's tantamount to a dinner gong,' declared Charlie.

'My turn to rustle up some grub for us, I think.' Luke rubbed his hands together. 'Any volunteers to help?' He raised his eyebrows at Bridge who turned her head away in avoidance.

'I'll come,' said Jack, brushing cobwebs from his sweater. He'd missed a long stringy one. Mary had an urge to dust it off, in the way Princess Margaret had once dusted a piece of lint from Group Captain Townsend's jacket, thereby signalling to anyone with an ounce of gumption that she was in love with him. But Mary's hand didn't stray to Jack. She wished her heart would catch up with the brain that was playing those words over and over like a stuck record: *Notice you when you're not there. Notice you when you're not there.*

'I'll have a game of draughts with you in the meantime, Mary. Set them up,' said Charlie. 'Winner gets first choice of the chocolates that I'll get out of my suitcase later.'

'You sneaked chocolates into your suitcase?' said Robin. 'Think of your cholesterol levels!'

'Oh, bugger off. And yes, I bought some, in case you didn't buy me any,' parried Charlie.

But Robin had. His favourites. From Patrick Roger in Paris, presently sitting in his suitcase, and he hoped that come Christmas morning, Charlie scoffed the lot, one after the other until he was full.

*

'So you make vegan scones then, do you?' said Luke to Jack, as they hunted through the pantry. 'How do they taste?'

'Very, very good,' replied Jack. 'We . . .'

Jack's voice trailed off. He had a recollection of Mary standing by his desk. *'Can I just say that I think veganism is going to be a booming business, and the company should really look at producing vegan scones that taste as good as the others.'* He cringed inwardly as he remembered dismissing her with a patronising, *'Yes, thank you, Mary.'* Then a year later, the head of product development had said the same thing and Jack had jumped straight on it, because that boom had already started happening and he'd almost missed the boat.

'You were saying,' Luke prompted him.

'We had to work hard on the recipe though, the road to success was paved with a lot of failed attempts. Firstly they were too dry, then bland, but they still sold quite well.

Finally, we thought ... *er* ... we thought we should go back to the drawing board and revamp the recipe. Eventually.' Mary again: *'I hope you don't mind me saying but the vegan scones aren't great, Jack. They taste cheap and dried out. They have to be better. They have to be more moist ... and buttery.'* And that time he'd listened.

Because of Mary his output had increased by ten per cent and growing, they'd won a baking industry award and a bounty of positive PR for the 'Butterfly Buttery Vegan Scone'. And he'd given the head of product development the bulk of the credit for it, upped his salary. He'd given Mary a 'Thanks for your input on the vegan scones' compliment in passing once. Having time away from the office and to think really was showing him up to be a prize prick.

'We should talk, I'd be extremely interested in buying some for Plant Boy,' said Luke. 'By some, I mean a lot.'

'Happy to. I'll give you my business card before we leave and I'll take yours.'

Luke hunted through the fridge, pulled a tray out, read the packaging label. 'Ah, nut cutlets from Hollybury Farm, wherever that is.' Local farm shop, he presumed. Most of the clingfilmed trays on the shelves bore the same brand sticker. 'These will do nicely for us all. Thank goodness the landlord had plans to cater for us lot as well as you carnivores tomorrow.'

'You're a fully-fledged vegetarian yourself then?' asked Jack.

'I wasn't when I started Plant Boy, but I more or less am now. I've done a lot of homework and I find the diet suits me for many reasons. I wanted people to have good tasty alternatives to meat so they could make changes that weren't too painful or going to break their banks. More than half our products are suitable for vegans, and they're good.'

'So Bridge was never part of your business then?'

Luke's features gathered in a semblance of horror. 'God no. It was bad enough living with each other, never mind working together as well.'

He opened up the freezer to hunt for something to go with the nut cutlets and found inspiration in the second drawer.

'Ah, frozen pitta breads. That's sorted then. We'll have veggie kebabs for lunch. We shall grill these and serve them up with cheese, diced red onion, tomatoes. I'll rustle up a makeshift tzatziki, says the man who six years ago would have had to consult the internet on how to boil water. Ha.' He laughed at himself. 'You can be on chopping duty, Jack. Grab a knife, a cucumber and some garlic.'

Jack let Luke direct him on how much of what to chop.

'Do you think you and Bridge will eventually find a friendship going forward?' he asked.

'No idea.' Luke shrugged. 'I'd like to think we could. We've done all the fighting we can, there's nothing left to throw at each other. I even think we enjoyed it in the beginning, all that anger made us forget the hurt.' He smiled ruefully. 'Now, with the wisdom of hindsight, I realise so many things about our marriage; given time to let the waters settle, I see clearly what being with Bridge brought me.'

'Like?' prompted Jack, expecting the answer to be: *an ulcer*.

'This rich, calm bloke with his shit together that you see before you grew from the soil of my time with her. I wouldn't be here now had it not been for Bridge. I see that. And I'll stretch my neck out and say that she wouldn't be the shit-together, rich ... maybe not calm though, woman she is if it hadn't been for me. We were each other's stepping stones to contentment.'

Luke turned on the grill to defrost the pitta breads.

'Tell me more about Butterly's. Give me some background. How did you start the business?'

'Well, actually it was my grandfather who set it up,' began Jack. 'He was just a man employed in a bakery who had an idea that he could make more money selling the baker's products on markets for a cut of the profits. Then he realised that if he produced the scones himself and sold them, his profits would be even bigger. So he taught himself to bake in my great-grandmother's kitchen, set on some of the family as bakers, then bought premises, then a factory. Then Dad took over, then me . . . That's about it, really. What I've done with the business isn't anything like as impressive as you setting one up from scratch.'

'But you must have expanded it? Or did it always produce two million scones per day?'

'Yes, I expanded it. I've trebled production in four years. And extended the lines. My father wouldn't have even entertained the thought of vegan scones, he thought veganism was a "flash in the pan" that would peter out in no time.'

'Ha,' exclaimed Luke.

The success of that product had encouraged Jack to break away from the long-held company policy of keeping it simple, and in doing so, he'd made himself an extremely rich man. He didn't want to think how much he owed to the Butterly Buttery Vegan Scone.

'You've got a good team working for you?' Luke enquired of him.

'Yes, they're . . . all very efficient. At least they are now,' answered Jack. 'I had to get some new blood in when I took over.'

'Oh?'

'Dad was . . .' *Oh, how to put it delicately* – there wasn't really a way. 'He . . . wasn't a great businessman. He thought he was, because he was lucky: the basic product was first-rate and he had excellent salesmen, but he also had too much chaff in with the wheat. Most of the management did as little as possible for their inflated salaries and the product development chef hadn't developed a single thing in years. Dad hadn't wanted anything developed, though; that was the problem. So the chef sat in his office, picked horses from a newspaper and smoked.'

'Tell me you got rid of him,' said Luke.

'Oh yes, he was first to go.'

'Let me guess that there weren't any women in senior positions.'

'No.'

Jack thought it best not to elaborate on his father's attitude to women, it felt disloyal to his memory. He remembered then his father describing Mary as being 'surprisingly good at her job for a silly young thing'. Just because she was a woman under thirty, she was automatically dizzy. And just because people like the company chauffeur Fred were men, they were robotically to be respected. Mary was the best at what she did and Fred was a lazy old goat, but his father would have refused to see that.

'Men were good, women were bad. That was the prism through which my dad saw the world.' Jack hadn't realised he'd spoken that aloud until Luke answered him.

'That's not how you think about them though, surely?'

'Dad had a bad divorce. He used to call women "bullets in make-up".'

'Ooh, that's bitter.'

'And no, to answer your question. That's not how I think about all men and all women.'

Luke grinned at him. 'You must be the most eligible bachelor in town. I bet women are all over you like a heat rash.'

'Do you know what, Luke? I think I'm . . .' Jack waved the rest of the sentence away.

'What?' prompted Luke. 'You can't stop there, I'm intrigued.'

'What I was going to say is pathetic.' Jack sliced down hard on the cucumber.

'Let me be the judge of that.'

Jack blew the air out of his cheeks. 'Okay' – *here goes* – 'I think I'm slightly scared of women. There.' It was too easy to talk to this man while they were making vegetarian stuffed pitta breads. He hadn't even discussed this with his old friends.

Luke hooted. 'Join the club, mate.' Then he curbed his laughter, respecting Jack's confession. 'Okay, I'll kill the flippancy. Why?'

Jack hunted around in his brain for a starting point. 'Dad was very much a man's man, didn't want his wife going out to work, wanted his tea on the table when he got in, shirts ironed, that sort of thing. He couldn't understand how my mother could be completely bored of being trapped in a six-bedroomed domestic box with a swimming pool, even less that she saw fit to disobey him, got a part-time job . . . and then ended up leaving him for someone she met there. Dad was justifiably upset, in fact I'd go so far as to say that it warped him. It didn't help that Mum never fought for me, that played right into his hands. It was too easy to believe Dad's diatribes that women were terrible creatures.'

'Right.' Luke mused. 'So ... you pick women who don't last long, women you can't fall in love with. Women who don't possess the power to hurt you, how am I doing so far?'

Jack's jaw fell open. It was as if this man grilling pitta breads had seen into his soul. Luke seemed amused by his expression.

'Thought so. Jack, mate, piece of advice: you're doomed if you don't break your pattern of picking women you don't really fancy that much but think you should. What's the point in having all the trappings of success if you have no one to share them with?'

'I know,' said Jack. 'I hate going home to a big echoey house every night. I see my friends and what they have: wives, children, laid-back houses, sensible cars and smiles on their faces and I want it so much but ... there's a barbed wire fence between their world and mine.'

'No there isn't,' Luke refuted. 'Your brain has imagined it there to give you the illusion that it can't be yours, the excuse. But it can, trust me. You just need to do what you've done with your business and step out of your comfort zone or you'll be running around in it in small circles for the rest of your life.'

Jack let Luke's words sink in. Could it really be that simple?

'You're very wise,' he said.

'I've made a lot of mistakes. People who have and who've learned from them usually are quite savvy.' Luke left it a beat before continuing. 'Mary's lovely.' It was written all over the woman's face in emotional Sharpie what she thought about her boss. Jack must be blind if he didn't see it.

'Yes, she's ...' Jack was going to say efficient again, '... awfully good at her job.'

'Oh, Jack, get over yourself. She's also a woman. You

should take off your office glasses and see her as a man would.' Luke put the second batch of pitta breads under the grill.

'Don't be ridiculous. As I told you before, she sees me as her boss. I've never given her the slightest bit of encouragement to think otherwise either,' said Jack, dismissing the notion outright.

'I can well believe that,' said Luke, turning his attention back to making lunch.

Everyone was ready for something to eat by the time they brought it through. The six of them sat at the long table, passing around dishes of the various ingredients and, simple fare as it was, it felt like the best kind of banquet. The lounge had been fully warmed up by the fire, which cast a cosy orange glow into the room in stark contrast to the bluey-white snowy exterior beyond the stone inn walls.

Radio Brian gave out a grim warning of ceaseless snow for the next twenty-four hours at least. No one would be home or in a luxury Scottish hotel for Christmas Day.

'So looks like we're all going to be lumped here together tomorrow,' Charlie said with considerable glee. 'We should prepare.'

'Prepare?' asked Jack. 'Whatever do you mean, Charlie?'

'Celebrations,' explained Charlie. 'We have to make merry for Christmas Day of course.' He bobbed his head towards Mary. 'As the Norwegians would do, by making the best of our situation.'

'Precisely,' Mary added to that. Playing draughts with Charlie had salved her injured feelings no end. 'We should cook a Christmas dinner. There's plenty of ingredients in the larder for it and they'll probably be wasted otherwise.

We'd be doing the landlord a favour.'

'Absolutely,' said Luke, high-fiving Mary for her altruism.

'I was hoping to have mine cooked for me by a Michelin-starred Scottish chef,' said Robin in a grumbly voice. 'But, as the Norwegians would' – he also gestured towards Mary – 'I will embrace the alternative with gusto.'

'That's the spirit,' said Charlie.

'Let's do a Secret Santa,' suggested Luke, clapping his hands together with childish glee. 'We'll each go on a hunt around the inn and find something to wrap up for someone else. We don't have to keep it and get arrested for stealing when the owner comes back. It's all about the opening anyway.'

'Sounds good,' said Bridge. She got up from her seat and tore a page from Mary's notebook on the bar. She ripped it up into six, wrote their names on the pieces, folded them and put them in a dimpled beer glass.

'Right,' she said, returning to the table, 'pick a name out of the hat. If you pick your own, put it back and pick another. We'll carry on until everyone has someone else's name. Don't say who you've got, it's *secret*.'

It took three attempts but eventually they all had a piece of paper that didn't bear their own name.

'We should each put one of our socks in front of the fireplace to fill,' said Mary, as the idea came to her.

'Ooh, I like that,' said Robin, standing to collect the plates. Bridge started to help him.

'Who's for a coffee and a mince pie?' asked Robin.

'Oh, why not,' said Charlie. 'And see if you can find some brandy butter while you're in there.'

'Cholesterol!' barked Robin, and Charlie chuckled.

'I'm going to decorate the tree this afternoon,' said Mary.

'And make some paper chains, that'll pass some time.'

'I'll do the chains while you do the tree,' Bridge threw over her shoulder as she headed to the kitchen to help Robin.

'Jack and I will get some more logs after we've finished eating,' said Luke. A mini video hijacked his brain: he and Bridge with two carrier bags going into the park to collect snapped-off branches for kindling and any stray logs. The park keeper was a bit keen so they had to hide behind trees when he was patrolling, trying not to giggle. They'd been so very much in love, he couldn't get enough of her. She was mad and exciting and loving and damaged and he wanted to mend her. He wondered if he had now, after damaging her more first.

Bridge brought in a big jug of coffee and Robin a plate of warmed mince pies, a bowl of brandy butter and one of rum cream. Robin opened his mouth to remonstrate as Charlie loaded his pie with a huge blob of the butter, closed it again, let him be.

'If this is the start of a nuclear winter and we are discovered by scientists years later, they will wonder why our skeletons are so fat,' said Luke, through buttery crumbs of pastry, which made them all laugh.

'You can't have a fat skeleton, idiot,' said Bridge.

'I bet you can if you eat like this for a while,' Luke argued.

'I can't see this clearing for days, can you?' said Robin with a sigh. 'I do hope the travel insurance company don't class this as an act of God and refuse to pay up. I shall tell them that I'm an atheist and see how they like them apples.'

'Are you?' Bridge asked him. 'I wouldn't have had you down as a non-believer.'

'If it means I'll get our money back for the hotel in Aviemore, I'll say I'm a Jedi Knight,' said Robin. His voice softened then. 'I'm a good Catholic boy. Well, a bad one actually. Lapsed – very lapsed in fact. But I do know going to church is no guarantee of being a good person. I think it's far too late for me to go back to it properly. If I went into a confessional booth to catch up with all my undisclosed sins, I'd not come out for a year.'

'I don't believe that for a second,' said Bridge.

'What about you, Charlie?' asked Luke. 'You a believer?'

'I am,' said Charlie, already on his second mince pie. 'Plus I *want* to believe in a heaven after all this. It would be a shame for the things we have learned and the connections we have made to be for nothing in the end. I just hope I'm following the right god, that's all. The one with the kind face and nice beard. What do the Norwegians say about the afterlife, Mary?'

'Oh, they're big believers in the afterlife,' she answered.

'I'm a dyed-in-the-wool atheist myself,' said Luke. 'I think afterwards is the same as what we had before – the wheel turns and we come back to nothing, oblivion. In saying that, it would be good to be proved wrong. I think as humans, we've over-evolved, made it too complicated for ourselves by not accepting we simply stop and that's it. All we can be sure of is the here and now.'

'How cheerful,' said Bridge, deadpan.

Charlie was drinking every word in though. 'That's . . . insightful, Luke.'

'If I'm wrong, then I have no fear of a god on judgement day,' said Luke. 'Just because I don't believe, that doesn't mean I don't have a pronounced sense of right and wrong. You don't need a god to tell you that you should look out for your fellow man.'

He expected Bridge to chirp up again, but she didn't.

'Not sure what I believe either,' put in Jack. 'If I could

have a sign, that might help any faith issues.'

'Faith is having a belief without the need for proof, though,' said Mary.

'You have such a wise head on your young shoulders,' said Charlie. 'I wish I was part-Norwegian.'

'I believe in God too. I don't go to church or push my faith down any unwilling throats, but I say my prayers at night before I go to sleep,' said Mary.

'Are they ever answered?' asked Bridge.

'Some,' she replied, and the way in which she said the word told that she had no plans to elaborate.

Mary had prayed very hard for God not to let her dad suffer at the end of his life and he hadn't. She'd asked God to please make the six wives of Henry VIII turn up on her A-level history exam paper because she knew everything about them, and it had. She'd asked God to *please* let Jack Butterly somehow find out that she fancied him, no more, because she wanted him to do all the work if he fancied her back. That prayer remained unmet. She'd also prayed for guidance before she set off on this trip with him and – oh boy – he'd really answered that one.

Chapter 14

Wearing Charlie and Robin's wellingtons, padded gloves and snow coats, Jack and Luke ventured outside to bring in some logs. The wind was howling, tossing the snowflakes up in the air as if juggling with them. At this rate the inn would be buried in days.

Across from them, the unoccupied buildings of Figgy Hollow looked chocolate-box pretty under a felting of snow. In summer, this must be such a picturesque and tranquil place to stay, thought Luke. He'd like to bring Carmen here one day, maybe even hire one of the cottages for the weekend.

The wood store was packed solid with logs, chopped up in readiness, bigger ones on the left, thinner ones for kindling on the right. There were some hessian sacks and a bank of newspapers tucked in the driest corner, dated from years ago, the headlines seeming to be from another age: *Tony Blair Wins Labour Leadership Bid. Mandela Becomes First Black President of South Africa. Madonna Tells Letterman to 'Smell my Pants'.*

'Well, that's a mix of news,' said Jack. He flicked through

one, for amusement purposes and read aloud: '*Why the New American Series* Friends *is Doomed to Fail, by TV Tim.*'

'Wonder why I haven't heard of TV Tim,' said Luke. 'It's a shame to burn these papers, it'll be like burning history books. Look: *Channel Tunnel Finally Opens.*'

'*Stolen Masterpiece* The Scream *Recovered.*'

'*Britain's First National Lottery Rollover Winner Nets £17.9 Million.*'

'*The World Welcomes Genetically Engineered Tomatoes.*'

The raging gale rattled at the shed walls as if to remind them why they were there. They stopped reading and filled up four enormous sacks with wood and papers. As they dragged them from the log store, the wind pushed at them from behind as if hurrying them back to the sanctuary that the inn afforded.

Charlie passed a crystal angel up to Mary who was standing on a stool to reach the higher branches of the tree. He didn't ask but he wondered what had happened in the cellar between them when she and Jack were looking for games, for it was a different Mary who had returned to the one who went down the steps. She had been almost fully restored after their cheerful game of draughts and a nice lunch. Almost but not quite.

Charlie was very intuitive and he was rarely wrong in his summings-up. If ever there was a woman more like a real-life Anne Elliot than young Mary, he was yet to meet her. So proper and capable and far too lovely to sit on a shelf waiting for her Captain Wentworth while her bloom faded. He fancied her heart had already been set on someone, a heart that would not settle for second best, so it waited for love to be requited, love she had for Jack, her boss, because there was a light that turned on in her eyes when he was in her physical orbit.

He liked these people in his present world far more than the short time they had been together should have allowed. Bridge: he wasn't sure about her at first, but yes – she was a soft kernel fiercely protected by her case of hard nut. Luke: a darling fizz of a man who had completed a long journey. But it was Jack who intrigued him most. He seemed off-kilter with the world, as if he didn't quite understand it, but wanted to. Maybe that's why he was such a good busi-nessman, because he devoted his time to where he was best placed. But that didn't necessarily make him a happy man, or one that could see the fruits for the taking in front of his eyes, because those eyes were too focused on attaining the illusion of the horizon. A fruit in the guise of the so proper and so very capable Mary.

'There's an empty branch for the angel, my dear,' Charlie pointed out.

'Yes, Charlie, but we have one nearby. I need a robin there, I think.'

'Someone call?' said Robin, scooping out some ash from under the fire and putting it in a metal bucket to cool.

'Get back to the housework,' said Charlie.

'Are you intending to sit on top of the tree yourself or is there a prettier big fairy in the box?'

Charlie gestured towards him while addressing Mary.

'Do you see what I have to put up with?'

Mary chuckled. She was well on the way to ador-ing Robin and Charlie. That they cared for each other deeply was clear as the crystal angel she was about to add to the tree.

All eyes then turned to the opening door. Jack walked in

dragging sacks like a bright orange Father Christmas, Luke in his wake.

'Good God,' said Bridge, feeling the blast of cold air from outside as she sat at a table constructing a paper chain.

'Oh, Bridge, we're old friends, just call me Luke,' he said, which Bridge ignored.

Jack's eyes fell on Mary standing on the stool, decorating the Christmas tree, taking care to do it properly, he had no doubt. But then that was Mary all over. Whatever she did was right, even down to the coffees she brought him in. Never a spill in the saucer. She made a capable job of everything. *No one so proper, so capable . . .* so Charlie had said about that woman in the Jane Austen book.

'Good to be home, it's bad out there,' said Luke. And a part of him genuinely did feel that relieved to be back in the inn. He only hoped that Carmen was okay in the bosom of her family and that there was nothing for him to worry about. He hadn't been away from her for as long as this before and he was feeling their separation keenly. Especially now.

The inn was an oasis of contentment. Charlie was happily acting as Mary's assistant, Robin was tidying up around the fireplace and Bridge was making her chain. Radio Brian was playing Doris Day singing 'Have Yourself a Merry Little Christmas'. It could have been a scene ripped from the pages of a 1940s magazine.

Jack and Luke emptied two of the sacks, arranged some of the wetter logs on the hearth to dry out, banked up the hungry fire, which started tucking into the woody fodder with the zeal of Charlie tucking into the mince pies. Doris finished crooning and Radio Brian commenced talking in his best toothless tones.

'Anyway, I'm going to have some snap now,' he said. 'It's well past lunchtime isn't it? I think Mrs Brian Bernard Cosgrove has got something meaty in store for me.'

'I hope he puts his teeth in if he's having a steak,' tittered Bridge.

'. . . Maybe a glass of mulled wine and why not,' Brian went on. 'So I'll leave you with a little-known radio show that always makes me chortle even though it's quite a few years old now: *Sir Colin of Castle Street*, and this is the Christmas 1952 special. I'll be back later, everyone. Don't go anywhere.'

'Fat chance of that,' said Bridge to Mary. 'Never heard of Sir Colin of Clifton Street or whatever he said.'

But Mary was smiling with recognition. 'Then sit and listen to it. My dad used to love radio plays; he'd split his sides at Sir Colin – it's very funny. People have fallen away from radio shows but I think they'll have a renaissance. Audio books are big business these days, I gather, so I reckon it's only a matter of time. I don't think we ever lose the childish joy of listening really, it just gets buried under adult stuff.'

'*Jackanory*,' said Robin with fond remembrance. 'How I loved that as a boy.' As if a lock had been sprung on a box, his head suddenly flooded with images of June Whitfield, Spike Milligan, Richard Briers, Thora Hird. People from a yesteryear that was stable and solid, one flavoured with jam sandwiches and Vimto. When he was a little boy who had no idea of what was lying in wait for him, around the corner.

'*Sir Colin of Castle Street* was recorded in front of a live studio audience,' announced a plummy male radio voice as a vintage tinkly tune revved up to cheers and voracious clapping from the audience's hands.

Bridge, who was preparing herself to audibly block out a load of unfunny old duffers performing stuff about the war, found herself pleasantly surprised at the antics of Sir Colin, a pensioner who 'had it on good authority' he was descended from royalty and acted as such. He was also tight as the proverbial duck's arse and got his words horribly muddled up. On paper, it was about as humorous as an anal abscess but the actors breathed magic into the script and the audience were in fits. Mary's bubbling brook of laughter as she tarted up the tree infected the others. Tears started to roll down Charlie's and Robin's faces as Sir Colin was mistaken for the vicar at a children's church nativity service. Luke, warming himself by the fire with Jack and Robin, secretly watched Bridge chuckling away to herself as she looped the strips one around the other. She looked like a different woman when she laughed and didn't scowl. They'd laughed so much in the early days. Laughed at their empty pockets, laughed at their attempts to make meals out of the barest ingredients in their food cupboard. They'd laughed out of bed and in it. When had they stopped?

At the end of that half hour of hilarity, the six of them all broke into applause along with the live studio audience who were probably not very live any more, their laughter preserved, pinpointing a moment in their personal history when they were squeezing every drop of enjoyment from the here and now like the big juicy orange of time that it was.

'What a tonic,' said Robin, his cheeks aching.

'Did someone say gin and tonic?' asked Charlie.

'No they didn't,' said Robin, shutting him straight down.

'Or one of Radio Brian's mulled wines, maybe?' Charlie suggested. 'Ever since he mentioned it, I've been fancying one.'

'I make a cracking mulled wine,' said Mary. 'It's laced with port. Shall I go and make some? We can all sit around the fire and listen to carols and fill ourselves with Christmas.' She draped the last snake of tinsel around the bottom branches of the tree, nudging it into shape.

'I'll come and help you,' said Robin, pressing his hand towards Charlie as if he had offered instead. 'You have a rest, love. You must be exhausted sitting in that chair and passing decorations to Mary.' Then he winked at him.

'Mind if I make some of that chain with you after we've had the mulled wine?' Luke threw across to Bridge.

He expected her to tell him to bugger off. Was pleasantly surprised when she said:

'If you want.'

Chapter 15

Robin took three bottles of red wine and one of port from behind the bar and he and Mary went into the kitchen. He looked around for some spices and found some in a well-stocked rack. Mary put a large stewing pan on the stove and poured the wine in and a generous slug of port, adding some brown sugar, cinnamon sticks and cloves, while Robin, at her request, was zesting an orange.

That done, Robin checked his watch, started talking to himself in a low voice.

'Just making sure I know where I am with Charlie's tablets,' he explained, picking up a wooden spoon and beginning to stir the slowly warming wine. 'Good job he has me.'

'Yes, it is,' said Mary, her voice soft, thoughtful.

'This rich food will do nothing for his indigestion. Or his wind. And it's me that has to suffer during the night if he overdoes it.'

Mary reached behind her, pushed the door shut to give them privacy.

'The tablets in the green bottle,' she began. 'The ones

I gave Charlie when you were outside at the car. The Oxycophine.'

'Yes, love. What about them?' said Robin.

'I know what they are.'

'Charlie has dreadful heartbur—'

'My dad had the same ones,' Mary cut him off. 'He was one of the first people to get them. They'd just rolled them out after successful trials.'

Robin stopped stirring, turned his head towards the wall shelves. 'Now I'm sure I saw a jar of maraschino cherries somewhere. Charlie loves those.'

'I know what those tablets do, Robin. I know why people take them. I know *when* people take them.'

A palliative drug. The name of it stamped on a part of her brain that wouldn't ever forget it.

Mary placed a hand on Robin's arm and that simple, small touch knocked down walls within him. Walls he had kept erected, dam walls holding a lake back. He dropped the wooden spoon on the floor, his hands shot to his eyes, his shoulders began to judder. Then as quickly, he recalibrated, forced himself to rebuild, dashed away the shiny drops of tears from his face for the irritations they were.

'Look at me, what a fool,' he said, bending to pick up the spoon then rinsing it under the tap.

'I didn't know whether I should say anything or not,' said Mary. 'I'm so sorry if I upset you.'

'Don't you apologise, love,' said Robin, giving himself a shake as he tried to steady his ship. 'To be honest, it's a blessed relief to let go, even for a few seconds, take myself off the boil. I feel sometimes as if I'm ready to burst.'

Mary's arms wrapped around him and Robin lowered his

head against her shoulder; she felt the wetness of his tears on her own cheek.

'Oh look, I'm getting you all soggy,' he said, pulling himself sharply away, striving once again for control. Kindness was a pin in his balloon of decorum. 'I'm okay. I always said that I'd fold afterwards, when it's over, not before. I don't want Charlie to ever see me upset.'

Mary knew how hard it was to keep up that façade, to pretend that everything was 'normal' when your stress levels were constantly off the charts.

'How long has he been given?' asked Mary gently, taking an apple from a fruit bowl, chopping it into quarters. She knew the finishing line was in sight when Oxycophine was prescribed.

'Not long,' said Robin. 'This will be our last Christmas together, we know that, hence why I pushed the boat out and booked the hotel in Aviemore with all the bells and whistles. Charlie can't fly now or we would have gone to Austria, he loves it there.'

'The Oxycophine really helped my dad.'

'Did it?' Hope thick in Robin's voice.

'Very much,' said Mary. 'Dad didn't want to carry on going to hospitals any more. He was sick of them, so he made the decision to enjoy what time he had left, which would be shorter but the quality would be much better. And it was. He didn't have to avoid this or that, so long as he didn't overdo things. He looked forward to his big brandy every night. It made him feel as if he was living a full life, a *normal* life rather than one filled with lots of restrictions.'

'How ... how long was he on it for?' asked Robin, his voice wavery with emotion.

'Three months. He felt good on it – really well, like ...

old Dad. He slept properly, he had the appetite of a horse too. We knew it was the drug masking the symptoms but that was okay. The hard part was trying to accept the fact that he wasn't getting better, even though he looked as if he was. The Oxycophine propped him up all the way until the end.'

'Charlie's accepted it more than I have,' said Robin, stirring the wine, hanging on tightly to the spoon as if it was giving him some form of comfort. 'I can't think about it. He wants to talk to me about what's happening and I won't. I can't. "*Just sit with me for half an hour, Robin*" he keeps asking and I know it's only half an hour but I don't want to hear what . . . Oh fucking hell.' He shooed away a fresh flurry of tears, sniffed back the rest that were forming inside him before they made a show.

'Will you take a little advice from someone who knows,' said Mary. 'Let Charlie talk to you.'

A dull echo of a similar scene played in her head.

Mary, can I talk to you about what's going to happen?

No, Dad, I can't. I really can't.

'No, Mary, that's one ask too far,' said Robin, defiantly.

'My dad wanted to talk to us,' said Mary. 'He wanted to make sure that everything was in place for when he'd gone. It would have given him some peace that he could go with all his ends tied up, all his wishes known. And we didn't because none of us could face it. And we were wrong to deny him that, we saw that . . . when it was too late.' Her own voice broke then, she coughed to clear tears clogging up her throat. 'I'll never forgive myself for being a wimp. So if Charlie wants to have that conversation, don't deny him, please. It's only half an hour of your time and then you can forget about it but it's important to him and it *will* make his passing more peaceful. Believe me.'

'I can't,' said Robin. 'I really can't. I would if I could. I'm not good with words, putting feelings into sentences ... Charlie is, he's so emotionally intelligent, so eloquent, but I'm not. I can't.'

'Yes you really can,' said Mary firmly. 'Because you would be doing it for Charlie.'

'I love him too much to even think about losing him, never mind talking to him about it, Mary,' said Robin, his voice dissolving into his sadness. Mary tore off a piece of kitchen roll, handed it to Robin to mop up tears as they fell.

'It's just our way of coping when we try to pretend that things are carrying on as normal. Those pills are very good at masking the real truth too, making us believe that they're doing more than they are. It's time to work with the Oxycophine, Robin. They're giving Charlie a new lease of life, so let him live the best version of it with all his loose ends tied up. Please.'

*

'Ah here they are,' said Charlie as Robin walked into the room with the large stewing pot and a ladle stuffed in his back jeans pocket. Mary went behind the bar for glasses; she found some ideal ones with glass handles on the stems.

'Well doesn't that smell Christmassy,' said Luke as Robin lifted the lid and the aroma of warm wine and spices drifted out into the air.

'I think we overdid the apples,' said Robin. 'There's half an orchard in there.'

Mary began to ladle out the wine. 'It's always better when it's left for a while, but who wants to wait?'

'Not me,' said Charlie. 'Robin, go and get the chocolates from my suitcase. You can't have mulled wine and no chocolate.'

'Yes you can,' rebutted Robin. 'Your cholesterol levels will be through the roof, Charles Glaser.'

'Mary has to have first pick as promised after she thrashed me at draughts,' Charlie nodded towards her. 'I haven't forgotten.'

'I shan't argue with you, Charlie,' she returned.

'Oh go on then.' Robin relented and went to fetch them.

Radio Brian was now back from his lunch and sounded as if he'd had a couple of glasses of mulled wine himself as he was slurring his words. He'd just introduced that famous carol, 'While Leopards Washed their Clocks by Night'.

Everyone sat absorbing the music, clustered around the crackling log fire, and sipped, feeling the warmth of the spicy wine spreading through them.

'This is bloody strong, Mary,' said Luke. 'Well done.'

Mary stuck a thumb up by way of an answer as she had just bitten into a chocolate cherry. A burst of cherry brandy flooded into her mouth and out through her lips.

'Oh yes, I meant to warn you about those,' said Charlie. 'They're like little bombs. I buy them from a chocolatier in Lincoln. They're called Cherry Grenades.'

'They're gorgeous,' said Mary, when she had swallowed enough of it to talk. She had a small blob of chocolate on the side of her lip that made her look totally endearing. Bridge wished that Jack would reach over and wipe it away with a tender thumb, or better still kiss it off. He did neither.

'I wish it could be Christmas every day,' said Charlie with a yearning sigh. 'I love it. We haven't had snow like this at

Christmas for so long, have we? I prayed for it this year it and it seems I've been answered.'

'Stop praying, Charlie,' said Jack. 'You're obviously too magic for your own good.'

'Or at least pray that I'll win the lottery,' said Luke with a snort.

'The wind's dropped,' said Robin, pointing to the window. 'The snow is falling straight down instead of blowing all over the place. It looks a little calmer out there.'

'*All is calm, all is bright*,' trilled Charlie. 'We should go carol singing.'

Five heads turned to him.

'I think you've had too much of that wine,' said Robin.

'No, I mean it. We'll pair up and sing at the door and the most tuneful wins a prize.'

'I'm not going out there for anything. Not even to rescue a naked Hugh Jackman standing by my car,' said Bridge, resolutely.

'My friend and I used to go carol singing,' said Robin. 'We'd earn a small fortune, by kids' standards anyway. We stood by the Jolly Butchers and tapped into the stream of benevolent drunks coming out of it.'

'I'm not surprised, you have a beautiful voice,' said Charlie.

'I don't, I sound like a goose having a seizure,' he replied and swung a pair of twinkling hands around to his partner. 'Now Charlie here, he's hiding his singing light under a bushel.'

'Well if we do go carol singing, I'll volunteer to join up with Charlie,' said Jack. 'There, you heard it here first.' He smiled and Mary thought that she'd seen him smile more in the past twenty-four hours than she had in the last six and a half years.

'My, it's weathery out there,' said a half-sloshed Radio Brian. 'The other BBC met office has announced that it's minus twelve out there at the moment but the wind factor will make it feel like minus twelvety-two . . . I mean twenty-two. Oops.'

'Did he just fart?' asked Bridge. They all heard it. Brian's 'oops' both highlighted and confirmed it.

'Wind factor,' said Luke. 'It's like the X factor only smellier.'

Which wasn't the best joke in the world but somehow they all started laughing, feeding each other's hilarity until their sides began to ache.

'What I can't understand,' said Robin, wiping his eyes, 'dear me, is if you went outside and it was minus twelve, which is bloody cold isn't it, how much colder can it feel? I mean what's the difference between minus twelve and minus twenty-two?'

No one could answer, no one even wanted to think about it. They were all too mellow, too comfortable and in Jack's case, too content to even check his phone for any messages.

Chapter 16

Charlie and Robin fell asleep in the armchairs, lulled by the soft feathery voice of Radio Brian and his melodious Christmas tunes. Jack banked up the fire and then helped Mary carry the glasses into the kitchen to be washed. As usual she felt as if the surface of her skin buzzed with electricity when he was near to her. Someone, one day, would invent some spectacles and when people who were in love were viewed through them, they would be lit up with an orange glow, as if they'd eaten up five whole boxes of Ready Brek like the old TV advert used to show.

'Can't believe a pub hasn't got a dishwasher,' said Jack. Tiny as the kitchen was, it surely would be a standard piece of equipment. 'I mean why would the owner invest in that huge German coffee machine that takes up half of the available work surface but rely on this minuscule sink to cope with all the washing up? Makes absolutely no commercial sense.'

Jack might not have looked at his phone for a little while, but his head continued to spin on the logistics of business.

It was certainly a kitchen not conducive to more than

one person working in it at a time, or two who wanted to become better acquainted. Three could possibly lead to impregnation.

'You wash, I'll dry,' said Jack.

'Okay,' said Mary, trying to sound a lot more at ease than she felt. Her brain knew she had less than no chance of a romantic liaison with Jack. He had done nothing other than keep her at his very long arms' length for years and yet here was her stupid heart quivering in her chest at being so physically close to him. Her brother's gently taunting voice singing 'The Boy from Ipanema' drifted into her mind. Jack really was him, long and lovely and about as attainable as Brad Pitt. Probably less so. Plus she could quite happily appraise Brad without her nerve endings doing weird things.

She filled up the bowl with hot water and a squirt of washing-up liquid. Jack went to the drawer filled with tea towels. All different designs, age-old presents to the landlord probably: Souvenir of Blackpool; a long poem: 'The Italian Who Went to Malta'; the commemoration of Prince Charles's wedding to Lady Di.

The profile of his back made Mary's heart beat almost as fast as his front profile did. Her involuntary reactions were truly starting to annoy her.

Mary dunked the first glass, rubbed at it with a sponge, checked that the stubborn gluey wine had gone, gave it a quick rinse under the tap with fresh water before placing it on the draining board.

'You even do the washing up properly, don't you?' said Jack, curious grin quirking up one side of his mouth.

'I try and do everything properly,' replied Mary. 'It only takes a little extra effort to do a good job rather than a mediocre one. That's what my dad taught us.'

Jack lifted up the glass, began to dry it.

'Do you still miss him? Even after . . . two years is it now?'

'Yes,' said Mary, dipping another glass. 'I've got past the floppy, crying all the time stage but that doesn't mean he's not in my thoughts. I still think "I must tell Dad" when something happens that I know he'd like to hear about or when I want to run something past him. And I still feel sad that I can't ring, but I talk to him, and if he's around, he'll hear me, and maybe he'll guide me. Dad wouldn't want me to mope and be miserable, he'd tell me off. If I had children and I . . . left them, I wouldn't want them to miss me so much that they didn't enjoy things any more.'

'Do you think you'll have children one day?' asked Jack.

The question surprised her; he'd never asked her anything as personal before, but she tried not to let that show as she answered him.

'If I found someone nice to have them with.'

Admittedly her thoughts, on occasion, had strayed to pictures of herself and a nice man walking through a park: she pushing a buggy, he holding the lead of a collie they'd taken in from a rescue centre, like the sort of dog her family had when she was growing up. But she would never attract someone who was truly interested in her as long as Jack was occupying her thoughts, because she wouldn't flag up on the dating radar as available. Presently, she was like a nun, married to the Church. And tomorrow she would be twenty-five years old. Time to make things happen, not dream stupid dreams any more that would never come to anything.

'What about you? Do you ever think about having children?' she threw the question back at him.

Yes he did, imagined him kicking a ball over the vast lawn at the back of his house or holding a little girl's hand as she prattled on and he tried not to chuckle at her. But he wouldn't have children if it meant he didn't have enough time to read a story to them, or worked so long and hard that he had to send them away to boarding school. He wouldn't have them if his marriage wasn't rock-solid and if, by any chance, it broke down afterwards, he would do his damnedest to make sure his child wouldn't get caught in the crossfire or be dragged into the poisoned lake that stood between warring factions. He knew his father hadn't meant for that to happen, but still it had. No, better not to have them at all than risk he might replicate his mistakes.

'I'm not sure I will,' said Jack, setting the dried glasses on a tray to take back through to the bar.

'Why not?' said Mary.

'I'd be worried I wouldn't be a good enough father.'

'Well that's just rubbish, if you don't mind me saying, Jack. All parents make mistakes.' *Ooh, was that a bit rude*, said a voice inside her. She jumped in quickly to pat her dissidence down. 'I mean, my parents made loads. They were only human. My dad never went to any of the plays my older siblings did at school, which he regretted, he said, because he came to the ones I did and he realised then what he'd been missing. And my mum always said she was a bit soft on us. For instance, my older brother made a mess of his GCSEs and Mum was really cross at herself for not coming down harder on him for playing truant at school. But then again, maybe if he hadn't cocked up he wouldn't have tried so hard to make up lost ground. He's a chartered surveyor now and lives in a massive house. Maybe his wrong path turned out to be the right one in disguise.'

She shut up, not even sure if that made sense.

'I don't know if I have a healthy family template to copy,'

said Jack. 'I don't want others to suffer because of things I get wrong.'

He meant Reg of course, Mary knew. Reg was a hard man, totally work-focused. He was gruff and rough, his manner brusque and he'd been warped and damaged by being rejected for another man, but he never missed an opportunity to boast about his son. *'Oh that lad of mine has got us into Waitrose, I knew he would'*; *'I told him, I said, our Jack's the man to talk to about that, he'd know'*; *'Jack'll take this place to heights I'm not clever enough to do'*.

Mary took in a fortifying breath. She was about to over-step the mark and, again, she'd probably get shot down for it, but what did she really have to lose now?

'I can tell you without any doubt, Jack, that your dad loved you very much and he was so proud of you. And just in case you're wondering how I know that, it's because he told me he did.'

Jack's hand stilled on the glass he was drying. 'Did he? When?'

'Loads of times. He'd put the phone down after talking to you and sort of smile as he said, "That was my lad on the phone."'

She could go further, decided she should.

'He once said to me: "I'm proud of our Jack, Mary. You mark my words, he'll take this company to new heights," and he was pleased as punch when you got the Waitrose order. He once told me he'd sent you away to school because he wanted you to have the best education he could afford, as there was no point in having money if you couldn't spend it on those you loved.'

She saw Jack swallow before he asked her, 'He said that? Really?'

'I wouldn't lie for effect, Jack,' a nip in her voice. 'I remember taking tea in for him one time when he'd just come off the phone to someone. He was smiling and he turned to me and said, "If only I'd known I had it in me to have a son like our Jack, I'd not have waited so long and I'd have had a dozen of 'em."' She imitated Reg's broad Yorkshire accent as she said it. 'And I said to him, "You should tell him that, Mr Butterly. He'd be chuffed to bits."'

She looked up at Jack to see that he was waiting for her to continue, so she did.

'... And he said, "I'm not that sort of bloke, Mary. He knows anyway without me having to say it."'

The expression on Jack's face as those words sank into him told Mary that Jack hadn't had the slightest inkling that 'he knew anyway'. He looked rocked to the core and she had an overwhelming urge to reach out and touch him, hoping to transmit somehow by proxy the love Reg had for his son, and which she had witnessed. She didn't but she told him instead something her own dad had said about the set-up at Butterly's when she'd spoken to him about it.

'Some people, especially in that generation, found it hard to say how they felt, as if it was a weakness. I got the feeling that old Bill Butterly wasn't exactly a loving, hands-on father and maybe your dad never learned from him how to articulate his feelings. Maybe, just maybe he wanted it to get back to you what he was thinking without having to speak the words himself. Maybe that's why he told me, because he could only manage to say what he felt in an indirect way, because a direct way was just too difficult for him ...'

Mary's words tailed off because Jack looked felled, and that wasn't the effect she'd hoped to have on him. She went into a momentary panic, cross at herself, expected him to say, *'Yes, thank you, Mary'*, in that same dismissive way he'd used when she'd told him he should be making vegan scones. Then, barely above a whisper, he said, 'I wish I'd known.'

'I did try to—' She stopped herself, poured the water out of the bowl, silently cursing herself for heading towards a conversation that she didn't want to stray into.

'Try to what?'

'Nothing.'

'It isn't nothing.'

'Okay then, I did try to tell you once but you shut me down.'

Jack looked somewhere between dumbstruck and horrified. 'When? When did I do that?'

'When you came back to work after your father had died. I knew what you were going through, I knew that you could never have prepared for the impact and I stopped you in the corridor one day to tell you what your dad said to me about you. I thought it might help you. But you said, "Whatever it is, it'll have to wait, Mary."'

'Did I? Did I say it like that?'

'Exactly like that.'

'Why would I do that?'

His lack of self-awareness made Mary prickle with an annoyance that fuelled her next words.

'Because I'm just Mary who files your correspondence and makes your coffees. Not someone to take any serious notice of.'

There, she'd let it out; it had been sitting inside her for years.

The words seemed to hang in the air for a moment, with long tails of echoes. Jack had never blushed in his life, but he felt heat rise in his cheeks and when he spoke next, his voice was drained of volume.

'I'm really sorry if I did that, Mary. I can't remember it, but if I did, then please accept my belated apology.'

'Don't worry about it, it's fine.' Mary acknowledged the admission, dried her hands while thinking that she wouldn't have dared say all that to Jack had she been scared of getting on the wrong side of him. It was the first step in letting him go. The realisation triggered a wave of both relief and sadness at the same time.

Chapter 17

'Well this is very pleasant isn't it?' said Luke to Bridge as they sat opposite each other at the table constructing a paper chain. 'And the most polite we've been to each other in years.'

'Don't forget we need to sign and swap those documents before we get out of here,' said Bridge. 'That would be too ironic, being holed up together for days and then forgetting to do that.'

'I promise I won't if you won't,' said Luke and licked a strip of paper. 'Ugh, that awful gluey-glue taste.'

Bridge made a grumbling noise of agreement, tried not to think again about the last time she had made a paper chain with Luke. But the taste of the glue had jogged his memory too.

'Ooh, déjà vu,' he said. 'I had a sudden flash of doing this before with you, making a chain. We can't have though. We were never the making-paper-chains sort of people, were we?'

'No, it's déjà vu,' she said. *He'd forgotten then*. Forgotten that day when the chain they'd spent putting together all afternoon ended up as a flattened, unusable, broken pile of scrap paper. So why hadn't she? Why was the memory half-fluorescent, half-neon lights? She looked forward to some modern technology where you could go to a clinic and have selected memories zapped out of your brain with lasers.

'Can you remember, that first Christmas we had in the flat?'

'Not really,' she said, lip curled like a disgruntled toddler.

Luke grinned.

'Yes you do. There's nothing wrong in having memories. We were married, we can't airbrush ourselves out of each other's history.'

'Sadly.'

'Even if you did once say I was the reason why God gave you a middle finger.'

She couldn't help but laugh at that.

'There's been enough bad blood between us, we can walk away from each other with civility,' said Luke.

'You are not now and never will be on my Christmas card list,' said Bridge. She'd been at loggerheads with Luke for so long, she couldn't think of a sure path out of it. Like Hansel and Gretel, they had strayed deeper into a dark wood of mutual enmity one footstep at a time, getting lost in it, questioning how they could have wandered so far into such a hostile place and carried on fighting long past the point of remembering what they were fighting about.

'We were young, daft and very much in love once,' Luke said, softly.

'Daft being the operative word.'

'I've never met anyone like you, Bridge. Still haven't,' said Luke.

Bridge stopped sticking. 'Go on, say it: "Thank God."'

'I wasn't going to say that at all. You are an incredible woman. I've seen how far your star has risen and I've been really glad for you. Okay, I admit that on occasion I was happy it had because I intended to take half your business, and before you open your mouth I bet you were secretly glad Plant Boy was doing well for exactly the same reason.'

Say something nice in return, Bridge, prompted a voice inside her.

'. . . I'm glad you've done okay too. I was wrong to scoff at the only good idea you had in all the time I knew you.'

He laughed at her barbed compliment.

'I'm not sure I would have had half the success without the name. Do you remember the day you came up with it?'

'How could I ever forget?'

'Ha. Plant Boy was an inspired name for a company. I didn't lie to the solicitor about the company worth, for the record. I haven't tried to hide anything.'

'Yes, well I haven't lied about Bridge Holdings either.'

'Never thought you would.'

'Ha. You'd have been wrong then because I did think about it,' said Bridge. And she had. Initially she wanted to haunt him for the rest of his life, keep using the Palfreyman name to piss off any future wife, claim a lump of his pension, screw him for every penny she could, even though she didn't need it. She'd pored over his accounts looking for how much she could claw into her own bank to kick him in his financial bollocks if not his real ones, but then she knew if she did, he'd fight back harder and she didn't want to hand over the fortune she'd worked so tirelessly for. Sense prevailed in the end. Sense and decency.

'So, do you still call yourself Mrs Palfreyman?' he asked.

'All my documents are now back in my maiden name.

I am once again Miss Bridge Beatrice Winterman. I . . . I didn't think it was fair on Carmen.'

'I can imagine Ben's happier about it too.'

'Of course,' she added quickly.

'What does he do? For a living.'

'Mind your own business. *Bugger.*' She'd ripped one of the strips.

'Oh, Bridge, put your guns down for goodness sake.'

'Okay then, he's in IT,' said Bridge. 'People consult him about important things. He's very clever and he works for himself. That do you?'

'Does he make you happy?' Luke's voice was tender, genuine.

He saw the small swallow in her throat before she gave the single-word answer.

'Yes.'

'So what will your new married name be?'

'I'm not sure I want to take another man's name. Even Ben's.'

A picture rose up in Luke's mind of sitting at the kitchen table with her as she practised her new signature:

Bridge Beatrice Palfreyman

She never used 'Bridget' because it reminded her of a life before him that was unhappy and dysfunctional and full of the worst mistakes that would resonate through her whole life. Watching her form the letters carefully, a tongue of concentration sticking out at the edge of her lovely mouth, he'd been totally zapped by the happiness fairy. He was sure they were forever.

'Why's that?' Luke grinned. 'Has he got a funny name?

Would that make you Bridge Bottom, or Bridge Dick, Bridge Overtheriverkwai?'

Despite not wanting to, Bridge smiled.

'No, none of those,' she said. 'I just think that I should keep my own name. It's stood me in good stead.'

'It might have stood you in better stead if you'd called the company BBW Holdings.'

'Oh my goodness, imagine,' said Bridge and they both laughed, easily and openly. The first time they had laughed together like this in a long time. And they used to laugh so much together.

'When the divorce is all finalised, we should go out – the four of us. Carmen and me, you and Ben,' said Luke. 'For dinner.'

'Er, no,' said Bridge. 'Let's not.'

'Maybe you're right.'

Charlie gave a loud snore, woke himself up, settled immediately back to sleep. Bridge and Luke both smiled at him, as if he was an aged uncle they were both fond of.

'We had some good times, didn't we Bridge?' said Luke. 'I mean, I know we were poor as church mice, but we got a lot of pleasure from the small things, didn't we?'

'Did we?' asked Bridge. She really didn't want to take a detour down memory lane. There were too many houses on it, where a lot of pain resided behind the shiny doors.

'That carpet the old lady across the road gave us when she got a new one, do you remember? The brown and orange and yellow one. It was as ugly as a dropped pie but it felt so much better than the bare floor.'

Bridge remembered. It must have been twenty years old, but it looked virtually new. She'd even given them the underlay and when she and Luke had fitted it, in comparison to the cold cement floor, it had felt as bouncy as a trampoline. Then that same day they'd christened the carpet by making love on it and squashing their paper chain.

'I remember your foster mother giving us her old suite,' said Bridge. Upholstered in blue corduroy, it didn't go with the carpet one bit, or the pink armchair that she'd bought from a car boot sale.

'Did we have anything that matched?' Luke asked, guffawing.

'Not sure we did,' said Bridge. Including themselves. They didn't match either, but like the furniture it all worked somehow. For a while.

'Do you remember the weird and wonderful meals we used to make? They always tasted so good, didn't they?' asked Luke.

'We were bloody starving all the time, that's why.'

'Hot buttered toast, Laughing Cow cheese and chopped-up red onion.'

'Bread dipped in a cup of Bovril.'

'Tinned tomatoes and cheap white bread.'

Bridge was sure her mouth was starting to water slightly. 'It feels like another lifetime ago.'

'We had everything then and didn't know it,' Luke said, his smile fading. 'It was all waiting inside us to flower.'

Bridge saw his Adam's apple rise and fall as he swallowed. The show of sunshine in their conversation slipped behind a cloud.

'Well, that was then and this is now,' she said, as Jack and Mary walked in from the kitchen.

'I'm glad we both found another happiness,' said Luke.

'I'm glad you're glad.' A flash of a smile, no more.

Luke pushed back the vision of them both lying on the

springy new-old lounge carpet crushing the paper chains they'd spent the best part of the afternoon putting together. She hadn't remembered and neither should he. It had no right being in his head any more.

Chapter 18

Radio Brian gave himself a break from Christmas carols and revved up a mambo from Pérez Prado, which cut into Charlie and Robin's sleep and woke them up. They both stretched like synchronised Siamese cats.

'How long have I been out for the count?' asked Robin, eyes roving around the lounge looking for the clock that he was sure was on a wall somewhere.

'Months,' replied Luke. 'It's now June.'

'I do hope not,' said Charlie on a yawn. 'I don't want to miss Christmas Day.'

'Oh yes, we all need to go present-hunting, don't forget,' said Robin.

'Ooh, I see the paper chain is up,' said Charlie, admiring Bridge and Luke's joint effort. 'And you've finished the tree, Mary.'

'You've just reminded me.' She sprang up from her seat and trotted over to it. 'Are you all ready?'

'For what?' asked Robin.

'This. Ta-da.' Mary bent down, pressed a switch. Christmas tree lights. Twinkling and red like large holly berries.

'Perfect,' Charlie declared.

'Do you know what the difference between a Christmas tree and a Christmas tree light is?' asked Luke.

'I have no idea,' said Charlie.

'Forty calories,' said Luke and exploded into laughter.

Groans ensued. That triggered off an idea in Luke's head.

'I tell you what, I'll make some crackers with my best jokes in them for tomorrow.'

'I hope they're better than that one, Luke,' Mary said, holding up crossed fingers.

'Trust me, they won't be,' replied Bridge to that.

Outside the snow continued to fall, but softly so; the wind was taking a rest.

'So, are we going to have the full Christmas dinner shebang then?' asked Bridge. 'I mean, all that food the landlord's bought in would go to waste otherwise, won't it?'

'I'd like it to go to my waist,' said Mary, which made Robin and Charlie chuckle. 'I'd love to cook the Christmas dinner for everyone.'

Noises of protest came from all concerned.

'We will cook it together,' said Charlie and licked his lips. 'Do you know, I don't think I would ever get fed up of Christmas food. I could live off it every single day.'

'You might have to if this snow doesn't go,' said Bridge.

'Which brings us to the question of what to have for dinner tonight,' said Robin. 'Anyone fancy a jacket potato?'

Robin wrapped lots of large white potatoes up in tinfoil and put them in the bottom of the oven. He returned from the kitchen wearing a huge smile and carrying something behind his back.

'Look what I found,' he said and pulled out a large toasting fork. 'We can make toast.'

'We can anyway, there's a grill in the kitchen, Robin,' said Bridge.

'Oh, but this way is much more fun,' argued Robin, settling back into the armchair. 'And marshmallows. There's a bag of them in the kitchen, suitable for vegetarians – I checked. And you can get about six marshmallows on each of these big prongs.' He looked around. 'Where's Mary?'

'She went upstairs for a sock,' said Bridge.

'I thought she'd been picked off by the murderer among us,' said Robin. 'And then there were five.'

'No one in their right minds would pick off Mary first,' said Jack. 'She's too . . .' His voice trailed into silence as he realised he'd spoken a thought aloud.

'Efficient?' Bridge supplied the word, flavoured with a tone of mischief.

'Capable, I'd have said,' stated Charlie. 'No self-respecting murderer would want to get rid of someone who would be his greatest ally if things went awry.'

'Maybe Mary could be the murderer though,' said Luke. 'Has anyone thought of that?'

Mary appeared at the bottom of the staircase and everyone fell into a semi-awkward silence, as happens when the subject of conversation unexpectedly turns up.

'We were just saying,' said Robin, eventually cracking the ice of hush that had formed over them, 'it really is like being in an Agatha Christie story. All of us here, marooned together. Just like Charlie said yester—' He stopped to think, patting his lip with his finger. 'Was it only yesterday that we came here? Feels so much longer.'

'Time flies when you're enjoying yourself, doesn't it, Bridge?' said Luke, turning to her for affirmation.

'Oh yes, the hours are simply zooming by,' replied Bridge snarkily.

'Well, here's my sock,' said Mary, placing it on the hearth. It was long and red. Part of a pair she'd brought to go under her new red boots, which were destined for a refund. She'd never wear them anyway, she'd always be reminded of this failed trip and she didn't want any memories of that going forward.

Radio Brian announced that he was signing off for an hour or so as he had to go and chop some logs for himself and Mrs Radio Brian, or Cath as she was better known to his regular fifteen listeners. But he was leaving his flock with some Christmas carols from the past.

'He can hardly leave them from the future, can he?' scoffed Bridge.

'There might be no future,' said Robin. 'Looking out there, it would be easy to think the sun has died. Maybe we're all starring in a real disaster movie. *The Christmas Armageddon.*'

'The Apocalypso Carol,' said Luke, playing a riff on some imaginary drums. 'Ba-dum tish. Right, I'm going for my sock.'

'I'll come up with you,' said Jack.

'I might as well get ours,' added Robin, attempting to heave himself out of the comfort of the armchair. Having only just sat down, he found himself reluctant to leave it. Bridge held out her hand to help him up.

'I'd better go and get mine too,' she said.

She and Robin followed the others, leaving Charlie and Mary alone. He looked at her intently and smiled.

'You know, don't you?' he said.

'Know what, Charlie?'

'About me. It was how you handed over the tablets to me this morning, with that lovely smile, but it was powered by forced cheer.'

Mary opened her mouth to deny it, but she knew she wasn't a good liar.

'My dad was on the same medication,' she said instead. 'As soon as I saw the name on the bottle, I knew, yes.'

Charlie nodded slowly. 'I intend to have a wonderful Christmas Day and make some memories for Robin to keep,' he said and leaned in close. 'To be honest, it was Robin's idea to go to Aviemore, not mine, but I couldn't spoil it for him by saying I wasn't that keen. He wanted to push the boat out. I just wanted some snow and I was going to hire a machine to make it and blow it all over the garden.' His blue-grey eyes sparkled, reflecting the firelight. 'I'm having the most perfect time here with everyone. It's people more than places that give the greatest happiness.'

'Good. And you're right,' said Mary and when Charlie's hand reached out to hers, she took it, felt him squeeze her fingers hard as if transmitting feelings he couldn't – or didn't want to – put into words.

'Did … did the pills work for your father?' Charlie asked then.

'Right to the end,' she answered him honestly. 'There was no sudden decline. He went to bed after watching the last-ever episode of a box set he'd enjoyed, he had a belly full of fish and chips, chocolate fudge cake and his usual big brandy and he … never woke up.'

'Ah. I'm sorry for asking.'

'I don't mind, really,' returned Mary.

'I want to make it easy on Robin when I go, you see,' said Charlie. 'I don't want him to be traumatised.'

'He will be anyway, Charlie. Because he loves you.'

Charlie sighed in understanding, and let go of Mary's hand, aware that he was in danger of cutting off her blood supply. It was the letting go of Robin that concerned him most. He knew he'd hurt.

'I hope you find your Captain Wentworth in life, my little Anne Elliot,' said Charlie. 'The good ones are always worth waiting for.'

There comes a point where hanging on becomes wasting your life, though, thought Mary, just as Jack appeared at the bottom of the stairs, waving a sock. One of a striped Paul Smith pair. She recognised them because she had bought them for him last Christmas, part of a set of three designs.

'I'd better not lose it,' Jack said, 'it's one of my lucky pair. Every time I put these on, something good happens. I was going to wear them for my meeting with Chikafuji.'

Mary wondered if he remembered who had bought them for him. Probably not, but at least she hit the bulls-eye with her present, unlike he had with his Christmas presents for her. Not even a single '1' on the dartboard of suitability.

Charlie's sock had a red, blue and green argyle pattern on it, Robin's was a white cushioned sports sock. Bridge had a long black one, Luke's – not surprisingly – was covered in pictures of lumps of cheese with whiff marks coming out of them.

'How very mature,' said Bridge, playing straight into his hands.

'Mature ... cheese ... like it,' he said and played another drum riff.

'What are we having on the baked potatoes?' asked Charlie after his stomach gave a plaintive keen of hunger.

'How about plain old butter and salt,' said Mary. 'Nice and simple. We can eat them out of the tin foil and pretend we're camping.'

'That sounds delicious, Mary,' said Bridge. 'Sometimes the simple things are the best.'

'Aw cheers, Bridge.'

'Shut up, Luke.'

'So how are we going to organise the filling of the socks ceremony?' asked Jack, aware that everyone then looked to Mary for direction.

She pondered for a moment before she answered him. 'Well ... we have to be in bed before midnight or Santa won't come,' she said, setting off ripples of 'of course' and 'quite right' in response. 'So if we all go up at the same time, we can sneak down at five-minute intervals. We'll draw lots to determine when that is. That work?'

'I think, Mary, you are missing your way in life,' said Charlie. 'You should be in charge of something multi-national that needs your most excellent skills.'

'Maybe,' she said. 'I'm ready for a change.'

It was a slip of the tongue, but she went with it, forced herself not to look at Jack in case she saw him nod in encouragement.

'Want me to tell you what you missed earlier on, Mary?' said Bridge with quiet relish, as they were preparing the baked spuds in the kitchen. 'You'd gone up for your sock and we were talking about being picked off by a murderer and

Jack said that you wouldn't be picked off first as you were too ... and then he shut up. But he was obviously going to say something nice.'

Mary didn't miss a beat, but carried on slashing crosses in the tops of the potatoes.

Bridge huffed loudly. 'Well I am disappointed, Mary. I thought you'd be delighted to hear that.'

'The missing word was probably *industrious* or *indispensable*, or most likely *efficient* – that's one of Jack's words. He wouldn't have said I was too *gorgeous* or too *stunning* to be picked off.'

'He might have,' said Bridge.

'He meant that any killer among us would want me to hang around and make the coffees or take down a dictated account of how he murdered people for posterity.'

'Now you're being silly. But ...' Bridge took a breath, '... if you ever do feel like a change, as you said out there, I think you'd fit into my company like a size three hand in a size three glove. My PA is going on maternity leave in the next couple of months and I have a feeling that she won't be back. So ... I'll just park that with you.'

'In Derbyshire?' asked Mary, which wasn't an out and out refusal, Bridge noted.

'The Hope Valley. It's very pretty. You'd relocate from Yorkshire, I expect but I'd throw in a place to stay. I've got plenty of rental properties on my books; one beautiful little cottage comes to mind that would suit you down to the ground. And it's not that far from Yorkshire, for when you wanted to drive back and see your family.'

'Thank you, Bridge,' said Mary. 'I'll consider it.'

'These potatoes smell divine.' Bridge swapped the subject back to food, not wanting to over-egg the job offer pudding, and dropped a knob of butter into each of the slits that Mary had made, but she could sense the cogs turning in the younger woman's brain. At least she hoped they were.

They all enjoyed more carols from the radio and buttery baked potatoes in front of the fire, everything washed down with red wine except for Charlie who had a gin and tonic with a maraschino cherry dropped in it.

'Charlie has a real thing for cherries,' said Robin. 'I brought a jar with me in case they didn't have any in Aviemore. Emergency cherries, as I call them.'

'Maraschino cherries always smell of Christmas, I think,' said Charlie. 'I don't have them at any other time of year but in December, because it makes me giddy and full of silly anticipation. Plus they count as one of my five a day. Along with the juniper berries in the gin, I've got two covered.' He gave a little-boy chuckle and Robin rolled his eyes.

'Three if you count the potato, Charlie,' said Jack, tucking in to his.

'Ooh yes, of course,' Charlie's musical chuckle extended a few bars.

'These jacket spuds are wonderful,' said Luke. 'Simple and fabulous grub.'

'I usually have cheese on mine but I'm not missing it at all,' said Bridge.

'We're developing a vegan cheese,' said Luke. 'The ones out there presently are awful. I'm determined to crack a good recipe. I'm working with an actor whose roles dried up so he learned how to make cheese and started his own company, Praise Cheeses – terrible name; terrific cheese, though.'

Bridge noticed how fired up he was talking about his

business. He really was unrecognisable from the Luke she married, who once nearly set the kitchen on fire when trying to make cheese on toast by using a toaster upended onto its side. The Luke she knew.

Jack licked some butter off his fingers, then scrunched up the tin foil.

'That was perfection,' he said. 'We used to do these at school. We'd sneak out through the dorm windows and make a fire, bake potatoes in the hot coals. The whole process used to take up half the night.'

'Boarding school?' asked Luke.

'Yes.'

'Posh sod.'

'Was it brutal?' asked Charlie.

'No, it was good. First year was a bit tough, when we were all pushed around a lot by the bigger boys. But I liked it. I'm still friends with a lot of them who were in my year. Plus I had an excellent education.'

'Uni?' asked Bridge.

'Oxford.'

'Posh sod,' said Luke again.

Jack laughed. 'Bit of a waste really. I was always going to join the family firm and not become a history professor. But I loved the subject and I enjoyed my time there.'

'Did you go to university, Mary?' asked Charlie.

'No, I left college and went to work at Butterly's,' she replied. 'I was lucky really because Jack's father was looking for a secretary and I walked straight into the job.' She knew she wouldn't have got it had anyone else applied for it. Especially someone older and therefore 'more sensible' – and not being a brunette helped. 'I'd had enough of studying, I wanted to get out there and earn some money.'

'I'd have read English had I gone to university,' said Charlie. 'I would have taken my fill of Jane Austen and her works until my appetite was slaked. Robin would have read geography.'

'How do you know what I'd have done?' asked Robin, giving him a dirty look.

'Because you love to travel and you know everything about everywhere.'

Robin contested that suggestion. 'I might have done theology, for all you know. My mother wanted me to be a priest. Well, she did before she knew what my proclivities were.'

Charlie laughed at that. 'You'd have made a wonderful cardinal whatever your proclivities. You look so fetching in red. Cardinal sin.'

'Oh do stop, my sides are splitting,' said Robin, holding himself, pretending to be in pain.

'You're like a double act, you two,' said Bridge, smiling along with the others, enjoying the interchange between their two most senior members.

'We have a lot of fun together, don't we?' Charlie grinned across at Robin, his eyes full of laughter.

'We do, Captain, we do,' said Robin. The moment hung between them for a long second, full of warmth and affection.

'Right, I'll clear up . . .' began Luke.

'No, you will not. *I'll* clear up the dishes,' said Charlie and would not be stopped.

'I'll make my crackers then,' said Luke and went off hunting for things to make them with.

Bridge decided to go and find something for her secret Santa present. She'd pulled Luke's name out of the hat, which was the one she really didn't want.

'Fancy a game of chess?' Jack asked anyone who'd answer.

'I will,' said Mary. She already knew what to give for her Secret Santa present. It was a bit corny, but she hoped it would be okay.

'I must warn you, I was captain of the school team,' said Jack.

Mary checkmated him within fifteen moves.

Chapter 19

'I can't believe this is Christmas Eve,' said Robin who was sitting next to the fire, toasting marshmallows on the large fork. 'Charlie, what in God's name are you doing?' He watched as Charlie dropped a maraschino cherry into his hot chocolate.

'It's a Black Forest special,' he replied. 'Stop worrying. There's no cholesterol in cherries.'

'Smile, everyone,' said Luke, lifting up his phone and taking a selfie of them all sitting around the fire with their hot chocolates and faces glowing from the light of the flames. He snapped, preserving them in a perfect smiling shot that oozed cosiness. He wished he could send it to Carmen to show her he was okay, wished he could talk to her and make sure she was okay too. It felt a very long time since he last saw her.

'In a weird way, I'm actually looking forward to tomorrow,' said Bridge. 'I think it'll be fun.'

'What were your original plans?' asked Robin.

'Just spending it alone,' said Bridge, quickly adding, 'I mean, the two of us alone, obviously. Ben's a great cook.'

'You obviously have a type, then,' said Luke with a wink.

'Oh purr-lease,' returned Bridge. 'I remember when you thought a lentil was a support for a door hole.'

'Well there's nothing we can do about not being where we should be, so I suppose we should make the best of it,' said Robin, passing around the plate of toasted marshmallows.

'I bet we wouldn't have had these in Aviemore,' said Charlie.

'You'd have been chucked out of the hotel if you'd started putting cherries in your hot drinks. Whatever next? Tangerines in your cappuccino? Dates in your lapsang souchong?'

Charlie shuddered. 'Ugh, don't be disgusting, Robin.' Then he bit down on a marshmallow and chewed it blissfully.

'Top hot chocolate, Jack,' said Bridge. 'Perfect, in fact.'

'Oh ... oh, thank you, do ... do you think so? Really?' said Jack and beamed bashfully. 'I was always the one who had to make them for others at St Christopher's because they said I got them so on point.'

'Were you someone's fag?' asked Robin.

'Yes, I was,' said Jack, sounding proud of it. 'Nothing sinister. In the first year, you were sort of expected to be a bit of a servant for the older boys. I ran a few errands and made a hell of lot of hot chocolates. The boy I fagged for was a thoroughly nice chap, government minister's son. He gave me thirty pounds at the end of each term. I rather enjoyed it, felt quite honoured actually.' The nostalgic smile on his face reflected that.

Bridge studied him. Unlike the others who'd been the same since the moment when she'd first met them, Jack had changed. He'd started to drop his astute businessman's guard and was letting them peep at the man behind the mask, one who probably hadn't had a lot of personal compliments, judging by how he handled someone saying he made a good hot chocolate. He had impeccable manners, she liked that in a man, and was full of small considerations like banking up the fire more than anyone else, making sure everyone was served before himself when they ate and drank. And when he spoke to someone, he gave them his full attention, she'd noticed. All telling, positive traits. He was still a posh twit mind you; though she'd demoted him from posh twat.

'Deliciously frothy, with just the right amount of chocolate. Neither too runny nor too thick.' Luke appraised it as if he were a wine connoisseur.

'Hear hear,' said Charlie. 'Would be very nice with a splash of rum in it.'

'Cherries and rum?' said Robin, throwing him a look. 'Revolting.'

They sat and sipped, while in the background Radio Brian, returned from his log-chopping, was playing some wonderfully festive Renaissance music. He'd made them all splutter their hot chocolates by announcing that he 'had been first gripped by the madrigals at the Cambridge Folk Festival'.

'Wonder if that had anything to do with his teeth falling out?' asked Bridge, adding to the hilarity and Luke was reminded of what a quick wit she had, every bit a match for his. She'd made him laugh a lot, as well as cry, scream and punch walls.

'I for one can't wait for Luke's crackers,' said Mary. 'I could hear him giggling to himself as he made them.'

'They are really good, if I say so myself,' said Luke, taking the opportunity to preen. 'I think I've discovered another new hot-shot business venture.'

'Cracker Boy?' queried Bridge, wrinkling up her nose. 'Doesn't really have the same ring.'

'You should throw one at me tomorrow and see what name comes out,' returned Luke, soft full mouth curved in a puckish smile. For a moment, they were the only two people in the room.

'So, the plan tomorrow is . . . ?' asked Robin, to the group in general.

'I think we should all get up at the same time to open our presents,' said Bridge, clicking back to them.

'We should divvy up the jobs tonight,' suggested Luke. 'We can't all fit in the kitchen together so we'll need to be as organised as the SAS.' He popped another marshmallow into his mouth and chewed. 'These are so good, Robin. Do you want a job working for Plant Boy as head chef?'

Bridge yawned. 'I'm tired,' she said. 'It's exhausting doing nothing except eating and listening to Christmas music.'

Mary fetched her pad from the bar and drew a grid on a fresh page.

'Are we bothering with starters?' she asked.

'I'm more than happy to go straight to the main,' said Charlie and everyone nodded in agreement.

'I would like to volunteer to prepare the vegetables,' said Luke, raising his hand as if he was a small boy in class who wanted to go to the toilet. 'I can do amazing things with a parsnip.'

'I'll help. I can be your sous chef,' offered Jack. 'Or fag,' which made him chuckle to himself.

'I'm happy with that,' said Robin. 'I'll prepare the turkey

and ... oh, what will you two have instead?' He waggled his finger between Mary and Luke.

'Leave that with me. I can sort our turkey alternative out when I'm doing the veg, no problem,' said Luke.

'I'll do the washing up,' said Bridge.

'I'll help with that,' said Mary. 'And the clearing up.'

'Perfect.'

'What about me?' asked Charlie.

'You can do the toast, Charlie. The raising a glass sort of toast, not poking bread onto Robin's big fork and waving it at the fire toast,' said Bridge.

'And say grace,' said Robin. 'That can be your contribution.'

'It's not enough,' said Charlie. 'I'll dress the table as well. I have unsurpassable flair for these things so I will employ all my best skills.'

'You do indeed,' affirmed Robin. 'I'll also help anyone who needs it. Preparing the turkey won't be that big a job.'

'Now that was easy,' said Luke. 'What a diplomatic lot we are.'

Brian's voice came on the radio.

'And that's it from Radio Brian for tonight, folks. Sleep well and remember to leave out your stockings for Father Christmas. I'll be back with you all in the morning. I'll play you out with Nat King Cole roasting his chestnuts on an open fire. Goodnight.'

'That sounds as painful as being gripped by the madrigals,' said Robin, and got up to look out of the window.

'How is it out there?' asked Bridge.

'I'm seeing it's a "White Christmas",' he trilled by way of response.

'You really do have a lovely voice,' said Mary. 'Very Bing Crosby.'

'Oh get away with you, lady. It's probably the whitest Christmas we've ever seen in this country. The snow is deep and crisp and even.'

'Like Good King Wenceslas's pizza,' said Luke, laughing. 'Deep pan, crisp and even.'

'I hope that isn't one of the jokes in the crackers,' said Bridge, 'because it's at least one hundred and fifty years old.'

'Nope, they're all originals from the brain of Luke Palfreyman.'

Luke had made crackers that last Christmas before it started to go wrong, before the sea change, Bridge remembered then. The jokes were terrible. They had laughed until turkey and cheap plonk came down their noses and had a Christmas bonk before they dished up a Black Forest gateau bought from the cheap frozen food stall in the market. They were always so very good at sex; both loved the urgency of it, both came together like express trains. *God, I'd kill for a shag*, she exclaimed inwardly, then felt herself freeze and blush at the same time as there was a noticeable hush in the room that suggested she'd said that thought aloud. Luckily, she hadn't.

Jack collected the mugs and took them into the kitchen to wash up. Bridge turned off the radio and the Christmas tree lights.

'Well, I'm going upstairs to Bedfordshire,' said Robin, glancing over at Charlie and taking in how tired he looked. These days he could be the life and soul of the party one minute and the next, a punctured lilo.

'We should all go then,' said Luke. 'What about the stocking-filling procedure?'

'Has everyone got their presents organised?' This from Bridge.

A chorus of 'yes'.

Mary tore a page from her writing pad, ripped it into six strips, wrote on them.

'Okay. Each of these has a time on it, five minutes apart, commencing in ten minutes. Pick one and don't be late or you could end up revealing your identity.'

They waited for Jack to come back and then Charlie chose first.

'Isn't this exciting?' he said. 'I can't remember having a Christmas where I smiled as much as I am now.'

'Oh, thanks very much,' said Robin with a tut.

'You know what I mean,' said Charlie, giving him a playful tap on the arm.

'Here's hoping you have many more, then,' said Bridge. 'I mean the smiling part, not the being trapped in an old pub with a bunch of strangers part.'

'I hope so too,' said Charlie, with a soft smile.

Robin turned away, picked up the poker and started prodding the half-burnt logs. 'Don't want these falling out and causing a disaster,' he said. Mary recognised that look on his face, when you felt yourself slipping as you tried so hard to be brave. She knew that Robin must be mentally exhausted and probably physically too, as dreams would kill the quality of his sleep, propelling him to a fearful consciousness when he needed most of all to gain strength through rest.

'First up gets everyone else up,' said Luke. 'To make sure everyone does come downstairs at the same time. I can't believe I'm so excited about all this.'

'You need to get out more,' said Bridge, even though she knew what he meant. He was just making the best of their enforced circumstances, as she was. But Ben would be fretting about her, because that's what he did and she wished there was some way to let him know she really was all right. On a more practical level, she needed to go upstairs to wash some pants so she had a clean pair for the morning.

'What time does everyone want to rise?' asked Jack.

'Don't make it too early, we aren't five,' said Bridge.

'Shall we say not before nine, then?' suggested Mary.

'Perfecto,' said Charlie.

They filed upstairs, issuing goodnights like a festive version of *The Waltons*. Bridge checked the piece of paper that had her stocking-stuffing time on it. She had fifteen minutes to do her little bit of laundry.

'I've got loads of spare pants if you need them,' Mary offered when she realised what Bridge was doing in the sink. 'I always pack too many. Seven pairs for an overnight stay.' She didn't say that one of those pairs cost thirty pounds and were silk and she wanted to wear them for dinner with Jack in the Tynehall Country Hotel in the hope they'd make her feel sexy and seductive 'from the fuff up' as her sister Maggie would have said. She'd probably never wear them now. She had no occasion to and by the time she did have, at this rate, they'd have disintegrated.

'Thanks for the offer but it's no trouble. So long as the radiator works some magic and dries them for me.'

Mary put her hand on it; it could have been warmer.

'Stupid me,' she said then and pulled her handbag over. 'Why didn't I think . . .'

She took something out of a side compartment and started fiddling with the radiator.

'What are you doing, Mary?' asked Bridge.

'I'm bleeding it,' came the reply.

'You carry a radiator bleeding key around with you?' asked Bridge.

'I've got all sorts in my handbag,' said Mary. 'Scissors, screwdriver, sewing kit . . . You just never know, do you.'

A sister soul, Bridge thought. Between them, they probably had enough tools to build and plumb an extension to the inn.

'Ah, listen to that lovely hiss.'

The radiator gave a satisfying long, slow fart of air. 'That's it,' Mary patted it as if it were a pet. 'It's heating up properly now. I'll go around the house and do the others in the morning. Then again, it's nice to be chilly enough for us to want to huddle around the fire isn't it?'

Bridge wrung out her pants and then draped them over the radiator.

'You don't mind them being here do you?' she asked Mary.

'Why should I?' Mary assured her. 'If it doesn't sound a bit weird, they're beautiful pants.'

'La Perla,' said Bridge. 'Ridiculously expensive. Something I never thought I'd be able to afford, but I can now, so extravagant lingerie is my go-to indulgence.'

'Mine would be handbags,' said Mary. 'I've always wanted a Coco Chanel handbag. I'm not really a labels person because we've never had the money for stuff like that, but I think I should really love one of those one day.'

'They keep their price. Even second-hand ones are extortionate,' said Bridge. 'Some of the vintage ones fetch higher prices than they did when they were new.'

'A pipe dream for me,' said Mary with a sigh.

'Did you notice that Charlie had a Chanel scarf on yesterday? Though he was wearing it as a cravat.' Bridge squeezed some toothpaste onto her brush.

'I noticed his cravat but I didn't realise it was Chanel,' replied Mary. 'It suited his image. I bet when he was younger he looked like one of the three musketeers.'

'They're a funny couple, aren't they?' mused Bridge. 'I mean Robin runs around after him like a servant. I know there's a lot of years between them but are they partners or master and slave?'

Mary recalled the comment Bridge had made about hoping Charlie had many more Christmases to come. She'd wondered whether to say anything, torn between breaking a confidence and preventing Bridge from saying something clumsy out of ignorance; decided she should.

'I should tell you something about them,' said Mary.

'What?' asked Bridge. Mary had her full attention.

'This is the last Christmas Robin and Charlie are going to spend together. Charlie's ill.'

'How ill?'

'He's dying.'

'Really? Oh fuck, oh no, God how awful,' said Bridge, her voice hushed with shock.

'I didn't want you to put your foot in it.'

Bridge looked pensive, then she cringed.

'Thank you for telling me, Mary. I already did though, didn't I, wishing he'd have many more happy Christmases to come. Me and my big mouth.'

'You weren't to know.'

'How did you?'

'When I went to fetch his tablets earlier on. I recognised what they were.'

'How ... how long does he ...?'

'I don't think he has long. You only get them right at the end. They don't extend your life, but they help you enjoy what time you have left. Charlie knows I know.'

Bridge felt a rush of sadness hit her from left field. What really did she have to complain about in life when compared with that? Poor lovely Charlie. She would make sure he had every consideration she could give him while they were there.

Mary checked her watch, stirred into action.

'Anyway, I'd better just nip out, I have something to do. See you in a couple of minutes.'

Bridge smiled. This was absurd, all six of them sneaking downstairs at five-minute intervals just to slip a present into someone's sock. So why was she brimming with this ridiculous sense of anticipation?

Chapter 20

Mary knelt down by the fire and stuffed the small item into the toe of the sock. She hoped he wouldn't think it was too ridiculous or cheesy or make him sad, but she was driven by her conviction that this was totally the right present for him. She was the first down. All the socks laid out reminded her of being a little girl at home. They'd had a real fire, just like this one, and her dad would empty a three-pound bag of flour onto the hearth and stamp his big boots in it to make it look as if Santa had stepped there. Mary had the sudden yearning to crawl back into that past when they were together: Mum, Dad, Sean, Maggie, Rob and their collie Barney. But they all had moved on and found a new family nucleus for Christmas Days. Would she ever find hers, so she could look forward with hope, instead of back with longing?

Perfectly on time, Bridge stole downstairs and over to the fire. She would like to have stayed down here for a while and sat by the dying embers, but she needed to be quick so the next person could come. She didn't have a real fire in her house but she soon would. She decided that when she got home, she'd have the arty gas fire ripped out and an inglenook fireplace built in its stead. It might be more faff having to clear out ash, but the pleasure would far outweigh the trouble.

As she stuffed her present into the sock, she knew she had the perfect gift for the owner of it. Maybe not the most conventional, but one that she hoped would convince him that the battle lines were trodden into the dust, finally and forever.

Charlie hurried downstairs as fast as he could, despite having promised Robin he would take it easy. He hadn't felt this able for weeks; there must be magic in the brandies or the toasted marshmallows, possibly the cherries ... or maybe he was just enlivened by the wonderful company he was keeping.

He had made his present himself and he hoped that it would work, because if ever anyone needed some guidance it was *him*. *He* was Charlie years ago, barricades up, letting no one in and nothing of himself out. If Robin hadn't been so damned persistent, Charlie would have ended up a lonely, sad old man. Instead he'd had a lifetime of love and joy and he wanted the same for this person.

He hoped *he'd* read the words of a contented old Yorkshireman and learn from his hard years of experience. It would be a shame for it all to go to waste.

Robin was next. His hand was trembling as he put his present inside the sock. He didn't want to go through with it, wished he had thought of something else now, but he knew that the recipient wanted this more than anything and he had to think of him before self. It would make him as happy as it would make Robin sad, as if they were on opposite sides of an emotional see-saw. But he owed him this. For all the wonderful years they'd shared, for all the love, the fun, the laughter. But he was dreading the giving of it.

Luke tiptoed downstairs. This time next year his Christmas would be very different. A new era awaited, one he never imagined would be his.

He had to stretch the sock to fit his present in it. Stupid but full of meaning. It represented a time in his life when he didn't think his lot could be any better. Okay, so he hadn't exactly been aiming high at the time where luxury was concerned, but he had everything his unambitious heart wanted. Life was so much better now, but in a different way. It was comfortable and calm and easy. Before, it was raw and exciting and edgy and that had been a fit for the Luke he was then. He had needed to be him first, the blank sheet of paper to be written on, the rough copy. It was just a shame that the grateful thrill of the simplest pleasures had become collateral damage of his evolution.

He hoped his gift would mean something to her, that she'd take from it what she'd meant to him once. The page may have turned and they may have skipped forward chapters, but it was still there, an integral part of their book. Of them.

Jack was the last one to go downstairs; all the other socks were filled except the long red one. Present-choosing was never his forte, which was why he tended to delegate the duty to those who would pick something more suitable than he could, because he didn't want to get it wrong. He felt ridiculously apprehensive about putting his gift into the sock. Maybe it was too subtle, maybe it was overstepping a mark, crossing a line. Maybe it wasn't crossing it enough.

He had the luxury of time, being the final stocking stuffer and sat in the armchair for a moment, enjoying the peace. Something cracked, as if it was the inn settling down to sleep, resting its old bones. How good it would have been to sit somewhere like this with a lovely woman in the armchair next to him, enjoying a nightcap after a mad half hour putting their children's toys under the tree. He did want what his friends had, that shift of focus from the material to the personal. They all still worked damned hard, but now what they did had more purpose, because they were building for a family. It made them both tougher and softer at the same time. They'd changed and he wanted to change with them. He did want children, wanted them to have the things he didn't have, things his dad had missed in pursuit of giving him what he thought was the most important. Because he'd loved him.

Finding this out from Mary, and that his dad had been proud of him, had meant everything and, if what she'd said was true – and he had no reason to doubt it – he could have discovered it a lot sooner had he not rebuffed her in a corridor. It sounded crazy but it was as if he had just met her, this kind, thoughtful, accomplished … *woman* – yes, woman – who had always been as far from a 'silly young thing' as it was possible to be. Why hadn't he realised that Mary existed outside the frame of a PA before? Luke, Bridge, Charlie, Robin had made him view her through their eyes, because they had seen more of her true worth in the day and a half they had known her than he had in six and a half years. He felt confused by the absurdity of it and something else he couldn't quite pin down that defied definition, like someone blowing a hint of warm breath on his nerve endings, setting them to shiver with a frisson of delight and trepidation when she was nearby.

All he did know for certain was that he wanted Mary to comprehend what his present was meant to say, what he was getting at: that she was class, a woman of quality. He hoped that the subtlety of that message would come through loud and clear to her.

Chapter 21

'Mary. You awake?' Bridge whispered tentatively, not wanting to disturb her if she wasn't.

'Yep. Can't sleep.'

'Me neither. No idea why. I usually have no problems and I can't blame the bed. I slept like a baby last night.'

'Me too,' said Mary. 'I could never sleep on Christmas Eve when I was young. I used to be terrified I'd be awake when Santa came and he wouldn't leave me any presents. One time, I awoke and saw him, this red suit in the corner of my bedroom and I turned over and squeezed my eyes shut. I reckoned if I couldn't see him, he couldn't see me. I must have scared myself into a coma because my mum woke me up the next morning as I'd slept in.'

'Ha! You must have been the only child in the country not to be up before five o'clock.'

'It was Dad, of course. When he died and we were clearing some of his things out of his wardrobe, I found his Santa costume. He'd kept it all those years.'

'How sweet,' said Bridge. She'd never get her childhood

back, but on their first Christmas Luke dressed up in a red jumper, fur-trimmed hat and a beard he'd made out of cotton wool and cardboard and put her presents in a pillowcase at the bottom of the bed. She'd woken up, asked him what the hell he was doing, and he'd pretended to be Santa, told her in a deep voice to get back to sleep. He'd bought her a Polly Pocket Fashion Star, a Fuzzy Felt, the Mouse Trap game and other stuff she told him she'd put on her Christmas lists when she was a kid but never got. He'd hunted them down on eBay. Another memory resurfaced that she'd buried with all the other Luke detritus.

'He sounds like a nice man, your dad,' Bridge went on.

'He really was, Bridge.'

'Were you very close?'

'Very. I was a proper daddy's girl.'

'I never knew my dad,' said Bridge. 'I had a stepdad. More than one actually, but I stayed as far away from them as possible.'

'That's sad.'

'No point in complaining about it. The past made me resilient. Luke was the first person who gave me any real affection. I think I repaid my debt though because I gave him the idea for Plant Boy.'

Mary levered herself up onto her elbow. 'No way.'

'Yes way,' said Bridge, with puffed-out-chest pride.

Next door, Luke asked Jack if he was awake, even though it was obvious with all the tossing and turning and disgruntled blowing out of air that he was.

'Sorry, can't sleep. Didn't mean to disturb you,' Jack answered.

'It's fine. I can't get to sleep either.'

'It's too quiet, isn't it?' said Jack. 'I'm not used to this countryside muffled snow silence.'

'I know what you mean. I moved from the city into a hamlet recently and it took me ages to get used to it.'

They both listened to the nothingness for a few beats before Jack spoke again.

'Interesting name, Plant Boy. Where did it come from?'

Luke grinned. 'Bridge. It was an insult she levelled at me, accompanied by a large head of broccoli, which gave me a discoloured, if not quite black and blue eye for a couple of days. Her words, paraphrased, ran on the lines of, "*Here you go, plant boy, make a million out of this then*."'

Jack gave an impressed whistle. 'Wow, that's ... remarkable. Not a strong enough word I know, but suffice to say you grew a hell of a plant from that small verbal seed, pun intended.'

'Jack, I'm under no illusions that the unwittingly donated company name has been instrumental in my success, even if I did make Bridge mad enough to clobber me with a vegetable, and boy she really was furious. Admittedly I had just told her that I was thinking of walking out of my job on a whim because I wanted to give everything I had to a new business venture making vegetarian food – me, who couldn't boil an egg.' He laughed at the farcical nature of it, though it hadn't been that funny at the time because it was the most insane of impulsive gambles. Plus, he'd always been of the belief that vegetarians were akin to circus freaks, along with the four-legged lady and the man with an arse for a head.

'The name stuck in my mind, accompanied by her shrill

delivery,' continued Luke. 'Every time I hit a stumbling block, I replayed her screaming it at me and it drove me on. I couldn't bear her to think I'd fail.'

Jack could easily picture the scene. Bridge, he imagined, could make Medusa look reasonable.

'She didn't try to claim credit for the Plant Boy name, then?' he asked Luke.

'Course she did; just after we split up for the final time, she told me she was coming after me for three-quarters of everything it had made, and that would have been a lot to hand over because I was making money faster than I could bank it.'

Jack's eyebrows raised. 'Split up for the *final time*? How many times did you split up in all, then?'

'I did hear that it takes couples about five or six false attempts before they make that decisive break. I think with us the number was about thirty-two,' Luke said with a long drawn-out sigh.

'How did you and Luke meet?' asked Mary, sitting up in bed now, not even thinking about nodding off.

Bridge sat up also, her action mirroring Mary's. 'Remember I told you that I once worked in a plumbing factory in Derby? Well, the day after I'd twatted that boss for slapping my bum, I was walking to work rehearsing what I was going to say if I was pulled in by HR to explain my actions. It was winter, the ground was covered with snow, I wasn't looking where I was going because I was preoccupied and I tripped, and this man appeared from nowhere with a smiley face and angelic mad hair.'

'Luke.'

'Yep. That was the start of it.'

'And you say you gave him the idea for Plant Boy?' Mary's fascination was clear.

'We'd been together about eight years. I was working for a company selling property by then. I took Luke to a works dinner with me and the vegetarian option was lazy, some disgusting boiled cauliflower with paprika sitting in what looked like wallpaper paste, everyone was complaining about it. At the time Luke was trying to find something to sink his teeth into work-wise. He wanted his own business, so he said, but if get up and go was dynamite, Luke wouldn't have had enough to blow his own nose with. So I was joking when I said something on the lines of that he should look at making vegetarian food more interesting because there was obviously a major gap in the market. Luke had only just learned how to pour milk on his cornflakes, so I had no idea what I'd kick off with that remark.' Bridge shook her head in the dark, remembering the scene she had walked into the day after. Luke had spent all the rent money on food they wouldn't eat, and not only that but he'd skived the day off work to buy it. 'To cut a long story short I ended up throwing some broccoli at him and told him to make his first million out of it. I called him Plant Boy. I was so fucking cross.'

'Wow,' said Mary. 'Just wow.'

'Yes, and he did make his first million out of a broccoli burger. You couldn't make it up.'

'All that from throwing a sprig of broccoli at him?' Mary gave an impressed whistle.

'It wasn't a sprig, it was a massive head of it,' said Bridge. She thought she'd fractured his eye socket, although bloody-mindedness had prevented her from giving him the slightest hint of apology or concern. But then, it had been a time when she thought all her softness had gone forever, when she'd lived off a diet of frustration and self-loathing.

'Crikey.'

'I watched him change before my eyes in a matter of weeks from a feckless drifter into this manic creature with an obsessive drive. He became someone I didn't recognise. Still, I thought he was on the road to nowhere. I had no faith in him. Not a bit. I thought he'd gone batshit insane.'

'Did that lead to you breaking up?' asked Mary.

Bridge gave a long outward breath. 'Oh, Mary, there were about a million reasons why we broke up. I don't even know where to begin answering that.'

'Must be weird being here with Bridge,' said Jack.

'Weird isn't the word,' said Luke with a dry chuckle.

'When did you split up?'

'Four years, nine months and three weeks ago. I can give you days, hours and minutes if you like because the exact moment when I walked out of the door for the very last time is tattooed on my brain.'

'That's a long time to be battling,' said Jack, raising his long thick line of eyebrow in acknowledgement of the fact. 'My parents' divorce was done and dusted within six months and they despised each other.'

'My solicitor explained to me that there are two types of acrimonious divorce,' began Luke. 'Firstly, where the couples hate each other so much, they can't wait to be free and just want it all over and done with as soon as possible. Secondly, where the couples hate each other so much that the desire to hang on and hurt becomes more of an aim than the parting of the ways. Crazy stuff. The flipside of love can be very ugly.'

'I see,' said Jack, although he knew that already.

'I used to marvel how I could hate someone with as much passion as I used to love them,' said Luke. 'Once upon a time, I'd have cut out my heart for her. Now, she'd let me.'

Jack shuddered at the mental image. 'How did you meet each other in the first place?'

'I was nineteen, walking to work in a factory early one snowy morning and a woman went arse over tit right in front of me. I helped her up. Turns out she was heading to the same place I was. We worked in the same building but didn't know it. Then again, so did a thousand other people. And that was the start of us. After that, I seemed to bump into her all the time and I couldn't wait to bump into her either. I fell hook, line and sinker for her, the full soulmates fairy story. We were married within the year, not a penny between us, trusted love would sort out any problems and we really thought it could solve everything. We struggled, had good times, bad times, really bad times, we fought, made up … until we ended up fighting more than loving. We tried to stay together, we had a dog that we both wanted to keep, but there was too much going on. We were both terrified that we'd try and claim each other's hard-earned profits. Bridge got a new boyfriend and I was jealous as hell, then I got a girlfriend and she went nuts. Well, even more nuts, because nuts was her default setting.

'Then … I met Carmen and Bridge met Ben and they were both for keeps, which accelerated the need to get this sorted, and somewhere in the last year, I grew up. I decided that if Bridge tried to fleece me for half my business, I'd just let her have what she wanted to make it all stop. Turns out she'd grown up too, and thought the same as me. So we both waved a white flag and called a ceasefire. We started to talk to each other as we should have done at the beginning, made the decision at last to walk away from each other cleanly, make the split final and forever, not take a thing from each other.'

'And the dog?' asked Jack.

'She died,' said Luke in such a way that told Jack that subject was off limits.

'She's quite . . . formidable, Bridge,' Jack went on, which made Luke snigger.

'That's conservative. Bridge is a tornado, a volcano, a tsunami. If she was born a horse, she'd have been a bucking bronco.' Jack smiled at that. 'But yes,' Luke continued. 'She's most definitely formidable. I admire her more than I can put into words.'

'Do you?' Jack couldn't work out what Luke's true feelings for Bridge were at all.

'Jack, I thought I had a crap upbringing but it pales into insignificance alongside how Bridge was dragged up. We both came from households with no discipline, no care, no love, permanently hungry stomachs, no Father Christmas visits. We were just kids people had, by-products of careless contraception, not wanted. Bridge ended up in the care system, which failed her really badly, made her borderline feral. I at least moved into a wonderful foster family at thirteen that unknotted some of the damage. Bridge didn't know what it was to love or be loved until we met and she both wanted it and couldn't handle it. She craved normality, the stuff that she'd seen other kids have; you know, the stuff people like you probably took for granted.'

Jack didn't commit to any comment.

'And she was so bright, but she hadn't a GCSE to her name because she'd messed about at school, trying to get attention in all the wrong ways. She realised this and decided to make up for it in the world of work, show all those people who'd written her off just what she was capable of. She'd stand outside estate agents' windows and look at the big houses. She'd tell me that one day we'd live in a pad like that. And we do, but not together.'

Luke gave a small groan. 'Sorry for giving you the long version. The short version is that Bridge was bonkers and I didn't pull my weight enough. Bridge tried to buy her mansion one quid at a time, I preferred to dream about it in a pot-filled haze. I didn't want to sell things, build things or write about them at a desk. I was, without putting too fine a point on it, a lazy, selfish arse.'

'I don't get it,' said Jack. Luke was anything but the past portrait he'd painted of himself. 'What was that catalyst that changed you?'

'Looking back, it's pretty clear I was a singular piece of touchpaper waiting for the exact match. And that, my friend, was also supplied by Bridge's vituperative gob.'

Oh, how to explain where it all went wrong, thought Bridge. 'We didn't believe in each other. I laughed at Luke for wanting to be a leading light in the food world. He laughed at me when I said I wanted to buy and sell property. I had big ideas for someone who had to pawn her engagement ring to pay the electricity bill.'

She remembered the woman in the pawn shop's derisory tone when she offered her an insult of cash for it. *'If I had a strong enough magnifier in my loupe to see the* diamond *you say is there, I might have given you a fiver extra.'*

'I wasn't a very nice person when I was younger,' Bridge went on. 'I was screwed up and defensive and aggressive and I nagged Luke into the ground to get him to change. I can't remember how many pieces of crockery I threw at the walls in exasperation, but the neighbours must have thought we had a Greek wedding in our flat every night. And then I announced I wanted a child by him and I fell to bits when I found out I couldn't have them. Thank God, really. I'd have been a shit mother.'

'I'm so sorry to hear that, Bridge. That must have been hard for you both. And I'm sure you wouldn't have been a shit mother.'

'It was my fault that we couldn't have them anyway. You were so lucky you had the upbringing you did, Mary. I don't even think I had a childhood.'

'No job fitted or interested me. I hopped from one to the other like a dysfunctional frog between lily pads. I was happy enough living hand to mouth, but Bridge wanted *everything*: big car, big bank balance, big house, his and hers walk-in wardrobes, swimming pool, Koi carp ...' Luke explained to Jack. 'She was working for a property auction place at the time, loving it, she was excited by it, aiming to end up running it. I thought she had no chance. Incidentally she didn't end up only running it, but she ended up owning it.' He pulled himself up into a sitting position because even the short version of this part of the story would run on a while.

'Anyway, she saw a job advertised in Calvers Frozen Foods, in the product development department, told me if I didn't apply she was leaving me. I thought I'd hate it, a fair assumption, me being king of the workshy, but I didn't. They were a great bunch, it was a buzzing atmosphere and there were people there who had a real passion for putting ingredients together, constantly trying to make recipes better for Calvers. I started to enjoy going there every morning, even stayed behind later at nights, went in weekends sometimes. In fact, I was there so much, Bridge thought I was having an affair, which caused more rows. But the only affair I was having was with myself. I don't know what happened to me there but I discovered something – a place I fitted. I was infected with enthusiasm. But it wasn't enough. I wanted to work for myself and not anyone else, but I couldn't think how. Then Bridge dragged me along to an office dinner event and all the people who had picked the vegetarian option were moaning how awful it was. Bridge said something to me on the lines of how much untapped potential there was in the vegetarian food market . . . and it was like a bomb going off in my head. I skived off the job the next day to go around supermarkets and buy bags and bags of vegetarian food that we couldn't afford for essential research purposes. We were in so much debt at the time too, hence why she threw the broccoli at me and, along with it, the insult, *Plant Boy*.'

'You're lucky it was just broccoli.'

'I'm not sure we had any crockery left at that point. Anyway, I turned from being the world's laziest knob into a man possessed. I knew Plant Boy was going to be big, don't ask me how but I had a feeling I couldn't shake. And round about this time Bridge found out that she couldn't have kids. She'd had an op in her teens that went wrong but she'd never known how much it had damaged her inside. She was absolutely desperate for a child and it broke her heart that she'd never be able to carry one.'

'Did you think about adoption?'

'Bridge didn't want to go down that route. She *needed* the whole pregnancy thing from fertilised egg to giving birth; she wanted to bake the bun herself, make sure the baby was nourished and loved and safe from the off. I suppose it was because of her past, though I didn't really understand that back then – insensitive twat that I was – but now I do. One of many things I've learned in the past few years . . .' His voice tailed off, as if he was snagged in a net of regret. 'I didn't want kids, I didn't want the responsibility. Bridge went for tests without telling me anything about it and when she got the results she had a full-on meltdown. I wasn't there for her.' He'd never quite forgiven his former selfish self for that.

'And do you feel any different now you're with your new partner?' asked Jack.

'Yes,' said Luke. 'It couldn't be more different.'

Jack couldn't see it, but he could feel the heat of Luke's smile in the dark.

'I couldn't have children because I had a botched abortion when I was fourteen that totally knackered my insides.'

Mary's hand flew to her mouth. 'Oh, Bridge, that's terrible. I don't know what to say . . .'

'Nothing you can say, Mary. Luke didn't want kids anyway. Ironic really because I think he'd have made a fab father. He'd have stepped up to the mark, I know he would have. A child would have saved us. I know it's the wrong reason for having one, before you say anything, but in a parallel universe somewhere is a happy Bridge with a child, still married to a Luke who decided to pull his finger out for his family and made Plant Boy happen from love, not hate. There was so much hate in our relationship towards the end. It was like the flipside of our coin, because we loved each other so much in the beginning. I'd have done anything for him. Anything.'

'Plant Boy started off with just one product: broccoli burgers. I got them right. They were good, really good, and I was selling loads to vegetarian restaurants in the area, then countrywide,' said Luke. 'My pal was a journo and did a piece on how successful I was and how a supermarket giant had been in touch, total smoke and lies. Then the buyer of a supermarket giant read the story and really did get in touch because he wanted to get in first. I borrowed cash to rent the smallest factory on the planet with kitchens, hired workers. We couldn't produce them fast enough. By then I was working on a fake fillet steak. I hired an ex-chef who'd been in prison and needed a break. What he didn't know about food and nutrition wasn't worth talking about.'

'You still employ him?' asked Jack. His father would have promoted women to executive positions before he'd have had an ex-con in his factory.

'I do. And his wife, son and daughter,' said Luke. 'When Plant Boy got big, I moved all my best people over to Manchester with me. I have a shit-hot team, great products. But it was the name Plant Boy that spun the magic, the buyers loved it.'

Jack raised his eyebrows. 'That's insane isn't it?'

'Tell me about it. Bridge was starting to do really well at the time too. She'd just made a stack of money from selling a plot of land she'd bought for peanuts.'

'You could have been a power couple.'

'We could have.'

'What was the thing that finally split you up then?'

'A lie,' replied Luke.

'What finally split us up?' Bridge repeated Mary's question back to her. 'He slept with my best friend,' she replied. 'So I slept with his.'

*

'Oh?' A small sound but nevertheless one full of Jack's curiosity.

'At the time Bridge and I were on yet another break. I holed up with an old pal of mine, James. His wife Tina and Bridge got on in the beginning, they were like best mates but then Bridge pulled back, said she didn't quite trust her, she got the feeling that Tina was a bit jealous of her.'

Luke left out the irrelevant detail that Bridge also thought Tina had a head shaped like a football.

'I didn't realise their marriage was in such bad shape until I stayed with them. They argued more than Bridge and I did, and that's saying something. It was quite uncomfortable and awkward and I was actually packing to go and stay in a B and B when it happened.'

In the dark Jack heard Luke's long outward breath as he waited to hear what *it* was.

'I heard James storm out. Tina was crying hysterically, craving comfort, she wanted a hug . . .'

'Ah.' A picture was forming.

'No, I didn't in case you're wondering,' Luke answered the unsaid recrimination. 'But she told me she didn't love James, because she was in love with me, in fact she said she'd been in love with me for a long time and wanted us to be together. She said she'd seen the way I looked at her, she knew I felt the same and that's why I'd walked out on Bridge and gone to her. I swear, Jack, I hadn't a clue what she was talking about. I felt like I'd run off from a frying pan and ended up in a vat of boiling oil. I backed right off as you can imagine, told her she'd got the wrong end of the stick; she went bananas, accused me of leading her on. I was out of the house with my bags in five minutes flat. And so she used me as a weapon at James, and she used James as a weapon at me. She told him I'd slept with her. He believed her. And he told Bridge.'

'But you didn't?'

'No, I would never have done that.'

Jack winced. 'Oh shit. That's a mess. That's a real mess.'

'There's worse. Bridge and James got their own back. A revenge fuck. A revenge fuck for a revenge fuck that never happened in the first place.'

Jack made a pained, strangled sound.

'And that was the real end of us. Our marriage was no longer on life support, in intensive care; that yanked all the tubes out and pulled the plug. We were dead.'

It sounded like a horror story. It sounded like Jack's parents' marriage, so much heat and hate, intensity and fury, jealousy and bitterness. Something to be avoided at all costs. As soon as relationships got complicated and involved, Jack cut and run, sensing that inevitability of walking in his parents' footsteps. It never occurred to him that it might not happen.

'I was so hurt when James told me what Tina and Luke had done,' said Bridge. 'He used me to get back at his wife, I can see that. I was manipulated, stabbed in my sweet spot where all my greatest insecurities sat. Luke and I couldn't recover from it. He swore to me that he hadn't slept with her and I chose not to believe him and was just hell-bent on getting my revenge. I've wondered since if I did that because it gave me the perfect out from a marriage that had limped on way past the finish line. I couldn't forgive adultery, and I knew Luke couldn't either.' She made a deep huff sound. 'Do you know, Mary, I've studied what happened to us so much over the years that I could have done a PhD in it, and yet it still doesn't make any sense. If we were then who we are now, we could have conquered the world.'

'Tell me you didn't stay friends with James and Tina.'

'No I did not. And I punctured all four tyres on her BMW with a screwdriver late one night. At that point in my life I was made up of hurt and anger and tears and nothing else.'

'Who left who first?' asked Jack.

'Moot point. Bridge will tell you she did. But I left the moment I discovered her suitcases packed at the bottom of the stairs. So I beat her to it as far as walking out of the house for the last time goes.' He sighed heavily. 'It mattered to my ego that I'd made the break first, when I was young and stupid. Now, I couldn't care less about point-scoring.'

He realised that he sounded as if it had all happened decades ago and not a mere half of one. Those five years had seemed so much longer, he felt as though he'd collected a century's worth of wisdom and sense and maturity in them.

'It must have been a relief then for it to finally end,' Jack surmised, thinking back to a sticky relationship he'd had years ago that had been a nightmare to get out of.

'You'd think so, wouldn't you, but I missed her for ages and I really had to force myself not to pick up the phone. I did come to realise that I was addicted to that high-octane theatre, the kissing and making up that almost felt worth the dysfunction. It was like a drug, and when I was weaned off, I learnt that life was so much better and deliciously uncomplicated without it. I had plenty to keep me busy, of course, the business seemed to boom overnight. I had a couple of short-term relationships, nothing serious, just pleasant interludes. But on the weeks when I had the dog with me and it was just us, I found peace in my soul. Then I started seeing Carmen and the peace just got better.'

In the dark Luke made a long sound of regret. 'Bridge and I were a car crash, but . . .'

He didn't go on and Jack didn't push. That 'but' was loaded with a lot of emotion. He wasn't even sure if Luke himself knew what those emotions were.

'My life began with Luke,' said Bridge. 'I don't count anything that came before it. I might have given him the idea for Plant Boy, but he gave me stability and a home and joy that I'd never had before and more than that, made me believe I was someone worth loving.' Bridge's voice cracked. She coughed the strength back into it. 'I cut my teeth on him and I hurt him.'

'Are you really sure you're ended?' asked Mary. Whatever Bridge was saying to the contrary, there was an awful lot of feeling for Luke still there, thick in the voice that had started to break. 'Is there no way back for you both?'

'We're happier without each other than we were with each other,' Bridge said. Something she had told herself over and over until she had been forced to believe it. 'Goodnight, Mary. Let's try and get some sleep. I've bored you long enough.'

Christmas Day

The magic of Christmas day is silent
You don't hear it, you feel it
You know it, you believe it

Chapter 22

At quarter past nine Luke knocked on Charlie and Robin's door with a jaunty rat-a-tat-tat.

'You up?' he called.

'We are. Just give us five minutes,' replied Robin. 'Charlie's on the loo. He's reading *Persuasion*.'

'Oh, tell the world,' Charlie shouted through the bathroom door.

'It's only Luke, not a *Daily Mail* reporter,' Robin barked back at him. He took a tablet out of the orange-coloured bottle and was standing waiting like a sentry, hand extended, when Charlie exited the bathroom.

'Is this the one that makes things taste of fish?' asked Charlie.

'Yes, but you have to take it,' Robin insisted.

'Well I'm not. It's not an essential one is it? Not like the ones in the green bottle.'

'No, it's the orange.'

'Robin, I don't want to eat turkey and Christmas pudding and have that off-salmon flavour infiltrating my tastebuds.'

'Charlie, it's a pain relief.'

'I know what it is but I'm not taking it. And you can't force me. I'm not a suffragette for you to stuff it up my nose.'

Robin's hands flew to his hips. 'Whatever do you take me for, Charles Glaser?'

Charlie's hand came out to rest on Robin's arm, his voice was soft when he answered that. 'Someone who cares deeply, that's what I take you for. I know how much you want to make this ... this stage easy for me, but I'm not taking that one in the orange bottle any more. It ruins my pleasure in eating. I can put up with a little pain if it means I can immerse myself in the full Christmas epicurean experience, otherwise I might as well have been hooked up to drips in a hospital.' Charlie smiled. 'No point in having the appetite of a shire horse and not being able to enjoy stuffing my face.'

Robin huffed with frustration, 'It's your funer—' He sliced off the word, shook his head at his verbal blunder.

'Yes, my dear Annie, it is my funeral. Eventually. Not yet. Don't let my last meals be fishy-flavoured. Please.'

Robin, purse-lipped, put the tablet back into the bottle. He would guide but never bully. If Charlie felt strongly about something, then he had the right to run his own show, they'd agreed that from the off.

The one stipulation he had managed to adhere to was Charlie's insistence, after his diagnosis, that they continue as normal wherever possible. Let them carry on with their merry bickering; and Robin had carte blanche to be his usual nagging self, so long as it all fitted within the parameters of *normal,* because this was what would help Charlie deal with it mentally more than anything. But normality was an eggshell veneer, a shimmering illusion, and Robin could feel the cracks in himself destroying it a little more each day.

The fishy-tablet had stopped working anyway, though Charlie hadn't said anything, not wanting to cause concern. He'd been spitting it into his hand out of Robin's sight for a few days now, so it was time for a little honesty, but not too much. He had begun to ache everywhere, a bone-deep nag that was becoming harder to disguise and made it more difficult for him to sleep properly. Except, it had to be said, for the last two nights here in the Figgy Hollow Inn. He'd slept solidly like a milk-drunk baby and the pain was a mere low murmur in the background. He felt, this Christmas morning after a solid, restful sleep, as close to feeling fresh as a daisy as it was possible for someone in his condition to feel.

He put the book down on his bedside cabinet for later. Becoming reacquainted with the characters in *Persuasion* was like the cherry on his cake.

'Right. Let's go and see if Santa's filled my stocking,' he said, clapping his hands together. He grinned at Robin, who thought again how his grin never aged, how it lit up his blue-grey eyes and let him glimpse once more the Charlie Glaser he had fallen in love with three full decades ago. How would he ever be able to exist without this man?

It was funny how simple pleasures were often the best ones, thought Bridge, who had put on her pants warm from the radiator, then remembered how she used to always put them on the radiator whenever she stayed over at her posh schoolfriend Jane's house. Jane lived in a semi-detached on an estate but they had central heating, which her dad used to leave on during the night, and their tiny box bedroom had a piano in it, which Jane's mother called 'the music room'.

Other snapshots of that portion of her past wriggled to

the surface of this surprise memory pool, dislodged from the settled silt by the sensation of warm pants against Bridge's bum. Jane's mother had a tea service in a glass cabinet that was called 'Eternal Beau' and was used only on special occasions, and she only ever drank 'Italian champagne' called Asti Spumante that she bought in Marks and Spencer. Bridge hadn't thought about Jane in twenty years but here she was, large as life, swimming in the waters of her mind. Jane's mother split up their friendship in the end, deeming Bridget Winterman too common. And Bridge had really wanted Jane's mum to like her enough to think about adopting her.

'Bridge?' Mary's voice prodded her, burst the bubble of her reverie. 'You nearly ready?'

'Sorry, Mary. Two ticks,' Bridge replied, pulling on her jeans, zipping herself into them. 'There, now I'm ready.'

Mary smiled excitedly. 'Isn't this all crackers?'

'It's certainly that. I'm not sure if I'm in a bad dream or a good dream,' said Bridge, lifting her shoulders in a gesture of 'WTF' but really knowing that, while it might have all started off as a nightmare, she had the exact giddy feeling about going downstairs that she should have had as a child on Christmas morning. And not because she wanted to rip into her own stocking – her expectations of what might be in it were low – but because she wanted to see *him* opening his present. Not something one would find in John Lewis, but she reckoned she'd got it right on the button.

'Okay everyone, you can come out now.' Luke's voice on the landing.

A ripple of anticipation tickled down Mary's spine as Bridge opened their door.

'Happy, happy Christmas, everyone,' said Charlie.

'And happy, happy birthday, lovely Mary,' added Robin, putting his arms around her and squeezing her.

'Yes of course, happy birthday, Mary,' said Bridge, annoyed that she'd forgotten.

'Happy birthday, Mary,' said Jack, not quite sure if it was appropriate to accompany his words with any physical gesture, and so missed the boat as Charlie moved in smoothly for a hug.

'A double celebration,' said Luke. 'Let's not waste another second.'

They filed downstairs in jolly expectancy. In the lounge, the Christmas tree lights were already on, the radio was playing on low volume, the logs spitting and crackling a Christmas morning cosiness in the hearth.

'Aw, who did all this?' said Charlie. 'How thoughtful.'

'Santa, obviously,' said Luke.

'I feel as if I've just walked into a Christmas card,' said Bridge, wondering if Luke had sneaked down earlier to set the scene for them. It was the sort of thing he'd do. He was always full of the small, considerate gestures.

'Happy Christmas everyone,' said Radio Brian from the speakers. 'I hope you're all enjoying opening your presents on this beautiful snowy morning and are safe at home with your loved ones. Here's the magic voice of Sammy Davis Junior singing "It's Christmas Time All Over the World".'

Luke wished he were at home with his loved ones. He'd prayed to God before he'd gone to sleep, told him that though he hadn't believed in him since school, if he could make sure Carmen was safe and well, he'd take that as a sign that maybe his atheism was cock.

The lounge looked beautiful and Christmassy: the hearth, the tree, the decorations, even a contribution from the three front windows, framing a triptych of snowy scenes like paintings in a gallery.

'Are we having breakfast or presents first?' asked Charlie.

'Presents!' came a hearty, synchronised chorus by way of reply.

'Come on everyone, and sit by the fire,' said Mary.

'Let's open them one by one,' suggested Bridge. 'Left to right.'

'Oh yes, let's, because that makes mine first,' said Robin and picked up his sock, peered inside. 'Ah, how lovely and traditional. An orange and some nuts.'

Mary's brow creased in puzzlement. She hadn't put those in there.

Robin tipped the nuts in their shells and the clementine into his lap, not expecting to find anything else until the tiny package fell out. He unfolded the tissue and there was a mobile telephone number written on a slip of paper, along with Mary's friendship bracelet. He knew exactly why she had given it to him. A token of true kindness. And friendship.

'Oh, Mary, this means so much to me already,' said Robin, leaning over to plant a kiss on her cheek, then asking her to fasten it immediately onto his wrist. The small blocks each bearing a letter: C.M.W.Y.N.A.F. *Call me when you need a friend.* He would be calling her, because he would indeed need to.

'Me next,' said Charlie.

Robin passed his sock to him; his also had been stuffed with an orange and nuts. One of them must have come down and done this. The same thoughtful person who had built the fire and switched on the radio and the tree lights.

'Keep going,' urged Robin when Charlie thought he had

emptied the sock of all it had. He reached into the toe and found the rectangle of paper. On it was drawn an imitation cheque, signed by Robin Raymond.

I promise to pay the bearer: half an hour of my time to use as you will.

Charlie looked squarely at Robin to make sure he had understood correctly.

'Half an hour of your time?' he asked.

Robin nodded slowly, emphatically.

Charlie's hand came out to his, grasped it firmly and his eyes became glassy.

'Thank you, Robin. Thank you.'

'What's this? Is it saucy?' asked Luke.

'Sexier than you could imagine,' said Charlie. 'Let's leave it at that.'

'It's obviously hit the spot,' said Jack, hoping his present hit the spot too. Inside him, two lots of fingers crossed as Mary picked up her sock.

'More nuts and an orange,' said Mary. 'Who put these in here?'

'Elves,' said Jack, who suspected either Luke or Robin as the most likely culprits, if it hadn't been Mary.

'I do hope it's a Chanel handbag. I know that's what you were hoping for,' said Bridge, mischievously.

'Somehow I don't think so, but that's okay,' replied Mary, pulling out a slim red diary, House of Quill stamped in gold at the bottom. No prizes for guessing who this was from because she'd opened the parcel in which it had arrived. Jack had ordered it to give to Mrs Chikafuji as a present. It cost over a hundred pounds and was absolutely beautiful. For a diary.

'House of Quill,' said Charlie with a whistle. 'Very nice.'

'To whoever bought me this,' began Mary in the spirit of 'secret' Santa, 'thank you, it's beautiful. I shall treasure it.'

She tried not to look disappointed, tried to see something other than a glorified diary. A typical Jack present, a complete gift mismatch to the recipient, at least when the recipient was her. Her formal Christmas present from him, given to her the day before they set off for Tynehall, had been a tartan headscarf, shopping bag and a box of jellied fruits. Presents from a person who didn't know her at all and had no intention of ever getting to know her. The diary was functional and practical and reliable and boring. This was how Jack saw her: an office *thing*.

'You shouldn't treasure it, you should use it,' said Charlie.

'Oh I most certainly will.' Mary maintained her bright smile for the benefit of her new friends; she couldn't look at Jack, though, because her eyes would have made a lie of her words.

'Me next,' said Luke, with more excitement than a room full of Labrador puppies finding a stash of toilet rolls. He picked up his stocking, shook it. More nuts and a small orange. And a matchbox. He opened it to find it was full of ash.

'Ash?' A present from Bridge, he knew. No doubt she couldn't find a piece of coal to give him, as Santa rewarded the kids on the naughty list.

'Well, cheers, whoever you—'

'It's symbolic. I'm going to give you Sabrina's ashes,' said Bridge, interrupting him. 'I know as presents go it's a bit weird but I also know you'd treasure them.'

Luke, for once, was speechless.

'A dog or a cat?' asked Charlie gently because he could see how taken aback his new friend was.

'Dog,' Luke and Bridge answered together.

Bridge had kept their dog's ashes because she could. Luke had asked if he could have half of them, to bury in his garden, grow a rose over the spot. She'd refused just to be arsey, even knowing how much such a concession would mean to him. She'd confused kindness with weakness before she'd grown up to realise there was a dignity and strength in the quality. She had kept Sabrina's collar; Luke should have the ashes in their entirety.

'This means a lot, Bridge,' said Luke, swallowing a ball of emotion lodged in his throat.

'I know it does,' she said as she reached for her own sock, which was the fullest of all of them. She scooped out the nuts and the small orange before pulling out a can of plum tomatoes. Then she laughed.

'Memories,' she explained for the benefit of the bemused others. Her eyes drifted to Luke and stayed there. 'Happy memories.'

'We were very happy once, believe it or not, Bridge and I,' said Luke, addressing them all, before his eyes locked with Bridge's.

They'd chopped up the tomatoes and heated them in a pan on the fire because they had no coins for the electric meter. They'd stirred it with loads of salt and pepper and dipped cheap white bread from the bargain shelf in the local shop into the pan and it had tasted like a feast. Neither Bridge nor Luke had ever been able to unlink the sight of a humble tin of tomatoes from that night, however much water had gone under their bridges since. It was a symbol of what they once were to each other. What they had needed to be to each other in order to be what they were now.

'Thank you,' said Bridge, the two words holding a bucketful of emotion.

'Okay, Jack, your turn,' said Robin.

Jack picked up the sock, did a quick calculation and realised that whatever was inside must have come from Charlie.

'I hope there's a diamond in here,' he said, addressing no one in particular.

'There is, in a fashion,' Charlie said. 'It's certainly one of the most valuable things you'll ever have.'

Jack was intrigued.

There was a small, thin notepad in the bottom among the fruit and nuts. One of the Figgy Hollow Inn pads that they all had in their rooms on the dressing tables, with an accompanying complimentary pen. On the cover, in spidery handwriting, the title: *Rules of Life by a Man who Lived Well.*

Jack flicked through the book; each mini philosophy took up a page.

'Follow that and you won't go far wrong in life,' said Charlie.

Jack read aloud.

'Say good morning and goodnight to your cleaners. Treat kings and commoners with respect.'

'That is a sterling piece of advice and one I was given many years ago by my first employer, a very rich man who had survived a concentration camp in the war. He came to London with nothing but the clothes he was wearing. A man who had seen the worst of life and its best.'

Jack turned to page two.

'Never let an unsaid thank you sit in your heart undelivered.'

'Everyone underestimates the power of a simple please and thank you,' Charlie explained. 'You can change someone's life with the smallest act of gratitude.'

'I never knew you were so wise,' said Robin, playful smile on his lips.

'I was wise enough to let you into my heart,' said Charlie and tapped his temple. 'That should tell you that I have an adequate number of marbles in here.'

'That's debatable. Anyway, do you want your half an hour now or later?'

'Now,' said Charlie. 'Then we can get on and enjoy our Christmas.'

'Come on then,' said Robin, rising from the chair with a loaded outward breath. 'Let's get it over and done with so I can stuff the turkey.'

'Wahay,' exclaimed Luke.

'Cheeky boy,' said Charlie and winked at him.

Mary gave Robin and Charlie enough time to get to their room and then she beckoned Luke and Jack to lean in close.

'I think I know what Robin's present is,' she said in a low voice. 'He wants to give Charlie the opportunity to say . . . uncomfortable things. I should tell you, Charlie isn't a well man.'

'Really?' said Jack.

Bridge and Mary nodded together.

'Oh hell,' said Luke. Both he and Jack looked rocked by Mary's revelation, slapped from the side by an unseen hand. 'Thanks for letting us know so we don't say anything else inappropriate.'

'How poorly is he?' asked Jack.

Mary gave the slightest shake of her head, which said everything. A few moments of contemplative silence ensued and then Luke smacked his hands together.

'Then let's give him the best Christmas we possibly can. All the bells and whistles we can muster,' he said. 'Right, Jack, let's go and peel some spuds.'

Chapter 23

Upstairs in their room, Charlie sat on the bed and patted the space next to him.

'Come on, I'll be gentle with you,' he said.

Robin sat, his hesitation apparent. Charlie appreciated more than he could know, the sacrifice he was making.

'Do I need to take notes?' asked Robin.

'If you think it necessary,' said Charlie. So Robin pulled his phone out of the drawer, opened the Notes app, waited for Charlie to begin.

'Firstly, I've written most of the disbursements I want you to make on my behalf and stored them with my will in the safe. But some have changed. I want you to give the Chanel handbag to Mary. Don't give it to Rosa, she'd sell it but Mary will treasure it.'

'Good,' said Robin, managing to transmit in that one word exactly what he thought about Charlie's niece.

'Tell her though that she must promise to carry it with all the chutzpah she can find in herself. And give Bridge my Chanel scarf. She'll look lovely in it, like the queen she is.'

'I'll do that for you,' said Robin. 'Any other disburse-ments? Do you want me to give Jack your car and Luke your Rolex?'

Charlie laughed. 'I'll think of something for them and write it down for you to execute. Now, in the locked left cupboard of my desk at home, you'll find all the information you need on investments and bank accounts, national insur-ance number, insurances, passwords. I've got all the financial affairs organised. I've been in contact with the funeral direc-tor and given him a running order of the service already so you don't need to bother about all that.'

'You didn't have to do this, Charlie.'

'I wanted to. It helped me come to terms with things, gave me some control. In a way it was quite comforting. What would haunt me is looking down, seeing you flum-moxed by having to make decisions your head just doesn't want to deal with at that time. But there are some extras I wanted to talk to you about.'

'Okay,' said Robin, seeing how much this meant to Charlie and feeling a tinge of regret that he'd shied away from doing this before. It wasn't as traumatic as he'd imagined – so far.

'I want Christmas foliage on my basket coffin. Holly and poinsettia flowers. And mistletoe.'

'If it's available out of season,' said Robin, tapping this into his phone.

'We both know I'm not going to last until the bluebells come out, darling. Now music. There's a change. I want, "I Wish It Could Be Christmas Everyday" and—'

'You can't have that,' protested Robin. 'It's far too jolly.'

'Every day has been Christmas with you, my dear capable Anne.'

Robin gave his head a wobble, a sharp intake of breath to steady himself.

'You can stop that as well. Making me emotional. This is the longest half hour of my life already.'

Charlie nudged him affectionately with his shoulder.

'I've left Dotty five thousand pounds in my will but I want her to have ten.'

'Eh? She'll be the richest cleaner in Hertfordshire.'

'She's been a godsend. And put her wage up.'

'Shall I transfer the deeds of the house to her as well?'

'It'll be your house when I pass, you do what you like with it. What song did you think of having in the middle when everyone is supposed to have bowed heads and sentimental thoughts of me?'

'"Ding Dong The Witch Is Dead",' said Robin, which made Charlie hoot.

Robin drew his eyebrows together. 'I don't know. I don't want to think about this stuff at all.'

'You have to. And sorting it out now is better than after when it will be so much harder work because you'll be tired and confused. Can't you remember the state I was in when my mother passed?'

Robin could. He hadn't been far behind Charlie in the upset stakes either. He'd adored Charlie's mother.

'Let me tell you what I've picked. It can only be Vera singing "We'll Meet Again",' said Charlie.

'Ooh, that's naff.' Robin winced.

'I don't care, I want it. And I want people to sing along, and to sway as they're doing it. And don't even try to negotiate probate, I've left instructions with Reuben to do all the legal stuff. You can trust him, you know you can.'

Reuben was Charlie's nephew, both he and Robin were

very fond of him. Not so much his sister Rosa who strangely had only started visiting when they'd heard Uncle Charlie was ill. Circling like a starving vulture, Robin had said. He wasn't fooled by her sudden concern for her uncle's well-being.

'I've left the clothes I want to wear in the third bedroom wardrobe. In an old Savile Row suit box. I thought I'd meet my maker in the dark grey suit we got married in. Yellow cravat and I'd like a white Yorkshire rose in my buttonhole, just like on the day.'

They'd had bespoke matching suits, even down to the matching shoes.

'Underwear, socks, it's all in there. You can leave off the top hat. It made my head sweat.'

'You've done that too?' Robin looked at him incredulously.

'Yes, Robin. I want to save you as many duties as possible. I know you, you'll dither for ages worrying that you've picked the right things – *are these the socks he would have chosen?* – so I've taken it upon myself to do this. Don't come and see me lying there inanimate in the Chapel of Rest, remember me as I was.'

Robin nodded. He was grateful for that because he didn't think he could bear seeing Charlie lying there still. Charlie and still didn't go together, he snored and twitched even when he was deeply sleeping. 'Is it okay if I come and sit with you though?'

'Of course,' said Charlie. 'Just don't expect me to converse. I've also been having a think about where you can scatter me. Best to cremate me first.' He nudged Robin who let out a spurt of laughter, despite the tears pricking his eyes now.

'Don't, Charlie.'

'We could always find humour in anything, you and me, Robin.'

'Not in this.'

'I want maximum black regalia, no bright colours or rainbows. I want full blown gravitas, black horses, no flowers except from you – something with white roses in it and feel free to stink the place out with Stargazer lilies, I've always liked those. Donations in lieu of flowers to The Little Hospice down the road. This is all in the letter stapled to my will.'

'Then we don't need to talk about it.'

'I want to. I need to explain so there's no surprises for you, no shocks. Your brain will be the equivalent of a mashed beetroot. Anyway, I want Father Derek to conduct the service in Tuckwitt Church, not that awful Father Aubrey who talks ad infinitum and bores everyone stupid, then I'll go on to the crematorium by myself and—'

'You will do no such thing.' Robin refused that request, point blank.

'Yes I will. You say goodbye to me at the church, then go and play host at Tuckwitt Manor. People will need to be fed and watered by then and you should mingle, it'll cheer you up. As for my ashes . . . in the letter it says I want them to go at the bottom of the garden but I've changed my mind. I'd like to be sprinkled with my mother and father in the sea at Whitby. I don't think I'm going to be leaving Yorkshire alive, Robin. I shall end in the place I started.'

'Don't be so bloody stupid.'

'There's a certain serendipity in dying in the area in which you were born. It's as if I've come home for that reason.' Charlie had said his goodbyes to the south when he set off. He wouldn't be back this time, he knew it.

'Don't forget to keep up with my donations to the Yorkshire greyhound rescue centre,' he continued.

'I won't.'

'Oh, and don't let Rosa convince you that I want that "Do not stand at my grave and weep" poem read out at the service, I fucking hate it.'

Robin chuckled again, even as his tears fell.

'I promise.'

'She'll lie and tell you it was one of my favourite poems. It isn't. It's morbid. I want a limerick. *There was an old jeweller called Charles. Who traded in diamonds and* parls . . . *but he wasn't one for the* garls. Something like that.'

'I am not doing that. I'll find something classy.'

'I wish I could hear your eulogy. Will you speak of me in glowing terms?'

'No, I'll say you were a ridiculous old fart.'

'You'll do me proud, I know you will. I'd like to be there at my own funeral. I will do my best to attend.'

'Well sit at the back, otherwise I'll have a heart attack and end up joining you,' said Robin. 'The two of us can end up in the sea at Whitby then, distributed from the same urn.'

Charlie smiled. 'I will try and come back and let you know I'm all right, but it won't be in the form of a white feather or a robin or a Red Admiral because that's overdone, isn't it? What shall it be then? Let's decide now.'

'A diamond dropping from the sky. One big enough to give me concussion.'

'Too obvious.' Charlie thought for a moment. 'I'll leave a cherry on the floor somewhere.'

'Oh very clever, so someone slips on you and goes flying.'

'A cherry, not a banana skin, Robin. All right, something else then.' His eye caught the beautiful scene framed by the large picture bedroom window. 'I know, I'll come down to see you in snow form. You can stand by the French window and watch me fall gently into the garden.'

'I'll be in Bermuda with my new lover for the winter months so I'll miss you dropping by, sorry.'

'Freak snow, like this. You won't want me popping by every five minutes, you'll have your new life to lead. But when the weathermen are scratching their heads because the snow is unexpected, you can presume I'm partly to blame for it.'

Their volley of banter stalled now. Robin couldn't respond because his heart was breaking in his chest. Who could ever hope to fill Charlie's huge, solid, perfect footsteps?

Charlie lifted the phone from Robin, put it down on the bed, took his hand; it was shaking like a frightened bird.

'I want you to find someone who makes you happy.'

'I have and he does. Mostly.'

'You're a young man, Robin.'

'I feel ancient. Fifty-five isn't that young.'

'Fifty-five is spring chicken age. I was forty-seven when we got together romantically, if you remember. I won't stand for you moping around covered in cobwebs like Miss Havisham, do you hear me?'

'White's not my colour.'

'I know, it makes you look bleached.' Charlie felt the weight of Robin's big hand in his own. Solid, strong, tender – this hand stood for the whole of him. 'Find someone that makes your heart sing, my darling, you aren't meant to be lonely. Someone should have the gift of you after I've gone. I shan't rest easy knowing you're being maudlin and crying yourself to sleep.'

'Don't kid yourself, I'll be clubbing every night. Off my tits on cocaine.'

Charlie let loose a froth of laughter at that. 'Don't be frightened of falling in love. Just be careful and don't let anyone love the money more than you. I don't have to tell you this, you're sensible, but you might just be a bit vulnerable. What about Reuben's friend, the architect? He's very good-looking.'

'Ugh. He smells of yeast. I just couldn't.'

'What about Daniel, Sol's widow?'

'Daniel bores me rigid. He has three topics of conversation, himself, himself and politics. I imagine Sol threw himself into the grave head first to escape.'

'Find someone gorgeous who'd love you if you were rich or poor, like I found you. There are lots of diamonds out there waiting to be discovered.'

Robin broke down then.

'Charlie, how do I live without you?'

'For goodness sake, don't go all LeAnn Rimes on me.'

Robin snorted involuntarily. 'Oh look, tears and snot. What a mess you've made of me.'

He stood up to get some loo roll to clean himself up, came back into the bedroom to find Charlie sitting, smiling like a beatific Mother Teresa.

'Thank you for this Christmas present. It means the world.'

'I love you,' Robin blurted. 'I never said it enough. I hardly ever said it at all, but I hope you know I do and I will always love you.'

'LeAnn Rimes *and* Dolly Parton. I'm impressed.' Charlie stopped joking then. 'I know you do, my dearest Robin and—'

'But you needed to hear it more, Charlie. You're my soulmate, I don't feel worthy enough for you. You're the kindest, most beautiful man in the universe and I don't know what I did to deserve you but whatever it was, I'd gladly do it again. The thought of being without you—'

Charlie reached over to his bedside drawer, pulled something out. A ring box. He placed it in the centre of Robin's palm. Robin opened it to find a stunning thick platinum hoop studded with yellow diamonds. It was beyond exquisite.

'Something to remember me by. Something to remember this perfect moment by,' said Charlie.

'It's never real is it?' Robin half-gasped.

'I don't do fakes. You know it's real.'

Robin put it on; the diamonds twinkled like sunshine as he moved his hand around. Of course it fitted, because Charlie had designed it and he was a master at his craft.

'Merry Christmas, Robin. You have made my life happier than I could ever have thought possible and whatever your future holds, and whoever it is with, I will be looking down on you with my love and wishing you well.'

Robin crumpled against Charlie, who held him and they both savoured the closeness of each other, pressed it and shaped it like a diamond, to be kept for a treasured memory.

Chapter 24

'Disappointed with your Christmas present?' asked Bridge, taking logs out of a hessian sack to put in the basket next to the fire. She had been deliberately watching Jack's face as Mary opened up her present and he seemed keen for her to like it.

'No, it was lovely,' said Mary with a fixed smile, the two rows of her perfect neat teeth butted together, like soldiers defending the untruth.

'A voucher for a snog in the woodshed would have been better though, eh?'

'Shh,' said Mary, checking behind that Jack hadn't chosen that moment to walk into the bar lounge.

'To be fair to Jack, it was a tough call finding something around the inn that would be suitable as a present. I mean' – Bridge gave a little laugh – 'I got a tin of tomatoes, for God's sake.'

'It clearly meant a lot to you, though.'

'Because Luke and I have a long-shared history.'

'Yes, well.' Mary shrugged, she wasn't convinced.

'House of Quill stationery is stupidly expensive. Don't

you think that he might have given it to you because it's an indicator of how he sees you: someone of quality and worth coveting?'

'No,' replied Mary, flatly. 'I think it's an indicator that he sees me as an old young fuddy-duddy. Useful yet boring. He's never been that great at Christmas presents if I'm honest.'

'Oh?' said Bridge, wanting more.

'The first year I became his PA, I got some hand cream and a giant bottle of old lady perfume. Then the next year a talcum powder gift set and fudge. This year, a tartan headscarf, a matching shopping bag and a box of jellied fruits. Presents you give to frumpy aunties, not to women that might cross your mind outside office working hours.' Mary lobbed a log onto the fire, which told Bridge exactly what she thought about Santa Jack and his bum gifts. Bridge opened her mouth to say something of comfort, realised there was nothing she could offer and just let out a long breath of frustration for Mary instead.

In the kitchen Jack took a few moments to look through Charlie's book of wisdom. He wondered if these were his standard mantras or if Charlie could read his mind because they seemed to have been tailor-written for him. The last one particularly hit home.

Don't expect to get a good woman if you aren't a good man. Meet the requirements of your requirements.

His list of requirements wasn't that long – but hypocritical, he realised. He'd wanted to be trusted, without trusting himself. He'd wanted to be appreciated for who he was, not his bank balance, and yet he'd used the trappings of his wealth as a magnet. He'd wanted to be loved, without letting the lock on his heart open in order to love back.

'Penny for them,' said Luke.

'Sorry,' said Jack. 'I was just looking through Charlie's present to me. He's a very sagacious man.'

'May I?'

Luke put down his peeling knife and took the notebook from Jack's hand, flicked through it.

'*Be the best version of yourself that you can be.*' He nodded. 'One of my sayings. I think I am the best version of myself now that I can be. I'm certainly in sync with my expectations of myself.'

'I'm not,' said Jack.

'*Meet the requirements of your requirements,*' Luke read aloud. 'Yep, he's right again. Oh boy, is he.' He laughed then, as if he were sharing a private joke with himself. He turned the page. 'Yep, he's right about the comfort zones too. I like this very much. *Ships are safe in harbours but that's not why ships are built.* Oh yes, praise be.' He handed the book back to Jack. 'We didn't talk much about your business last night, did we? It was all opera singer stuff.'

'Pardon?' said Jack, bemused.

'*Mi-mi-mi-mi-mi-mi,*' trilled Luke, as if he was tuning up to perform 'Nessun Dorma'. 'Sorry, couldn't resist. Anyway, tell me, what was it that drove you to take Butterly's out of its comfort zone and turn it into such a behemoth, Jack?' He tossed him a bag of sprouts then for him to prepare.

'I just saw the potential in expand—'

'The real reason, Jack. What caused the fire in your belly to burn so fiercely?'

Jack put the book down on a shelf so it wouldn't get stained and picked up a knife. 'Not sure really.' An obvious lie.

'Okay,' said Luke, preparing to trade, 'with me it was getting back at Bridge. I wanted her to not only eat her words, but to throw them up with nauseous jealousy and eat them up again. I wanted to show her what I was made of. There's a lot of juice in hate, so I thought. Looking back I don't think it was hate, I think it was pain. That's what turned the ignition on in me. Now you.'

'Okay then. My father,' said Jack. 'I wanted him to be proud of me. That was my fuel.' He gave a nervous laugh, scratched the back of his neck before continuing. 'Sounds pathetic, doesn't it? A grown man wanting his father to notice him. I never knew what he truly felt about me, you see. For a long time I thought he sent me away to school because he didn't want me around.'

'Not at all,' said Luke. 'I get it. Ironically your dad's *froideur* probably helped you make that business what it is today. Maybe if he'd showered you with his affection, you wouldn't have tried so hard to make him proud of you.'

Jack thought about that, then dismissed it. 'Maybe if I'd known that he did love me, I'd have worked even harder for him.'

Luke flashed him a wry smile. 'You'll never know. All you do know is that you – *you* – made Butterly's big. Jesus, Luke, two million scones per day, that's like – wow. Now take a leaf out of *my* book of philosophy and work to live, not live to work. And Charlie's right about the requirements thing: you want a partner, but your missus will want a partner too. Make sure you don't keep her waiting around in the background for you to give the crumbs of your attention to, while you give the full cupcake to people you do business with. Find some balance. In fact, Jack, in the nicest possible way ... get a life.'

Jack nodded. Luke had just exposed the template of his father's existence. A man who had died rich, bitter, unhappy, successful . . . and so very lonely.

*

'So what did you people out there get for Christmas then?' Radio Brian asked his captive audience. 'I got some Brut, because it's always nice to have smellies at Christmas, isn't it, and a book with a very intriguing title: *Captain Corelli's Mandolin*. I wonder what that's about?'

'Surely he's heard of it,' Bridge curled her lip Elvis-style. 'I thought everyone had.'

'I thought it was Captain Corelli's mandarin,' said Luke. 'Isn't it about an Italian who loves oranges?'

'Idiot,' said Bridge.

'. . . And my favourite chocolate – a giant Toblerone,' Brian went on.

'He'll never manage to bite into one of those with just his gums,' said Charlie, polishing the cutlery with a Souvenir of Yorkshire tea towel before he put it on the table. 'He'll end up sawing half his face off in the process. I would have thought he'd be much better off with something gentler on his mouth, like Turkish delight, unless Mrs Radio Brian enjoys the floorshow.'

'Or jellied fruits,' put in Robin, newly arrived from the kitchen having popped in there to check on his turkey.

'Yes, because nothing says you don't care about someone more than a gift of jellied fruits,' Luke replied.

Bridge noticed that Mary's head gave a slight reactive jerk. Jack's, however, didn't.

'Lazy present,' said Robin. 'Charlie's niece Rosa always

buys him a box of those for Christmas. She's never once taken the time to ask me what would be a good present fit for him.'

'Okay, what else constitutes crap presents?' asked Luke, sitting by the fireside with a pre-prandial glass of sherry. Mary had insisted they all had one. Nothing conjures up the anticipation of the Christmas dinner to come like the aroma of sherry, she'd told them as she'd poured them out.

'I know, perfume, when it's a stab in the dark,' said Charlie. 'No one should ever buy perfume for someone else without knowing what will suit their skin chemistry. Arpège smells divine on Robin and I love it, but on me it smells like cat pee.'

'Charlie always gives the best presents,' said Robin, twinkling his newly decorated hand. Luke wolf-whistled at it again; Robin had been showing it off since he and Charlie came downstairs.

'Does Jack give good presents? I do hope so,' Bridge asked Mary, eyes glittering with impishness. Mary could have thrown a cushion at her.

'Er, yes,' she answered. 'Really nice. Anyone for a fill up?'

'I'm going to check on my trifle,' said Luke.

'You've made a trifle?' Charlie gasped with joy. 'Please tell me there's sherry in it.'

'Of course. You can't have a Christmas dinner without a trifle and you can't have a trifle without sherry in it,' came the reply.

'*More* sherry?' said Robin. 'Haven't you had enough, Charles?'

'Never. Put some cherries on the top please, Luke.'

'Especially for you, Charlie,' said Luke and pushed

himself out of the chair. Since Mary had told them about Charlie, Luke had gone over and above the call of duty in the kitchen.

'Remember those bath cubes you used to get that you had to take a mallet to?' said Bridge. 'The ones that never dissolve properly.'

'Yes, that's what Charlie's niece buys me every Christmas.' Robin sniffed. 'If you happen to sit on them, they embed themselves in your arse like shrapnel.'

Mary giggled and followed it up with a cough because sherry came down her nose and it stung.

'Now our cleaner Dotty always gets us a big tub of Quality Street, doesn't she, Charlie. We love those.'

'When you open up a tin of Quality Street, the smell of Christmas rushes out at you, doesn't it,' said Radio Brian, as if he were joining in with the conversation.

'Sadly you don't get that effect from the plastic tubs they come in nowadays, Brian,' Robin replied to the radio. 'It's not the same.'

Bridge nestled back into her armchair. It was Christmas Day and it felt every bit like a Christmas Day should. The only thing missing from the scene was some chestnuts roasting on the open fire, which was crackling cheerfully. The sherry was mellowing her like she couldn't remember being mellowed for years and her thoughts strayed south to Ben. She'd bought him a Mont Blanc pen for Christmas, something he'd always wanted but would never have bought for himself. He deserved it; he was the kindest, sweetest man she knew. She hoped he wasn't eating his Christmas dinner alone and had braved the elements to go and join his sister and her family who lived less than half a mile away.

Charlie dropped a fork and almost toppled over trying to pick it up. Mary leapt up to retrieve it for him.

'Thank you, Mary. You know, I never had children but if I had, I would have wished for a daughter like you. I think your parents were a very lucky couple.'

Mary beamed. 'Oh, thank you, Charlie. That's such a lovely thing to say.'

'It's important to say all the things that are sitting waiting in your heart to be said,' he replied. 'You never know what's around the corner.'

Robin nodded in agreement. He was so glad he'd had 'that' conversation with him this morning. It hadn't been as morbid as he'd been expecting and he knew it had given Charlie great comfort. And himself. He wouldn't have regrets now that he hadn't told Charlie how much he felt about him; he'd said important words that had been sitting in his own heart unspoken.

'I'm presuming neither of you have children, then?' asked Bridge.

'No, but I would have liked them,' said Charlie. 'When I was young, the idea of a gay man raising a child was not something to be considered. The world is a far more tolerant place for us now than it was back then. When I was eighteen, I smiled at a man in passing in a park. He not only beat me up very badly but had me arrested, said I'd accosted him, which was a lie. I spent three months in prison. The judge said I was in danger of infecting men with homosexuality, whatever that means. So, never in my wildest imagination did I think during that horrific time that one day men would be able to marry each other and bring up children together.' He shuddered as terrible memories were nudged to the surface.

'Did you have families who supported you?' asked Mary to both Charlie and Robin. It was horrible to think such archaic attitudes were actually just over the leaf in history's book.

'Not me,' said Robin. 'I was an only child, a great disappointment. We skirted around the elephant in the room when I was growing up. My father forced me to box and play football. If he could have injected me with testosterone, he would have. Then one day, when he'd had too much to drink, he asked me if I preferred boys to girls, he told me to be honest with him. And so I was. And within the hour I was thrown out with my suitcase. I was seventeen. They carried on being Christians, going to church, collecting money for the poor, listening to sermons about kindness and tolerance while turning their back on their only child. My cousin let me know when my father died, but he'd had it written into his will that I wasn't to come to the funeral. I reached out to my mother after a respectful waiting period but . . .' He paused, breathed. 'She didn't want to know me. I was dead to her. She'd also had it written into her will that I wasn't to come to her funeral either. And that was in the 1980s.'

'And yet my mother couldn't have been more different,' said Charlie. 'She was a Londoner who had moved up to Yorkshire when she married my father, but after he died when I was eight she went back home to live with my grandmother, and the two of them brought me up between them. I think it was quite obvious from an early age that I wasn't going to marry a nice girl one day and continue the family line. They hoped I'd grow out of it but when they realised it wasn't to be, they both came to terms with it and accepted me for who I was. Mum married again. She met a charmer of a man who whisked her up the aisle after getting her pregnant with my sister. After their wedding, he changed from Dr Jekyll into full-on Mr Hyde and decided to thrash my sexuality out of me. When my mother found out, she thrashed the living daylights out of him with her best frying pan and that was the end of that marriage. My mother and my grandmother stood by me when I went to prison and they were both waiting at the gates to take me home when I came out, battered and bruised.

'I worked my bones off to give them everything they deserved for their unstinting love. Years later, I took them to a Royal Variety performance in the London Palladium, dripping in diamonds they were. They had their picture taken with the stars of the day since I knew most of them personally, because I'd loaned or sold them jewellery from my shops.'

'We've got pictures of them all over the house,' said Robin. 'I never met Charlie's grandmother but his mother became every bit my mother too. She was the best lady who ever lived. That's where Charlie gets it from.' Robin's face melted into a soft smile.

'And my father,' said Charlie. 'I've often wondered if he knew, even then, because I remember him saying to me, "Charlie, you are what God made you, don't you ever forget that."'

'How the world has changed,' said Bridge.

'I don't much like the world as it is,' said Charlie. 'There's so much hate flying around. And that's why I'm enjoying this glorious bubble so much, just us, new friends and nothing but loveliness in the room.'

'Anyone for Yorkshire puddings while I'm in the mood

for making some batter? Speak now or forever hold your peace,' called Luke from the kitchen.

'YES,' came the united answer.

Chapter 25

Luke had made everyone hats out of old broadsheet newspapers. Bridge hadn't got him down as the origami type, but then she didn't really know this version of Luke Palfreyman at all. Mary's hat had tinsel around the top. The birthday girl hat, Luke called it. Charlie looked like an admiral, Bridge like a nurse. They put them on before taking their places at the table; Robin draped a tea towel over his arm and assumed the role of sommelier, filling everyone's glass with red, white or rosé wine, according to their choice.

Jack and Luke brought out the turkey and bowls full of vegetables, Yorkshire puddings, stuffing, various sauces and pickles, everything that a Christmas dinner should consist of and more. There was barely enough room for it all on the long table, which Charlie had made an excellent job of dressing. He'd found a surfeit of red tablecloths and Christmas-patterned serviettes in a wooden sideboard, waiting in readiness for the paying diners who should have been turning up today. He had also found some 'luxury' crackers – according to the box – in there too, but seeing as Luke had gone to so much trouble with his home-made ones, he'd left them where they were. Also in the sideboard was a box of long, tapered red candles and an elaborate five-armed candelabra worthy of a place on Liberace's piano. It made a fitting centrepiece. Luke's newspaper crackers didn't look at all out of place, positioned by the forks. In fact, co-ordinating with the hats, it could almost have been a designer ploy. But then Bridge had the belief that 'shabby chic' had started because someone had made a total cock-up of painting a chest of drawers and sold it with sales patter bullshit as a style that could really take off. And it did. You could pass anything off as anything else and charge a fortune for the privilege if you had enough chutzpah – and a fool with a fat wallet to fall for it.

There wasn't a more festive room in the whole of Christendom: lit candles, log fire, soft snowflakes falling outside, snow on snow; Perry Como, Frank Sinatra et al singing in the background; a table groaning from the load of Christmassy food with its heavenly host of aromas competing with each other for dominance in the air; and most importantly there was a cornucopia of conviviality. Charlie's heart felt as Christmassy as if it were stuffed with Radio Brian's carols. What a precious memory in the making this was. The others wouldn't feel the intensity of it as he did, but he hoped they'd keep this picture in the treasure boxes of their minds, bring it out to look at occasionally, remember it all – and him – with a smile.

'We would like you to say grace, Charles, before we plough in,' said Luke.

Charlie got up from his chair, a little stiffly but he wanted to stand. He thought for a few moments before he began to speak. Heads dipped, eyes closed.

'Dear God in heaven, thank you for the food we are about

to receive. Look after the loved ones whom we cannot be with today, keep them safe and may we be reunited with them soon. And may the people around this table here be joined together by the spirit of Christmas in peace and love and take everlasting happy memories of this time with them, wherever our journeys take us. Amen.'

They opened up their eyes, no one saying a word. Charlie's prayer had touched them all deeply, they knew he had chosen every word with care.

Jack picked up a cracker, held it out towards Mary. It was made out of newspaper and the inside of a toilet roll, the ends twisted and tied with red string that Luke had found under the bar.

'You have to say "bang" when you pull,' Luke commanded.

'Really?' said Bridge, her nose wrinkled.

'Yes, really,' said Luke, adding proudly, 'I had to decimate six toilet rolls in the store upstairs to make them. I came over all *Blue Peter* and channelled the god that is John Noakes.'

Bridge shook her head, bit her lip to stop herself grinning. They'd had a framed photo of John Noakes and his dog Shep in their bathroom. The mad-bonkers presenter had left *Blue Peter* before they'd even been born, but he was one of Luke's idols nevertheless. This new Luke reminded her a little of John Noakes: fearless, magnetic, hair that defied a comb.

'Okay, I'm ready,' said Jack.

'Yep, me too.'

Everyone shouted 'BANG!' Jack won the lion's share. He offered it to Mary but she pushed it back at him saying he'd won it fairly and squarely. Jack pulled out the joke, scribbled on a rectangle of paper. He read.

'What did one snowflake say to the other?'

He was met by a sea of faces eager for the punchline.

'He didn't say anything in case it offended him.'

A tumbleweed silence and then groans of laughter rapidly ensued.

'Or her,' put in Bridge, with mock indignation.

'Oh shut up,' said Luke, picking up a sprout and pretending to lob it at her.

'What's the present inside, Jack?' asked Charlie.

Jack poked around to try and extract it because whatever the present was, it had lodged inside the toilet-roll inner.

'Oh, it's one of those things that you put your fingers and thumbs in and open and close. We used to make them at school,' said Bridge, when Jack had succeeded. 'What were they called?'

'Not sure I ever knew they had a name,' said Mary. 'Fortune tellers, maybe?'

'What do I do?' said Jack.

'Oh come on,' said Bridge with incredulity. How could anyone not know that?

'I'll show you.' Mary reached over, pushed her two index fingers and thumbs into the paper corners. 'Pick a number between one and four.'

'Four.'

She moved her fingers in and out. 'One, two, three four.' She read from the choices that were revealed when she stopped on 'four'. 'Pick from a car, a plane, a helicopter or a bus.'

'A helicopter.'

Mary unfolded the paper, lifted the flap. 'Oh.'

'What does it say? Come on, Mary,' urged Charlie.

It couldn't have been any worse.

'"I love you",' said Mary.

Bridge noticed Mary's cheeks had started to flush. She grabbed the fortune teller from her hands in an effort to divert attention from Mary and onto herself.

'Luke, pick a number.'

'Four. Then I pick a helicopter.'

'Absolutely not.'

'Okay, three.'

'One, two, three. Bike, ship, skateboard, submarine.'

'Submarine. And I swear to you, I have no idea what I wrote behind it.'

Bridge unfolded, swallowed hard.

'What does it say? Come on, Bridge,' urged Robin this time.

'You never left my heart,' she said, reading automaton style, distancing herself from the words with a deliberate lack of emotion. 'Word of advice, Luke, don't take up fortune telling if your company folds.'

Or do. Because his prophecies had just hit two bullseyes.

'I want to pull my cracker,' said Charlie, holding his out to Robin.

'BANG!' everyone yelled.

Charlie won, unfolded his joke first, read it silently and then began to giggle in the way a schoolboy might while looking at an old page three of the *Sun*.

'Come on, share it,' said Robin, catching Charlie's laughter.

'What do you call snowman poo?'

'I don't know,' everyone chorused. 'What do you call snowman poo?'

'Marshmallows.' Charlie dissolved into fits. The others laughed more at his reaction than at the joke. Tears started to roll down Charlie's cheeks as he kept reigniting his hysterics by repeating the word 'marshmallows'.

'That's the worst joke I've ever heard,' said Robin, rubbing his sides in order to relieve the ache in them.

'It's terrible,' agreed Jack, consumed by hilarity to the extent that he had to wipe the tears spouting like a leaky tap from his own eyes.

So that's what he looks like when he really laughs, thought Mary. She hadn't ever seen the phenomenon before and was fascinated by it. The sight of Jack's lips stretched wide, teeth showing, the crinkles gathered at the corners of his eyes . . . he was so perfect. Something pinged against her heart, like a thick elastic band, causing a sharp sting, a dilemma. She had decided what to do about Jack, but suddenly she wasn't so sure any more.

'Oh dear, Luke, you really have missed your way,' said Robin. 'You should be a comedian, not a Plant Boy.'

'He absolutely shouldn't,' said Bridge, in near paroxysms.

They couldn't stop laughing. As soon as they tried, the silence felt like a pressure bubble that needed to be burst. Then Charlie pulled out his cracker present, which was a marshmallow and that set them all off again. Minutes passed, joyous wonderful minutes in which nothing else seemed to exist but these six people laughing at the word marshmallows in an inn on the snowy moors of Yorkshire.

Eventually they were spent, everyone else pulled their crackers and the jokes were as bad if not worse. The other 'presents' inside were a shower cap, purloined from the stock cupboard upstairs, a pickled onion wrapped in clingfilm, a long green balloon with green lines drawn on it and a tag reading: 'Grow your own cucumber' and a keyring, made from a square of corrugated cardboard and a reshaped paperclip for a hoop. Luke had written 'Figgy

Hollow Six' on one side, today's date on the other. Robin had been delighted to win it and said he would treasure it for all time.

The Figgy Hollow Six. That's what they would be forever, Charlie thought. He liked that. Their collective essence was woven into the air of this place now, their little gang was part of its history. Even when he was gone, he would still be one of them. For always.

Everyone declared Luke's crackers the best, worst ones they'd ever had. It would be difficult after that to go back to shop-bought ones, said Robin, and asked if Luke would give him his email address so he could put in an order for next year. It was a joke that was immediately punctured by the burden of knowing that there would be no Charlie next Christmas. He drowned the thought with a throatful of Pinot Grigio blush.

'We'd better eat before all this food goes cold,' said Bridge.

'I'll carve the turkey,' said Robin, jumping up.

'And I'll carve our nut roast, Mary,' said Luke, who'd managed to cobble together something from chopped-up nut cutlets bound together with root vegetables and lashings of sage and onion.

Charlie had spent a lot of money in his lifetime on dining out and this lunch was right up there with the best of them. The roast potatoes were crisp against his teeth, fluffy on the inside, the turkey tasty and on the right side of dry, even the honeyed parsnips set his palate sighing with pleasure – and he hated parsnips usually. And there wasn't as much as a hint of fish hovering around his tastebuds. They ate in a wonderful genial silence, entertained in the background by Radio Brian and his musical choices. Then one by one they set their closed cutlery on the plates, sat back in their chairs and the smiles on their faces mirrored the smiles in their stomachs.

While Bridge and Mary cleared up the plates and delivered them to the kitchen, Luke went to fetch the pudding and the trifle and Jack added more logs to the fire that crackled and hissed cheerfully as if joining in with the celebrations.

'I can't remember eating so much for ages,' said Charlie, embarrassed then as a long, satisfied burp escaped him. Robin looked across at him and his heart seemed to swell in his chest. There was a rosy glow on Charlie's sunken cheeks, and Robin couldn't recall the last time he'd seen it there. Charlie had lost so much weight in the past months that he'd needed new clothes because nothing fitted. He'd asked Robin if it was really worth it and Robin had been furious at the very thought and taken him expensive shopping.

'Perfect, wasn't it,' said Robin. 'It's all so perfect.' A perfect bubble where all was well and he wished he could stay in it for a long time.

The fire spat a salvo of cracks and pops as if demanding attention.

'Ah, the fire is so delightful,' Jack said.

'And as we've no place to go,' added Charlie to that.

'We did, we had Aviemore,' said Robin and gave a small sigh. Charlie would have had every luxury he wanted or needed there on tap. He'd made sure of it.

'I wouldn't have enjoyed Aviemore a fraction as much as this,' said Charlie with a grin of contentment. 'I wouldn't have heard rude jokes about Rudolf and his yuletide log or won my own personal piece of snowman poo in a cracker, or even learnt that it is possible to love a parsnip. Even the

Cipriani hotel in Venice would be sadly lacking by comparison and you know how much I love it there.'

'That yuletide log joke was disgusting,' said Robin, a grin squeezing through the outrage.

Mary came back carrying dessert dishes and started to distribute them around the table.

'I feel blissful,' said Charlie, rubbing his stomach. 'I am crammed to the gills full of lovely food and wine, I'm warm down to my bones and Radio Brian's music is like soothing olive oil in my ears. I've got absolutely no discomfort and if I fell asleep in this chair and didn't wake up, I think I'd be quite happy to let go.'

'Don't you bloody dare, Charlie Glaser,' Robin warned him.

'Not before pudding please, Charlie,' said Mary, adding a gentle admonishment of her own. 'Luke's put all those cherries on the trifle especially for you.'

They knew the truth about him now, Charlie could tell, but they weren't pussyfooting around him. He was just one of them, a fully paid-up member of the Figgy Hollow Six, as special as any of them, but no more, and that felt marvellous. *Normal*.

'Go and get some champagne and mark it down on the notepad, Robin,' said Charlie. 'We should have champagne today.'

Robin didn't protest. Whatever Charlie wanted he should have. There was a fridge under the bar where various wines were chilling. Robin hunted around in it.

'There's a couple of cold bottles here. Not exactly Dom Perignon, though.'

'Perfect.'

'And it's pink. That all right?'

'Even more perfect.'

Robin took six flutes down from a shelf, popping a maraschino cherry in the bottom of one of them. He fell into step with Bridge who was carrying Luke's trifle from the kitchen, closely followed by Luke who paused with his tray by the bar to douse the Christmas pudding in brandy before placing it in the centre of the dining table.

Robin popped the cork from the champagne and carefully poured out six glasses of fizz, handed them out.

'Aren't you supposed to toast the pudding?' asked Jack.

Luke started to raise his champagne in Bridge's direction.

'Don't you dare,' she replied, narrowing her eyes at him.

'I think you toast the haggis at New Year,' said Mary, 'not sure about the pudding, but if the cap fits . . .'

'Yes why not, let's toast the pudding,' said Jack.

Luke struck a match, held it near to the brandy-sodden pudding and the ghost of blue flames appeared.

'A toast then, to the pudding,' said Luke, then swept his glass-holding hand around the table. 'And to us. The most eclectic but joyous set of *strandees* it is possible to be holed up with. May love find you and keep you, may it be Christmas every day in your hearts.'

Everyone raised their glasses then chinked them against the glass of everyone else.

'So, we have rum custard, brandy butter or clotted cream,' explained Luke, introducing the choices to accompany the pudding.

'I'll have all three,' said Charlie. 'And a spoonful of trifle on the top.'

'Cholesterol!' barked Mary, who was feeling a bit squiffy.

'Fuck cholesterol,' said Charlie, reaching for the jug of custard.

Robin didn't argue with him. Charlie had always loved his food. They'd eaten in the best restaurants all over the world in their years together. When Charlie became ill and lost his appetite, Robin felt as if an integral part of his lover had died ahead of the rest of him. The wonder drug Charlie had been prescribed had given him back his love of food, his love of life because the two went hand in hand for him. It revived him so much, Robin wanted to believe the doctors had it wrong, that he'd get better, that all Charlie needed to do was give his body the chance to heal properly and eat healthily. And so Robin had pored over nutrition books, drawn up menus, trusted in superfoods, cruciferous veg, whole grains, unrefined this and organic that in the desperate hope that they would restore Charlie back to him. But a stuffed pepper couldn't bring the sort of smile to his face that the Christmas pud had just put there.

'Can I really fit some pudding in?' asked Bridge, who felt as if her weight had doubled in the last half hour.

'Course you can. Women have a second stomach especially reserved for it,' said Luke. It was what Carmen said in restaurants. She always had dessert. She judged the worth of a dining establishment by the quality of their dessert menu. It was one of the funny little things he loved about her. And there were many funny little things that he loved about her.

'Tremendous pudding, Luke. Did you make this yourself?' asked Charlie.

'Nope. According to the label it's another product from Hollybury Farm. They must keep the pub supplied with their products.'

'Local farm shop I reckon,' said Bridge. 'I might try and find it on the way home. So far everything from there's been top-notch.'

'There is a hamlet called Hollybury in this area,' said Charlie. 'They used to have a May Day fair every year. I remember my mother taking me and I won a teddy bear on the hook a duck stall. My, I'd forgotten all about that. It just shows you, doesn't it, what's lying there in the depths of your mind waiting for something to entice those recollections to the top.'

Charlie marvelled how the mere word 'Hollybury' could have unearthed such a wealth of technicolour memories. The bear was brown with a yellow ribbon around his neck and a red belly and he'd called it Robin. How could he have forgotten that?

'I wonder what the people who should have been having their lunch here today are doing instead,' Bridge said, to no one in particular.

'Eating cheese sandwiches, the poor sods,' replied Robin, his spoon diving into the pudding. 'Think of the favour we are doing the landlord. All this food would have rotted. At least, the stuff that wasn't in the freezer, anyway.' He picked up his champagne. 'He should be paying us really. We've kept the place aired for him, we've taken care of perishables and no doubt we'll give him a glowing report on Tripadvisor.'

Jack clicked his fingers. 'I knew there was something I meant to tell you. I bet no one's looked at the photographs on the wall.'

There was a general shaking of heads. Mary, in passing, had noticed some small postcard-sized photos in frames, but not taken much heed apart from that.

'Well look more closely, they're everywhere and so interesting. And they all feature Figgy Hollow as it was in its heyday. Although to be fair, "heyday" is probably pushing it a bit.'

'I simply cannot understand why I've not heard of this place,' said Charlie. 'There are so many small villages around here and I know them all, in fact their names could be my specialist subject on *Mastermind*: Slattercove, Hollybury, Briswith, Winmark, Little Loste, Ren Dullem . . . what an odd place that was. Like something out of a John Wyndham novel. I went as a boy and remember there were no women to be seen and some of the menfolk staring at my mother as if she were some kind of bizarre creature.'

'Bloody northerners, they're all weird,' said Robin, winking at Mary.

'There was definitely something weird about that place.' Charlie shuddered. 'They were breeding mutants or harbouring aliens or something there. I mean the village we live in is quite insular and I like that, it's quirky, but Ren Dullem was right off the peculiar scale.'

'Where do you live, Charlie?' asked Jack.

'We live near Tring, beautiful part of the world. In a village called Tuckwitt, please don't laugh.'

Too late: Jack exploded and his pudding shot out of his mouth, much to his embarrassment and Mary's amazement.

'Yes, it's an unfortunate name,' Charlie continued. 'There's a movement to change a vowel and make it slightly more respectable. We have yet to see if one day we will be Tockwitt or Teckwitt. The local rag rather enjoys running headlines about Tuckwitt councillors.'

'I hope you folks won't mind me taking the rest of the day off,' Radio Brian interrupted their conversation. 'Mrs Cosgrove is about to serve up and I wish I could send you the aroma coming out of our kitchen via the radiowaves. I will be back tomorrow, and until then I'll leave you with some of my favourite carols to eat your dinner by.'

'Wonder what he's having?' asked Charlie.

'And in case you were wondering, we're having a leg of pork,' said Brian.

'That's so spooky,' said Bridge. 'It's like he's listening to us.'

'I hope it's not too tough on his gums,' replied Robin. 'He'll not fare well with crackling.'

They ate up their pudding and Luke's most excellent trifle while Brian played on with his pre-recorded tracks. *Silent night, holy night. All is calm, all is bright . . .*

Charlie listened to the words of the carol he had heard so many times before but the lyrics struck a chord with him today. *Sleep in heavenly peace.* He felt he really would sleep in peace now that Robin had given him the gift of his time, let him say all the things he wanted to say.

As if Robin knew he was being thought about, he turned to Charlie and smiled. Smiled at the wonderful man that life had blessed him with, a man who had given him everything: a job, a family, a home, security, love. He felt tears welling up behind his eyes and stamped down on them hard. He would grieve Charlie when he was gone, not before. This was a time to savour, along with the pudding and the trifle. The here and now.

Chapter 26

Bridge couldn't remember the last time she had put so much food away. Ben would have approved of her not counting any calories today. When they'd first met, she'd been ridiculously skinny, cheekbones pushing through her skin and he'd brought home-cooked food to her door to fatten her up. Professionally she'd been storming it, personally, she was a wreck: drinking too much, eating nothing, surviving on whisky and cigarettes and vitriol. He'd helped her find some balance in life. He was a good man, the best and she couldn't wait to give him a big hug.

'Anyone for coffee and a mince pie?' asked Mary after all the spoons were downed.

'You are joking,' said Luke, falling against the back of his chair and framing his pushed-out stomach with both hands. 'Hell yes.'

'Well said, Luke, Let's have the full works,' added Robin. 'It's not Christmas every day, is it.' He cast a fond gaze at Charlie who returned a grin so wide, he could have posted envelopes through it.

'I wish it were,' said Jack with a contented sigh. He was

decidedly tipsy by now. 'In fact, I wish it were this sort of Christmas every day.'

'But may I suggest an interval,' said Charlie. 'Let's have our carol singing competition. In our pairs, we must go outside, sing and be rated by our peers.' He spread his hands out towards them, looking not unlike da Vinci's Christ at the Last Supper.

'You want us to go outside?' said Robin. He twisted around in his seat to peer out the window. 'Actually it doesn't look that bad. I think the snow's stopped. A little fresh air might invigorate me because I'm in some danger of nodding off.'

'I'm up for it,' said Luke. Charlie's wishes were theirs to grant. 'And the losers make the coffee.'

'That sounds fair,' said Mary.

'Extra points for harmonies,' added Bridge, presuming the other half of her pair would be Mary, until Jack said, 'Come on, Mary. We'll go first.'

Outside the door, Mary stood in Charlie's jacket, which engulfed her, with her size four feet in size eleven wellington boots. She felt as if she were in fancy dress, but she didn't care. The snow was two foot deep, more here where it had drifted against the inn walls. It stretched as far as her eye could see and she had the sudden urge to run across it, stamping footprints into it like a five-year-old, but Jack was waiting for her to pick a carol.

'What about "Good King Wenceslaslas",' said Mary and then hiccupped very loudly; the fresh air and alcohol combo wasn't doing much for her street cred in front of this man her heart refused to shut the door on.

'Okay, that works. Are we doing to go all the verses? I mean, going to do all the verses?'

'Do you know them?' Mary would have been surprised if he did.

'I think so. I used to. My memory retains useless stuff like that, don't ask me why.'

'Okay then. Let's do them all.'

'Do you want to be the page or Wenceslaslas?' Jack asked.

Crikey, it was catching. Mary sniggered to herself, hearing Jack struggle over the word. *He has Wenceslaslasitis,* she thought.

'Be funnier if you were the page,' said Mary.

'Okay. After three. Then. That's one-two-three and then start, not one-two and start on three.'

'*Mmmmm.*' Mary sang the elongated note so Jack could grab the key.

From inside, the remaining four listened to the carol being performed. Two strong voices for the first verse and chorus, then Mary's solo in a deep, robust tone; the good king, enquiring of his page information about yonder peasant. Then the page sang his response about where the peasant lived.

'That's never Jack is it?' said Bridge. Blimey, he had let his corset strings out.

'He makes a very good castrato,' said Robin.

'I hope not, for Mary's sake,' said Luke.

So Luke also knew that Mary had a crush on the posh twit, thought Bridge. It seems there was only Jack himself who didn't. *Or maybe he does,* said an insightful voice in her head, from a place unaffected by the alcohol. *Maybe he just doesn't want to reciprocate. Don't interfere, Bridge. Let what will be, be.*

She knew only too well that love wasn't always a

high-speed dual carriageway; sometimes it was a round-about, too often a one-way street.

Outside Mary was as gobsmacked as any of them that Jack could achieve such a nuts-in-a-vice piercing falsetto. He was smiling while he was singing, his mood oiled by wine, champagne and probably the dessert too as Luke seemed to have a very generous hand where alcohol in puddings was concerned.

They joined together for the last verse. Gave it their all.

'. . . Shall yourself find bleeeeeeeeeessssing.'

They dropped the last note totally synchronised, but it continued to hang in the air like the echo of a bell. Jack and Mary stood silently, without moving, as time stretched the long second and Mary's brain was plunged into a sobering icy pool of clarity. If ever Jack was going to make a move on her, it would be now. If he didn't, then he probably never would.

Had Mary always been that pretty, Jack thought. Alcohol was supposed to dull the senses, but the opposite was occurring. Her eyes were quite lovely, light and shining, a mix of sea greens and blues, the colour of a mermaid's tail, he fancied as he stood there, slightly swaying. Her lips full, soft, he could imagine how they'd feel against his own. That weirdness swirled inside him again, a confusion of trippy emotions ruffling his senses. It would have been the easiest thing in the world to lift up his hand, thread it in the golden silk of her hair and kiss her. His hand twitched upwards, then common sense slapped him into temporary sobriety. He'd be taking advantage, he'd embarrass himself – and her. He'd have overstepped a boundary that couldn't be un-overstepped. But how he wanted to. He should ask first. *Mary, can I kiss you?*

His mouth formed the first word: 'Mary . . .' – just as she turned from him.

It wasn't going to happen. And she couldn't stand there any longer looking up at him all doe-eyed waiting for his rejection. The moment had passed. The last vestige of hope detached itself from her, drifted away into the cloud-clogged sky.

'Yes, Jack?'

Dithering idiot. 'Well done,' he said, and swallowed hard.

'Yep, we did good.' Mary opened the door, and they walked back into the inn to be met by thunderous applause, and some loud whistling from Luke.

'Fabulous,' said Charlie. 'The best version of "Good King Wenceslas" I have ever heard.'

Mary took an exaggerated bow, overcompensating the jollity. She didn't want to give a hint of what she really felt, because inside herself, she was crunched into a corner crying hard.

'Us now,' said Luke, getting up keenly. 'Come on, Bridge.'

Bridge gave a drawn-out sigh. 'If I must,' she said and put on the wellies and coat that Mary had just vacated.

'You look like a lagged pipe,' Luke laughed at her.

'I feel like one.' The coat that fitted a man of six foot two was no fit for a five-foot, eight-and-a-half-stone woman.

Luke opened the door, waved her forward.

'Look, Mr Tumnus is over there,' he yelled and pointed into the distance. Bridge's head whirled round, then she realised what he was talking about.

'Knob,' she declared him.

'Isn't this beautiful? It really is like Narnia,' said Luke, turning a full circle to view the surroundings from all sides. 'And how cosy does the inn look through the window?' It did too; a friendly orange glow shone gently out, as if there was a sun trapped within the walls.

'Which carol are we going to sing?' asked Bridge, dragging his attention back to the job in hand. It was freezing and she wanted to be inside again as soon as humanly possible.

'"Jingle bells". It's my lucky song,' said Luke, while fiddling behind his back. 'Look, secret weapon.' He'd taken the bell that sat on the bar, which a landlord might use to announce last orders. 'We'll wow them with the sound effects.' He gave it a little shake to demonstrate.

'It doesn't exactly jingle, more of a dong,' said Bridge, eyebrows crunched together in exasperation.

'Who doesn't love a dong?' said Luke and then hooted and Bridge found her automatic disapproval of him melting into a chuckle. *This is what we were like, always laughing, joking, larking around.* She'd forgotten. He'd been an irresponsible Great Dane pup and she'd loved him for it. Once upon a time.

'Okay, ready?' said Luke, ringing the bell, which sounded as if he was a teacher announcing to pupils it was the end of playtime. He counted down on his other hand.

'Three, two, one. *Dashing through the snow . . .*'

He really did have a terrible voice, thought Bridge. He couldn't hold a tune with a pitchfork. He attempted a harmony in the chorus, at least that's what she thought he was doing. And then a yodel. Who yodelled while they were singing 'Jingle Bells'? She steadfastly kept to the melody and tried to increase the volume to drown out his efforts, then was belted by the realisation that she was actually taking this competition seriously. She'd got too used to winning, beating down other competitors, even here and now in trying to avoid making the after-dinner coffees. She throttled back, let his bizarre a cappella attempt shine.

Luke ended the song with a mad flurry of dong-jingles.

'We've so lost,' said Bridge with a laughing sigh.

'Wrong. That was amazing. It was highly original and if I'd had the sense to record it, I would be sending it to Simon Cowell as soon as I got a signal. Now let's go inside and receive our bouquets.'

They opened the door to a scene of hilarity equalled only by marshmallow-poo-gate.

Charlie and Robin were cackling like lunatics, Mary was clapping merrily and Jack was sitting mouth agape.

'What. The. Bloody. Hell. Was. That?' he asked.

'See?' said Bridge, throwing a hand up at Luke before answering Jack. '*He* insisted on too many factors.'

'Look, the melody – i.e. you – was strong and when the basics are rock solid, you can experiment around them,' explained Luke, as if that was his business template as well as his carol-competition-winning strategy.

'Bravo,' said Charlie, clapping loudly. 'You're in my top two so far.'

'I preferred the first couple,' said Jack.

'Us now,' said Robin, turning to Luke and enquiring, 'How cold is it out there?'

'If you're asking that in order to pull a favour so we don't have to go outside then don't bother, because out we are going,' Charlie admonished him sternly.

'Absolutely, you have to go outside,' said Jack. 'This is serious stuff. No concessions.'

Charlie smiled at him. 'Thank you, Jack,' he said.

'Come on then, Captain,' said Robin. 'Let's show 'em how it's done properly.'

'Ooh, my wellingtons are lovely and warm,' Charlie said then, putting them on straight after Bridge had taken them off.

Robin opened the door, Charlie followed him outside and they stood in wonder for a few moments, looking around them. The snow was just starting again, falling like feathers on them. Robin turned a slow full circle, smiling blissfully, arms extended, hands open, catching the flakes and the image struck Charlie as familiar, and at the same time not at all – like déjà vu in reverse.

'It's beautiful, like fairyland,' gasped Robin.

'Isn't it magnificent,' said Charlie. 'Look at all that snow. If I'd been a few years younger, I would have just bounced in it.' A memory from his childhood rolled into his mind then. 'I remember my mother buying me a pair of wellingtons, bright red ones, just so that we could go sploshing in mud together.' A loaded sigh. 'What a fabulous woman she was. I wonder if she's up there wait—'

Robin cut him off, he didn't want to hear it.

'She'll be shouting down, *Pick a carol you naughty boy and get on with it because Robin is freezing his Jacksons off.* So what will it be? "The Little Drummer Boy"? "In the Bleak Midwinter"?'

'Something jolly, not a dirge,' said Charlie.

'"Away in a Manger"?'

'Do I look three?'

'No but you act it mostly.'

Charlie flapped his hand at Robin in mock exasperation. '"Deck the Halls" then.'

'I only know the fa-la-la-la-laaa bit.'

Inspired by the snow everywhere, Charlie clicked his fingers, began to sing, confident this was the one. Robin knew it, everyone did.

'White Christmas'. Charlie's voice, Matt Monro-mellow, nailing notes with a precision that Luke could only dream of. On the repeat, Robin attempted a harmony, easy enough though he'd never done it before, secured it. He figured he'd heard the song so many times, the score had been imprinted on his brain. Flawless.

They both held the final note, then Charlie made a cutting gesture and they let it float away on the snowflakes.

'Ah,' said Charlie. 'I think we've won.'

'Hands down,' said Robin. He opened his arms and Charlie walked into them.

'I love you,' he said.

'Ooh, twice in one day. I am honoured,' said Charlie.

'Don't,' said Robin, squeezing him tighter.

'And I love you. And this has been the best white Christmas in history.'

Robin took his dear face between his chilled hands and kissed him.

'Love of my life,' he said.

'Love of my life,' Charlie said back to him.

A prick of tears behind Robin's eyes, a sign to go in before he broke down completely, dissolved into the snow at his feet, in the air.

Charlie pushed open the door and he and Robin were met by a rapturous round of applause. Mary was wiping her eyes surreptitiously, but there wasn't a lot that got past Charlie.

'That was perfection,' said Bridge. 'I think it's safe to say you two aren't doing the coffees.'

Charlie gave a deep bow as Robin dropped a curtsey.

'I thought our bell was inspired,' said Luke, feigning hurt.

'Yes, it inspired everyone to vote us last, you *bellend*,' said Bridge, presuming that's where they were on the leader board.

'Come on then, Bridge. Let's get started. We can't be brilliant at everything.'

In the kitchen Luke tipped some beans into the fancy-dancing coffee machine and checked the water level, while Bridge busied herself getting out some mugs. She spooned some brandy butter into a dish, switched on the grill to warm up the mince pies. They'd been home-baked by someone and there were old metal biscuit tins full of them.

'I am actually hungry enough to eat more than one of these,' she confessed. 'How can that be?'

'A renewed appetite for food signifies a renewed appetite for life, that's what my spiritual guru always says.'

'You have a spiritual guru?' asked Bridge, as a picture of Luke in a kaftan, folded into the lotus position shot through her brain.

'I'm joking, Bridge. I have no idea. If you're hungry, maybe it's your body telling you to eat. People don't listen to their bodies when they cry out for attention, but they should.'

'Aren't they more likely to cry out for water or nutrition than mince pies?' she asked with a slight note of scoffing in her voice.

'Maybe your body is crying out for what mince pies represent: laughter and company and warmth.'

'Bollocks,' said Bridge and unpeeled the plastic wrapper from a packet of After Eights. But it wasn't bollocks, it was right on the money.

'Have you planned your wedding yet?' asked Luke.

'Well seeing as my first one was ... low-key, I thought maybe Chatsworth House this time. The full works. Champagne reception, five-course meal, lots of bridesmaids, white dress ...'

She waited for him to make a comment about that but he didn't even look tempted to.

'Fixed a date yet?' he asked.

'Not much point fixing a date when you're still married to your husband,' answered Bridge with a humph. 'Why, have you and Carmen?'

She presumed he'd say they were going to fly off to the Maldives or Hawaii as soon as the decree absolute came through. He was loaded now so it was bound to be a showy affair. They'd probably get a dolphin to swim up the beach to deliver the rings to the priest. But he surprised her.

'I think we might just slip off to a registry office and do the deed without any fuss. Party afterwards for close friends and family. Why isn't this coffee machine working?'

Bridge leaned across, pressed a button and the machine burred into life.

'Ah, cheers. Remember our wedding, Bridge?' said Luke.

'How could I ever forget it?' she said.

He in a suit he'd bought from a supermarket, she in a dress she'd bought from a charity shop. Luke's foster mum had taken in the waist for her, Luke's foster dad had put a ribbon on his ancient Volvo estate and driven them to the town hall. Her mother hadn't been there even though Bridge had decided to invite her. She forgot, she said. Bridge was glad really, because she'd have only spoiled it.

Bridge remembered fizzing with excitement as she recited her vows, feeling as if she were on the brink of something special with this man. Luke got his words mixed up, stumbled over parts where she was word perfect because she'd been rehearsing them for weeks.

Until death do us part.

They thought they'd be together forever. She'd loved him so much and she'd felt his love for her, like an energy that was almost tangible.

'How are your foster parents?' she asked him, knowing that Luke would always stay in touch with them because he'd loved them like his own. More than his own, in fact.

'Good. I say good although Phil's riddled with arthritis, but living in Portugal in the sun helps. Sandra loves it out there. Ducks to water.'

She knew he'd bought them a villa in the Algarve. She'd seen his financial records, pored over them with her accountant.

'Have you seen anything of your mother at all?' Luke asked.

'You are joking.'

'I'm really sorry, Bridge.'

'Don't be. I've not had any relationship with her for—'

'I didn't mean about her. I meant I'm really sorry. About us.' He had turned fully towards her. He had taken both of her hands in his.

She hadn't expected this, didn't know what to say. For once, Bridge was dumbstruck. This short but massive word could have changed their history, but he'd never said it before. Not ever. She felt the warmth of his skin pressing against her own as he carried on speaking.

'I think back often to how hard you worked and what you wanted for us both. I should have been a better husband to

you. I let you down on so many fronts. I let you think you
were wrong when you were right.'

It wasn't all you, she wanted to say. *And it wasn't all bad, it
really wasn't.* But she couldn't; the words lodged in her throat.

The coffee machine picked that moment to buzz to say it
had done its duty and delivered coffee from bean to jug. It
couldn't have timed its intervention better.

'Yeah well, it's all in the past.' Bridge pulled her hands
from his in one smooth movement. 'And we both have a
bright, shiny new future to look forward to, don't we?'

'Mary was just saying that Boxing Day breakfast is the best
meal of the whole season,' said Robin to Bridge and Luke
as they walked over to the table with the mince pies, mints
and coffee.

'Oh, I totally agree,' said Luke.

'I've never heard of a Boxing Day breakfast,' said Jack.

'What?' exclaimed Luke. 'Where have you been living,
under a rock?'

Jack sometimes wondered if he had been. Life in Figgy
Hollow was like a life in a different solar system. He couldn't
remember the last time that he didn't have any inclination
to check his emails or care about where his phone was. His
hand usually twitched towards it every few seconds, when
he wasn't seated at his Mac or laptop. It was the first thing
he looked at every morning, the last thing every evening.

Bridge sat down and picked up a mince pie. Whoever
had made the pastry had been heavy-handed with the butter
because it crumbled delightfully against her teeth. She wasn't
drunk but there was definitely a fair amount of wines, both
fortified and not, sloshing around inside her. Funny thing
about alcohol sometimes, she mused, it split the brain, made

one half see things through a distorted lens and the other see them with hyperlucidity. She looked across at Charlie who was smiling serenely, listening to the table conversation. He didn't look ill in the slightest. Maybe Mary had got it wrong. She hoped so. Someone at the end of their life wouldn't have had the strength to sing so beautifully about a white Christmas in the whitest Christmas they'd seen in decades, surely? Her eyes travelled to Mary then, her body language telling as she was leaning away from Jack on her left and towards Robin on her right. Luke was explaining to Jack that Boxing Day breakfast was a pan-fried mash-up of all the uneaten components of a Christmas dinner. She barely recognised him from the Luke of old. He looked like an older brother of himself, a sensible sibling, who cared for himself, worked hard and also reaped the fruits of his labours to enjoy with extended leisure. A man who had carved his place to fit him comfortably. The rough draft of the Luke she knew was long gone, refined out of existence. She hoped the rough draft of Bridge was long gone too.

Chapter 27

After the dishes had been cleared and washed up and the excess food decanted into bowls and put in the fridge for the morning, Jack stoked up the fire and they gravitated to the chairs placed in a crescent around it.

Jack couldn't remember the last time he had done nothing and been able to enjoy it. He was a hard taskmaster on himself, always trying to run and be first across a finishing line that seemed to constantly move away from him; but now, here, today he felt like a marionette whose strings had been severed, forcing him to collapse.

'Doing nothing is an acquired art,' said Charlie, as if he was reading Jack's mind. 'But, take my advice and do acquire it. I was lucky, I had a mild heart attack when I was sixty that made me sit up and take notice.'

'First time I've heard anyone say that a heart attack was lucky,' said Jack, raising his eyebrows.

'It saved my life, ironically,' replied Charlie. 'After that Robin insisted I retire. I didn't need to work, we had more than enough money, so I sold the businesses and we *lived*, didn't we Robin?'

'Oh we did,' agreed Robin, nodding emphatically. 'We

toured the world, we went on safaris, dived into lakes as deep as forever, travelled to the top of the world and the bottom, swam with dolphins, went whale spotting, gambled in Vegas, schmoozed with glamorous glitterati, sunbathed on sugar beaches . . .'

'Sounds blissful,' said Jack.

'It was.' Charlie sighed. 'I've had a good life, done almost everything I wanted to. Including, might I add, have a white Christmas this year. I wanted snow, lots of it. I wanted it to blind me with its brilliance.'

'Well you certainly got your wish, Charlie,' said Jack.

'I'm lucky that I have my loved one here to share it with me though,' Charlie said. 'You'll be glad to get back to your lady, Luke and Bridge her dear Ben. And poor Mary, your family must be worried silly about where you are. It can't last much longer, can it? Though I think I could survive forever in a world full of Christmas trees, log fires, mulled wine and mince pies.'

'Cholesterol!' yelled Luke, for comic effect.

'After all this food, I think I'm mainly constructed of cholesterol now,' said Bridge. 'If I cut myself, I bet I'll ooze brandy butter before blood.'

'I do hope Radio Brian's having a lovely day too,' said Robin. 'I've missed his voice since he went off air.'

'I have enjoyed his pre-recorded playlist though,' said Charlie through a mouthful of mince pie. 'It's as if he's made it from all my favourite Christmas songs.'

'Shall we play a parlour game?' suggested Luke. 'What about charades?'

'Ooh yes,' said Charlie. 'I haven't played it for years.'

'I haven't played it ever,' said Jack, deciding that his work/life balance really was crap.

'It has to be Christmas themed,' said Bridge.

'I'll start,' said Luke. 'I've got a good one.' He stood in front of them all, opened his mouth and drew some invisible notes out of it.

'A song,' said Charlie. 'A carol?'

Luke stuck up his thumb, then four fingers.

'Four words.'

One finger.

'First word.'

Luke held his stomach and bobbed up and down.

'Wind?' suggested Robin, then jumped up excitedly. '*Wind in the Willows*? "Wind Beneath My Wings"?' Sadly neither were right so he sat back down.

'Full?' This from Charlie.

Luke pointed to his wide-open smile.

'Laughing?' tried Mary.

'He looks in pain to me,' said Bridge. 'Pancreatitis? Duodenal ulcers?'

Luke ignored that with the disdain it deserved. He gave up on the first word for now, held up three fingers. The third word. Then he gave his ear a waggle.

'Earrings? I know – hearing aid,' said Robin.

'Sounds like,' Bridge corrected him.

Luke's mime involved a lot of thrusting forward of hands.

'Throw?'

'Launch?'

'Bat?'

'Overhand balls? Is he playing cricket?' asked Charlie.

'Looks more like tennis to me,' said Jack. 'Ace? Smash? Björn Borg?'

'Lob? Is it something to do with volleyball?' asked Robin.

Luke waved his hands as if to wipe his last efforts away, then drew a circle above his head.

'Hair?'

'Static electricity?'

Charlie squealed. 'I've got it, "Angels With Dirty Faces"!'

'Oh for fu—' Luke cut off the profanity, recalibrated, held up four fingers. The fourth word. He pretended to take off what appeared to be his trousers.

'Strip?'

'You lot are shit at this,' said Luke, exasperated.

'Shh, you aren't supposed to talk.'

Once again, Luke repeated the mime, then he held up his imaginary clothing, threw it away and pointed to his groin area.

'Dick,' said Bridge with relish, which earned her a dirty look from her soon-to-be ex.

'Removing your jeans, suit, slacks?' Robin was throwing everything at it.

'Drawers?' said Mary. The look Luke gave her suggested she was closer than any of them so far. He made an encouraging *come on* motion with his hands, wanting more from her. 'Shorts? Knickers?'

Luke grinned. Took off his pretend pants and pointed to his groin again.

Robin made a vigorous leap from his chair, convinced he'd got it now. 'Take your knickers off, Father Christmas.'

'Ah yes, that well-known children's carol,' said Bridge to that, rolling her eyes.

'It's something definitely to do with knickers,' said Charlie, which triggered near ecstasy in Luke as he once again wriggled out of some pretend underwear.

'Knicker-less?' said Bridge. 'Of course, I've got it! "Jolly Old St Nicholas".'

Luke stuck up his thumbs and collapsed forward in exhaustion.

'Where did the volleyball fit in, I'm confused?' said Jack.

'I was trying to say, "sounds like *sent*". When you didn't get that I drew a saint's halo above my head.'

'Ah,' said Bridge. 'Well, that wasn't an ordeal at all. Anyone want to go next?'

Robin stood up and entertained them all with a very funny – if quite indecent – mime of 'Fairytale of New York'. Then Mary followed with 'O Little Town of Bethlehem'. Then they had a break for mulled cider, which Luke had also made that morning so all the spices had plenty of time to marinate. It could have fuelled a rocket up to Mars, said Charlie, coughing after his first mouthful before quickly returning for a second. Luke had been delightfully liberal with his addition of Calvados to the mix.

'You really have turned into Superman haven't you?' said Bridge, nodding with approval at the taste.

'I'll take that,' said Luke.

'And what is your kryptonite then?' asked Jack.

'I don't have one,' said Luke. 'I turned all my weaknesses to strengths.'

'Everyone has a weakness,' said Bridge. 'Mine is not being able to resist a bargain. If I sniff even the smallest profit in a plot of land, I have to have it.'

'Mine is cherries,' said Charlie. 'I'd do anything for one of those cherry grenades.'

'What's yours, Jack?' asked Luke.

'His posh twitness,' Bridge answered for him.

'*Bridge,*' said Luke, with disapproval.

'No, Bridge is right,' said Jack. 'All education and no

common sense.' He couldn't shake the image of Mary's lovely face upturned to his when they were outside.

'What about a nice sedate game of bingo?' said Mary, a distraction from anyone asking her what her weakness was because he was there, sitting next to the fire with his eyebrows knitted together in consternation. When the idea was greeted with tipsy enthusiasm, she got up to distribute bingo cards and counters from the box to cover the numbers. Luke volunteered to be the caller and got very much into the spirit of things straight away.

'Are we all set? Eyes down, ready for your first number. One and two – three. Leg and a fat lady – eighteen.'

Bridge was going to ask him if he had to be a twenty-four-seven clown but she didn't want to risk stifling his bingo lingo creativity. Looking at Charlie with his foot-long grin, eagerly awaiting Luke's next call, she was glad that he hadn't traded that daft-as-a-brush essence of himself for money and success. They played five games. Charlie won the last one with the most serendipitous of numbers.

'The Figgy Hollow Six . . . number six of course.'

'House,' yelled Charlie, throwing his hands up in the air and sending all his counters flying. 'What do I win?'

'An overnight stay in a top Yorkshire hotel,' said Luke, putting on his best announcer's voice. 'With a five-star Boxing Day mash-up breakfast thrown in.'

'Wonderful, I'll take it,' said Charlie.

No one suggested any more games, they were beat. They relaxed their backs into the armchairs and let Radio Brian's playlist sink into their souls. Judy Garland serenaded them with 'Have Yourself a Merry Little Christmas'. Their hearts were light, their yuletide had been gayer than gay. Robin tried not to read deeper meaning into the lyrics, about their troubles being miles away. Sitting there in a merry crescent around the fire, it was too easy to believe the world would carry on turning for him – for Charlie – as it had done for the past thirty-odd years, and so he allowed himself to believe it.

He yawned, and set off a chain reaction. A day of cooking, eating, drinking, singing, parlour games and laughing had started to take its toll on some more than others.

'I might have to turn in,' he said. 'I need some sleep to generate enough energy to eat my breakfast.'

'We will feast like kings tomorrow. I can't wait,' said Charlie, his expression filled with glee.

Jack smiled at Robin and Charlie struggling to their feet, leaning on each other for support.

'Goodnight, one and all,' said Charlie. He stood for a moment, beamed at them. 'Thank you for making it special for me today. It's been joyous. I will see you in the morning, God willing.'

'We *will* see you in the morning, Charlie,' said Jack with emphasis. 'Sleep tight, you two.'

A salvo of more goodnights ensued, then the oldest members of the Figgy Hollow Six lumbered noisily up the stairs, leaving the remaining four, contentedly soaking up the last of the Christmas Day hours in front of the softly flickering flames of the fire. Mary's eyes were shuttering down; she was too comfortable and struggling to fend off sleep as a result.

'I think we gave Charlie a good day,' said Luke.

'He laughed at all your jokes,' said Bridge. 'Even I did, Luke. You haven't lost your touch.'

'Praise indeed. Thank you, kind lady.'

'You should have been a redcoat at Butlins really, shouldn't you?'

'If I'd been born a few years before, I probably would have gone for it,' replied Luke. He turned his head towards Bridge. Her hair was mussed, tousled, natural, though he imagined she wore it straightened like a copper sheet these days. When he met her it was down to her waist and looked like fiery flames trailing behind her. Jack had said she was formidable and she was, and so much more. Small and elfin as she was, she could take up a whole room simply by being in it. Ben was a lucky man.

'I'm not sure I can keep my eyes open much longer myself,' said Bridge then, arching her back and stretching her arms up into the air. 'I didn't sleep all that well last night. Took me ages to get off.'

In the next chair, Mary emitted a little snort. Bridge leaned over to give her hand a gentle shake as she didn't want to leave Mary asleep here. Mary's eyes sprang open.

'Yes I mean it, I'm leaving, I'm handing in—' She'd clearly been jettisoned at speed from a dream and was disorientated. 'Oh sorry, I thought I was at work.'

Jack turned to her. 'Was I keeping you back to do one last job?'

'Sorry? Oh yes, something like that,' replied Mary, not catching his eye. She felt as if the dream had followed her out of her nap and was becoming reality.

'I'm going up to bed, Mary,' said Bridge, in a soft voice. 'I just thought I'd let you know.'

'Yes, all right, fine. I'll ... er ... come with you,' said Mary, getting up from her chair.

'I presume we're staying for a nightcap?' Luke asked Jack. He didn't wait for an answer before heading off to the bar.

'Goodnight, boys. See you tomorrow.' Bridge said it for both of them.

'Goodnight, Bridge, Mary.'

Jack's eyes followed Mary as she walked across to the stairs. She'd sounded quite cross when she'd awoken and said she was leaving, said she was handing in ... what? It could only be her notice. It was strange really, but people who worked for Butterly's tended to stay working for them. It hadn't crossed his mind, until that moment, that Mary would ever find another job and leave. Why would she be dreaming about it if she wasn't thinking about that?

'Here you go,' said Luke, handing over a generous measure of malt. They'd have no problems sleeping tonight.

'My dad used to drink this,' said Jack. He should have been smashed for the amount of alcohol he'd put away today; maybe he was, but the thinking part of his brain felt remarkably sober. 'I could never stand the smell of it until about five years ago. Maybe I'm turning into him more with every year that passes.' His expression told Luke that wasn't the most welcome of prospects.

'What did he look like? Like you?' asked Luke.

'Quite short, bullish though, big neck, oozed aggression and he marched everywhere as if he had a seriously urgent purpose. I seem to remember him being different before my mother left to how he was afterwards, less brittle, less stiff. She set off a stick of dynamite inside him and he never recovered from the blast.'

'You couldn't manage to keep a relationship going with your mother then?' asked Luke.

'She walked out on us both and didn't look back. I tracked her down when I was sixteen but she had a new family with her second husband and I was part of a complicated past she'd painted over.'

Luke sighed, shook his head. He could never abandon his child, never relinquish the mantle of parenthood once it had been placed on his shoulders, couldn't understand how people did.

'Patterns don't have to repeat themselves you know, Jack,' he said. 'I wouldn't be the sort of father my father was to me.' Luke took a sip from his drink. 'And Bridge definitely wouldn't have been the sort of mother hers was either. She has a bank of love in her heart to spend.'

'Why did you give her a tin of tomatoes for Christmas?' asked Jack.

Luke gave a small chuckle. 'We once made a meal out of them when we were totally broke. It tasted like nectar because we were happy. Just before we started to realise that you actually do need other things apart from love to live on, it's not that romantic to be permanently worrying about where the next rent is coming from. That's why I donate a percentage of the Plant Boy profits to low-income families, because I've been where they are and not all of them find their rope ladder to climb out of the hole.'

'That's noble of you,' said Jack, then in case that came out as patronising added, 'I really mean it. We should do something like that at Butterly's. I've always taken a comfortable life for granted. Dad always chanted, *Charity begins at home* whenever anyone approached us for donations.'

'You sound very different to him.'

'I loved him, Luke, but I hope I am.'

Something was weighing down Jack's eyebrows.

'Penny for them,' Luke asked eventually, as there was definitely some intense activity going on behind the wall of Jack's skull.

'I'm not convinced my present to Mary went down as well as I'd hoped,' came the reply.

'What did you expect to achieve from it?' asked Luke.

'I don't know,' said Jack. 'I'm ...' He shifted forward in his chair, leaned over to Luke not wanting to chance that he might be overheard. 'I'm confused about what's happening ... there.'

Luke wasn't sure what he meant. Jack, he had come to realise, was not great at putting emotions out there. Hearts worn on sleeves risked a battering, but that was the chance you took for enjoying the feeling of light and sunshine on them, for being willing to win the prize of love.

Jack chewed on his lip. The large malt was levering up his internal portcullis. He wasn't used to letting people see inside the castle walls.

'When Mary said just then that she was dreaming about leaving, about handing in her notice – I presume, I had a real moment of panic about that and I don't know why. I felt something,' Jack swallowed, pressed at his chest. 'For Mary. I don't know what though. Possibly reverence. Have you ever seen *The Admirable Crichton* ...?'

This was painful, thought Luke, pinching the top of his nose with exasperation.

'Jack, for fuck's sake, you need to man up. I'll tell you this for nothing. You are never going to find what you most want in your safe zone. What was Charlie's life hack about ships not being built to sit in harbours?'

'Yes, I see what you mean. Right. I have to ... sail out there into the open sea.'

'Exactly, my friend.'

Jack looked down into the glass of malt and found an idea in it. A perfect idea. At least, it felt like it at the time.

'What were you dreaming about that made you shout out that you were leaving? You sounded very adamant,' asked Bridge after she turned out her bedside light.

Mary groaned, plunged her head deep into her pillow.

'That I'd told Jack I was handing in my notice.'

'Yes, well, that was obvious.'

'Was it?' Mary's horror was refreshed.

'Of course, but that's because I know what's going on in your head,' Bridge replied. 'So *why* were you dreaming about telling Jack you were handing in your notice is the big question.'

'Because ... that's what I'm going to do in real life,' said Mary. She might have been well past tipsy, but on this she was clear. 'I'll lose all self-respect if I stay. It would be so much easier if I could winkle him out of here' – she patted the part of her breast where her heart lay – 'but I can't. I've tried, and it's pathetic how sad I feel when one of his leggy girlfriends turns up and how elated I get when office gossip tells me she's off the scene. So no more. I'm leaving.'

'You should. Come and work for me. Whatever he's paying you, I'll more than match it,' said Bridge. She might have been well past tipsy, but she meant every word.

Mary took a deep breath. 'Yes, I accept.'

Bridge nodded, smiled. 'I'm delighted, Mary.'

'It's started to hurt me to be around him.'

'Then it really is time to leave,' said Bridge.

*

'Robin, are you awake?' Charlie asked in a hushed voice.

'No, I've been asleep for half an hour,' came the weary reply

'I've thought of something for you to give to Jack and Luke as a present. I'm going to write down my instructions and put them in my suitcase.'

'As if I won't have enough things to do,' said Robin with a groan. 'All you've done at me for over thirty years is bark instructions. Robin, drive me here; Robin, arrange for Securicor to deliver that necklace to Lady blah–blah; Robin, book us two tickets for Vegas.'

'Would you have had it any other way?' asked Charlie softly.

'No. Now get some sleep,' said Robin, and tumbled back into the dream he had temporarily vacated.

Boxing Day

Christmas is a holiday so powerful

that it requires another one, Boxing

Day, to be observed right after it

Chapter 28

'Well it's stopped snowing ... oh hang on, no it hasn't, but it's very fine.'

Robin stood by the window, curtain pulled back, looking out. 'I doubt Aviemore in its prime could give us this much snow. It'll be interesting to ...' His voice trailed off as he turned back to Charlie and noticed how still he was.

'Charlie?'

Charlie was lying on his back, a faint smile on his lips. Still. Charlie was never still.

'Charlie?'

Nothing.

Robin crept over to the bed, his heart increasing in tempo with every step.

'Charlie, wake up.' Robin shook him rudely by the shoulders and Charlie's eyelids sprang open.

'What? What's the matter?'

Robin sat on the bed, his spine seemed to collapse.

'Thank God, I thought you'd shuffled off.'

Charlie closed his eyes again.

'Would it be such a bad thing to have gone in my sleep?'

'Yes. I'm not ready for you to go.'

'If you think I'd have gone and missed that marvellous-sounding Boxing Day breakfast, then you don't know me at all.'

'I do know you, you stupid old bugger.'

'I had planned to croak on a ski-slope in Aviemore doing a black run slalom.'

Robin allowed himself to smile at that. 'I should have known you wouldn't miss any food. I'm half-expecting you to turn up for the buffet at your wake.'

'If you promise to put on creamed asparagus vol au vents, I'll be there like a shot. And I want loads of mince pies. Add that to your notes.'

'There will be Gregg's sausage rolls and not much else.'

'Ooh, I love a Gregg's sausage roll,' said Charlie, squeezing himself with glee.

Robin looked at him with open-mouthed shock. 'When have you had a Gregg's sausage roll?'

'Dotty brings me a secret one every Tuesday morning when you're out washing the car.'

Robin's jaw snapped shut. 'Does she indeed?' he said then. 'I'll be having words with her when we get home.'

Charlie stretched. 'This bed is so comfortable, Robin, I haven't slept as well for months.'

Neither of them had slept well for months, that was for sure. Charlie's sleep had been disturbed by dull aches, Robin's by bad dreams. Sleep quality was even worse in the overnight hospital stays, as plush as the private suite was. Charlie had called a halt to all that; he said he wasn't going to spend another night away from home, apart from the hotel in Aviemore. When they got back after this trip, their bedroom would start looking more like a hospital though.

The palliative care team would be coming to assess Charlie and their regime would begin. Daily visits, twice daily, three times daily . . . more.

Charlie swung his legs out of bed with a new ease. He stood up, then leaned over and touched his toes ten times. He hadn't been able to do that for weeks. Robin applauded him.

'Very good, Olga Korbut. I thought you'd be worse for wear this morning. I bet Jack's head is spinning. He was pissed as a fart.'

'*Au contraire*. I feel as if I could run a marathon,' Charlie declared. 'I imagine I'll feel even better after my shower.'

'I'm delighted for you,' said Robin, leaning across himself to rub his shoulder. Charlie came over, massaged the nag of arthritis for him. The first crumble, as Robin called it.

'Mmm, that's better,' said Robin with rapture. 'You have such a magic touch.'

'I know. I'm a man of many talents. I'm going to have a word with Bridge today, Annie,' said Charlie.

'Oh, and why's that?'

'Because I can spot a fake when I see one, that's why,' said Charlie.

'Breakfast in five minutes, folks.' Everyone heard Luke's voice travel up the stairs.

'I'm not sure I dare go down,' said Mary. In her head she held the memory of standing outside carol singing with Jack, looking up at him with a 'kiss me' expression on her face, which he totally ignored. Minds being what they are had distorted this to her standing there for minutes with her lips puckered. Even if the recollection was mostly false, there had definitely been an unmistakable long second when electricity had arced between them, and then absolutely nothing had happened. How much more of a fool could she make of herself? Because, as she told Bridge last night, it was hurting now. She might have made up her mind to leave Butterly's and work for Bridge when she was the worse for wear from the mix of drinks, but her decision was still the same in the sober light of day. She'd tell Jack when they got home, she didn't want to make things awkward, especially on the drive back. She'd just have to bear keeping the words unsaid until then.

'Mary, listen to me,' said Bridge, putting her hands on the younger woman's shoulders, looking at her straight in the eye. 'You made a big decision yesterday, your new life starts here if you want it to. But I know we were pretty hammered last night, so if you made a choice influenced by alcohol and have changed your mind, I'll understa—'

'I didn't,' cut in Mary, her voice unwavering. 'I do want to work for you.'

The prospect of no longer having to worry about what Jack thought of her was as delicious as a glass of cold lemonade on a dry throat. But lying there in the core of her heart was also a sadness that felt like a rock. The end of an era was nigh. She loved the scone industry, took pride in the differences she'd made to the business, even if she'd never been formally credited for them. Yes, time to move on. Time to make differences somewhere else where her efforts would be recognised. She was doing the right thing, she knew.

'Fabulous timing,' said Luke, when Mary and Bridge walked downstairs. The fire was blazing in the grate, everyone else was seated at the table, while Luke was spooning out portions of chopped-up Christmas dinner, bound together with buttery fried onions and mashed potatoes from a huge frying pan.

'Morning everyone,' said Bridge, brightly.

'Sleep well, girls?' asked Robin.

'Oh yes,' replied Mary, and Bridge added, 'Out like a light. You?'

'The beds are like clouds, aren't they?' said Charlie.

'Did you sleep okay, Jack?' asked Bridge.

'Perfectly, thank you.'

Luke knew that was a lie. Jack had been rotating as if he were on a spit and mumbling unintelligibly. He'd been impressed that Jack hadn't woken up clutching his head and crying for ibuprofen.

'There's a vegetarian option for anyone who wishes to give it a go. The first draft of a new addition to the Plant Boy range, the Boxing Day mash-up,' said Luke, indicating his creation, which sat in a second pan.

'So this is a sort of festive bubble and squeak then?' asked Jack.

'*Bauble* and squeak,' Luke said with a roar of laughter at his pun. He dropped a large dollop onto Jack's plate, which landed with a *clud*. Jack studied it dubiously before picking up his fork. It looked like a train wreck of food.

'I'm going to try the vegetarian option,' Bridge announced.

'Certainly, madam,' Luke said.

'This is good, this is really good,' said Jack, sounding surprised.

'It's absolutely divine,' said Charlie. 'I shall be diving in for seconds. Pass the gravy please someone.'

'Cholesterol!' barked Jack, who was decidedly jolly this morning, Bridge noticed. She raised her eyebrows at Mary but Mary's expression remained blank. Jack was on a quick-defrost setting. Shame it was too late now. His loss would be Bridge's gain.

'So Christmas is over for another year then,' said Bridge with a sigh of lament.

'Absolutely not,' said Charlie in protest. 'This is only the second day of Christmas. It doesn't end until Epiphany. The twelfth night. The Christmas season is getting shorter and shorter and it should be illegal. I always think of the poor workers forced into shops today to sell goods.'

'This weather will be a blessing for them in that case,' said Robin.

Jack didn't say that he would have been in the office by now had he not been snowed in. He knew how sad that would have made him sound.

'I think we need to hear from Radio Brian,' said Mary, getting up from the table. Bridge saw how Jack's eyes followed her all the way across the room. *Interesting*, she thought. Mary, oblivious, switched on the radio and Brian's dulcet tones emerged mid-flow.

'. . . had a lovely Christmas. I was talking to my friend Malcolm this morning and they're having a Boxing Day leftover breakfast fried up in a pan with some butter.'

'So are we, Brian,' Jack called over to him.

Robin gave him a sideways glance. Was this really the same stiff suit he had been introduced to only three days ago?

'The weather outside is indeed frightful but the other BBC is telling us that a thaw is on its way, starting tonight, so if you're going to go out and make a snowman, you'd better do it today,' Radio Brian continued. 'There's a lot of snow to melt, isn't there, so I expect to hear flood warnings.'

'Oh my goodness, I hadn't thought of that,' said Charlie. 'All this snow has to go somewhere, doesn't it?'

'Snow, floods, what's next – locusts, boils, frogs?' Robin asked the air. 'I tell you the end of the world is nigh. We'd better paint a red cross on the door.'

'Oh, shush and eat your breakfast, Robin. You're putting me off, talking about boils,' Charlie admonished him, tucking in with the zeal of someone not put off in the slightest.

'. . . reports of intermittitent phone lines working . . .'

'*Intermittitent*,' echoed Bridge with a snigger.

'Bless him,' said Robin.

Jack responded to that nugget of news like one of Pavlov's dogs switching on anticipation at the ringing of a bell, but then again his phone was upstairs and he decided he'd check for any communications later, if he remembered; he was in no rush to leave the table. No sooner did he think that than there followed a freeze-frame moment in which he marvelled at himself for having thought it.

I don't want to get back to reality, said Robin inwardly. He felt protected here in this odd little inn. It was as if it was enchanted, like the Beast's castle when Belle walked in and found all the luxury food waiting for her. He wouldn't have been at all surprised if clocks and candelabras had started dancing around the room singing 'Be our Guest'. Charlie had been like his old self; they'd located sunshine again in Figgy Hollow after months completely smothered by shadow. If it meant Charlie could be well, he'd stay in this spot forever, letting it be Christmas every day, even if it meant an eternal diet of cold turkey and cranberries.

'My friend Malcolm's just been around to his neighbour, he says, for a carrot because they used all theirs up yesterday and his grandson needs one for the nose of his snowman and no one's got any. He's had to use a beetroot.' Radio Brian began to laugh heartily as if he'd told the world's funniest joke.

'I think he's been on the mulled wine again this morning. Either that or he's read your cracker jokes, Luke,' said Bridge, nevertheless infected by Brian's laughter.

'I haven't made a snowman since I was a boy,' said Charlie. 'I want to make a snowman. I know, let's have a snowman-making competition today.'

'I'm up for it,' said Luke.

'There's a shocker,' replied Bridge.

While Mary and Robin were tidying up around the fire, and Bridge and Charlie were in the kitchen washing up, Jack slipped upstairs and into the middle bedroom like an SAS soldier on a mission. Mary had made his job easy for him because the red diary he had given her was on the dressing table. He opened it, and scribbled, 'Dinner with Jack, Firenze' against January 11. His mouth was dry with anxiety and his heart had migrated into his eardrums and was keeping pace with the William Tell Overture. Firenze was the most fabulous restaurant in the whole of Yorkshire; there was nothing subtle about this move. Then he put the diary back in the place he had found it, and returned downstairs with no one any the wiser that he had taken the first step out of the prison of his own making. Maybe Mary would ignore it, save them both a pie in the face moment, or maybe she wouldn't.

Jack felt the ship in his comfort-zone harbour jerk upwards on the anchor.

Chapter 29

'I can do these by myself,' said Bridge, filling up the bowl with water and Fairy Liquid. 'Why don't you go and rest by the fire, Charlie.'

'I insist,' he said. 'Now, do you want to wash or dry?'

'I'll dry,' said Bridge, going over to the drawer for a clean tea towel. A 'Yorkshire Dictionary' one this time. It was like a different language, she thought, reading it until Charlie had given her something to dry.

'So when are you going to tell Luke that you're still in love with him?' Charlie asked, sponging potato from the first plate.

Bridge's attention snapped to him. 'What?'

'You heard. When are you—'

'You're right, I did hear,' said Bridge, her tone almost defensive, 'but I'm not.'

'I can spot a fake a mile off,' said Charlie with a soft, knowing smile.

'Sorry?'

Charlie reached for Bridge's left hand, lifted it as if he were a prince about to kiss it.

'I can spot a fake a mile off. I can *smell* one in fact, I'm that good,' he said, tapping her engagement ring. 'That's not a diamond. It didn't fool me and you don't either. Now you're not the type to wear a fake diamond on your hand, so what does that tell me? That you're here to sign divorce papers but you don't want to, and so you're hiding behind this ring.'

Bridge snatched her hand away. 'Come on, Charlie. Let's get these plates done.'

Charlie dunked another plate into the water, put it on the draining board and Bridge picked it up and began to dry it. Another plate and another. Then Bridge broke the silence.

'Ben's my neighbour. He's a wonderful man. He's in his late fifties, unmarried, writes Midnight Moon romances under the pen name Benita Summers for a living and he writes them surprisingly well considering he's never been romantically interested in women, or men for that matter. He considers himself quite lucky, being oddly free of that complication, he says. He's beyond kind, a true friend and I adore him. That's his happy place in life: friendship. He shops for pensioners, he looks after people's cats if they're on holiday and he makes cottage pies for his screwed-up neighbour when he thinks she's too thin.'

'Ah,' said Charlie, not missing a beat as he rinsed the suds from a mug.

'I haven't gone into a lot of detail about him, so I don't trip myself up with any lies. Most of what I've told Luke is true; that he's clever and funny and caring, and he is. Sadly Ben and I will break off our "engagement" soon, before our wedding plans get too much underway.'

'But, my dear Bridge, why even invent a fiancé?' asked Charlie.

'I don't know, pride I suppose. Luke had someone serious and I hadn't. I didn't want him to think I was unlovable.' She smiled, a sad smile, kept her eyes lowered.

'You're very lovable, Bridge. If I weren't a married gay man, I should be courting you with diamonds.'

Bridge hiccupped a laugh, wiped a rogue tear from the corner of her eye with the heel of her hand.

'Luke is too,' said Charlie. 'I imagine once you have loved him, it would be very hard to unlove him, wouldn't it?'

'Luke and I aren't good for each other. We don't work. We had great sex but it came at too high a price. He and Carmen sound amazing together.'

Charlie nudged her shoulder.

'Cupid's a little bastard sometimes, isn't he?'

Bridge laughed. 'Yes, he's a total wanker.'

'You and Luke, Jack and Mary. One of you with a golden arrow stuck in you, the other one he's pinged full of lead.'

'I want what you and Robin have,' said Bridge. 'Nothing less.'

'I've been lucky,' said Charlie. 'I had to kiss a lot of frogs though before I met my prince. One who's been barking "Cholesterol!" at me for years.' He tutted then, affectionately so. 'I'm going to miss him, but I hope I have a lot of time to wait until he joins me.'

Bridge folded, Charlie opened up his arms and wrapped them around her: he felt the weight of her head against his breastbone and tears seeping through his shirt.

'A new year's around the corner, it'll bring some magic, I promise you, Bridge. And no more need for fakery. Just you wait and see.'

*

'Fancy a game of something, Mary?' asked Jack, tapping her on the shoulder as she stood by the window, her brain miles away from her body.

'Er, yeah, okay. Buckaroo?' she suggested. She didn't have the headspace for chess at the moment.

'Okay. I've never played it before, you'll have to show me what to do.'

Mary brought over the box from the pile of games on the floor by the Christmas tree and set it on a table by the window. She took out the mule, pressed down its hind legs and attached the plastic saddle onto its back. It struck her how calm she was: emotionally distancing herself from Jack was liberating; she wasn't second-guessing what he might have thought about her choosing Buckaroo over something far more mature. Her second choice would have been Snap.

'We have to take it in turns to hang things on the hooks. The person who overloads the mule and he bucks, loses the game,' she explained.

'Right. You go first. Show me how it's done.'

Had Mary looked at him then, she would have seen something new in his eyes, something sparkling and hopeful and slightly scared, but she didn't.

She picked up the coiled rope and carefully attached it to the saddle.

'This looks easy,' said Jack, who duly hung on the spade and the mule bucked. It startled him enough for him to jump. 'Cripes, not as easy as it looks, is it?'

'You have to sneak up on him,' said Mary. 'He's lazy, he doesn't want to carry anything.'

'I see. Okay, one nil to you then.'

Mary reset the mule, chose the bedroll this time.

'I'm sorry about your Christmas present yesterday,' said Jack. The words came in a blurt, as if his voicebox had pushed them out before they had a chance to hurry back to where they were formed. 'Everyone else's presents were so inventive and personal.'

'It was nice,' said Mary. 'It's a nice diary. Handy. For a handbag.'

'I couldn't think of what to wrap up for you. Well, for anyone really. So whoever I picked out of the hat would have probably got the diary.'

That didn't quite come out the way he'd expected it to. He should have said that he was terrible at picking presents so it might have been the easiest option, but for anyone else it wouldn't have held the same meaning, it wouldn't have symbolised their most excellent qualities as it did with her. Mary's hand slipped and the mule bucked.

'One all,' she said. She really was doing the right thing, said a voice in her head, one that was standing there, arms folded and head shaking slowly from side to side with disbelief.

'I mean—'

'Charlie's book of life hacks was brilliant,' she spoke louder, cut off whatever useless crap he was going to come out with to mitigate what he had just said.

Jack picked up the pan and hung it carefully.

'Yes, I particularly liked, *Ships are safe in harbours but that's not why ships are built*. It's about comfort zones and reaching beyond them.'

Mary felt some heat in her cheeks, willed it to go away. Had he drawn the right conclusion from what she'd said last night when she'd been half asleep in front of the fire? Did he suspect that she planned to desert him, hand in her notice and leave her currant- and sultana-filled comfort-zone harbour to work for a property magnate in another county?

'Why did you give Robin your bracelet? Was there a hidden meaning?'

'A friend gave it to me after my father passed; a reminder that whenever I needed someone to talk to, I should ring her and she'd be there for me.'

'And did she keep that promise?'

'She did. As I shall be there for Robin when he needs a friend.'

Jack smiled. 'That's incredibly generous of you, Mary. Such a thoughtful gift to give someone.'

She used to love the way he said her name. He elongated the 'a', an ever so slight roll on the 'r', the 'y' became more of an 'e' than an 'i'. It made her sound like a lady, a countess, someone who wore a crown.

'And thank you for the Christmas present you gave to me in the office, it was very kind of you,' he went on. 'I haven't opened it yet so I don't know what it is. It's waiting at home. I was saving it for Christmas Day.'

She always took ages to source something to give to him for Christmas; this time she'd bought him a travel kit for overnight hotel stays. It was a mini hard-shell suitcase and had an atomiser for cologne, a soap pump, razor, nail clippers, scissors, a styptic pencil, even an emergency flannel that folded into a tiny magic square of material. It was a gift perfectly matched to him.

'I hope you like it. It took me quite some time to find.' She couldn't resist emphasising the trouble she'd taken, the thought.

'Did you open your present from me?'

'Yes, thank you.' Though the least said about that the better. She picked up the plastic guitar, added it to the mule's load.

'Remind me, what . . . what did I buy you for Christmas?' said Jack then.

He couldn't even remember. This decision to go was just getting easier and easier, thought Mary as Jack attached the gun holster to the saddle.

'A tartan shopping bag, a matching headscarf and a box of jellied fruits,' she said, imbuing the words with contemptuous neutrality.

'What? Did I?' said Jack. His mind rewound to the conversation they'd all had about crap Christmas presents and how jellied fruits were right up there with the worst of them. He swallowed. 'What did I buy you last Christmas, can you remember?'

Did he go shopping in a trance, Mary wondered.

'Erm . . . a folding rain hat and a colossal jar of mint imperials,' she answered him.

'What?' His eyebrows were low, knotting together in the middle. 'And the year before?'

'A Flowers of the Valley talcum powder trio and a box of clotted cream fudge.'

Jack visualised the presents as if they were laid out in front of him in all their frumpy glory. He let out a long breath of annoyance before speaking again. 'I've never known what to buy you, Mary, so since you came to work for me, I've always asked Kimberley to choose your presents on my behalf. She said she knew what you'd like.'

Well that explained it, thought Mary. *Bloody Kimberley.* She'd always had a chip on her shoulder and she'd climb over everyone to be first in the queue for the coveted position of Jack's new PA as soon as it became vacant. It might have explained it, but it didn't excuse it.

Mary picked up the dynamite, balanced it expertly.

'Your turn, Jack.'

She flicked her eyes up to him and he thought that they really were beautiful: the colour of a blue lagoon with just a hint of green, with thick dark eyelashes. How could he have worked with her for so long and never noticed? How many other things had he missed from seeing only work in his line of vision? He was more of his father's son than he wanted to be. He should have checked what Kimberley had bought and wrapped for Mary. Actually no, he should have chosen something himself for the woman who gave him the idea for vegan scones, who had the guts to tell him the ones he produced were awful, who reached out to him when his dad had died to comfort him, only for him to snub her, as his father would have done to a 'silly young thing'.

'Mary, I promise you, I shall have some severe words with Kimberley when we get back to work. I don't know what she was thinking of.'

He sounded cross and she was sure he would take Kimberley to task, but she wouldn't be there to see what she got for a present next year from him.

'Don't even give it another thought,' said Mary sweetly.

'Gather round everyone, we have a nice pot of tea for you all,' Charlie announced as Bridge followed him in with a tray and so called a halt to their game. Just as the mule kicked off Jack's addition of the water canteen, which looked remarkably like the sort of frumpy shopping bag that Kimberley had bought for Mary.

*

They all sat around the fire, drinking tea and listening to Radio Brian, who was now rabbiting on with tips for what to do with leftover Christmas food and booze.

'Who has leftover booze at Christmas?' said Robin. 'We don't, do we, Charlie?'

'Not so much as a dreg of Cherry B,' Charlie replied. 'Talking of which, any cherries around?'

'I'll get you one from the bar,' said Luke, and sprang up to bring him a cherry on a cocktail stick. Or two, as it happened.

Charlie popped them in his mug and Bridge made an 'ugh' noise.

'My tablets play havoc with my tastebuds,' he explained. 'I've had some very weird cravings the past couple of weeks, haven't I, Robin?'

'He has. I did wonder at one point if he might be pregnant,' replied Robin.

Mary didn't say that the same thing had happened to her dad. He developed an obsession for bacon, burnt to a crisp and dipped in vinegar. She didn't say it because her dad was very near the end then. It was like a switch going on, weird cravings revving up. Jelly cubes rolled in salt, toast slathered in mayonnaise. He didn't even like mayonnaise usually.

'Whatever lights your candle, Charles,' said Luke.

'... my wife and I like a turkey curry,' Radio Brian announced to them. 'And my friend Malcolm makes frugal soup from the outer layer leaves that you strip off your sprouts. He says it's delicious.'

'Malcolm sounds like a laugh a minute,' was Robin's response to that.

'It's minus two outside but it will feel like minus ten,' said Radio Brian.

'All the more reason to stay within arm's length of this glorious fire,' said Bridge.

Luke cast his eye towards the log basket. 'I think we need some more wood from the shed.'

'I'll come with you,' said Mary.

'You will not,' said Charlie. 'Not while there are young, hunky men around.'

'This is the age of sexual equality, Charlie,' Mary said, wagging her finger.

Charlie wouldn't have it though.

'Women and men cannot be equal, there are too many biological differences. Men cannot bear children and women cannot grow beards.'

'I've been out with a few who could,' said Luke with a snort.

'All the lines are blurred these days, Charlie,' said Bridge. 'Best not to stray into that territory.'

'Charlie is right from a propriety perspective,' said Jack. 'I couldn't sit here while a lady is braving the elements on my behalf. I'll come with you, Luke.'

'Lady, eh?' said Bridge, quirking her eyebrow at Mary when Jack and Luke had gone out. Mary didn't respond. It was just a word, it meant nothing.

Jack had to put his shoulder to the door of the log-store because it appeared to have frozen in the jamb. It gave after the second mighty heave and Jack went flying through it and landed on the wood pile. 'Yep, this is the way my day is going,' he sighed, as Luke helped him up.

'Why's that? I thought we were all having a good one.'

'I've been giving Mary probably the world's worst Christmas presents. Headscarves and tartan shopping bags, old-lady toiletries, mint imperials. And jellied fruits.'

'Good God, man, she's twenty-five, not one hundred and five. Why did you buy her those?'

'I ... er ... actually I charged someone else with the task of buying something suitable for her,' came the answer.

'Wow, what a bitch,' said Luke with a crooked grin of astonishment. 'Why didn't you just buy her something yourself? It's not that hard, even if you're the world's crappiest present-picker. A John Lewis voucher never fails to hit the spot as a failsafe.'

Because you're your father's son, that's why, came an unwelcome voice in Jack's head.

'And if you must know, I'm feeling awfully ashamed of myself where Mary is concerned. Quite a few things have come to light over the past few days.'

'Like what?'

'This is going to sound really bad.'

'Try me,' said Luke.

Jack took a deep breath. 'I have patronised her,' he said, with the same tone someone might have employed to confess that they had shagged a zebra.

Luke waited for more and when nothing was forthcoming he waved his hands in the air as if to encourage the 'more' to come out.

'I've treated her as if she was a young woman who should really stick to what she was paid to do and not as someone with a brain capable of working outside the parameters of her job.'

'For instance?' asked Luke; the disclosure didn't exactly shock him.

'Do you know, Luke, it was Mary's idea that the company should make vegan scones. I remember thinking at the time when she suggested it, *Thank you, but you'll find I know more*

*about all this than you do and can you please ring the dry-cleaner
and ask if my suit is ready to be picked up.'*

'Yep, that really is patronising,' said Luke, nodding.

Jack cringed. 'Then vegan scones hit the market, were an
absolute wow, and our head of product development said we
should follow suit. We could have led, not followed, if I'd
listened to Mary. But we weren't too late, thank the lord,
and they were a massive hit ... and I gave product development the credit for the idea.'

'Ouch,' said Luke.

'It gets better – or rather, worse. The vegan scones wer-
en't good enough at first and it was Mary, not the bakery
team, who told me we needed to revisit the recipe. And
she suggested we use red cheese instead of white so the
cheese scones would look more obviously "cheesy" and she
suggested we make luxury short-life ranges exclusive to
high-end stores. All of these were brilliant ideas.'

'All of these brilliant ideas from the mind of a young
woman who shouldn't be thinking outside her box?' Luke
suggested to him. Jack couldn't bear to see himself mirrored
in those words.

'And there's more ...'

'You're kidding,' said Luke, which didn't help.

'I wasn't as sympathetic as I could ... *should* have been
when her father died. I asked the same woman who bought
the presents to enquire when Mary would be returning to
work. I did tell her to say there was no rush, but it appears
she left out that part of the email.'

'*Bitch* is too kind a word, I think.'

'Yes, quite. Then last year my own father died and
Mary was ... was kindness itself. Held the fort while I
was off.' He gave the front of his head a rub of angst. 'I've

just had the most awful, uncomfortable game of Buckaroo with her.'

Luke snorted, tried not to laugh, covered it up as a cough.

'I said all the wrong things. I can't even repeat what I said about that bloody diary.' A growl of frustration. 'Anyway, after our conversation last night I decided to take the bull by the horns and I went into Mary's room and I wrote in the diary that I'd like to take her out to dinner.'

'Blimey,' said Luke, knocked back by that. 'I'm impressed.' And he was. Hardly the most direct approach, but for Jack it was leaps and bounds.

'Luke, over the past few days, I've felt as if I'm viewing Mary through other people's eyes. Everyone likes her and respects her here, don't they? And she's such a lovely person. Why have I seen her and yet not *seen* her before?'

'You're seeing her now,' said Luke, opening up a sack and starting to throw logs into it. 'Better late than never.'

'I don't want to be my father. I never realised until I came here how much I was like him. I don't want to be that man.'

'Then don't be him,' said Luke. 'Simple as that.'

'I want what you have with Carmen and what Bridge has with her new man. I want to be as loved-up as Charlie and Robin. I want someone to smile at me the way they smile at each other.'

'Yep, it's good. It's worth having,' said Luke and smiled at the thought of what he had with Carmen.

'I almost kissed Mary yesterday, you know, after we were carol-singing. I looked at her in that huge coat and those ridiculous wellingtons and I wanted to pick her up and plant my lips on hers.'

'Then maybe you should have, Jack,' said Luke.

'I don't know what she feels about me.'

'I don't either,' replied Luke. It wasn't his place to make it easy for him. Jack needed to learn first-hand from Charlie's life hack that he should meet the requirements of his requirements. Everyone deserved as much.

Chapter 30

When Jack and Luke got back in, there was no one around.

'We're up here, looking at pictures,' called Robin from upstairs.

Jack and Luke took off their coats and wellies, piled up a few logs at the side of the fire to season them and joined the others. They were checking out the photos framed and hung on the walls. Not only photos though as there were also yellowing pages taken from an old book, the title of which could be seen in small ornate lettering at the top.

History of Figgy Hollow Hamlet of Yorkshire

'Hiffftory of Figgy Hollow of Yorkfffyer,' Mary struggled while reading aloud.

'Be careful putting "f"s where "s"s should be,' Robin warned her. 'You can get yourself into all sorts of trouble.'

'It sounds like it's been written by Radio Brian,' said Charlie and chortled.

'I give up, I can't make out the lettering even with my glasses on,' said Robin, taking them off and slipping them back into his shirt breast pocket while stepping out of the way so that Luke could get closer to read.

'Fays here that Figgy Hollow waf an Anglo Faxon fettlement,' said Luke.

'Ah, "hollow" means "valley",' said Bridge, reading sensibly.

'"Valley of figf"?' questioned Luke. 'I wonder if it was originally *Valley of cigs* then. Maybe Figgy Hollow is where all the Vikings got their duty-free fags from.'

'Stop being an arse, just for a little while please,' said Bridge, even though she could see Robin, Mary and Charlie giggling like toddlers who had just heard the word *fart*.

She read on, expertly translating the 'f's into 's's where it was appropriate to do so: '"The name Figgy Hollow is said to originate from the production of fig plants brought over by the Romans and farmed from the thirteenth century by monks in the nearby monastery. The valley, i.e. hollow, and tributary stream gave perfect sheltered and watering conditions for the figs to flourish and the monks both traded in the harvested fruits in the markets along the east coast and made *figgy beer*, wine, and brandy." Ah, so figgy really does mean *from the fig* then. "The monastery was destroyed by troops of Henry the eighth in 1540, but the industry endured. The stone was reclaimed to build local houses, the old inn and, in 1641, the church of St Stephen, which stands on the site of the wasted monastery."'

'How fascinating,' said Charlie.

'I bet the monks were wasted as well with all that figgy booze,' joked Robin.

'Maybe those cottages were once filled with workers who used to reap the fig harvest and tread on them, or whatever you do with figs destined for bottles,' said Luke. 'I shouldn't think it's still going as a local delicacy, though, I haven't heard of it.' And he would have, at a food fair.

'I wonder if the church owns all the buildings, then?' said Bridge, cogs turning in her head.

'You'd buy it?' asked Luke, instinctively knowing where her thinking was going.

'If the price was right. With a bit of TLC, it could be one of those places that turns up on the prettiest villages pages on Pinterest. Like Cockington or Bibury.'

If the photos were anything to go by, Figgy Hollow was very pretty once upon a time, with its central stream and tiny village green. The church and nearby run of cottages appeared to have been designed by an architect who'd discovered a secret cache of figgy brandy before he'd picked up his drawing tools, but the overall effect was quaint and perfectly imperfect.

There were foxed sepia photos of children playing on the green; a man with a huge moustache, in a smart waistcoat, standing proudly outside the inn, smoking a clay pipe. An elderly lady in a bonnet and shawl sitting in a wicker bath-chair outside one of the cottages; a soldier in uniform by the bridge with a bride in a long white dress holding a posy. He had one leg and a crutch held under his arm, an older woman and a man at the other side of him, dated 1918 at the bottom.

'Fascinating,' said Mary. 'He must have come back from the war and married his sweetheart. Poor man.'

'Marriage isn't that bad, Mary,' teased Luke.

'I mean poor man because he lost his leg, not because he'd got married,' replied Mary, giving him a playful nudge.

'Here's some later ones,' said Robin, following the wall around to where there was a series of colour photos with subjects reflecting the fashions of the era. A group shot of giggling women in miniskirts, then two men with mullets and flares, another bride and groom, this time both sporting mad eighties perms. And the last of them, a grinning gent in an enormous jumper with an impressive browny-grey combover and a short, portly woman wearing an apron. They were standing outside the cottage furthest away from the church, their feet planted in snow.

'Figgy brandy sounds fantastic,' said Charlie, licking his lips.

Bridge, however, was thinking what an opportunity to not only inject new life into this part-time patch of Yorkshire, but resurrect an ancient industry as well. Exciting, very exciting.

Charlie's stomach gave a grumble and Bridge offered to knock up some sandwiches. Mary said she'd help. She buttered silently, things clearly on her mind, so Bridge let her get on with the job without trying to drag her into conversation. Mary would talk to her if she wanted, but it looked as though she needed some thinking time. She had some not-so-small changes to plan for.

They delivered lunch to the others who were listening to Radio Brian, who was thrilling his audience with some advice on what to do with unwanted Christmas presents.

'I know some people around here who donate them to local charities as they're always looking for things to raffle. My friend Malcolm saves them in his shed and gives them to other people for presents the following Christmas. He has a notebook to record who gave him what so he doesn't end up passing the same present back.'

'I could have guessed his friend Malcolm would be like that, I really could,' said Bridge.

Radio Brian continued. 'Now me, I couldn't do that. I take mine to the Maud Haworth Home for Cats, but I can tell you that if I get stuff like jellied fruits, they go straight in the bin because no one wants to win those on a tombola, do they?' And he chuckled at the very idea.

Mary didn't move a muscle but out of the corner of her eye she saw Jack shift uncomfortably in his armchair.

'So, lots of practical ideas there for your unwanted gifts,' said Radio Brian.

'Thank you, Brian,' said Luke, munching on a cheese and pickle breadcake.

'Present-buying is very simple, I've never understood why it's such an ordeal for some people,' said Charlie, shaking his head impatiently. 'A gift carries a message and that message should always be one that shows appreciation, whether it's for a service or love or friendship. If you don't care enough to put some thought into it, you shouldn't bother at all.'

Jack hadn't blushed since he was five, but he found his cheeks heating up faster than halogen rings on a hob.

'Bridge used to buy the best presents,' said Luke. 'Every year she used to give me a stocking full of things from pound shops, joke shops and car boot sales.'

'In other words, crap,' said Bridge, though she'd underplayed it because she'd taken a lot of time to select things that would make him laugh, hoot, smile. Things that were great to open but had no use: a fart in a bottle, a jelly spider that crawled down the wall, a stress ball that you could draw the face of your worst enemy onto.

'I liked them,' he replied.

'Anyone for some mulled cider? We still have plenty left,' Jack asked, eager to move the conversation away from unsuitable gifts.

'Oh yes,' said Charlie, 'and bring some mince pies, Jack. I haven't quite filled up on them yet.'

'Righty-ho, Captain Charlie,' said Jack, heading towards the kitchen.

Mary watched him walk away and a dull ache filled her heart. It would be hard not working for him any more. The prospect of change scared her slightly because it would be a *big* change, big changes plural, actually. She'd have to move house as well as start a new job and she wouldn't be ten minutes' drive away from her mum any more. But Charlie's life hack: *Ships are safe in harbours but that's not why ships are built* had struck a chord with her as well as Jack.

She suspected 'working Bridge' would be a little more serious than 'stranded in an inn Bridge' but that was fine. Mary had faith in her abilities as a competent and reliable PA and she was ready to impress a new boss, one that didn't give her any romantic complications. But she'd really miss the world of scones. Okay, so her office desk was from last-century MFI and her window looked out onto the bin store. And the catering facilities were sadly lacking, i.e. a hatch in a wall from where drinks, prepacked sandwiches and buttered scones were dispensed by a grumpy old woman called Edna, who had been there so long that many believed the place had been built around her. But the people who worked there were fun and friendly, apart from shitty Kimberley and the slimy head of product development, who liked to take credit for ideas that weren't his. Banter flowed in the packing area, it batted between the workers, many of whom had worked together for decades because there was something that kept people at Butterly's. It was like a home to their hearts, as it was to hers.

While Bridge was in the shower that morning, she'd written

a letter of resignation on a sheet of Figgy Hollow headed paper that she'd found in the drawer of the dressing table.

26th December

Dear Mr Butterly
    Please will you take this letter as notice of my resignation. I realise that I do have to work a notice period but have holidays untaken which could be offset against it, so I would like to be released at your earliest convenience in order to enable me to start my new position.
    I have greatly enjoyed my time at Butterly's and wish you and the company all the very best for the future.

Yours sincerely
Mary H.C. Padgett.

It was straight and to the point, no emotional content. She wouldn't waste any more of that on Jack Butterly.

Everyone was singing 'The Twelve Days of Christmas' along to the radio when Jack walked back into the lounge carrying first, a plate of warmed mince pies, then on his second trip, the pan of cider and a ladle. Someone had got the glass cups out in readiness from behind the bar.

'Come on Jack, join in for the last bars,' said Luke. 'We're all singing a line clockwise round. *Five go-hold riiinnngggsss.*'

Robin covered his ears. Luke really did have the most appalling singing voice.

'. . . And a partridge in a pear tree,' they all sang together, Jack included, and applauded themselves.

'We thought we'd build up a bit of a thirst,' said Robin.

'And some more facts about Christmas that you might not be aware of,' said Radio Brian. 'Did you know that Boxing Day gets its name from the money collected in boxes in churches to give to the poor on this day? And servants were allowed to go home after they'd looked after their employers on Christmas Day and these rich people would box up presents for them to take to their families, although hopefully no jellied fruits.' Brian laughed heartily and Jack thought that he was pushing this jellied fruits joke too far now.

'. . . And tradition has it you should eat at least one mince pie on each of the twelve days of Christmas for luck.'

'I like that idea,' said Charlie.

'. . . And Rudolf's red nose could be the result of a parasitic infection of his respiratory system.'

'Brian, that's gross,' Bridge wrinkled her nose up in revulsion.

'How can a fictional reindeer have a parasitic infection?' asked Luke. 'It's like saying Snow White has crabs.'

'Dirty bint,' said Robin. 'I always thought she seemed too whiter than white to be true.'

'I'm sure this cider has grown more potent overnight,' said Bridge, taking a glug. 'For the record, I'm not complaining.'

Luke bowed in his seat. 'Thank you, madam.'

'Are you going to be doing a Plant Boy mulled drinks range then, Luke?' asked Mary.

'I very much doubt it. It's all about getting healthier and I'm not sure my diet over the past few days fits in with the Plant Boy manifesto.'

'Well I feel the best I have in ages,' said Charlie. He certainly matched his claim with his pink cheeks and bright eyes; even his hair seemed thicker and lusher. Sitting regally in the armchair, he looked every inch the subject of a Renaissance portrait in oils.

'How many of you listeners have popped the question at Christmastime, or even got married at Christmas?' asked Radio Brian. 'I married my wife in the heat of August's blaze, hoping for a guarantee of good weather but it absolutely threw it down with rain. We were drenched.'

'Bridge and I got married at Christmas,' said Luke.

'Did you? And was it lovely and romantic?' asked Robin.

'Depends what your definition of romantic is,' said Bridge. 'The registrar had a really snotty cold and Luke's foster grandad couldn't find his braces and his trousers kept falling down.'

'My suit came from a supermarket, Bridge's dress came from the PDSA charity shop.'

'I made my bouquet from plastic flowers bought in Poundstretcher.'

'We had our reception in the Little Mermaid fish and chip shop. Six of us. Us two, the best man, my foster dad, foster mum and her father.'

'We went to a beautiful hotel in Matlock for our one-night honeymoon, which Luke's lot paid for.' The bed was enormous. *Enough room for an orgy*, Bridge remembered Luke saying as they sat in it drinking house champagne and eating complimentary popcorn.

'It was a bloody brilliant wedding,' said Luke. 'Snow fell like confetti when we were having the pics taken outside; the Salvation Army were playing carols and we washed the fish and chips down with pots and pots of tea and a bottle of their finest Liebfraumilch. God, we felt so sophisticated drinking that.'

He looked across at Bridge, and just for a moment, she

saw the Luke she had married, the young, gawky kid with the cheeky grin and wonky front teeth – now fixed and whitened. The boy who had made her heart thump and her body sigh for more.

'We had all the key ingredients there to make a wedding happy,' said Bridge, with feeling. *Us. In love. Two against the world. Planning a future together.* She felt a swell of emotion rise in her like a tidal wave and she braced herself against it washing her away, taking her to shores where old broken memories lay like driftwood.

'Sounds perfect,' said Charlie, smiling benignly at them.

'But that was then and this is now,' Bridge said, breezily, like a schoolmistress telling her pupils to chop-chop. 'It was a long, long time ago.'

'In a galaxy far, far away,' added Luke. Because their past was that far away. And in another galaxy.

Chapter 31

Robin realised he'd drunk too much of that damned cider when he walked up the stairs to get Charlie's tablet. He hadn't got full control of his limbs, that was for sure. He sat down on the bed for a few moments to steady himself. He could have quite happily lain on it and taken a nap, but he didn't want to miss a moment of this lovely day. He was glad they'd found this place, these people. Aviemore wouldn't have been a patch on Figgy Hollow. Charlie wouldn't have revelled, laughed, relaxed as much there as he had here, despite the best champagnes, the caviar, the seven-course Christmas lunch and entertainment, spa, sauna.

He caught sight of his own reflection in the dressing-table mirror and saw that he was smiling. No wonder, he was a lucky man. Who would have thought when he'd been thrown out of his home with a couple of changes of clothing that he – Robin Raymond – would have the life he had. He and Charlie had summered in Monte Carlo, had dinner with Frank Sinatra in Las Vegas, posed artfully by the Taj Mahal like Princess Diana. One lifetime wasn't enough with Charlie, though. There were still so many things they hadn't done: gone down a Siberian salt mine, spent a night in the Four Seasons Hotel in Moscow, met Celine Dion. But they had re-enacted that iconic 'I'm flying' scene from *Titanic* aboard an American billionaire friend's private yacht in the Maldives, featuring Charlie as Kate Winslet and Robin as Leonardo DiCaprio.

'*Robin, I'm flying.*' Charlie's arms held out like a crucifix, Robin behind him holding on to his waist, warning him to stop leaning forwards or he'd end up falling overboard and straight into the jaws of a great white. Robin closed his eyes, picturing the scene. He could hear Charlie's excited voice so clearly. 'Robin, look at me.'

Robin opened his eyes. Charlie's voice was not in his head.

'Robin, look at me. ROBIN.'

Robin pulled himself off the bed and rushed onto the landing. Bridge was standing by the window at the top of the stairs looking outside.

'Robbbiiinnn.'

She beckoned Robin quickly to her side. He had to do a double-take at what he was seeing.

'Look at him, the bloody idiot.' Charlie was lying in the snow, arms and legs moving outwards and inwards. Robin opened the window and yelled through it. 'What the fucking hell are you doing, Charles Glaser?'

'I'm making angels,' said Charlie. He struggled to his feet, chuckling at himself before lying down again next to his imprint and repeating the action. He got up then to show Robin his pair of perfect angels pressed into the snow before falling backwards once more.

'I'm going for a holy trinity.'

'Don't come crying to me when you get hypothermia and I'm supposed to thaw you out with hot water bottles,' Robin shouted down.

'I don't care, I'm enjoying myself. Come on, Annie,' Charlie shouted up, his voice brimming with glee.

'I'm on my way,' Robin said, shutting the window, but he carried on standing there, watching Charlie flapping his limbs, his brain recording this precious memory in the making.

Bridge sensed this, put her arm around him, felt a great sigh leave his body.

'You know, Bridge, he used to be twice the size he is now,' said Robin. 'He was a huge man when I met him, solid as the rock of Gibraltar, a *bon vivant*. He didn't age for twenty-five years, I thought he was an immortal, a god among men, but that bloody disease has taken him bit by bit, pound by pound from me. I've tried to be strong, for Charlie, but I can't bear that one day soon he won't be there any more. What am I going to do without that ridiculous old fart, Bridge? He's my world, my everything.'

Tears tripped down his cheeks unhindered, he just let them fall, one after another.

Bridge didn't know what to say. She'd never lost any person who was close to her but she'd been hollowed out by grief when her dog had died. It had been as if something had reached within and scooped her insides out and kept coming back for more until she was completely scraped empty, and then it filled the space with hard jarring rocks that hurt when she breathed.

'All I can do, Robin, is roll out the platitudes,' said Bridge. 'Grief is a tough road to travel and a lonely one. Time is a great healer . . . like I say, all the usual clichés. I know that's of absolutely no help. Enjoy the here and now, like Charlie obviously is; don't think ahead too much and miss it.'

Robin sniffed his unspent tears back, dragged his hands

down his face to dry the escapees. 'I think I can just about get my head around part one: that he'll die. We'll have a funeral, I'll do the paperwork, people will come and visit and we'll all have a cry and I'll be strong, because I'll have to be since despite how much of a wreck I look, I'm prepared … *we* are prepared for the inevitable. But it's part two that I'm not ready for, Bridge: that I won't ever see him again. I'll have to live out the rest of my life without him in it. He won't be there when I wake up, I won't be able to kiss him goodnight. I'll lose half of myself when he goes.'

'Cross every bridge when you come to it, Robin. Don't try and rehearse it in your head, it won't do you any good.'

'Robbbiiinnn.' A yell from below. 'Where the bloody hell are you?'

'Go on, squeeze every moment out of this Christmas. Make it count,' said Bridge.

Mary sprinted up the stairs, met them at the top.

'Come on, get your coats on, you two. If you can't beat them, you know what they say.'

When Robin, Bridge and Mary got outside it was to find Charlie stomping all over the virgin snow just like he used to go mud-sploshing with his mum in his red wellies. Jack and Luke were lying side by side in the snow flapping their limbs also making angels; they were even sharing tips.

'If you put your arm at ninety degrees and only flap up, then leave a bank of snow, then flap down, your angel will have arms as well as wings,' said Jack.

'Okay, let's do this,' said Luke.

Mary could not quite equate this Jack with the one who strutted from meeting to meeting, furrows of concentration wrinkling his brow, a constant down-turned cast to his mouth. He should drink mulled cider more often.

They were all dressed in Robin's and Charlie's coats and boots, which fitted the men a little more snugly than the women. Bridge was lost inside Charlie's scarlet fleece, Mary buried alive in Robin's green hoodie. They looked ridiculous and cared not a jot.

Bridge glanced over at Charlie and felt overcome with emotion. He looked like an old young boy, kicking snow up in sprays. Nevertheless, she picked up a handful of snow, patted it into a ball and threw it at him. It landed squarely on his back.

'You little minx,' he shouted, bent, rolled up some snow and retaliated. It fell short onto Jack's midriff. Mary threw one at Bridge and it exploded in her face.

'Ow. Mary, where's your female solidarity?'

'Every woman for herself,' Mary returned.

'Right, miss. You asked for it.'

Jack and Luke scrambled to their feet, began to make snowballs and launch them at any human target. The air was thick with missiles and squeals and groans as the snow burst on shoulders, exploding into eyes and mouths. They all seemed to collapse from exhaustion together, breathless from the cold, the laughter, the effort.

'I'm absolutely pooped,' said Robin, checking how Charlie was, and discovering he seemed to be the most alive out of all of them.

'We can't go inside without building a snowman,' said Mary, remembering that Charlie had professed a wish to do this and a thaw was on its way. 'Come on, folks. Loser makes dinner.'

'Help me up, Bridge.' Luke held his hand out and Bridge

pulled back, her hand slipped and she ended up splatting backwards in the snow herself. She was laughing too much to get up and for a while she and Luke lay there like a pair of overturned turtles.

Jack and Mary were already well advanced, rolling up a snowman head and body when they did eventually manage to achieve a standing position. Luke sprang into action, scraped together a ball and began to push it forwards.

'Stop copying our technique,' called Jack.

'Sue me for copyright, you posh arse,' Luke called back.

'Wouldn't it be ironic if we went home and forgot to sign the divorce papers,' said Luke to Bridge, as she began to shape some shoulders into the white mass of snow.

'It would. We should do it tonight and get it over with. It'll only take a couple of minutes.'

'Yes, okay.'

'I'm just glad we got there in the end,' said Luke, hefting the snowman's too-large round head onto his body.

'Football head,' mused Bridge, standing back to admire it. 'Remind you of anyone?' Then she punched it straight in the middle where the nose should be and made a fist-shaped hollow.

'I didn't, you know,' said Luke, suddenly serious. 'Tina lied. I didn't even touch her.'

'It doesn't matter any more.'

'Yes it does. I need you to believe me because it's the truth.'

'If I do that, it makes what I did to get back at you totally unforgivable.'

'Forget it, Bridge. You were right about her, she was poisonous. We were both played like cheap guitars.'

She nodded slowly. 'Okay, I believe you.' It was hard for

her to say and he knew that, because it meant her shoulders were weighted with more blame.

'Good. Thank you.'

Bridge fashioned 'Football Head' the snowman a very fat nose.

'They stuck together you know, Tina and James,' said Luke.

'No fucking way.' Bridge's jaw dropped to her knees.

'I don't keep in touch with them, in case you're wondering. I heard from a mutual friend. They renewed their vows to wipe the slate clean and ended up having a full-on fight in the church. The police had to be called.'

Bridge tried to close up her gloaty smile, but didn't put that much effort into it. 'Couldn't happen to a nicer couple. I hope they stay together forever. I can't think of a worse punishment.'

'Me neither.'

Bridge fashioned a pair of inflated snow lips for Football Head.

'Some things you can't stick back together again,' she said. 'So why bother trying?'

She said it but she doubted her own words. If this Bridge were single and this Luke were single, maybe, just maybe, the glue that once held them might have been reactivated.

'Does our snowman remind you of anyone?' asked Jack.

Thin flat line of a mouth, piggy little eyes, nose like a blob of Play-Doh, pair of pneumatic boobs. 'Nope,' Mary replied. Subconsciously she'd been sculpting a snow Kimberley, but she would deny it if asked.

Jack coughed, prepared to say something that the cider had loosened from its holdings.

'Mary, I would just like to say that I truly appreciate all you've done for the company. I know that the vegan scones were your idea and I never gave you credit for them.'

Mary paused from smoothing down the snowwoman's neck, then carried on. It was only the cider talking, she decided.

'Thank you,' she said eventually.

'And for so many other suggestions you've made that have helped the business. Helped me.'

'Oh, okay.'

'I was thinking that er . . . when we get back, maybe . . . you might er . . . consider . . .'

Mary's breath went into suspension. Her heart literally stopped beating.

The length of the pause was ridiculous, tantamount to the length of pause when the host of *Love Island* was about to announce who was getting chucked off.

'. . . a pay rise.'

Mary's heart started up again, a heavy compacted thump, like a racehorse landing on the turf after flying over Becher's Brook. Disappointment rumbled through every cell and sinew in her body, before quickly segueing into annoyance, then it gathered speed and galloped on into full-blown anger.

'Jack, there's something I have to tell you,' she said. 'I'm not coming back. I've been offered another job and I'm going to take it.'

The cider had loosened her tongue too.

'Talk about the abominable snowman,' said Robin, stepping back to admire their handiwork. Their snowman was hideous, with a shrunken head and a scrawny neck, but at least classily dressed with Charlie's Chanel scarf knotted loosely at his throat. 'Who does he remind me of, I wonder?'

'He looks not unlike Daniel. My possible replacement,' said Charlie, tilting his head to study their creation.

'He's got much more personality than Daniel,' said Robin. 'And at least he's not boring us to death with his comparisons between the present prime minister and Ted Heath.'

Charlie bent, fashioned a snow sausage and stuck it on the snowman's groin, adding a snowball at either side.

'Better?'

'Yes, he's slightly more attractive now.'

'Don't be lonely, Robin,' said Charlie.

'Very kind of you to think about me, but I'm exploring the possibility of becoming a celibate. I think I'd look fetching in a nun's habit. A wimple would frame my face beautifully.'

Charlie chuckled.

'I'm so glad we didn't go to Aviemore.'

Robin smiled. 'I agree with you, for once. How are we going to better it for New Year? Shall I invite them all down for a party? I will ask for their addresses before we go to bed tonight.'

'Yes, do keep in touch with them,' said Charlie. 'I'd like them to come to my funeral.'

Robin opened his mouth to retaliate with a 'shut up', but he felt Charlie needed to be listened to now.

'I'm sure we could run to a few extra Gregg's sausage rolls.'

'Thank you.'

'Right, right,' said Jack, trying to process this shock of new information.

'I've written you a letter. I was going to give it to you

when we got back home. I've been at Butterly's since I left college and I think it's time for pastures new and I'd like to start as soon as possible.' Mary thumped a lump out of the snowman's back, her actions channelling all the feelings that her calm voice wasn't.

'I see.' Jack's thoughts were racing in panic mode, like motorcycles around a Wall of Death. Could he honestly blame Mary for seeking pastures new after he'd treated her so much less appreciatively than he should have? She was young and clever and lovely and all he'd done to her for four years was to treat her like his father treated people. Of course she wouldn't be interested in him romantically. Of course she wouldn't want him to wine and dine her in Firenze. What had he been thinking of, writing his invitation in the diary? He trusted she hadn't seen it yet. What an idiot he was. He had stepped out of his comfort zone, got burned and now it was time to retreat, hopefully with a little dignity.

'Well, the very best of luck to you, Mary. I'll agree to your terms, it's the least I can do,' Jack said and held out his hand to shake hers.

His grip was firm; her hand sat inside it as limp as a dead fish.

Chapter 32

'Robin, will you add five pounds to the money we owe the landlord, I'm going to take this book home with me,' said Charlie, holding up the copy of *Persuasion*.

'If you want,' said Robin, changing into a dry pair of trousers. 'It's a bit worse for wear though. You could buy a new one for that.'

'No, I want this one,' said Charlie. 'I have plans for it.'

'Sounds very Secret Seven. Am I allowed to ask?'

'You'll find out soon enough,' said Charlie, tapping the side of his nose. 'I have enjoyed dipping into it again. It's brought back some very happy memories for me. Everyone should read this book, it's full of life lessons.'

'You and your life lessons! Like what?'

'Well, no one should ever settle for anything less than their Anne Elliot or their Captain Wentworth.'

'Granted.'

'And that you can have a happy ending, even when you've given up hope of it. As I had.'

'If you're lucky,' said Robin. Charlie was more of a romantic than he was.

'Do you think Jack knows Mary is carrying a torch for him? Should we tell him, Robin?'

'Absolutely not,' came the firm answer. 'If ever there was a strong woman who needed a strong man it's our little Mary; someone worthy of success and notice, which I'm not convinced she'd get from Jack. Not at the moment anyway. He needs firming up a bit.'

'I do like Jack and I think he feels something for Mary too,' said Charlie, dropping his volume to deliver his next words, 'but, sadly, he is more of a Corporal Wet-Wipe than a Captain Wentworth, isn't he?'

'Precisely, so no, let neither of us be persuaded to interfere, excuse the pun. Look what happened in the book when Lady Whatsername stuck her nose in. Jack's mid-thirties, not mid-teens. Who wants a Wentworth with no balls?'

'You're right, of course,' said Charlie.

'Again,' said Robin. 'Now let's go downstairs and feed you. It must be ten minutes since you last ate.'

'He said what?' Bridge asked Mary, as they were changing out of their snow-wet clothes upstairs in the bedroom.

'He wished me luck and shook my hand,' said Mary. 'After I turned down his pay rise.' She imbued the two words with all the contempt that they could carry.

'I have no words. Well, I have a few, but I wouldn't want to shatter your eardrums,' said Bridge. She had really started to take to Jack, but he was such a limp lettuce.

Mary shrugged. 'C'est la vie,' she said, her voice wavery. She sat down on the bed, wiped a flurry of involuntary tears from her eyes, beyond annoyed at their appearance. 'I'm dreading the journey home. It'll be filled with awkward, horrible silence.'

'I'll drive you home,' said Bridge. 'It would only be a short detour for me. No arguments, it's settled.'

Mary wasn't even going to put up any resistance. 'He said I didn't need to work my notice if I didn't want to.'

'Oh, Jack, you fucking arsehole,' said Bridge to the wall, as if the words would travel through it and into his posh twit earhole.

'I'm not expecting you to set me on as soon as we get back, Bridge, I just said I wanted to start straight away because it came out of my mouth before I could stop it.'

'Mary, when you're ready. My PA will welcome you with open arms because you'll take loads of pressure off her. And you can always stay with me for a while until you're sure you want to move permanently; try us out, so to speak. I've got six bedrooms in the house. I don't want to push you and yet at the same time I do, because I think you'd be a marvellous addition to my team.'

'Thank you, Bridge.' Despite her grateful smile, Mary both looked and sounded as felled as a spruce cut down for Christmas.

*

Bridge and Luke were designated cooks for the evening. Their snowman was by no means the ugliest, which had to be snow-Kimberley with the icy knockers and slit mouth, but Bridge volunteered them to save Mary being trapped in the tiny kitchen with Jack. Before they commenced cooking, there was one job to do upstairs, in private. The signing of the letters of intent so their divorce could go through uncontested. They had both agreed to a no-fault split, neither was claiming anything from the other.

'I thought you'd shaft me somehow in the eleventh hour,' said Luke, handing over his signed sheet with one hand, taking Bridge's from her with the other.

'I have. I signed it *Donald Duck*,' said Bridge.

Luke's head jerked and Bridge laughed, 'As if,' she said and Luke patted his heart in relief, grinned back at her.

They both looked down at the signatures on the forms. After five long years of a tornado-grade war, the winds of rage had softened to a gust, a breeze, a mere ruffle in the air. They were here, at the end of the ride. The end of an era.

'The deed is done,' said Bridge. She felt inexplicably sad, empty. A fat teardrop plopped out of her right eye and ran down her cheek. She flicked it away, aware that he'd seen it. 'Sorry, I don't know where that came from.'

'I feel it too,' said Luke, snapping a pale pastel tissue out of the box on his dressing table and handing it to her. 'We've been part of each other for so long.'

'The first cut is the deepest and all that.'

'Precisely.'

Bridge blew her nose. 'Thank you for all the love you gave me.'

'Thank you for kicking me up the bum,' said Luke, which made Bridge laugh. 'We are where we are now because of who we were then.'

'We are the manure on each other's prize-winning orchids.'

Luke took Bridge's hand, held it between his own. It felt so small, delicate, fragile.

'Bridge.' A sigh. 'I'm going to be a dad. No one knows yet. Well, obviously I do and Carmen and probably her family by now because we were going to make the big announcement yesterday. I wanted to tell you to your face before the news got out.'

Bridge smiled, a fresh flurry of tears falling at the same time. 'Ah, that is the best news, Luke. You will make a ... a brilliant father. I've always thought so. Even when you didn't. I couldn't be happier for you both.'

She felt something give inside her, something shift, as if a door stuck in the ajar position, in hope, had finally closed.

Luke pulled her towards him, his arms circled her. She felt a different shape, softer, more pliant than he remembered.

'Don't say no to thinking about adopting a child one day, Bridge. You'd make a fabulous mum.'

'You think?' said Bridge.

'I really do think. Some kid like we were would be so lucky to have you loving them. Promise me you won't rule it out.'

That hit her right in the chest cavity, bullseye in the heart. 'Thank you, that means a lot,' she said.

'And thank you,' he said. 'Thank you for being with me on part of my journey. Thank you for sharing plum tomatoes with me, throwing the broccoli at me, loving a dog with me, giving me the name Plant Boy and earning me enough to buy my gorgeous green Aston Martin.' He felt Bridge laugh into his shoulder. 'Thank you for it all. Be happy, Bridge.'

'And you, Plant Boy,' said Bridge.

They pulled apart, the gap between them small and at the same time as wide as a canyon.

He loved her still, a different love, a grateful love. The lazy gawky kid and the girl with fire for hair had burned each other up, and from the ashes came the people they were now. They were stepping stones in each other's lives to the Bridge and Luke of today. A Bridge and Luke who didn't belong together any more.

*

Radio Brian was grieving the end of Christmas.

'Of course it isn't over really until Twelfth Night, which is when you eat the last of the Quality Streets, the ones that you try and avoid when you've got a choice. In my case it's the Coffee Cream but my wife always leaves the Peanut Cracknel.'

'Blimey, it must be a while since they've had a tin,' Robin commented. 'Those flavours haven't been around for years.'

'. . . but I think most people these days wave goodbye to Christmas when Boxing Day is over and done with. The holiday adverts will be on the telly in a couple of days and I know that when we go shopping next, there will be Creme Eggs on the shelves. And did you know we have had them in our shops for twenty-three years?' Brian went on.

'Must be well over that,' said Jack. 'I remember buying them from the school tuck shop when I was ten and that's twenty-five years ago.'

'It's starting to thaw out there,' said Robin, standing by the window. He could see water drips making holes in the snow.

'No signal yet though,' said Mary, checking her mobile, which she'd left on the bar. The first chance it sparked into life, she would ring her brother, let him know she was okay. She picked up the landline phone, but it was still playing dead.

'For anyone who needs to follow the snow, it's heading to Scotland,' said Radio Brian. 'Night temperatures of five degrees are forecast for the area. I'll put this record on for the last time because it's one of my favourites. My wife and I have had such a lovely Christmas this year that I'd like it to go on for a bit longer. Thank you for listening. This is Radio Brian playing "I Wish It Could Be Christmas Everyday".'

A cash register sound, cow bells, children's voices, those all too familiar lyrics.

'Our last night together then, from the sounds of it,' said Mary.

'It's been a blast,' said Charlie, beaming. 'Our past Christmases in Austria would take some beating, but this one has been my favourite of all time.'

Luke and Bridge came in from the kitchen half-walking, half-dancing, singing along to Roy Wood and Wizzard on the radio, carrying plates full of savouries, pickles, sandwiches and mince pies. Mary thought they both looked different somehow, smilier, lighter. They looked like friends.

They sat contentedly around the fire, tucking in to the last Christmas feast. Then Robin passed his phone around, asked them to tap in their addresses and numbers.

'Looks like we'll be going home tomorrow. Radio Brian has declared a thaw,' Charlie informed Bridge and Luke, just as a large chunk of plaster fell off the wall above the fireplace.

'I don't think the inn wants us to leave,' said Robin. 'I think it likes us being here.'

'And we all like the inn,' said Bridge loudly, as if she was speaking to it directly. 'It's been a friend to us these past few days. It's given us shelter and warmth and fed us and kept us safe.'

She wanted to buy this place. She was going to make a serious effort to do so in the new year.

Charlie cleared his mouth of turkey sandwich to speak.

'Robin's psychic, you know. He feels things.'

'I bet he does,' said Luke, which made Charlie snort.

'There's definitely a presence in this place,' said Robin

with absolute certainty. 'Benign. It enjoys company. I hope we've given it a good Christmas as well, a jolly one.'

'Will you go on to Scotland in search of more snow?' Bridge asked Charlie and Robin.

'No, we're heading home for a quiet, restful new year,' said Robin. 'How could we hope to better what we've had here?'

'What about you, Jack?' asked Bridge.

'Back to work for me,' he said.

'Minus your right hand,' said Bridge, giving him the chance to fight for Mary.

'What's this?' asked Robin.

'Mary's coming to work for me,' said Bridge. 'In sunny Derbyshire.'

'You're going to work for Bridge?' said Jack, sounding as if he'd just been thumped; he hadn't realised Mary had been poached from right under his nose.

'Oh, it's beautiful there,' said Charlie.

'You're welcome any time,' Bridge returned.

'Thank you,' he replied. 'But why the change, Mary?' Charlie hadn't been expecting that at all. What was Jack doing letting her go?

'New year, new opportunity,' she said, avoiding Jack's eyes. 'It feels like the right thing to do.'

'Goodness,' said Robin, as stunned as his partner. It was a good job he'd persuaded Charlie not to say anything. He hadn't seen that coming. Maybe Mary wasn't as keen on him as they'd imagined.

'Many people will be back at work tomorrow,' said Radio Brian, taking the conversation away from Mary's new life, 'so I don't think I'll have my listeners during the day any more. But, don't fret, I'll be here as usual just in case. I hope you've enjoyed listening to me over Christmas and that I've brought you some cheer as well as up-to-date weather bulletins. Cath hasn't been too great recently so we're hoping to bring in the new year in Whitby. If you can't listen to me again, well, I hope you all have a happy, healthy, smashing new year and it brings you everything you dreamed of. For now, I'll say goodnight and leave you with the magic voice of Peggy Lee and "The Christmas Spell". Goodbye, everybody.'

Bridge thought she was the only one who felt choked up at that, until she heard Robin sniff.

'Well that wasn't emotional at all was it?' he said.

'Poor old sod,' said Charlie and blew a kiss at the radio. 'Thank you Radio Brian, you are truly a master of your craft. We have appreciated your every word and tune.'

'It wouldn't have been the same without you, Brian ... and Cath ... and even Malcolm,' added Mary, a wobble audible in her voice.

'God bless him and his gums,' said Luke, blinking hard.

Jack stood up to clear the plates.

'I'll go and make some coffees,' he said, hoping no one had noticed that his eyes were every bit as glassy as everyone else's.

The fresh air, jollity and food had exhausted them. Yawns ripped around the room and not even Jack's supply of robust coffee could keep their eyelids propped up for much longer. They sat in a companionable near silence in front of the dying fire, enjoying the last of its heat. There were no more logs left in the basket.

'We'll all meet for breakfast though, won't we?' Bridge asked.

'Of course,' said Charlie. 'There must be something we haven't yet eaten in the kitchen.'

'Right, I'll say goodnight,' said Bridge. Mary got up from her chair at the same time.

'Me too,' said Luke. 'I want to be fresh for my drive tomorrow. Sleep well, ladies.'

'And you.'

Bridge and Mary went upstairs, Jack and Luke followed after they'd washed up the mugs. When they had gone, Charlie wrote his number on the pad, left it on the bar counter with a note for the landlord.

'We'll clear all the bill, whatever it costs,' he said.

'Cheap at half the price,' said Robin, turning off the radio and the Christmas tree lights. He noticed the branches were almost bare now, the puddle of needles underneath on the carpet.

At the bottom of the stairs, Charlie turned back to the bar lounge. 'Thank you, Figgy Hollow Inn,' he whispered into the dark. 'You've given me everything I wanted this Christmas and more.' He blew a kiss then switched off the light.

27 December

The magic of Christmas never ends

when we are loved by family and friends

Chapter 33

Bridge was woken by the clank-clank of the old radiator alongside her on which her washed pants were warming. She swung her legs out of bed, pulled back the curtain and saw large patches of grass where yesterday, there'd been snow.

She heard muffled voices coming from next door, Jack and Luke talking. She wished some of her soon-to-be ex-husband's audacity had rubbed off on Jack and that a miracle had occurred and he'd grown a pair overnight. She had considered taking Jack to one side and telling him a few home truths, but no; why should she? If there was one thing she'd come to know over the years it was that life was about learning lessons and the things hardest to get were the most satisfying to own. Mary deserved someone who didn't disappoint her, a knight on a white steed, not a shite on a seaside donkey. Besides, she was really looking forward to working with Mary. She prided herself on being a good boss, a kind boss. She was grateful, in hindsight, for the school of hard knocks having given her all that she had now. But she felt for Mary and the first chance she got to fix her up with someone who had balls the size of coconuts, she would.

'Morning,' said Mary, stretching. 'My, I'm going to miss this bed.'

She'd slept unexpectedly well, took that as a sign she was now set on a road she should be travelling.

'Morning,' said Bridge. 'Take care before you look out of the window. I think we've become snow-blind; the sight of a bit of green sent my brain into a spin.'

Mary crossed to the window. 'Wow,' she said. 'Grass and road and car colours.' She took a deeper meaning from the sight. The end of something monochrome, the beginning of something vivid.

She showered quickly, dressed and stripped her bed as Bridge had, left the sheets folded up on top of the mattress, began to pack.

'Do you want a diary?' she asked, holding up the one that Jack had put in her Christmas stocking.

She didn't want to keep it, didn't want the reminder.

'If you're sure you don't, I'll take it off your hands,' said Bridge.

Mary tossed it over. Bridge flicked through it, admiring the quality, spotted the entry next to the second Saturday in January.

Dinner with Jack. Firenze.

'Did you write this, Mary?'

'I haven't written anything in it.'

'Someone has,' Bridge said. 'What's Firenze?'

'A fabulous Italian restaurant. Why?'

Bridge showed her the page. Jack's writing. Mary could

pick it out of an identity parade of two hundred fonts. She felt a flutter in her heart, for one split second, before an angry boot stamped on it and crushed it. She looked as cross as it was possible for Mary's delicate features to look.

'What does that even mean, Bridge? Is that a message for me to discover? And when – as now – I have, what was I supposed to do about it? Go up to him and say, "So, I see we have a date?" and give him the chance to say, "I don't know what you mean," because he possibly wrote it when he was pissed and now he's sobered up? Or was I supposed to turn up at Firenze and wait for him to arrive at some point?'

Mary's hypothetical questions kept flying out of her and Bridge couldn't answer any of them. Jack had totally blown it. Faint heart never won fair lady and his was fainter than an exorcised ghost in an invisibility cloak.

'Are you going to do anything about it?' asked Bridge, cautiously.

'No I am bloody not,' said Mary and zipped up her case in a manner that told Bridge exactly what she thought about that.

'I hear stirring from next door. The girls are up,' said Robin to Charlie, who was lying in bed, face up, eyes closed. He went over to the window. 'I can see our Range Rover again.' The brilliance of their car colours, the road, blue sky, the grass all seemed to pop with further brightness after days of seeing only a vista of white. The snow clung on where it could, but it was fighting a losing battle against the warmer currents of air winning the temperature war.

He checked under the bed and in the drawers to make sure he'd packed everything. 'I expect the landlord will be visiting this morning. I hope he's not too cross about finding his larder raided and his emaciated alcohol supplies.'

No response from Charlie.

'Don't do this again to me, Charlie,' said Robin, arms akimbo. 'I nearly had a fit yesterday.'

Charlie looked pale in the harsh morning light, paler than he had yesterday.

'Charlie?'

Robin nudged him gently. Still nothing. He put his ear to Charlie's face, listening for his breath. Charlie gave a snore loud enough to wake himself up; Robin jumped a mile.

'What are you doing?' asked Charlie. 'You blocked my bloody airways.'

'What are *you* doing just . . . lying there?'

'I was sleeping, Robin. That thing people usually do in beds.'

'Well you've no right to sleep so soundly,' said Robin. 'I wish I'd checked to see if there was a defibrillator in this place.'

'Bit of an over-reaction if I may say. I hardly need one of those to—'

'I meant for me, you old fool. My heart stopped. It's going like the clappers now mind. And it's totally out of sync.'

'I was dreaming about something deep and significant,' said Charlie, shuffling to a sitting position.

'What?' Robin asked.

'About the meaning of life. About what the point of it is. In my dream I was lecturing to a big group of people.'

'So, Professor Hawking, what were you telling everyone from your pulpit?'

'Lectern,' Charlie corrected him. 'And I was telling them that there isn't any point.'

Robin took that in, then gave his head a rattle.

'Well, I'd wave goodbye to the Nobel prize for philosophy if I were you.'

'No, Robin, I really think I know what it is,' said Charlie, excitedly. 'At this point in time, everyone on the planet is equal. We all have the here and the now, just like Luke said on Christmas Eve, it's in the bag. The past is gone, the future is always beyond our grasp and heaven is a mere nice bonus if it exists, so I think the point of life is . . . that there isn't a point. It just . . . is. We should accept that and enjoy the moments we're in. I think we'd all be a lot happier, if we just embraced the here and now a bit more, don't you?'

Robin absorbed the words before speaking.

'We've always embraced the here and the now, you and I, Charlie.'

'We got it right, Robin,' said Charlie.

'We have a signal. I'd better ring Ben,' Bridge announced, as her phone buzzed just as they were about to head downstairs with their cases. An email came through, then another, then another. Lots of them, and texts and notifications from various social media sites. She felt them already start to drain her soul, so made an early new year's resolution to spend more time with her phone switched off. Mary immediately rang her tearful mother, who was still abroad and beyond relieved to know that her baby was not part of a glacier on the North Yorkshire Moors or buried under an avalanche. Then Mary gave her brothers and sister very quick calls to tell them she was safe and would be home in a couple of hours and she'd ring them again then.

'They were all a bit sobby,' said Mary. 'Nice to be missed.'

'Yes. They must have been very concerned about you,' said Bridge.

'Did you get through to Ben? He must have been out of his head wondering where you were,' Mary asked her.

'He worries like a mother hen. Obviously not my mother because she doesn't give a cat's fuck.'

'Must be lovely having a fiancé who cares and worries about you,' said Mary. 'I might find out one day.'

Bridge gave a hefty sigh. 'Mary, I should have told you before, Ben's not my fiancé. He's a neighbour. I'll fill you in with the detail when we're driving. Stupid to pretend otherwise. Pathetic, I know, before you say anything.'

'It's not,' said Mary. 'Sometimes you just have to do what you have to do to protect yourself. Have you ever seen the inside of a Dalek, they're all mush.'

Bridge chuckled. If ever there was a suitable parallel, it was that.

She had some work to do on herself yet, she realised. Luke wouldn't have lied and invented a partner to save face. She was still a work in progress, but she'd get there.

Downstairs in the bar, Luke and Jack were having coffee, toast and cheese. There was also a plate of mince pies on the table. The lounge was chilly and the inn looked different somehow, tired and shabby, as if it had aged overnight. The light reflecting in from the snow had been kinder than the watery sun, it seemed. The Christmas tree in the corner was naked of needles underneath the tinsel and adornments, and the branches drooped wearily.

'Good morning, ladies,' said Luke, smile bright and pinned on his lips and Bridge thought of how he had always been a morning person – a lark, not an owl as she was.

Jack looked up briefly from his phone to add his good morning before returning to it. Business as usual for him, thought Mary. He must have loads of emails to sort through. Probably hundreds. He had that solemn set to his features again, that downward cast to his mouth; his Jack Butterly, MD of Butterly's scones face. A Jack who didn't throw snowballs or sing carols. A Jack with clear demarcation lines around himself that lowly PAs should not cross. But that wasn't her problem any more.

'Here, let me pour,' said Luke, standing to pick up the coffee pot. 'Want some toast?' He nudged a platter full of buttered triangles and blocks of cheese over in their direction. 'The bread hasn't gone green yet.'

Bridge pretended to gag, but took some anyway. 'We're going to get straight off after this,' she said, referring to the mug. 'Looks like the roads will be clear enough.'

'I tried to check the travel news with Radio Brian but there's just white noise where he once was,' said Luke with a sigh of regret. 'I had to consult the "other BBC". All the major roads and most of the minor ones are passable now.' He'd call it the 'other BBC' for a long time to come.

'Sorry,' said Jack, turning his phone to silent as ping after ping came out of it.

'Mine was exactly the same,' said Bridge.

'And mine,' said Luke.

'Did you get through to Carmen?' asked Bridge. 'And is she all right?'

'All well, all good,' said Luke, and for her ears only, 'And it appears I'll be eating another Christmas dinner when I get home. She hasn't told her family yet, she wanted to wait for me.'

Bridge smiled at him. She was so happy for him. She

hoped one day she'd get to meet Carmen, and have a cuddle with their baby.

Jack's phone might have stopped pinging, but it carried on vibrating.

'It's a vicious circle that needs breaking,' said Luke, leaning back in his chair, hands behind his head, looking every bit the laid-back dude. 'Work might fill the empty spaces in your life but maybe you need to fill those empty places with other things instead, Jack. Take a leaf out of this happy but still extremely successful man's book. Streamline, delegate, don't trot halfway around the globe for meetings you can do on a video call. Find some*one* to care about.' His eyes flicked to Mary but her thoughts weren't at the table with them. There was no customary smile on her face this morning. 'You need a good woman, Jack,' he went on. Last ditch attempt to guide him.

'Or a good man,' said Charlie, appearing at the bottom of the stairs. Robin followed behind, struggling with a suitcase until Jack and Luke both got up to help him and Mary began to pour out coffees in readiness for the last two members of the Figgy Hollow Six to join them.

'Well here we all are again,' said Robin, patting some breath back into his chest, sitting down, reaching for the plate of mince pies to pass to Charlie.

'Here we all are,' echoed Luke. Even in jeans and a jumper that needed a wash, and his unruly white-blond hair stuck up at weird angles, he looked every inch a success story, thought Bridge. She wanted that contentment he'd found: having a million in the bank was absolutely no good if you were too busy to spend it. She had turned down one too many invitations from friends in favour of chasing deals. Things were going to change this year.

'Can I just say, a big thank you,' said Charlie, before he bit into his mince pie. 'If I can take something with me and keep it forever, I'd take my memories, and these past few days would be right at the top of the pile with the best ones.' He raised his mug in a toast. 'May all of us around this table enjoy every minute of what we have left,' he said. Five other mugs crashed into it.

A noise from above, as if something had fallen heavily.

'This place is dropping to bits around us,' said Robin, surveying the lounge. Funny, but he couldn't remember it looking as worn out as this. He hadn't noticed the holes in the plaster before, the general unkempt dullness of the place. He was sure the tables had shone with polish when they arrived. Relief at finding the place must have added the sparkle, he thought.

'How long will it take you to get back home, Robin?' asked Bridge.

'Too long. We were going to take the scenic route, but Charlie's a bit tired so it's the motorway for us. Safer anyway, I'm sure.'

After a few moments, finishing up his second coffee, Luke put his mug down on the table. 'I think I'm going to head off. I want to get back to Carmen and I've got a bit of a stretch to my car, unless anyone is going to offer me a lift to it.'

He was inundated with offers, but accepted Jack's. He had plans to make with him.

As Jack nipped upstairs to get his bag, the others stood to say their goodbyes. Luke embraced Robin, then Charlie – a little harder and tighter as if he was trying to press some strength into his bones. He didn't want to say the 'good-bye' word to him, he left him as if it was *adieu*. Then he kissed Mary on the cheek and gave her a rocking hug full of affection.

'Come and walk me out,' he said to Bridge.

Outside the thaw was continuing at speed: the colours of the grass and parked cars looked too bright, as if they had been painted.

'I'll courier Sabrina's ashes to you,' said Bridge. 'Put them somewhere nice in your garden.'

'I've changed my mind on that. There was a wood I used to take her to, she liked to jump into the water there. Her favourite place.'

Bridge smiled. 'That sounds perfect.'

'I wish you and Ben all the luck in the world,' said Luke, 'I really do.'

She nearly told him, pulled it back at the last second.

'I'm not sure he's my Mr Right, if I'm honest.'

'There isn't just one Mr Right in the world, Bridge. Or Mrs Right. If he isn't for you, kick him to the kerb. Don't settle for second best, ever.'

'Carmen sounds like she's definitely Mrs Right.'

'So were you,' said Luke. 'I just met you at the wrong time.'

Their arms opened together, wrapped around each other tightly.

'Be happy, Bridge. Find someone who makes your heart want to keep beating forever.' Luke pulled away, smiled. She saw again the young teenage boy still hovering in that smile. 'Goodbye Mrs Palfreyman.'

'Goodbye Mr Palfreyman.'

'Well, thank you for a mad few days,' said Jack. He shook Robin's hand, was pulled into an embrace before Robin passed him over to Charlie.

'Keep reading that book I made you, Jack,' said Charlie, trying his best to look stern.

'I promise I will.'

Jack didn't want to make a big thing about his goodbye to Charlie, but he gave him a second hug that said everything he needed to.

'Good luck, Mary,' said Jack. 'There will always be a job for you at Butterly's if you change your mind.'

This is your very last chance to stop her leaving you, screamed a voice inside him.

'Thank you, Jack. Good luck.' She stood rigid, missiling vibes that their business was done. Jack could even hear it in her voice, that she didn't want him to stop her.

He turned, picked up his bag, opened the door. Left.

Bridge and Mary washed up the breakfast dishes, leaving the kitchen as spick and span as they found it, minus a lot of food. Robin and Charlie waited for them so they could walk out to their cars together. Mary was silent as she dried and Bridge let her be. You couldn't make an omelette without breaking eggs, she'd tell her later, and Mary was a zillion-dollar lobster frittata in the making.

'I hope the place will be all right,' said Bridge, picking up her own luggage in one hand and a suitcase full of Robin and Charlie's boots in the other. 'My breaking-in skills don't extend to repairing locks.'

'I'm sure the landlord will be back today,' said Robin. 'Nothing we can do about it if he isn't. We had our own emergency to contend with.'

Charlie turned to look fondly at the inn, issued a silent thank you to it, for the homely Yorkshire welcome, for Radio Brian, for the Figgy Hollow Six.

Robin turned to the inn, issued a silent thank you to it for giving Charlie the perfect Christmas. A priceless gift.

'Goodbye, Figgy Hollow,' said Bridge, when they reached their cars. It was odd but she felt changed somehow by the events of the past few days. Recharged and yet more at peace with herself.

'And goodbye Bridge.' Charlie embraced her, held her. 'What a wonderful woman you are. Like a fire, I can feel your fabulous energy,' he said. 'I wish you joy and love and lots of great sex.' Bridge hooted, tried to rein in the sob threatening to break out of her. She couldn't return the word 'goodbye', had to substitute it with 'take good care'.

'My darling Mary,' said Charlie, beaming at her. 'I hope you get your Chanel handbag and carry it like the lady you are. You are a prize, to be earned. Don't you ever forget that. You hold out for your Captain Wentworth, Miss Elliot. Nothing less, you promise me.'

'I promise I will.' She hugged Charlie with all her strength and thought how frail he felt, so much more fragile than he looked.

'I'll keep in touch,' said Robin. They both knew what he meant.

Jack hung around until Luke had switched on the ignition, made sure he wasn't stranded with a dead engine.

'Good to go,' said Luke, 'thanks for the lift. We'll be in touch about those vegan scones after New Year.'

'Great stuff, I'll ask Mary to—' Jack pulled up his words. 'I'll get someone to ring you about them. It won't be Mary, seeing as Bridge stole her from me.'

'She wouldn't have let herself be stolen, Jack, if you'd

fought even a little for her to stay,' Luke said before pipping his horn perkily and hitting the road.

Robin had luckily only driven half a mile before he realised he'd left his orange jacket hanging in the wardrobe. He cursed his memory.

'I'm sure I'm going through the bloody menopause,' he said to Charlie. 'I'll have to go back for it.'

'Okay, dear,' said Charlie, half-asleep.

'I blame you,' said Robin, making an about-turn in the deserted road. 'You distracted me talking about the meaning of life this morning when I was in the middle of checking that I'd packed everything.'

Charlie's response was a baby snore. Leaping around like a lunatic in the snow yesterday had taken it out of him and even a full night's sleep hadn't been enough.

The inn was in the near distance. Robin could see that a few of the tiles were missing from the roof. Those noises they heard last night from above must have been clumps of snow dropping through. Something else the poor landlord would have to deal with. He hoped his insurer wouldn't try and fob him off with that old 'act of God' clause. At the other side of the road, the cottages stood in a crumbling row. The snow had given them roofs where there weren't any, disguising their age and wear, the rafters visible now like ribs. The church was a ruin, with part of the back of its stone tower missing. Funny how snow could deceive the eye. Nature's Touche Éclat, he thought to himself with a mini chuckle.

'Shan't be a tick, love,' said Robin, pulling the car up in front of the inn door. He walked inside; how cold it felt without the cheer of fire in the hearth now that the insulating snow had melted from the roof. He rushed upstairs, pulled his orange jacket out of the wardrobe and did a quick double-check for anything else he might have missed, but the coat had been a single oversight.

Their room had a morning-after air; it too had lost its festive spirit. The carpet seemed more threadbare and the wallpaper more distressed than he remembered. He left quickly, before the magic of the last few days dissolved any further.

He hurried back to the car, threw the coat on the back seat before belting himself in, starting the engine, setting off again.

'That didn't take long did it? Now, how's this for a plan: we get on the M1 and then stop at the first services we come to. You can have anything you like; buns, full English, cherries if we can find 'em. How's that suit?' He didn't expect an answer because Charlie was out for the count. 'You know, you've always been such marvellous company when we're travelling, Charlie Glaser. It's a good job I don't get lulled to sleep by the hum of an engi—' He glanced to his side, and again, then stepped hard on the brake; something wasn't right. Fingers of cold dread brushed past Robin's nerve endings.

'Charlie? . . . Charlie, love?' Robin reached over, shook his shoulder gently.

But this time Charlie wasn't in a deep sleep, contemplating the meaning of life.

Chapter 34

The paramedics were there within fifteen minutes, but it was too late. It had been too late before Robin had even rung them. Charlie had slipped away quickly and silently. He had fallen out of this world and into another, as easily as he had fallen into the snow the previous day to make his angels.

One of the paramedics sat with Robin, taking details, comforting him, poor fellow. He hadn't been up in this neck of the woods for years. There was no reason to, the road only led to a small place called Figgy Hollow, long deserted. To his shame, he'd been one of the gang who passed an entertaining morning throwing stones at the windows of the old derelict inn there trying to break the glass, until they were chased off by the old bloke who lived in one of the cottages opposite. Ancient, with no teeth and a long, straggling combover, he always wore jumpers knitted for someone twice his size and he broadcast his own radio station, called something daft like Radio Kenneth or Bert or ... Radio Brian, that was it. Hardly anyone listened to it. He died not long afterwards and his wife had to go into a home and that was the last of the people who lived in Figgy Hollow. Must have been twenty-five years ago: just after Yorkshire had the shock of that severe winter spell that was every bit as bad as this one had been.

He switched his attention back to the gentleman here. Never a good time to lose someone, but it always seemed worse at Christmas.

10 January

Ships are safe in harbours

but that's not why ships are built

Chapter 35

'So, what did you think about your first week working at Bridge Holdings?' asked Bridge, a hopeful smile on her face.

'It's great,' Mary answered. 'What's not to like?'

There was nothing not to like. Her office was next to Bridge's, it was light and airy and had a countryside view. There was a small café in the building that sold really nice sandwiches, soup and a hot meal of the day (vegetarian option also). The people were so friendly; Sonia, Bridge's pregnant PA who was showing her the ropes, was a peach. Even the toilets at Bridge Holdings were swish with touch-sensitive taps and the sort of glittery tiles suited to a nightclub. Bridge was a boss who said things like, 'Mary, you're a find' and made her feel as if she was actually a visible and worthy entity. Everything pointed to this being a great career move. Except ... how Mary missed the chaos of Butterly's. She missed the banter of the packing department. She missed Edna's grumpily delivered excellent tea and the scones that she buttered with a heavy hand. And she missed Jack. Not that she'd admit this to Bridge, who'd done everything possible to make her move as easy as it could be.

Mary didn't even want to admit it to herself, never mind anyone else.

She'd moved in with Bridge on the second of January because Mary's family had arranged for them all to bring in the new year together. Her brother was back from Australia and her mum was home from the Canaries. Mrs Padgett was convinced that Mary's dad had been watching over her as a guardian angel and helped her find the inn. Sean was more interested in the details of what had happened between her and Jack, holed up for days. He was mightily impressed that his little sister had told the Boy from Ipanema to jog on.

Bridge's house was not as Mary had imagined it: cavernous, huge windows, neutral, minimalist, it oozed expense, good taste, wealth; it was gorgeous – but it was a house, not a home. She suspected it mirrored an emptiness that Bridge felt within herself. Mary wondered if this would be her destiny one day, because she was determined to be successful and if riches came with that, then she too would buy herself a big house. But she hoped it would reflect a full and satisfied heart, have toys around the place, a dog basket, sticky fingerprints, a room just for handbags.

Ben was waiting for them on the doorstep when they got home that night. Since Mary had moved in, Bridge hadn't been staying in the office for hours after everyone else had gone. She intended to make sure her life/work balance sat on the scales a little more evenly this new year.

'You've had parcels delivered,' he called, rushing out to meet them. He was tallish but looked taller than he was, being built like a solid oak wardrobe; completely bald, always smiling, always looked happy to see them, like the human version of an overgrown Boxer dog with a permanently wagging friendly tail. He was the antithesis of drab in what he customarily wore and today he had on a yolk-yellow woollen jumper, a colour that suited him perfectly, Mary thought. She'd taken to him from the off, felt she had known him months, not days. He was sunshine in human form, like a younger, hairless version of Charlie running on super-charged batteries.

'Thanks, Ben,' said Bridge, taking the two parcels from him. A large one for Mary, a smaller one for herself. The address appeared to be written by the same hand. 'You coming in for a Friday wine?'

'I will have to pass, alas,' Ben replied, with an audible sigh of regret. 'I'm going to the pantomime. My niece is a dancing flower and it's the last night. I'll take a raincheck of course.'

'I wish you'd been my uncle,' Bridge said to him, meaning it. 'And of course. You can have the wine with added interest the next time you're free.'

'I'm free tomorrow. Chinese banquet at mine. I'm paying,' he threw over his shoulder.

'It's a date,' said Bridge, on Mary's behalf too.

Wherever he went, he seemed to leave a smile imprinted on the air behind him like the Cheshire Cat, thought Mary. How blessed he was not to miss the sensation of falling in love with someone, not to have the complication of yearn-ing for the soulmate to spend his life with.

'I wonder who these are from,' Bridge said, unlocking the front door.

'I have no idea,' Mary answered. Hers had been redi-rected from her old address.

They took them through to the kitchen, sat at the long island and began to unwrap them.

Bridge's contained a black box. As she peeled off the paper, the name CHANEL was revealed in white capitals.

'What the hell? Who's sent me this?'

Mary's much larger box was white, trimmed black at the edges, the name CHANEL written in black across the middle. She looked at Bridge with the same look of confusion as Bridge had for her.

Bridge eased the lid off the box; inside wrapped in tissue was a Chanel scarf she recognised, and a folded note. She read it aloud.

My Dear Bridge

I am sorry to have to tell you that my darling Charlie has left us. He died on the day we all left Figgy Hollow, just fell asleep and didn't wake up. There has been a lot to do, as you can imagine. His funeral is at Tuckwitt Church, where we got married, 25th Jan, 11am and I hope you can join us. We were a family for a while, the Figgy Hollow Six of us, weren't we? What a happy Christmas we had. The best.

Charlie was insistent that I give this scarf to you. He said you would look lovely in it, like the true queen you are. He was such an excellent judge of character. I have washed it, but sprayed a little of his cologne on it for you.

It will be bitter-sweet to see you again on the 25th. I do hope you can come. Dress code: black and fabulous.

Love to you
Robin (and Charlie) xx

Bridge lifted the scarf reverently to her nose. The base notes of cedar and lavender transported her back to the inn, sitting around the fire sipping mulled cider, nibbling on mince pies, Radio Brian's witterings in the background. She folded it, replaced it in the box, not wanting to wet it with teardrops.

'He died then,' said Mary with a long drawn-out sigh. 'I was hoping he would have had so much longer.' She wiped at her eyes with a piece of snatched kitchen roll.

'I'm glad it was peaceful though,' said Bridge. 'I really am. And of course I'll go to the funeral. I'll drive us.' *Dear lovely Charlie.* 'Open your parcel, Mary.'

A sea of tissue paper, and sitting in it, a rectangular black bag, double Cs on the turnstile lock. Mary's jaw dropped and stayed dropped.

'That is gorgeous,' said Bridge. 'What a sweetheart he was.'

Mary opened the accompanying note, her fingers fluttering with emotion.

My Dear Mary

My darling Charlie has left us now, but he was insistent that you have this to remember him by. He bought it for his mother who never used it but perched it on her dressing table and looked at it a lot as if it were a treasure. And so it seems fitting that this treasure goes to yet another treasure. But it does come with a stipulation: that you must always carry it with all the chutzpah you can muster, Charlie was most insistent about that. He became so fond of you in the time he knew you, as did I.

Charlie's funeral is at Tuckwitt Church, 25th Jan, 11am. Please try to come. Also — a heads up — I may be using my Christmas present from you soon and ringing you, as I will need a friend's cheerful voice. Your presence on the 25th is one of the few things about the day I will be looking forward to. Dress code: black and glamorous.

Love to you
Robin (and Charlie) xx

She turned the bag over in her hands and knew exactly how Charlie's mother must have felt. She could quite happily have put it on her dressing table and stared at it for hours. It must be worth a small fortune.

'I can't accept it,' she said. 'It's far too much.'

'Yes you can,' said Bridge firmly. 'Charlie wanted you to have it and enjoy it, so you must. For him. So long as you promise you'd parade it. It will have made him happy to think he was giving it to you. I shall wear my scarf to the funeral and you must take your bag. If that doesn't fit in with the dress code, nothing will.'

'Do you really think I should, Bridge?' she asked.

'Absolutely,' said Bridge. Charlie had an obvious soft spot for Mary. Who didn't? Bridge only wished she had been like this young woman herself at that age: someone who recognised her own worth, who was brave and competent while still retaining a gentleness.

'Then I'll keep it.'

Bridge crossed to the fridge, took out a bottle of champagne. She always had a bottle in there waiting for an occasion. Once upon a time, she thought it would be the most glamorous thing ever to do, so now she did it.

She ripped into the foil, twisted the wire, covered the mushroom cork with a tea towel as she popped it so it didn't fly off and break one of her very expensive glass lights.

'We are going to drink a toast, to Charlie,' she said, swooping up two flutes and filling them.

'To Charlie.'

They chinked and drank, the bubbles raced down their throats.

Bridge looked at Mary as she drank; she had changed even in the very short time she had stayed here, was shedding a previous self like a skin. Tomorrow, Mary was going to have a consultation with Bridge's hair stylist, Russ. Then they were both going shopping afterwards. Mary said she wanted a whole new set of clothes to match her new life: she was planning to buy something bright, something that would pull her out of the shadows.

Mary Padgett owned a Chanel handbag; Bridge would do her best to make sure her young friend never slid back into the shadows again.

Chapter 36

Mr Chikafuji was still giving Jack the runaround. He said, or rather his PA did, that he could not fit an appointment in to see Jack until August now. He persisted in being impossible to get hold of and his office was habitually lax in returning calls. Jack, in sheer desperation, took a leaf out of Luke's book and suggested a video conference, but Chikafuji would not be pinned down even for that. But in that first week of the new year, a much smaller bakery chain in Japan had approached Jack asking to do business with Butterly's. The MD, a Mrs Anmitsu, appeared as keen to start the ball rolling quickly as Mr Chikafuji wasn't. Mrs Anmitsu didn't have time for face-to-face meetings as she had a young family, so Jack and Mrs Anmitsu had trans-continental video calls and he realised he could conduct business quite adequately like that without having to stare into the whites of her eyes. Mrs Anmitsu was direct and completely devoid of bullshit so Jack took a chance that this Japanese bird in the hand was better than two in the Bonsai. He'd not only saved a lot of expense but time. And Jack was determined this new year to make sure that he had plenty of spare time in reserve – for life, and that he wouldn't fill it with work. He didn't want a life/work balance that resembled a see-saw with a toddler on one end and an eighteen-stone fully-grown bloke on the other. He wanted, as Luke had, as Charlie had found, balance.

Kimberley had been drafted over as a PA fill-in for Jack until he found a suitable permanent replacement for Mary. He couldn't look at her without thinking of the snow-woman with the slit for a mouth, small bird-like eyes and blob for a nose. She wasn't bad at the job, but she wasn't – *say it Jack,* said a voice inside him – she wasn't Mary. Not by a long chalk. Also, she seemed to have been morphing into a parody of Marilyn Monroe since she came back to work after the Christmas holiday and discovered that Mary had left. Kimberley had automatically presumed she was first in line for the position and was doing her level best to secure it, using all her feminine wiles. Her clothes had got tighter, her lipstick redder and she had started sashaying everywhere. Or trying to, which resulted in any drinks she was carrying being sloshed over the side of the mug and onto the linoleum.

Jack sipped the coffee she had just brought him – too weak, too much milk – and wondered if Mary had seen the entry he wrote in the House of Quills red diary yet. If she had, what had she made of it? What *could* she make of it? What was she supposed to even do about it? It was as weak as this awful coffee. He hadn't even specified a time, or what the arrangements were. Why didn't he write, *'Firenze, 8pm, Jack will pick me up at home'*, direct and strong – well, in so far as writing a sneaky note in a diary went. Why hadn't he bitten the bullet and asked her outright if she'd like to go out to dinner with him? Why hadn't he been a ship that sailed out of the harbour into an open sea of uncertainty, in pursuit of the treasures of excitement, pleasure, love, instead of sending out a rubber dinghy with an idiot pilot to act as scout?

Jack picked up a biscuit from the plate, a choice of a bourbon finger, a garibaldi and a malted milk. Mary knew he hated those, would have put a pink wafer, a jam ring and chocolate digestive on the plate. He'd barely noticed her when she was here and yet he felt her loss deeply now. Butterly's just didn't run the same without her, like a machine that functioned perfectly and all the cogs got the credit for it, until the oil dried up and the real master of operations was uncovered.

A knock on the door. Kimberley's boobs entered a moment before she did. He tried not to look at them, but it was difficult as they took up a good portion of the office.

'Someone's just dropped off a parcel for you,' she said and put it down on the desk. He caught a blast of scent newly applied, heavy and cloying. Mary's fragrance was light, like a summer flower garden on a warm, balmy evening. Funny, he didn't even realise he remembered it enough to compare.

'Thank you, Kimberley. Have a nice weekend.'

But Kimberley didn't leave, just continued to hover until he was forced to look away from his screen and up at her.

'Er, I was just wondering about the prospect of this position being permanent,' she said. 'Now Mary's left you in the lurch.'

He felt a mini flare of annoyance on Mary's behalf and decided, on the spur of that moment, to do something about it, as the opportunity had arisen.

'Why don't you sit down and I'll interview you for it now?' said Jack.

'Really?' Kimberley smiled and Jack thought her mouth looked strangely like a letterbox.

She sat in the chair at the other side of his desk after wriggling her skirt down, back straight, ready to convince Jack of her suitability.

'So,' began Jack, 'we can skip a lot of the preliminaries and get straight to the nitty-gritty. How long have you been working for Butterly's?'

'Four years and three months. I came from an agency for a part-time position originally but was taken on as full-time permanent staff almost immediately.'

'And what do you see as the difference between working for me as opposed to working in finance?'

'I'm a qualified PA,' she answered, as if that was self-evident. 'I've been waiting for an opening for a long time in my chosen field. I want to do what I was trained to do. I have qualifications in typing and shorthand and I am a competent audio typist and diary keeper. I can work by myself without the need for supervision and as a team member. And, as you ask for me personally to fill in on such occasions whenever your regular PA is absent, it would be easy to presume that my services are satisfactory to your exacting standards.'

Clearly, Kimberley had learned this by rote in preparation for such a dialogue, thought Jack.

'So you think you're a team player,' said Jack, tapping his pen against his desk. He really did have to address this point all guns blazing, felt a bubble of mischief fizzing in his voice box.

'I most certainly am. And I'd be a wonderful ambassador for the company.'

Right into my hands, thought Jack.

'And if I . . . for instance, asked you to procure a suitable gift for a client, in order to impress them, how would you be able to cope with that particular duty?'

Kimberley beamed, tossed a newly highlighted curl back over her shoulder.

'I'd be very confident. I have a good eye for quality and I love shopping.'

'What about . . . someone within the company? An important member of staff for instance?'

'The same,' said Kimberley. 'I'd make an informed match of product to person.'

'You wouldn't, then, buy a frumpy, insulting present for a woman in her early twenties.'

A pause. 'Don't think so.' That smile not quite so sure now.

'Or buy her a bottle of old lady perfume, a tartan shopping bag, a headscarf square for her or . . . jellied fruits?'

Kimberley's face went from porcelain to traffic-light red faster than his Maserati went from zero to sixty.

Jack continued. 'And if a member of staff was going through a particularly hard time in their personal life and I asked you to send them an email enquiring if they had any idea when they'd be returning to work, always mindful of the sensitivity of the situation so that they were in no doubt their welfare was considered . . . need I go on?'

Kimberley gulped, once, twice, opened her mouth to speak, closed it again, carried on colouring forward to puce.

'I thought not. I need to be able to trust a PA absolutely, the way I trusted Mary. You see, Kimberley, I can't tell you how good Mary was at her job, how brilliant, how perfect because she did it so well, I didn't notice until she stopped doing it. Ironic isn't it? She was too valuable to be let down in the way she was by Butterly's and I wouldn't want that to happen to any member of my staff again. I bear the responsibility of not writing to her myself when her father died, or buying her Christmas presents that reflected her worth instead of leaving it to someone else who put chagrin above duty to me. It was totally remiss of me to delegate in both cases, but still . . . I think you can guess where I'm going with this. Have a nice weekend. You'll be returning to finance on Monday, I'll organise a temp to fill in until I can find a permanent replacement for Mary, because I don't think you're quite what I'm looking for.'

Kimberley got up, her face reddening further, which Jack didn't think was possible. She looked not unlike a radish with high blood pressure and he appeared to have killed her sashay stone dead.

Jack smiled as the door closed. If only Mary had been here to witness the moment of revenge on Kimberley that was hers by rights. If only she could feel the regret that was sitting like a jagged boulder inside him so she could savour her revenge on him too. He should have stood by that slit-mouthed snowwoman and said, 'Look Mary, I don't want you to take any other job because you are the cleverest, most intuitive, best person I know and I don't want to imagine you not being in my life. I want you to accept a whopping big pay rise because I think you've more than earned it, and much more than that, I want to take you out to dinner because I think you're fucking gorgeous and I wish I'd kissed you when we were carol singing.'

But he hadn't, he'd shaken her hand and wished her well. His head fell into his hands and he groaned aloud. What a plonker.

He wondered what she was doing now, how she was faring working for Bridge who had been a PA herself and would recognise her worth without having to be starved of it first. He sighed, logged out of his Mac and remembered the parcel Kimberley had brought in. A rectangular box wrapped in brown paper, a handwritten address in beautiful script. He opened it up to find a note stuck to a brown box, bearing the insignia of a gold knight on horseback, the word BURBERRY underneath.

Dear Jack

I hope this finds you well.

I'm afraid to inform you that my wonderful Charlie passed away on the day we all left Figgy Hollow. He whispered away in his sleep, his end was peaceful, happy but always too soon. His funeral is on 25th January, 11am at Tuckwitt Church (dress code: black and dashing) and I would love for you to be there with us.

Charlie left me instructions to send you a gift for you to use, but also another for you to read. There's a note on the title page. Another one of his 'Rules of Life by a Man who Lived Well' and he did live very well, Jack.

Your presence on the 25th will be a light spot in a dark day and I do hope you can make it and the Figgy Hollow Six can be reunited for the last time.

Fondest regards

Robin (and Charlie) x

Jack made an audible 'ah' of sadness. News that wasn't unexpected, of course, but he'd hoped that Charlie was still with Robin, living out his last days in comfort and kindness.

He opened the box to find a folded cashmere scarf with a repeating pattern of an equestrian knight logo. Sitting on top of it was a copy of *Persuasion*, the old battered one that he'd brought down from his room on Christmas Eve so Charlie could read it. He opened it to the title page and read.

Love is a risky, frightening business. What if it doesn't work out? But my goodness – WHAT IF IT DOES! Be as brave as a knight in matters of love, my dear Jack, and read this book from cover to cover for guidance.

With my kindest wishes
Your friend Charlie Glaser x

It wasn't Jack's usual sort of read, but he would, for Charlie. Maybe he'd see why he and Mary had been discussing it so fervently. *Mary again*. All roads led back to Mary.

The notepad full of Charlie's nuggets of wisdom sat in his office drawer. Occasionally he would hear them, read out in Charlie's voice: *Meet the requirements of your requirements.* And the one about the ships in harbours had been branded onto the folds of his brain.

Jack closed up the office, he would not be coming back until Monday. He was switching off the phone, having lunch with Roman and Georgie tomorrow, moseying around an antiques fair on Sunday. He drove his Maserati home, parked up in front of his super plush dream house and pushed open the front door, switched on the lights. It had felt even emptier recently, more echoey. It was a beautiful house, but a lonely shell, not unlike himself. He wished he had someone to share it with, share *himself* with. And he could not get Mary Padgett and her blue-green eyes out of his head, nor the joie de vivre that hung around her like the best sort of perfume.

In short, he didn't just miss Mary, he *really* missed Mary.

Chapter 37

Luke walked into the house to find Carmen in the kitchen cutting tags off baby clothes.

'I know, I know, I shouldn't buy before the baby comes,' she said, 'but just a few. Look.' She held up a tiny white cardigan with ducks for buttons. 'Isn't it cute? I can't wait.' She pressed her hand to her stomach and addressed the growing bump. 'Are you listening, baby? Mama has clothes for you.'

Luke gave her a kiss. He loved everything about this woman: her accent, her scent, the feel of her, the look of her. He couldn't wait to marry her and they could make plans now the divorce was finally underway. It was weird how much spiritually lighter he felt not having the strain of it playing like a constant annoying backing track.

'Oh, Luke, there is some post for you. It came this morning.' Carmen reached over and handed him a small parcel wrapped in brown paper. The address was handwritten in elegant scroll. Inside was a black box with a designer logo — the head of Medusa.

'Versace?' said Carmen, her chin resting on his shoulder. 'Who has been sending you expensive presents?'

Inside the box was a note, and under it an elegant black wallet, again bearing the head of Medusa in gold, at the bottom right-hand corner.

My dear Luke

I hope this finds you well.

I have bad news. I'm afraid my wonderful Charlie sadly passed, not long after we waved goodbye to you. It was quick and peaceful, which in time will bring me some comfort I'm sure, but not at the moment. His funeral is at Tuckwitt Church, 11am on 25th January, dress code: black and smart. Please come, let us all be the Figgy Hollow Six for the last time.

Charlie asked me to send this wallet to you. He bought it but never used it. He always said he intended to give it away to someone whom it would suit more than him. The Medusa logo is very interesting because she had a gift of making people fall in love with her and making it almost impossible for them to unlove her again. You are as magnetic as she, Charlie said. We both grew so very fond of you in our short time together.

Please come and say hello to me on the 25th, and say goodbye to Charlie.

With my very best wishes
Robin xx

'Oh no,' said Luke, shaking his head regretfully. 'That's so very very sad. Charlie died.'

'Ah, I'm so sorry, Luke. You will go to the funeral of course,' said Carmen.

'I wouldn't miss it for the world,' said Luke.

25 January

Chapter 38

The weather couldn't have been more different than it was a month to the date ago. After the coldest December for many years, England was experiencing the mildest January on record. The sun had been bright in the sky since the new year and had fooled the bulbs of snowdrops, hyacinths and crocuses to pop out early from the soil. The trees were sprouting leaves and blossom buds were forming; the grass was verdant after being so hydrated. The day of Charlie's funeral could have been one of spring May, not mid-winter. Only more of the same was forecast.

Bridge and Mary filed into the small church. Or at least it looked small from the outside, but its narrowness was deceptive as it was disproportionately long. A bride in heels would have bunions the size of walnuts by the time she got to the altar, Bridge thought. The dress code had been strictly adhered to; everyone was in black, men were smart in suits, many women sported hats and fascinators. They slipped into a seat at the back on the left; the front half of the pews on either side were already full. The heady scent of Stargazer lilies drifted over to them from the surfeit of flowers adorning the ends of the pews and showy displays at the front: roses and Christmas foliage, great scarlet heads of poinsettias shouting in beds of holly and ivy. An organist was playing church musak, something halfway between a dirge and one of the less jaunty hymns. An air of respectful solemnity pervaded but also the mood prevailed that people were attending for love rather than duty.

Mary looked around for a familiar face, *the* familiar face. Would he come? She felt not unlike being sixteen and hanging around the entrance to the school disco hoping that the captain of the football team, Jock Briggs, would turn up. Then he did and it was as if someone had poured a jug of joy into her heart. It emptied when she found him snogging the school 'it' girl an hour later. She should have learned then to stay away from any boy whose name was a variation of Jack, it was bound to not end well.

Bridge read the order of service that had been handed to them when they walked in. On the front: *A Celebration of the Life of Charles David Reuben Glaser* and a photograph of him looking like a portrait by Van Dyck with his long, thick salt-and-pepper curls, moustache and pointy beard. He was sitting at a table in a garden, holding up a glass of champagne. In front of him was an enormous slice of cake, every inch the *bon vivant*. He was smiling and she imagined that behind the camera Robin was telling him that the cake was for photographic purposes only and he was strictly not to eat it. On the back was a black and white image of a much younger Charlie in a tuxedo, looking handsome and slightly vampiric with his long, dark locks and trademark arrangement of facial hair, standing tall and proud between a plump, smiling woman in a fur coat and an old lady with a stick, both of them 'dripping in diamonds', the façade of the London Palladium behind them.

'His mum and his granny,' said Mary, looking at the same photo. 'That must have been a wonderful night for them.'

Bridge looked around in search of Luke or Jack, gave Mary a nudge.

'There's Luke,' she said in a church whisper. She waved at him and he waved back, but he was being herded to the right side by ushers. He mouthed that he'd see them later. He was alone. She hadn't expected Carmen to be there, but she thought he might have turned up with Jack, still bracketing them together as a pair.

More people started pouring in as if a bus unloading had tipped its passengers straight through the doors. For a moment Mary thought she saw Jack among them and her heart responded with a kick against her chest, like a racehorse trying to break down his stable door, but it wasn't him. She thought she was over him with her wonderful new life just starting up, but she wasn't, not by a long stretch. She suddenly wondered if he'd liked the Christmas present she'd bought him, if he'd thought of her when he opened it.

'Will you all please stand,' said a loud male voice at the back.

As they stood, from speakers positioned around the church came the familiar cash-register introduction to 'I Wish It Could Be Christmas Everyday'. The woman on the row in front turned to her partner, wrinkled up her face in consternation at such a choice of tune. Bridge and Mary smiled, members of an exclusive club who knew why the song had been chosen. *The Figgy Hollow Six*.

Pall-bearers carried a basket coffin covered in holly, mistletoe, white roses and poinsettias. Behind them a vicar in robes, then a serious, thinner Robin, in a black suit, long black coat, a white Yorkshire rose in his buttonhole. He cut a desperately sad and lonely figure and both Mary and Bridge swallowed hard at the sight of him.

The vicar ascended the pulpit, asked the congregation to be seated.

'Welcome, friends. I am Father Derek and we are gathered here together to say goodbye to our dear Charlie,' he began, coughing a croak out of his throat. 'Husband of Robin, uncle of Reuben and Rosa. He would be touched that so many of you have come today from as far afield as Australia, Spain, California, Yorkshire, Derbyshire, Manchester and, of course, a huge crowd from London.'

Clearly the vicar knew him well. There was emotion born of familiarity in his voice.

'Charlie was married in this very church to Robin three years ago. Our first gay wedding. A happy and historic event in Tuckwitt. I don't think I've ever seen as many empty champagne bottles in my life.'

A gentle laugh rippled around the church.

'Robin and Charlie were together as a couple for thirty-two years. There is no one more fitting, more proper, more capable, to deliver Charlie's eulogy than him.'

The vicar moved aside, let Robin take his place. Robin breathed in, steadied himself, gripped on to the sides of the pulpit for strength.

'It is a cliché but Charlie was my rock,' he began, his voice wobbly. Bridge had the sudden desire to leap across the heads of everyone just to take his hand.

'He was born into an intolerant age, a hard world, he became wise through times of great hardship and prejudice because he was gay, but he was lucky, because in the smaller world of his family, he was brought up with the love of two amazing women, his grandmother Jessie and his mother Elizabeth.

'He was born in Yorkshire but when his father David died, Elizabeth went back home to live in the East End of London. When Charlie was twelve, his little sister Mim was born, and he was a loving brother to her all her life, before she sadly passed ten years ago. Charlie was only thirteen when he left school to work for a jeweller who had survived terrible things during the war and yet, Charlie said, this man was the kindest person he'd ever met. He became a substitute father to Charlie, taught him not only a craft but about life. Charlie always said that if someone could survive that sort of hell, then it was possible to survive anything.'

Robin went on to deliver a long, yet still not long enough, homage to Charlie. The laughter he generated while speaking gave him the strength he needed to carry on talking. Funny, touching, sad, hard to listen to in places, Charlie Glaser emerged as the best humanity could mould. There were quite a few references to his cholesterol levels too.

'And just in case you're wondering at my song choice as we walked in – well Charlie's song choice actually, because him being him, he had planned his own funeral down to the letter – it's because he loved Christmas and if he could have had it, he would have lived every day as if it were Christmas Day. When he knew he wouldn't be here for another one, he wanted his last one to be full of snow,' said Robin, his voice catching.

He stalled for a few moments, took back control. 'So I booked a five star hotel in Aviemore, every luxury you could think of, but we ended up having to take refuge in an old inn on the Yorkshire moors. There were six of us holed up for four days. I was livid. Imagine, when you know this is going to be the last Christmas you have together and you've got champagne and canapés waiting for you in Scotland . . .' He left a long pause, smiled. 'But we couldn't have wished for a merrier Christmas. We couldn't have wished for richer company, for kinder people, for better fun and feasting than we had. We left for Aviemore with Charlie trying his best to hide his pain from me and yet he spent Boxing Day lying in the snow flapping his limbs making angels, building a snowman and pelting snowballs. Christmas magic – it had to be. He ate too much, he certainly drank too much . . . he lived those last days to the full. He died healthier than I've seen him for well over a year.'

A sweet wave of laughter rolled around the church, took in everyone.

'On that last morning, Charlie told me he'd discovered the meaning of life, the point of it all.'

He left a dramatic break before enlightening everyone.

'He said that there wasn't one.'

Laughter again. From people who knew Charlie well enough to believe Robin's words.

'Charlie said that the point of life is living, here and now, being present in the moment. Watching a concert with your eyes, not trying to film it on a phone; living in a real world, not a virtual one, squeezing the juice out of every second, enjoying this journey for however long it lasts. Charlie took chances and he took risks; sometimes he failed, sometimes he succeeded and the successes more than made up for the failures. He always said that ships were never built to sit safely in harbours, they were meant for adventures and exploring. Never sailing into the open meant you were saved the storms, but you'd never find the beautiful tropical islands, the white sands, the blue lagoons.

'Charlie didn't need to be in anyone's life for very long before he made an impact. There are some people in this church who only knew him for those last few days, but what days they were. And people didn't need to be in Charlie's life for very long before he got the measure of them. He saw everyone as diamonds. Some cut and perfect, some needing a little shaping and polish, the others – cubic zirconia. He didn't bother with those, he could spot a fake from a mile off. He was a craftsman of jewellery *and* people.

'I just want to say thank you to you all for your friendship and love. Thank you for your kindness to Charlie. And if you were with him on those last days, I know Charlie would like to thank you for the cholesterol.'

'Cholesterol!' someone barked. One of their friends who was party to the joke, it seems.

'Charlie did say he'd try and attend the funeral,' Robin went on. 'He said he wouldn't arrive as a butterfly or a robin. We did discuss banana skins and cherries but he said he'd prefer to come back as freak weather. So if this sunshine gives way to a whirlwind, blame him, not the weathermen, for the bum forecast.'

The end of Robin's speech was greeted by a hushed silence, then a stray tentative clap as if unsure whether it was the done thing in church. Bridge backed it up with a clap of her own, Mary followed, as did more until everyone was applauding not only Robin, but the man who had inspired his words: their beloved Charlie Glaser.

En masse they belted out 'We'll Meet Again' along with Vera Lynn, swaying like a human field of wheat rippled by a strong breeze as a sequence of photos was projected onto a wall. Photos of Charlie as a smiling boy; photos of him as a smiling man, that smile a common denominator in every image. Photos of Charlie with film stars, in tuxedos and dinner jackets, in gold budgie-smugglers on a sugar beach. Photos of him with his arms around family and friends, cuddling a dolphin, hugging his new husband in a blitz of confetti and finally the last photo of him ever taken, in the middle of the Figgy Hollow Six, his face golden from the kiss of firelight, holding up his hot chocolate Charlie-style: Black Forest with cherries.

The vicar took the stand again to deliver a poem that Robin had written: a short, funny but fond one. There was no mention of not standing at his grave and weeping in it. And at the end of the service, on behalf of the family, he invited everyone back to Tuckwitt Manor hotel to talk, reminisce, drink champagne and eat mince pies because Charlie had insisted they had plenty of those. Charlie was taken from the church to an awaiting car bound for the crematorium to the accompaniment of Karl Jenkins' imposing 'Palladio', his most famous piece of *Diamond Music*. Robin followed the pall-bearers out, his face wet with tears, eyes straight ahead. Today would all be a blur for him, thought Mary, and she hoped he had friends who would tell him later that he was a bastion of dignity and had done Charlie proud, as people had told her after her dad's funeral.

There was a bottleneck at the church door so Bridge and Mary sat and waited for the crowd to thin. Luke cut across the line of leavers, bounced towards them. The last, and only, time Bridge had ever seen him in a suit was at their wedding. This ensemble was very different: black, tailored, waistcoast, silk tie, a snow-white shirt with a gold collar pin, polished patent leather shoes.

'Hello ladies,' he said, enfolding Bridge in a hug, before turning to Mary, a double-take before he embraced her. Was this preened and elegant creature before him really the same one who had been launching snowballs at him only a month ago? Her hair was shorter, shaped; a hint of warm caramel lowlights made her blue-green eyes pop.

'So how are you both?' he asked.

'Good, really good,' said Bridge. 'How's Carmen? Everything okay there?'

'Yep, we are all three fit and well.'

'Do you know if it's a boy or a girl yet?'

'No, and we don't want to. We'll wait.'

'I hope you'll let me know. I'd like to send the baby something,' said Bridge. Her brain recorded a freeze-frame of this second: talking with the ex she had waged war with for so long about his soon-to-be wife and baby. He had shifted to a different part of her heart now though, one reserved for cherished history.

Luke picked up her ringless left hand.

'Oh, Bridge, tell me everything's okay.' He sounded genuinely upset for her.

'Ah, it didn't work out. We both had doubts. It's fine though, I'm getting better at ending things amicably.'

Luke smiled. 'You take your time, Bridge. Find someone who deserves you. I mean it.'

The look on his face backed up his words.

'I will.'

'In saying that, you should check out Charlie's nephew Reuben,' he went on. 'He was sitting on the front row. Talk about a Norse god, you—'

'I think I'll pass for now, thank you,' said Bridge.

'Let's get to the hotel then,' said Luke. 'You two okay for a lift? Any sign of Jack?'

'Just about to ask you the same thing,' said Bridge. 'And thanks, but I've got the car.'

'I don't think he's come,' said Mary, giving a shrug. 'We would have seen him.'

'He said he'd be here,' said Luke. They'd spoken on the phone only days ago, arranged to meet up and talk vegan scones in early February. Jack had said he would be there at the funeral of course.

Mary hoped Jack had bothered to turn up. He must have known how important it was to Robin that he was there. If he hadn't, then Mary really would shut her heart on Jack Butterly for being disrespectful and lock him out forever. *I thought you had already*, said a voice inside her head.

Chapter 39

Tuckwitt Manor was old and crumbly and gorgeous with ivy growing up its stone walls in an attempt to peep in the very many small mullioned windows. It stood at the end of a tree-lined drive, lush green fields at either side with horses feasting on the grass, enjoying the weather windfall of January midsummer sun on their backs.

The car park was full. Bridge drove around slowly looking for a space, while Mary sat in the passenger side, eyes peeled both for somewhere to park and for an emerald green Maserati. Then she saw Luke waving madly at the side of a vacant spot, as if trying to direct a plane to a runway.

Inside the manor was just as quaint as the outside. A beautiful wide, wooden staircase dominated the foyer, leading to rooms no doubt every bit as pretty as everything else, Mary thought. She would love to be so rich as to stay in hotels like this at weekends and she was going to do her best to work hard, to make sure that one day she could. She and Bridge talked long into the night sometimes about all sorts of things. Mary had been inspired by Bridge's road to success, about her early dysfunctional years, about being so poor that a shared tin of tomatoes constituted a feast. The cheap can of tomatoes that she'd found in her stocking on Christmas morning sat on a chrome display unit in her office, looking not unlike a piece of priceless Andy Warhol art.

Mary had the energy to do so much more than type up someone's notes and arrange custard creams on a plate. She'd shown some good business sense at Butterly's, had sound instincts for what might work, even if she hadn't been given the credit for them. She might set up a rival scone firm, she'd thought while soaking in Bridge's enormous pool of a bath; that would teach Jack Butterly. *Jack Jack Jack*. All roads still led to him and she hated that they did.

Mary, Bridge and Luke followed the others from the funeral party into an enormous function room, with floor-to-ceiling French doors, café tables and chairs placed around the edges, a long table at one end, covered with great oval platters of buffet food. Liveried staff circulated with flutes of champagne and canapés so decorative it was a shame to eat them, thought Mary, trying not to scan the room, trying not to be that teenage girl again at the school disco waiting with a hopeful heart for Jock Briggs. She might as well have told herself not to breathe.

'That's Reuben, Charlie's nephew.' Luke gave Bridge a nudge as into view walked a man who could have just leapt off a Viking longboat. Shoulder-length, strawberry-fair hair, clipped beard, eyes ice-blue as a Nordic sea. Bridge felt a primal noise of desire scrape the inside of her throat. Luke heard it and chuckled. 'Told you,' he said.

'I think I'll just nip to the loo,' said Mary.

'That way,' directed Luke, pointing.

'Thanks.'

When they were alone, Bridge realised that she didn't feel the slightest bit awkward standing here with Luke, this man who had once been her everything. For the first time in her life, she felt emotionally grown up.

'Is that Charlie's?' asked Luke, pointing to the Chanel scarf at her throat. 'I seem to recognise it.'

'Robin sent it to me,' she replied, touching it affectionately. 'He also sent Mary a gorgeous Chanel handbag; she's brought it with her today.'

'How thoughtful of him. He sent me a wallet with Medusa's head on it,' said Luke, smiling, pulling it out of his jacket pocket.

'Looks like me,' said Bridge.

'Ha! She's far less scary than you.'

Bridge's turn to smile. 'Versace? Very nice.'

Luke's smile widened to his customary grin. 'Who'd have thought one day we'd be sporting Chanel and Versace.'

'If it doesn't sound too patronising, I'm really proud of you, Luke.'

'So you should be, I'm your best work.'

Bridge grinned now.

'And I'm proud of you,' said Luke. His dear familiar eyes held her hazel ones and Bridge thought, '*I'm okay. I don't feel the loss of him any more.*' It was a wonderful, blessed relief.

'So, how's having Mary in the company working out?' he asked.

'She's brilliant,' said Bridge, without any hesitation. 'In fact, she's too good. She's wasted running my diary.'

Luke was puzzled because her regretful tone didn't match her complimentary words. But Bridge was about to explain that.

'Luke, I would have made a vacancy for someone like

Mary in the company, but I never expected her to take up my offer. I gambled on Jack being man enough to stop her.'

Enlightenment. 'Ah.'

'But, as you know, sometimes your gambles don't work out.'

'You of all people should know never to say never,' said Luke, looking towards the door.

In the toilet, Mary stood in front of the mirror, ready to retouch her make-up. A stupid flurry of tears had caught her unawares. She was annoyed with herself. Annoyed that her stupid idiot heart had been expecting to see Jack today. He should have come to pay his respects to Charlie; she obviously didn't know him as well as she thought she did. Of course she would have been lying to herself had she not wanted him to be here for another reason: to see the Mary that Bridge had helped to build, to style, her gorgeous new hair, to show him how she had started to bloom and grow in an environment where she was valued as a woman armed with the momentum to reach her full potential.

She opened the flap of her Chanel bag and then realised she was opening up the flap of *a Chanel bag. And it was hers*. Given to her by someone who thought she deserved it, who had exacted a promise from her that she should carry it with bold self-assurance; it would, after all, be an insult to the bag, to Madame Chanel herself, and more importantly to Charlie, to carry it any other way.

She repaired her face, fluffed up her hair, straightened her back and walked back into the reception room where Bridge and Luke were standing with Robin. And Jack.

Chapter 40

'Oh, my darling Mary,' said Robin, his arms wide open to receive her in a bone-crushing hug. 'What a joyous joy of joys it is to see you.' He whispered into her ear, 'And Chanel of course. You're a perfect pairing.' He pushed her to his arm's length and then hugged her once more. 'You look beautiful, the same but not the same. Whatever you are doing, keep doing it because it's working.'

'Hello Mary,' said Jack. For a moment she thought he was going to hold out his hand for her to shake, but he bent, kissed her cheek and she was enveloped by his intoxicating, familiar, masculine cologne. Her brain sighed; she could have slapped it.

'Jack went with Robin up to the crematorium,' Bridge explained to Mary.

'Against Charlie's express orders. He wrote in his will that he didn't want anyone travelling with him,' said Robin. 'But I couldn't let him go there alone. So he'll be cross but I'm sure he'll understand.'

'I got held up in traffic,' Jack added. 'I just made it to the church, but I had to squeeze in at the back, so I was last in and first out.'

'Bridge,' said Robin, 'I really must introduce you to Charlie's nephew Reuben at some point. I've told him all about you and he's just desperate to say hello. He's tall, blond, extremely good-looking, he's wearing an Armani suit and handmade shoes. He's also rich, clever, lovely, witty and very single. Am I selling him to you?'

'God, Robin, you're selling him to me, never mind Bridge,' said Luke. 'Let's go and look for this man immediately.' He crooked his arm for Bridge to take.

'We'll be back shortly,' said Bridge. She and Luke were on the same page – for once. Give Jack and Mary some time and just hope that absence had made the posh twit's heart grow fonder.

Jack smiled nervously. This was Mary whom he'd known for years standing in front of him, but he felt as awkward as if they had only just been introduced. She looked the same, but not the same, as Robin put it. She looked beautiful, she smelled beautiful, like a garden of flowers.

'So . . . how is everything?' he asked her. His tongue felt too big for his mouth.

'Wonderful,' she replied. *But it's not Butterly's.* 'How . . . how is everything at Butterly's?'

'Normal,' said Jack, with a head-shake that said otherwise. *It's not the same.* 'How's it working out with Bridge?'

'She's great.' *She's not you and I miss you.* 'I'm really settling in.'

'Nice bag.'

'A present,' she said, stroking it fondly. She would never get tired of knowing it was hers. 'From Charlie.'

'Oh. Nice.'

'Yes, it's gorgeous.' *And so are you.* His suit oozed style and class. He oozed style and class.

'Charlie sent me something as well,' said Jack.

'Oh, what?'

'A scarf. With knights in shining armour all over it.'

'That sounds smart.'

'And an instruction to read *Persuasion*.'

'What?'

'He—'

Jack was interrupted as the noise level in the room rose; people were being drawn to the windows and then started to pour out of the French doors into the grounds.

'What's going on?' asked Mary. Her first thought was a fire, or some other sort of an emergency. She saw Luke and Bridge ahead waving them forward so she and Jack joined the throng, moved outside onto the terrace and straight into a blizzard of snow.

The flakes were the size of feathers, drifting down to the ground, defying the sun to melt them; the air was full of them dancing like tiny ballerinas from *Swan Lake*. Robin's joyful yell sounded from nearby. 'I knew it. I knew he'd show up to his own funeral. He said he would.' Robin turned a slow full circle, his mouth a deep, blissful curve of wonderment, his arms out, hands open, catching them as they fell.

Charlie. The Figgy Hollow Six were all here, present and correct.

Jack placed a gentle finger on Mary's chin, turned her to face him. He swallowed, kept a picture of that Burberry knight forefront in his mind.

'You pierce my soul, Mary Holly Clementine Padgett. I am half-agony, half-hope. Tell me not that I am too late. If you had any feelings for me, have they gone forever? I offer myself to you.'

He saw Mary's mouth drop open, her soft, full lips painted a dark rose pink that he really *really* wanted to kiss.

'It's misquoted to fit,' Jack went on. 'I'm no Captain Wentworth, I'm a posh cowardly twit but you are every bit Anne Elliot: proper, capable, worthy, a blossom. I read the book cover to cover. It was lovely. You are lovely. Dare not say that man forgets sooner than woman because I can't get you out of my head. Am I too late?'

Snow was landing on her long dark eyelashes, her cheeks, her hair. He was sure he could hear the beat of her heart, or maybe it was his own beating loudly enough for two, galloping like the steed of a knight. His hands came up to cup her face and his head bent. He tasted snowflakes on her lips.

Luke and Bridge stood with the others, in awe and delight, the snow falling now as heavily as if someone in the sky had split a giant pillow and was shaking goose down onto them.

Luke turned around for a second then gave Bridge a nudging alert.

'I think you just might have lost your new PA,' he said.

Bridge looked behind her, saw Jack and Mary in a tight embrace, bodies pressed together, snogging like teenagers, oblivious to everything except their magical snowy world of two.

'Halle-bloody-lujah,' she said.

The Following Christmas

Epilogue

Mary peeled off a first-class stamp and stuck it in the corner of the envelope containing Robin's Christmas card. She hoped he would be okay, this first Christmas without Charlie. They rang each other a lot to talk and he was doing well, considering. But then Robin had a fantastic circle of friends who looked out for him and cared for him. He was spending Christmas Day with Charlie's nephew Reuben, who was, according to Robin, a virtuoso in the kitchen. Reuben would be chef-ing to impress, as he would be cooking for Bridge too.

She and Reuben had been seeing each other since they first met at Charlie's funeral. 'Love at first sight,' Bridge had said, something about as expected as the freak blizzard. She had been a swooning mess of dribble for days afterwards, not to mention insecurity, but that was what new love did to people, made them live through that knife-edge uncertainty, sleep-robbing anticipation, trying to second-guess what the other was thinking. A rite of passage; and when the ship did steady, ironically that was the heady phase people hankered for again. As Anne Elliot in *Persuasion* so masterfully put it, *When pain is over, the remembrance of it often becomes a pleasure.*

Mary knew this first hand, because she'd had it with Jack for too long, but then it was his turn. For once, she'd been the one holding the cards. She knew she was in love with him, he conveniently didn't know that she'd been mooning over him for four years; it had been his time to work for it and worry that she felt the same, to stress over the uncertainty and parity.

She thought Bridge might have been annoyed with her for messing her about and leaving so soon after she'd moved down to work for her, but Bridge couldn't have been nicer about it. Although she made Mary promise that she would *not* return to work for Jack as his PA. So she rejoined Butterly's as 'executive office director', which was a newly created position with a wishy-washy job description because she had carte blanche to make it what she wanted. Her first duty was to spend some serious money on updating the offices: new desks, paint, carpet, blinds, flooring. There was an upgraded canteen too with smart tables and chairs, though Edna refused to relinquish the command post of her hatch but did allow the addition of a dishwasher to her den. Now when Mary sat in meetings, someone else took down the minutes and served the tea. Kimberley decided her talents were best served elsewhere and gave in her notice.

Robin was coming up to bring the new year in with them, and so was Bridge. And if Bridge came, Reuben would be there too, because they couldn't keep away from each other and they were a perfect match: she made him laugh loads, he turned her to a total love-mush. Ben was asked but couldn't join them, as he was off cruising in the Bahamas with a bunch of Midnight Moon author pals. Jack had invited Luke and Carmen over too, but they wanted a quiet one at home with Jorge Felipe Palfreyman, the world's most gorgeous baby. He had Carmen's olive skin and Luke's pale-blond hair and the bluest, brightest eyes. They saw quite a lot of Luke as Plant Boy had commissioned a range of their vegan fruit scones. Plans were afoot for vegan cheese scones (red cheese not white) and other flavours to be decided. What with the Plant Boy orders and Mrs Anmitsu doubling her order, Butterly's production output was now pushing two and a quarter million scones every day. And, thanks to some nifty negotiations via video conference, they now had four distributors in the US and two in Australia as well. Mary had brokered half of those deals.

Mary had moved in with Jack last month. Her family really liked him, they liked the respectful way he treated her. Sean couldn't believe she'd managed to make the posh Boy from Ipanema not only stop from walking by, but sit down with her on the beach towel, rub in some factor twenty on her back and buy her ice-cream. Jack smiled a lot these days and Mary didn't deny herself the credit that she'd put that smile there. She made sure these days that any due glory was hers for the taking.

She had been defeated in the one duty she wanted to fulfil before she left Bridge though and that was to find who owned Figgy Hollow, because Bridge wanted to make an offer for it. The Diocese of York said that English Heritage owned it, English Heritage said it was the Church. No one seemed to know. She'd tried the Land Registry, but they took their time even with straightforward queries, never mind one this complicated. So Bridge made a trip up there to ask around in person. She'd hoped that local Hollybury Farm, which supplied the inn with foodstuffs, might have been able to shine some light on the issue, but to her confusion she learned that it had been demolished years ago and a well-established housing estate now stood on the land.

Bridge had told her that when she'd gone back to Figgy Hollow, she'd found it unrecognisable, to the extent that it would have been impossible for them to hole up in the place now. The inn was completely derelict, the church forlorn and roofless, the cottages mere stones held together by luck and fair wind, the bridge over the stream collapsed; all too far gone to renovate without spending a small fortune, and nowhere near the picturesque spot she'd remembered it to be. She'd given up trying to find who it belonged to after that; it was as if it didn't want to be bought, she said. Besides, her energies had been otherwise engaged this year.

So much had happened that last Christmas seemed like a lifetime ago. They had all changed so much for being trapped in an old inn with a bunch of strangers. Robin's landscape was wholly different now and he was taking tentative steps into a new life. Bridge and Luke were in a relaxed state of armistice; she'd given him a great deal on some land so that he could set up another factory and she didn't need to pretend she had a fake fiancé any more because she had a real one. Reuben had surprised her with a ring on her birthday, a belter of a genuine diamond – Charlie would definitely have approved. And, if what Mary had discovered by accident hiding in Jack's ensuite was hers, she wouldn't have a naked third-finger left hand for much longer herself. She'd been practising her best surprised face. It was certainly an improvement on jellied fruits.

Mary Padgett thought that her dad would be extra-proud of her as he looked down on the person she had become, once the family baby, but always a daddy's girl. She was no longer a young lass tossed helplessly in a sea of unrequited love, because it was very much requited these days. She would always be so proper and so capable, one of life's Anne Elliots, but now she was the woman at the end of the book, united with her dashing Captain Wentworth, her heart content. And together they had cast off anchor, sailed their ship away from safe harbour and were on course to find everything they had ever hoped to find.

*Never grow up so much that you
stop believing in magic . . .*

CHARLIE GLASER
Rules of Life by a Man who Lived Well

Acknowledgements

You will forgive me for a couple of fallacies in this book. Firstly, there is no Oxycophine drug – it's totally made up. I remember reading how Stephen King had invented Novril in *Misery*, and if it was good enough for him, it's good enough for me. And also I might have mucked about with some weather history. And there is no A7501 (which is sort of 'lost' backwards)

Sir Colin of Castle Street doesn't exist, but he was inspired by the very funny Count Arthur Strong, who pulled me back to the joy of radio shows. And House of Quill doesn't exist either. Their diaries are too expensive anyway.

Apologies to lovers of jellied fruits. If we could invent our own planets, mine would be totally lacking in these monstrosities and marzipan.

So to the 'thank you's for this book. Where do you start with so many people who deserve top billing? I have always been blessed with good editors who help to make the silk purse out of the sow's ear. My copyeditor Sally Partington goes a shade greyer every time I work with her, but so far has never declined to work with me and I'm beyond thankful for that. I have to butter her up with either gin or craft beer for the next time, so I'm so glad that method works. My editor at Simon & Schuster Clare Hey directed me to where the story was lacking, where it was strong and I trust her direction implicitly – thank you so much you two belters.

The team at my publishers are so talented and devoted and hard-working. They come up with the goods every time, the marketing, the distribution, the posters, the graphics, the covers. Thank you to Ian Chapman, Suzanne Baboneau, Hayley McMullan, Sara-Jade Virtue (she also makes gin – stay on the right side of her, I will!), Rich, Gill, Joe, Jess, Dom, Pip and the so capable Alice Rodgers who never misses a trick. I appreciate you so much, one and all, and I hope I haven't missed anyone.

Thank you to Emma Draude and Annabelle Wright at ED PR. You are so amazing to work with and like magic fairies adding sparkle and glitter. Never leave me.

Thank to you my kick-ass super-agent Lizzy Kremer, who is the woman you always need in your corner, and the crew at David Higham Associates, especially Maddalena Cavaciuti, who should be cloned. And Brian, obvs, who dishes the dosh.

Thank you to Gallery Books over there in the US: Molly and Kate, and Christine, who does a sterling job of trying to translate Yorkshire into American. The editorial notes are fascinating and so funny sometimes. I'm learning a whole new language. And, I suspect, so are they.

Thank you to Stu Gibbins my web designer. Possibly one of the most talented blokes who ever existed and someone I'm glad to call my friend.

Thank you David Gordon of www.dcgbusinessplus.co.uk, my go-to knowledgeable bloke about legal stuff, in this case what to do if you've been stuck in a divorce impasse for over five years (shudders!). As always full of practical common sense. And obviously to Mary Smith there too, who is every bit as lovely and indispensable as Mary Padgett.

Thank you to my ever-patient family who are the reason I breathe (give or take my lungs). I would never have found a way into this business without having my sons as they were the key to the door. And my other half Pete keeps those coffees rolling in. And occasionally French Fancies. Mum keeps me supplied with the best one-liners and I hope Dad is up there watching us all and keeping us safe.

Thank you to Roy Wood for unwittingly giving me the title of this book. 'I Wish It Could Be Christmas Everyday' has been one of my favourites since I was a kid and I hope the song has played merrily in the background as you've read. As for the man himself: an icon in my eyes. Wizzard, The Move, ELO have produced so many songs that have been a backing track to my life.

To my friend Wayne Padgett of Haywood & Padgett Ltd, scone maker extraordinaire who pledged a large dollop of cash to the Barnsley Youth Choir in exchange for having a character named after a person of his choice. He chose his dad Roy Padgett, a man with twinkly blue eyes, common sense and a great love for his family. I hope I've done him justice. Had Wayne not won the auction, there would have been no scone factory, no vegan scones and probably no Plant Boy. So sometimes our fate is decided by these turns and I'm so glad on this occasion. Haywood & Padgett started small and, to press, produces a million scones a day. You can read all about them at www.haywood-padgett.co.uk. And you'll see first-hand what is possible with a small investment and some hard work and gumption.

Thank you to the family of my young friend Luke Palfreyman, to whom this book is dedicated, who sadly died in 2019. The family of Luke wanted his name to carry on in some way and it was an honour to call my Luke after him.

The real Luke was a trained mechanic, loved animals, was a keen horseman, raised money for cystic fibrosis charities because that's what Luke himself was born with. By the age of twenty-three his condition had diminished so badly that he only had ten per cent lung function. He was almost at the end when he had a double lung transplant that gave him *life*. What most of us take for granted – i.e. taking in a big breath – was a new sensation for Luke who was floored by how cold February air could feel. He gained weight, he picked up muscle strength, he had an amazing time partying with his many friends, even picking up a Proud of Barnsley award for his amazing achievements. Then an infection took hold that he couldn't fight off. But what a fabulous year he had – thanks to a generous gift from someone who believed in the power and magic of transplants. He was a dear, wonderful, kind and inspirational young man and I was honoured to know him.

I am proud patron of Yorkshirecatrescue.org and, like so many charities, they've struggled to keep afloat, especially in this awful year. But they have a lovely online shop and everything they sell goes towards helping cats. Do pop along and have a look. They have some top Christmas cards. And a book of very irreverent poems that I wrote called *A Cat-Shaped Space* (I ship worldwide from my website). All the profits go to the charity. The 'Maud Haworth Home for Cats' is them in disguise.

And last but by no means least – thank you dearest readers for your love and support and touching letters. Without you, us writers of novels are just unpaid hobbyists and so I'm glad that you've given me a job that allows me to pay the mortgage and buy Grand Marnier. If I've brought you cheer, respite, entertainment as you've told me, then my job is done. Thank you for giving me my dream.

Luke's Terrible Christmas Jokes

Why doesn't Santa have a private dentist?
Because he believes in the national elf service

What do ducks pull at Christmas?
Quackers

What smells like Polos and hangs on Christmas trees?
Ornamints

What football team did baby Jesus support?
Manger-ster United

Why are Christmas trees so bad at knitting?
They keep dropping their needles

Why should you never buy a coffee grinder from a Womble?
Because your coffee will either be underground or overground

Why do birds fly south for the winter?
Because the bus is too expensive

What do snowmen eat in McDonalds?
Icebergers

Why is it always cold at Christmas?
Because it's in Decemburrrrrrrrr

What's the difference between MPs and Christmas puddings?
Nothing – they're all fruitcakes

Why don't snowmen run off when it gets warm?
Because they've got slush for brains

What do you call Bigfoot with a six pack?
The Abdominable Snowman

How does a snowman impress a snowwoman?
He shows her his snowballs

Why did the snowman use dandruff shampoo?
Because he had a snowflaky scalp

What's ugly and stands outside houses collecting money warbling Christmas tunes?
A carol minger

Who's covered in diamonds and sings 'I'm Dreaming of a White Christmas'?
Bling Crosby

What goes on Christmas cakes and smells terrible?
Fartzipan

Why don't sheep sing carols?
Because they can only remember the first two baaars

What's more Christmassy than an Aldi Reindeer?
A Lidl Donkey

How do you make a slow reindeer fast?
Don't feed him

Where does Father Christmas go for his summer holidays?
Santa Parks

Why did Santa paint a picture of Mrs Claus in watercolours?
Because she was no oil painting

Why do the RNLI have the best Christmas parties?
Because they really know how to push the boat out

What do you call an alien who eats too much brandy butter?
An extra cholesterol

Is it normal to find a Christmas market selling just jelly, custard and cream?
No – it's a trifle bazaar

What position does Father Christmas play in football?
Santa forward

What sort of lions do you find at the North Pole?
Very cold ones

What's a Christmas trifle's favourite place in a police station?
The custardy suite

What's red with a fur trim and has a hundred legs?
A Santapede

What do you get if you cross a spruce with a dinosaur?
A Tree Rex

What vegetables do you find in igloo toilets?
Frozen peas

Why don't snowmen have a curry after a night out?
Because they prefer a chilly

Why is Boxing Day so called?
Because it's spent reboxing crap presents to sell on eBay

What do you get if you cross Father Christmas with a shark?
Santa Jaws

Knock knock
Who's there?
Wendy
Wendy who?
Wendy red red robin comes bob bob bobbing along

What's the definition of perfect Christmas snow?
White stuff that's so deep the family can't travel to you

What do you get if you cross Father Christmas with Sherlock Holmes?
Santa Clues

What sort of motorbike does Santa ride?
A Holly Davidson

Norway has 48 words for 'snow'
But that's nothing because women have 598 words for 'ex'

What's worse than a Christmas cracker joke with no punchline?

Why do family get together at Christmas?
To remind them of why they stay apart for the rest of the year

Where's the best place to stuff Christmas stockings?
In carol singers' mouths to stop the row

How do you make a reindeer stew?
Don't leave him out any carrots